Malika's Revenge

Phillip Strang

Dedication

For Elli and Tais, who both had the perseverance to make me sit down and write

Map

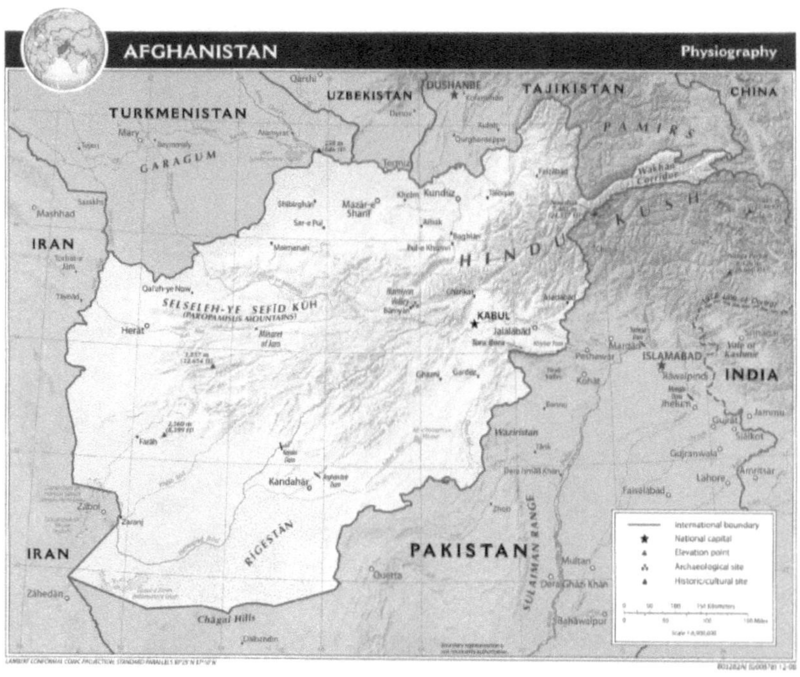

AFGHANISTAN
Physiography
TURKMENISTAN
UZBEKISTAN
DUSHANBE
TAJIKISTAN
CHINA
PAMIRS
Mary
GARAGUM
Termiz
Wakhan
Corridor
Feizabad
Mashhad
Shibirghan
Mazar-e
Sharif
Kholm
Kondoz
Taloqan
HINDU KUSH
IRAN
Sar-e Pol
Aibak
Maimanah
Pol-e Khomri
Baghlan
Qal'ah-ye Now
Bamiyan
Valley
Bamian
Charikar
SELSELEH-YE SEFID KUH
(PAROPAMISUS MOUNTAINS)
KABUL
Herat
Minaret
of Jam
Jalalabad
ISLAMABAD
Rawalpindi
INDIA
Vale of
Kashmir
Ghazni
Gardez
Farah
Kandahar
Waziristan
Jammu
Sialkot
Gujrat
Zabol
Gujranwala
Zaranj
REGESTAN
Lahore
Amritsar
IRAN
PAKISTAN
Faisalabad
SULAIMAN RANGE
Zahedan
Multan
Quetta
Dera Ghazi Khan
Chagai Hills
Bahawalpur
International boundary
National capital
Elevation point
Archaeological site
Historic/cultural site
0   50   100   150 Kilometers
0   50   100   150 Miles
Scale 1:6,000,000

Cast of Characters

<u>**Major Characters.**</u>

Tajikistan.

Malika Khalova - Drug-addicted prostitute in the drug smugglers' village – Tajikistan National.
Oleg Yezhov – Malika's lover in the drug smugglers' village – Gangster – Russian.
Yusup Baroyev – Drug lord – Tajikistan National.
Farrukh Bahori – Baroyev's man in the drug smugglers' village - Tajikistan National.
Rena Ilolov – Prostitute friend of Malika– Tajikistan National.
Gennady Denikin – Bratva, the Russian mafia's lead representative in Tajikistan - Russian.
Viktor Gryzlov – Gennady Denikin's bodyguard – Russian.
Igor Rothko – Assassin – Russian.
Pavel Suslov – Friend of Oleg Yezhov – Homosexual – Russian.
Yuri Drygin – Customs Officer - Panj-e Payon – Tajikistan National.
Andre Malenkov – KGB agent - Russian.

Afghanistan.

Najibullah – Drug Smuggler – Afghan.
Arif Noorzai – Taliban commander – Afghan.
Ali Mowllah – Businessman – Afghan.
Ahmad Ghori – Politician – Afghan.
Ashraf Ghilzai – Heroin producer - Former Taliban - Afghan.
Alam – Reluctant colleague of Oleg Yezhov – Afghan.
Farhana - Prostitute – Kunduz, Afghanistan – Afghan.

Russia.

Dmitry Gubkin – White-collar criminal – Drug-smuggling syndicate organiser - Russian.
Grigory Stolypin – Dmitry Gubkin's primary Russian mafia contact – Russian.

Boris Sobchak – Russian mafia – Colleague of Grigory Stolypin - Russian.
Ivan Merestkov – Russian mafia – Colleague of Grigory Stolypin - Russian.
Feliks Kalinin – Yusup Baroyev's Russian contact – Russian.

Minor Characters.

Anatoly – Dmitry Gubkin's bodyguard - Russian.
Georgy – Dmitry Gubkin's bodyguard - Russian.
Latif – Heroin production manager - Afghan.
Nazif Arsala – Minister of Defence, Afghanistan – Afghan.
Andrei Kholov – Rena Ilolov's pimp – Tajikistan National.
Artur Malenkov – Brother of Andre Malenkov – Russian.
Natasha – Oleg Yezhov's lover in St. Petersburg – Russian.
Ismail Samani – Provincial Governor, Kunduz, Afghanistan – Afghan.
Hammasa – Third wife of Ahmad Ghori – Afghan.
Lui – Prostitute in Kabul – Chinese.
Katerina Gubkin – Wife of Dmitry Gubkin – Russian.
Anton Davydov – Lover of Katerina, Dmitry Gubkin's wife - Russian.
Babak – Client of Malika's in the village – Afghan.
Azad - Bandit – Afghan.
Nozia – Farrukh's whore – Tajikistan National.
Aleksei Sidorenko – Gangster – Russian.
Abdul Sarabi – Politician – Hazara tribe – Afghan.
Tolib – Over-inquisitive gym attendant – Tajikistan National.
Nilufar – High-class escort – Tajikistan National.
Yudik Khujandi – State Committee for National Security, Tajikistan – Tajikistan National.
Mikhail Kandinsky – Senior agent, KGB – Russian.
Firuza Baroyev – Yusup Baroyev's wife – Tajikistan National.
Iskandar - Friend of Yusup Baroyev – Tajikistan National.
Rasul Dostiev – Employed by Boris Sobchak - Tajikistan National.
Khasan Boqiev – Employed by Boris Sobchak – Thug – Tajikistan National.
Yegor Luzhkov – Assassin – Russian.

Chapter 1

Malika Khalova sat dissolutely on the side of the dusty track, the main thoroughfare in the desert village in Tajikistan. A dirty, dishevelled man hovered over her, screaming abuse and waving heroin, the leftovers of the five kilos he had transported across the border from Afghanistan.

'Come on, if you want this,' he said.

She remained motionless, not because of what he had in his hands, but because, in a brief interlude, she had reminisced back to the pretty and innocent pre-pubescent child she had been.

In her fourteenth year, she smoked her first joint of hash, a dare from her friends. She had no chance; her genetics inclined her towards addiction.

By the time she was twenty-two, she was addicted to heroin and a promising future was over. Her parents, good people, lived in Dushanbe, the capital city of the impoverished country of Tajikistan, in Central Asia. It had cost them all their savings and assets to save her, but it was to no avail. Within two years, they were on the street and begging.

'Please forgive me. I will stop injecting myself and get a job. I will look after you,' she would say, but it was pointless. She would not regain her life and that of her parents.

Her father threw himself under a bus one Saturday afternoon, and her mother disappeared. Where Malika never knew, but in her heart, she was dead.

Over the years, she had attempted to wean herself off the heroin. The last drug rehabilitation centre had strapped her to a bed, let her scream until the effects of her previous fix had worn off and then let her scream again until the withdrawal symptoms had subsided.

She had left fresh and healthy, ready for a life of decency, full of self-worth, but the memories of her parents returned soon enough. Two days later, she sold herself in a back street of the capital for the price of a fix of low-grade heroin. It nearly killed her, but she was hooked again, and there was no going back.

***

It had taken five years before she found herself in a drug smugglers' village, waiting for the next man. Here, the transaction was not for money but for the drug. The supply was more plentiful and the quality better, but the clientele decidedly worse.

Her guilt over her parents was even more abhorrent than the vile and despicable Afghan, who intended to take her body and beat her. The melancholy, her only relief, would return after the next hit of heroin smuggled across the border from Afghanistan. The bruising, the scars, the thought of what she had endured, forgotten until the next illiterate peasant, gangster or corrupt Tajikistan policeman regarded it as his right to treat her as no more than an animal.

The occasional businessman in the capital had seen the beauty underneath the skin and treated her well, but that was the past. The present consisted of only the dregs of society. She was only twenty-seven but looked ten years older; the innocent beauty had long gone, and even now, the men were looking for fresher and more nubile meat to satisfy their lusts.

The drug smugglers' village, a ramshackle combination of makeshift mud huts, open courtyards and canvas shelters, was filled with the cruellest, vilest, most degenerate persons imaginable.

Those that came for her were invariably perverse in their demands, and she no longer cared what they did to her or what she did to them. She was unlikely to see her thirtieth birthday with no medicine, barely any food, and an addiction that was destroying her.

***

The next day, still feeling the effects of the abuse from the Afghan, one of the gangsters came for her. A sadistic killer-turned-drug-dealer, Aleksei Sidorenko was a Russian, a fat pig of a man. Daily, he ensured that he downed at least two bottles of vodka and took one of the women. Today, it was Malika's turn. Killing didn't pay the money he wanted, but drug smuggling did and if that included the occasional murder, so much the better. At least he could afford the beautiful blonde prostitutes in Moscow instead of a dark-haired, local whore who may have once been beautiful.

'How much do you want?'

'Treat me respectfully if you want my time,' she responded indignantly.

'I'll treat you as I want, and if you answer me back, I'll make sure you receive the back of my hand for your insolence,' Sidorenko responded. He had killed women and maimed them before. One more wouldn't make any difference, and who would care? There were as many as he wanted in the village, but he hadn't tried this one.

The pimps became nasty if the younger, fresh-faced whores were roughed up, and they were quick with a knife. He couldn't keep watching out for them when he was on top of a woman, asleep or drunk, which was most of the time.

'I want a fix. You give me a fix and some money for food, and then you can do what you like.' Her cravings were kicking in, and the man had what she wanted, even if he was ugly, fat and repulsive.

'I'll give you enough for a fix if you satisfy me or get nothing. Do you understand?'

'And some money for food?'

'What do I care if you eat or die? Go scavenge in the rubbish with the other vermin,' he said as he gave her the promised slap with the back of a heavy hand across her face.

It took ten minutes, with a man smelling of vodka labouring on top of her and attempting to throttle her until he was satisfied or incapable of more. He blamed her, not the vodka he had consumed or the obese weight he carried.

'You owe me some more drugs. We agreed.' He had only given her half of what he had shown.

'Agreed? What do I care? Go find a policeman and file a complaint.'

'I will,' she said, although she knew she wouldn't. Besides, the police were corrupt and in the pay of those trading the drugs. She knew that sex with the police chief in the town to the west would be the fee for him to swear that he would help when she knew he would not.

Only nine months earlier, the village had come into existence. The Taliban needed money and weapons, but mainly weapons and a kilo of heroin could be sold for two thousand American dollars. An AK-47 could be picked up for sixty dollars and sold back into Afghanistan for twice that price. The Taliban were becoming wealthy and well-armed, and dealing with a Russian was a small price to pay. They hated each other, but the Russian gangsters, especially Sidorenko, were of the same ilk. They were equally cruel, amoral and devoid of compassion or humility.

***

Najibullah was a small-time smuggler in Afghanistan with two frigid and passionless wives. The opportunity of a Tajik woman was some compensation, and Malika was good. Compared to his wives, she was beautiful. He had beaten her the day before Sidorenko, and both had treated her as no more than a dog.

'Did you enjoy the whore?' Najibullah asked.

'There are so many. It's getting difficult as to which one to choose,' the sadistic Russian answered.

'She'll take a beating.'

'True, but they all need beating.'

'You touch the new ones, and then you'll have problems with the pimps that look after them,' the Afghan commented, but then he knew. The scar across his left cheek had come about due to the beating he had given two months before to a fresh-faced girl, no older than sixteen, from a working-class suburb of Dushanbe.

Her pimp may have been effeminate, but he was fast with a knife. Surrounded by the other pimps in the village, there was no way the Afghan could respond. Besides, they would have killed him on the spot if he had. What was a filthy Afghan to them?

'Why should I care about their pimps?' Sidorenko pretended to be brave and strong, but he was neither. He was a coward and weak, but he would not let an Afghan tribesman, a religious lunatic, know. It was the tribesman's savage people that had killed his father fifteen years previous when the Soviet Army had liberated the Afghan's backward country.

'I will bring you more next week, an increased quantity,' said Najibullah. 'My master has instructed me to tell you.'

'Then I will be ready. How is the plan progressing?' asked Sidorenko.

'I am just a humble smuggler. The details of the plan, I do not know.'

'He must have told you something?'

'I was told that the plan progresses satisfactorily, and we will be ready.'

'Will your master come?'

'He does not become involved in such matters. I and others take responsibility for the deliveries. The route is dangerous. The chances of being caught or killed are high.'

'I thought you had it under control. Don't you bribe every official on the way?' Sidorenko did not believe the uneducated tribesman.

'Under control? It is in Afghanistan, but here in Tajikistan? Never.'

'What do you mean by never?'

'Not all can be bribed. There are some in the Tajikistan army who are incorruptible. They believe they must stop us.'

'Yes, there will always be deluded fools.' The Russian accepted the fact.

***

Dmitry Gubkin was as remarkable a man as he was a criminal. A tall, slim man with the body of an athlete and the silver hair of a man in his sixties, he was an aficionado of fine wines, opera and baroque furniture. A patron of the arts, a supporter of all things Russian and exceedingly patriotic, he was as well-known for his wealth as his generosity.

He had received his education in a small town west of Moscow in his youth, a degree in Business and Computer Studies from the Lomonosov Moscow State University. He could have been a professor, an academic, or a businessman, but he chose crime. Or, at least, it had chosen him.

He was descended from a family of leading criminals, mainly white collar, who used intellect rather than brawn. His father had pulled off the great banking swindle in Volgograd when ten per cent of the wealthiest people in the city had lost half their money.

Those who knew the details, the wealthiest and the most corrupt, never reported it. His father had been a smart man. He knew those he had fleeced would not want their financial dealings investigated. Some even paid him extra to keep quiet; others planned to kill him. However, he had let them know that he had a secret dossier and where it would end up if anything happened to him.

'Dmitry,' his father, Aleksandr, would often repeat as a bedtime story, 'being smarter than the next person is not a crime. It is a crime if you do not take advantage. How will they learn if we do not teach them?'

As he grew, Dmitry took the opportunity to put his father's wisdom to good use. In school, it was beating the others at cards. In University, seducing as many of the delightful females as he could with his good looks, elegant manners, and clever manipulation of conversations and situations. He ensured any competition was deterred by a couple of heavies he employed.

He plotted his future, the offer of smart and influential jobs in the city, and a couple of compliant females at the end of a phone line waiting for a call.

The women he kept until he had tired of them. As for the influential jobs, what use were they to him? At least the degrees had given him business acumen and computer skills.

His two heavies, Anatoly and Georgy, were strong and loyal, and where he was going, he would need protection. The first ventures were simple enough. Buy a succession of commercial properties through shelf companies and false names. Ensure they were suitably insured and then arrange for them to be burnt down, nothing obvious, perhaps a gas leak or faulty wiring. Some insurance companies suspected, but what could they do? If the insurance assessor started to make disparaging remarks or asked too many probing questions, he always had Anatoly and Georgy to call upon. If the attempt at a bribe failed, the assessor invariably had a family and *'you wouldn't want anything to happen to them.'*

Nobody, including the insurance company or the assessor, ever saw Dmitry. To him, it was too simple, and the money, good as it was, came nowhere near the flawless fraud that his father had committed.

His inheritance from his father and grandfather had ensured his wealth, and, to Dmitry, crime was an agreeable pastime. He thrived in its environment. Money laundering proved worthwhile; substantial partnerships in a few casinos were equally profitable. Then there were always the fraudulent real estate swindles. He boasted an impressive collection of expensive paintings in his mansion in Moscow and an appreciation of the best that money could buy. In time, a wife, Katerina – a former model and someone he truly loved – gave him the air of the complete man.

The phone call he received one afternoon in the office at his mansion intrigued him. He realised the person on the other end of the line was not the sort of person he would normally have communicated with, but business had become stale. The voice promised some degree of excitement. He accepted the invitation to meet.

***

The meeting convened twenty-four hours later at the Pushkin Café on Tverskoy Boulevard. The café had been modelled in the style of pre-revolution Tsarist Russia, with ornate wood panelling and its central chandelier the primary focus of attention. Even Dmitry Gubkin approved of the location.

'I'm from the Brotherhood, the Bratva,' Grigory Stolypin announced as they met.

'I came in good faith, assuming we were to discuss a business deal,' Gubkin replied. A pregnant pause ensued while he considered his position. The menu, elaborate and expensive, was presented by a waiter dressed in dark trousers and a white shirt, complete with a bow tie. They both chose blinchiki, Russian pancakes, the speciality of the house.

'That is why I am here,' said Stolypin. In his late forties, the self-pronounced gangster was well-dressed in an expensive suit. He sported a small, pencil-thin moustache above his upper lip, unfashionably inappropriate. His swept-back hair was a little too heavy on the hair cream for Gubkin's liking. Stolypin was tall in stature but rotund. He had the ruddy complexion of a man who drank too much.

Gubkin took an instant dislike to him. Stolypin wasn't the suave businessman's type of person, and associating in public with villains was not his usual modus-operandi.

'We have a proposal for you,' Stolypin continued.

'I don't do business with the Russian mafia or common criminals.'

'We are not common criminals. This is a business offer you will find hard to resist.'

'Continue, but I must warn you, if I see a familiar face enter the door, I will leave instantly.'

'No one will come through any door while we are here.'

'What do you mean?' The statement clearly stated caused Gubkin concern – the frown on his face visible to the gangster.

'The restaurant is closed until I leave.'

'What do you want?' Gubkin realised he was compromised. He had no option but to continue with the meeting.

'We're all criminals here, don't you agree?' Stolypin said in an almost sneering manner.

'I am an honest businessman.'

'Please, do not treat me as stupid because I do not have your social airs and graces.' Stolypin had little time for the eloquent Gubkin with his superior attitude. 'We know who you are and how you operate. It is why we are here talking today.'

'What do you want?'

'We want to employ you. We want to grant you the leadership of a select group on a project of the utmost importance.'

'I don't work for anybody, and why would I want to lead you?'

'It's a valid question. It's certainly not for money or influence.'

'Then why?' Gubkin realised that Stolypin was not as stupid as he first appeared.

'Your vanity.'

'Why should my vanity be of any interest to you?'

'It is because you will want to take the leadership.'

'What is this project?'

'Drugs!' the gangster said. 'How do you feel about drugs?'

'For a headache?'

'Don't be obtuse. You know what I mean.'

'Personally, I've no issue either way. If people are weak-minded or weak-willed to be seduced by them, that's their problem, not mine. Is this what this is about?'

'Yes, that's precisely what this is about.'

'I am a busy person. You are wasting my time,' Gubkin replied impatiently. 'Give me the facts and be quick about it.'

'My colleagues and I, we're gangsters. Old-fashioned gangsters who came up through the ranks from hustling on the streets, knife fighting, and killing when we had to. I'm one of the survivors, but I and others know our limitations. This is too big and too complex for us. We'll only end up fighting and cheating amongst ourselves.'

'What would be different if I became involved?'

'We'd swear an oath of allegiance to your leadership. No arguments, no debates and no fighting.'

'How could you hold an oath? The Russian mafia is not known for its sense of decency and fair play.'

'Gangster's oath. There's nothing stronger. Besides, anyone who breaks it is dead.'

'What's the project, assuming I'm interested?'

'You'll be interested. I guarantee you that.'

Trapped in a restaurant with a senior figure of the Russian mafia was not Dmitry Gubkin's idea of a good situation

– he was feeling distinctly uncomfortable. He was a respectable member of society who carefully maintained the illusion of honesty, even though he knew he was not.

Anatoly and Georgy were not far away, and unless he gave them a signal, they would sit mute, observe all and do nothing. He had no intention of doing anything rash. If there were to be a shoot-out, Anatoly and Georgy would be dead, probably himself. If he were killed or seen by the reporters in the aftermath, his respectability would be blown. He could see the headlines clearly. *'Dmitry Gubkin, patron of the arts and successful businessman, in a shoot-out with a leading member of the Russian mafia.'*

He shuddered at the thought. He decided it was best to sit it out and listen to what Stolypin had to say.

'Dmitry, I've told you I am a gangster, nothing more. I'm neither proud of the fact nor ashamed.'

'Get on with it. I don't want to hear that you came from a broken home, had no chance in life, or were abandoned on the street. Give me the facts.'

'Okay, I'll get on with it.'

'Thank you.'

'There's an intensive operation in Afghanistan to increase the number of opium poppies under cultivation in that country substantially.'

'Get to the point.'

'A third of the processed opium, heroin as you know, is shipped up through Tajikistan into Russia from Afghanistan.'

'What do you want from me?'

'We want to take it to sixty per cent, maybe more.'

'Why do you need me for that?'

'As I said, we would only allow greed and double-dealing to confuse the operation. We still have to deal with the person who controls most of the current thirty per cent.'

'I operate behind the scenes. I don't get involved in day-to-day operations, and I'm certainly not going to sit in an office and attend meetings.'

'That's what we want, you behind the scenes,' replied Stolypin. 'Look, there's enough money here without needing you to get personally involved. As I said, we want your organisational skills and will swear fealty to you. What you say goes, no questions asked, no dispute or argument.'

'And what's in it for me?'

'Five per cent of the profits, after expenses.'

'Five per cent? It doesn't sound like much.'

'Your five per cent will amount to several hundred million American dollars over time. It's more than generous.'

'Assuming I'm interested, how would you set this up with your colleagues?'

'You let me worry about that. You do not need to meet them. We'll just need to set up a line of communication. You will control the whole operation. As if we are trading wheat or coal.'

'Instead of misery and despair,' Dmitry added.

'I thought you didn't care what happened to the weak-minded or weak-willed.'

'I don't, although, with your sixty per cent, there's going to be many more people with their weaknesses exposed.'

'And you with your fortune. What do a few more junkies matter?' Stolypin said.

Dmitry Gubkin could only agree with the gangster's statement.

Chapter 2

Helmand Province in Southern Afghanistan had been a thorn in the side of the American invader, but they were no longer present, and the poppies were starting to grow in abundance once more. The Afghan army had attempted to control the increased production, but they were mostly ineffective and easily bought off.

Kandahar, the main city in the region, provided a suitable venue for two of the men involved in the audacious plan to substantially increase the number of opium poppies under cultivation to meet. They were both dedicated to the plan outlined by Grigory Stolypin in Moscow, although for differing reasons. The two Afghans neither respected nor liked the other and communicated with grudging disdain.

'Will Ashraf Ghilzai be able to process all the opium we send him?' Ali Mowllah asked. He was what the Taliban needed – an organiser for the venture, which would corrupt and demoralise the youth of a previous invader, the Russians.

Not only that, but it would also resurrect the power of the Taliban. The hoped-for resurgence of the fundamentalist organisation had stalled after the last invader had pulled out. The central government in Kabul was secure, not because of American support, but because the Taliban lacked manpower or weaponry. Bribing an Afghan officer down in Kandahar was one thing, but it was another to march on Kabul. The army would fight, and they would not be beaten.

Arif Noorzai, the man Ali Mowllah sat with while drinking tea had seen the situation clearly, even though he was a Taliban Warlord.

'Ghilzai says there is no issue,' he replied, 'although he will need additional equipment.'

As a Taliban military commander, Noorzai was exceptional. He had led raids against the Americans and killed many. As an organiser of such a plan, he knew he was incapable. Ali Mowllah had been his saviour but was not a believer, just a businessman looking for profit. He would let him have his profit for now. Another day, another year, he would deal with him.

'Will you be able to arrange the transportation of the additional equipment that Ghilzai requires?' Noorzai asked.

'My colleague will have no difficulty smuggling it in from Pakistan,' said Mowllah.

A shortish man, Ali Mowllah prided himself on his appearance. In his late fifties, he always wore a magnificent turban. His wealth was regarded as substantial in the small community of Sarobi, his ancestral home. The town, a hotbed of fundamentalists in the past, was located between Kabul and Jalalabad in Nangarhar Province, close to the border with Pakistan and the Khyber Pass.

His affluence had come from Pakistan, which was all he had revealed. The local community imagined it was trading. They never knew it was drugs. It was a secret he kept carefully guarded. He hoped he would remain a silent partner behind the scenes, organising as much as possible for the forthcoming upsurge in heroin production. He knew it was his analytical skills that the Taliban commander and his other colleagues, further to the north of the country in Kunduz, required.

'Good, then we tell Ghilzai to proceed,' Noorzai said.

'And the production of poppies, can we keep up with the demand?' Mowllah double-checked.

'I am assured we can, at least here in Helmand. What about down in Nangarhar Province?'

'We will maintain our quota.'

'Then soon we will have our revenge on the invader to the north and sufficient weapons and money to retake Kabul,' Noorzai said triumphantly.

Ali Mowllah was not as enamoured of the impending fight; however, until he had milked as much money as he could, he would only nod in acknowledgement. Besides, if the country degenerated to barbaric Taliban control, he could always retreat back across the border into Pakistan.

***

Latif had only one name and was an honest man involved in a dishonest pursuit. Neither a fundamentalist nor a businessman, he was a family man who produced a repugnant product. He regarded conscience as a luxury for the wealthy and the smug. It was poverty that drove him – or, at least, the innate desire not to return to the poverty that he had known.

His father had worked for the Russians during their occupation. A simple man with an aptitude for fixing motors, he was soon taken by the invaders as a motor mechanic working on their military vehicles.

Badakhshan in north-eastern Afghanistan, home to Latif, was a desolate, remote place before the Russians arrived. It changed little after, except they offered employment and, coupled with a severe and prolonged drought, his father, Tahir, had no option. He was forced to enter through the gloomy and depressing gates of the Russian army's compound. He hated them for what they had done to his country and his family.

His brother, Latif's uncle, had stood in front of one of their tanks as they entered the provincial capital, Fayzabad, early one morning two months previous, and they made no attempt to stop. The mangled remains after the tracks on the left-hand side of the tank had chewed him up were barely recognisable. The Russian commander apologised in a language he did not understand, but Tahir could see his men sniggering.

With no income, a wife and six children, he had no option but to work for those who had deprived his nephews of a father. Local custom decreed that he would take responsibility for them and his children – an honour he gladly accepted. He took the opportunity of the invader's money to give the male children a rudimentary education, and he learnt their language. In time, the hatred dissipated, but the anger always remained.

'Latif, take advantage of what they offer,' he would say.

'But they are our enemy, is that not so?' Latif would respond. However, he was young and, to him, everything was black and white, not grey, as with his father, who had to provide for an extended family.

'They are our enemy,' Tahir had said, 'but they have knowledge and wisdom. We can learn from them. Hopefully, we can use what we learn against them when that time comes.'

Tahir's wish was to come true when the Russians retreated back across the border to the north a few years later. He was not fixing vehicles then. He ensured that the weaponry against the Russians was in good working order. It was the final day of their retreat. In defiance and stupidity, he would fire a weapon in anger.

Standing unprotected, as the last vehicle cleared the city limits, Tahir fired a rocket-propelled grenade at a Soviet-built T-62M battle tank. He hit it with little effect, but the Russian soldier who raised his head out of the hatch on the top of the turret had no such problems. He was not more than ten metres away. The soldier took one shot from his Makarov pistol. Tahir was dead, and Latif was without a father.

Latif, now the only adult male, was thrust with the responsibility of being the provider for his family. With limited education, although better than most in the region, he opened a small pharmacy. It was basic, and the medicines were invariably old and of dubious quality, but he was a health-giver in a community sadly lacking in qualified doctors.

***

Business had been good that day when the man came into the shop. He had sold several packets of aspirin, two bottles of cough mixture and a dozen bandages. That day he would be able to feed his extended family and even be able to buy a couple of scrawny chickens. He realised the day after would depend on the business, and it may just be a weak broth with some pieces of lamb thrown in for flavour and some local bread.

'How much do you make here?' Ashraf Ghilzai asked as he casually checked the goods for sale. Latif knew him to be Taliban, but it did not concern him greatly. The shopkeeper was a pious man, pious enough to avoid any castigation from the increasingly evident and zealot black-turbaned men in the region.

'It is a modest living, but it provides for my family, thanks to Allah.' The pharmacy, a converted shipping container – the term 'modest' summed up the situation. Most days, it would keep his family fed, but there was no chance of an education for those in his care. Latif appreciated his father's insistence on receiving a sound education using the money the Russians had paid him.

'If you work for me, I'll double, maybe triple, whatever you are making here,' said Ghilzai.

'But what do you want of me?' replied Latif. 'I am an honest man making an honest living.'

'Honest and poor, isn't that the truth?'

'Yes, it is the truth.'

'We are processing opium poppies,' Ghilzai said.

'Into heroin to send to the West?' Latif ended the sentence the Taliban commander had started.

'Mainly into Russia. But, yes, into the West as well.'

'I have no love for the Russians. They killed my father and his brother and made our lives miserable.'

'They made everyone's lives miserable, but now we have a chance for revenge.' The Taliban commander knew of the honest, if desperately poor, shopkeeper's hatred of the Russians. He knew it was his Achilles' heel. 'You have received an education; you understand chemicals?'

'Yes, that is true.'

'We need someone to take control of the production of the heroin, to ensure the quality remains at its finest and to deal with the increased demand.'

Latif could see no tangible reason not to accept the offer. 'I will take the opportunity to take my revenge. And if that provides a better life for my family, then so much the better.'

*****

In the six months since accepting the offer from Ghilzai, Latif had enhanced his position as the leading production manager of heroin in the region. His children and those of his extended family were receiving an education, although he rarely saw them.

For the first three months, it had only been one makeshift laboratory, but now he oversaw ten, moving every few months whenever the police bribes became too severe and the Afghan army too inquisitive. He could never trust those working for him or the local villagers where the factories were. Most of his employees were drug addicts who wanted the drug, while the guards wanted to steal whatever they could to sell on the black market.

'Latif,' Ashraf Ghilzai said on one of his rare visits to one of the laboratories, 'we need to dramatically increase our production.'

'But we are at maximum capacity now. The men who work for us are no more intelligent than donkeys, and they are the best we can find.'

'Regardless of that, we must increase. Let me know what you need.'

'But why? Surely you are making a great deal of money already?'

'This is more important than money. We aim to accelerate the decline of the Russian invader's empire.'

It was an eloquent statement from Ghilzai, purely for his production manager's benefit. He knew Latif was an idealist, a believer in a better world. Ghilzai was none of those. All he wanted was money. Where and how he obtained it, it did not concern him. What his deluded Taliban comrades wanted in southern Afghanistan was fine as long as it didn't interfere with his aims.

***

Malika's life in the drug smugglers' village fluctuated between melancholy and depravity, although it was evident the depravity was winning. The drunken abuse by an Afghan smuggler or a gangster, Russian or Tajik, continued.

Her guilt over her parents continued to concern her until a fateful day in late February when the snow lay low on the surrounding mountains, and the night-time temperatures in the desert dipped well below zero. It was one of the new girls in the village, Rena Ilolov, who was to change her outlook on life.

Rena was the latest in a constant stream of otherwise attractive women, barely more than girls, who had made the trek to the village on the border with Afghanistan. Her story was similar, but in some ways, different to Malika, who was older and more mature. Rena was only nineteen and still beautiful and fresh. The men in the village immediately lusted after her.

No beatings for her, she was too valuable, and her pimp, Andrei Kholov, was neither effeminate nor gay. She was a drug addict, not as severe as Malika, but a drug addict nonetheless.

Malika's parents had been good people. However, Rena's had not; from the age of eleven, her father would rape her, as would her older brothers. When there was no money in the house, her father, a casual worker in a meat processing facility in Dushanbe, would sell her to his workmates or anyone else willing to pay. Her mother had protested, but she was weak, waylaid by the mentally damaging effects of too much alcohol. Rena's father would first beat his wife senseless as she moaned about how he could treat his daughter in such a manner and then thrust an open bottle of vodka between her swollen lips.

Her father would force Rena to smoke hash to deaden her resistance to the sexual abuse her young body was compelled to endure. Afterwards, they would blame her for what they had done to her, a sin in their religion.

'*It was her fault,*' they would always say.

'*If she did not dress provocatively,*' although she did not.

'*If she was not so beautiful,*' which she was.

'*If she did not tempt us with lustful thoughts, we would resist her.*' She was the temptress, the devil's agent – they, the mere pawns.

She had been a decent person, but as the degeneration exacerbated, and the belief that maybe they were right, she moved towards stronger drugs. Eventually, her father threw her out of the house. She had drifted aimlessly around the capital, getting laid when she could, getting a fix if she could. It did not take long before she ended up at the end of the road, at the drug smugglers' village.

'Your mother is still alive,' she said to Malika as they huddled around an open fire to keep warm.

'How do you know?' Malika replied.

'She came looking for you.'

'But where did she know to look?'

'It's not difficult. A heroin addict in Dushanbe, female and attractive.'

'She knows I'm selling myself?'

'Yes.'

'Does she know I'm here?'

'Nobody knows you're here. I remember only your name and her insistence to find you at any cost.'

'I am pleased she is alive, but I am dead,' Malika responded sadly.

'You are only dead when you accept it.' Rena still maintained some hope, although her future was as precarious as her new-found friend's.

Malika could not remain impartial to what Rena had told her. However, the strength of her addiction made it impossible for her to contemplate leaving and rushing to her mother's side, but if she could, she would have.

Mother, oh Mother, somehow, someday, I'll make it up to you, she thought, but it was only a daydream. It wasn't possible. Or was it? She was not sure.

Chapter 3

Oleg Yezhov, the son of a butcher and his wife, had grown up in a pleasant suburb of St. Petersburg, close to the Baltic Sea. His education had been adequate even if he had, at best, been a student of no more than modest academic achievement. He had tried, but the schooling frustrated him, and by his fifteenth birthday, he ceased to be interested.

His introduction into crime had been unusual and unexpected. Walking home from school late one afternoon, he unwittingly killed a youth.

A group of hooligans had waylaid a street dweller, down on his luck and looking for a handout. He had sought alcohol to help him through the impending freezing night-time temperatures and to deaden the pain of a gangrenous leg wrapped in a dirty, smelly bandage. The itinerant only had a coat and a blanket to protect him from the arctic winds.

No more than Oleg's age, the hooligans teased the man relentlessly. Pushing and shoving, ripping the blanket from his grip, offering to give it back and then pushing and shoving more, hitting when they could. Oleg entered the affray, initially to dissuade them from further abuse.

'Leave the man alone. Pick on someone your own age!' he shouted. He was of medium height, stocky and an amateur boxer of some note – he even boxed for his school.

'You're our age. Is that what you are saying? We should leave this old drunken vagrant alone and pick on you,' one of the three hooligans shouted back.

'That's not what I'm saying, but don't you have anything better to do?' Oleg was brave and fearless in the face of overwhelming odds, and, as a boxer, he had a reputation for never yielding, even when his opponent was beating him black and blue.

'We accept your challenge,' said another of the hooligans, who looked mean and tough.

'Please don't, or I'll be forced to deal with you severely.'

'Is that a threat?' the tall, skinny individual replied.

'I box for my school. I don't want to hurt you.'

'Hurt me? How? There are three of us, and I've got a knife.'

The three hooligans focused away from the beggar and towards Oleg. They did not realise he had a reputation for unnecessary violence, even in the boxing ring. There had been one occasion when it had taken four of his schoolmates all their strength to wrench him from inflicting repeated blows on an opponent. The opponent had questioned his manhood when trading blows in the ring. He ended up with two broken ribs and a severe concussion for the insult.

It was touch and go for a few days as to whether the amateur pugilist had sustained permanent brain damage. The school hushed it up, and the opponent's parents were paid enough to let it rest, even though they wanted to institute legal proceedings against the school.

Oleg discovered he had enjoyed immensely the thrill of the beating he had inflicted. His violence had been restricted to the ring, but three hooligans and an adrenaline rush proved too enticing.

The first of the three came at him with arms waving and chest exposed. Oleg took the opportunity to catch him clear in the central rib cage with a solid punch.

'Never leave your body exposed. Cover at all times,' his physical education teacher had drummed into him, time and time again. Oleg knew the hooligans had never benefited from training in unarmed combat. They had only ever watched the incessant nonsense on television, where the hero always wins regardless of his technique – invariably incorrect and unnecessarily flamboyant for dramatic effect.

With the first individual down on the ground, the second decided it was for him to show his mettle. He was more careful after seeing what had just happened. He sparred around Oleg, baiting him, calling him names, using as much bad language as he could muster, which seemed to constitute most of his limited vocabulary. After he had run out of swear words, he came in close, close enough for Oleg to get a clean punch to the side of his face. With blood emanating from inside his mouth, the would-be assailant retreated to lick his wounds.

It was then that the skinny individual felt he needed to show the other two why he was the leader of a bunch of poorly-educated hooligans. He had no intention of wasting his time with fists and posturing, aiming to look fierce and menacing. A knife was his solution, although he wasn't sure how to use it. His technique was to wave it menacingly. Oleg had the advantage. When he wasn't boxing, he was learning martial arts.

'You just remember the name of Sergei when you're lying in a hospital bed – if you're lucky to live, that is,' the knife-wielding individual bragged.

'You will remember Oleg when you're dead.' Oleg felt the need to respond.

Sergei came at him, jabbing this way and that with the knife, looking for an opening in Oleg's defences, but there were none. He kept trying, getting closer, more careless each time, until Oleg grabbed his knife arm, spun him around and twisted his arm around his back. The knife, still held firmly, pierced the hooligan's skin, and within two minutes, he was dead.

***

It had been impossible to convince the police that it had been an accident. Oleg, at the age of fifteen, a violent individual, when riled and with no criminal record, found himself incarcerated in an austere and foreboding establishment committed to the rehabilitation of the criminal youth of Russia.

It may have pretended to be there for rehabilitation, but it was not. The prison housed the most violent individuals, teenagers, although some were as young as ten or eleven. It was there that his skills were honed. Either you were strong, violent and cruel, or you were dead.

Oleg was released six years later, a hardened and dangerous criminal, even though he had gone in as a talented, unpredictable fighter who had only wanted to help a person down on his luck. The system that had aimed to protect and rehabilitate him had the reverse effect.

It was to be some time after his release before he killed again. He had killed while locked up inside, but the authorities didn't care. Sure, they asked questions and conducted investigations, but no one inside was going to squeal, and they soon lost interest. It was one less mouth to feed, one less individual to care about. As long as those in charge could keep the victim on the books, they could claim the payment from the government and keep it for themselves.

His parents could not deal with the ignominy of a criminal son, and the few times he had seen them since his release had been difficult and tense. Within a few months, he ceased to see them at all.

***

Oleg Yezhov's first criminal gang made a good living by offering protection to small shopkeepers.

'Either you pay us a retainer,' he would say, 'or your business will be burnt down or blown up.'

It was not an honest way to make money, but it was not long, only three months later, before he was driving around in a late-model BMW and seducing any woman he could lay his hands on. There was always a gangster's moll to be found, and Oleg was not a bad-looking man, tough after years of building up his muscles and well-dressed as would befit any respectable hoodlum.

It had been the first month of a new year when one of the shopkeepers, Artur Malenkov, had become difficult. There had been other criminal ventures – stolen cars, burglary – but Oleg Yezhov enjoyed the protection rackets.

Malenkov's store was near Catherine Palace, south of the city. He sold upmarket electronics, televisions, sound systems, and, as he said often enough whenever Oleg pressured him, 'My brother's a big man in the FSB (Federal Security Service of the Russian Federation). You touch me, and he'll be here soon enough to deal with you.'

It was not the first time Oleg had heard such a statement, and he ignored it. He was not a man to be intimidated and had a reputation within his organisation as the person who always brought in the money. He had no intention of allowing someone to get away purely because they said they had a powerful and influential relative.

'I don't care who your brother is,' he had said. 'We offer a comprehensive service. Plenty of criminals are out there, and I would not want it on my conscience if your business were to suffer. We're insurance, and it's only five per cent of your takings. It's not as if you can't afford it. You're making plenty here, and it would pain me personally to see all your hard work going to waste purely because we could not agree.'

'Don't give me your fancy words,' Malenkov replied. He was a big man, always well-dressed and eloquently spoken, with an air of respectability and self-assuredness. 'I know criminals when I see them. I know what you are. I've come across your kind before. Slimy thugs who think they can run roughshod over everyone else. You touch me, and I'll have the full weight of the FSB on your heads, and they don't mess around.'

'I'm sorry you feel that way,' said Oleg. 'I only hope you manage to survive without our assistance.'

There had been a few who had stood up to him over the years. Vasily Konev had been one. He had been a purveyor of men's clothing and good-quality handmade suits. He had resisted and said he was covered by insurance. At least, he did until the shop burnt to the ground early one morning.

He claimed it was an electrical fault. His insurance company disputed the claim. They said it was gasoline and accused him of doing it due to a downturn in business. The insurance assessor had been slipped the equivalent of five hundred American dollars by an associate of Oleg's and told to reject the claim. The last anyone heard of Vasily Konev was that he was attempting to sell shirts door-to-door and was no longer the brash, confident person who had continually rejected the enticements to sign up for an extended protection plan.

Anton Grechko had been another. He had thought his insurance company would protect his car maintenance business – high-end mainly, Mercedes, BMW, even the occasional Ferrari. It was a sad day, even for Oleg, who had found an appreciation for expensive motor cars, when a late model Ferrari and a couple of Mercedes went up in smoke. The insurance claim was invalidated due to negligence by Grechko, an arc-welding torch near an open fuel tank. It was bogus, but after that, there had been few who had resisted Oleg Yezhov's persuasive negotiating skills.

Artur Malenkov was a different issue. Perhaps he did have powerful connections, but let one off the hook, and the other shopkeepers paying in to Oleg's exceedingly agreeable lifestyle would start to question and cause difficulties. He had no intention of letting that occur.

***

The day had dawned fine for Malenkov. Sales were up, and the latest special offer on an excellent selection of televisions was bringing in the business. It had been three months since Oleg's assistance was rejected, and the shopkeeper had given it no further thought.

Some of Oleg's more recalcitrant clients were becoming difficult, wanting to negotiate rates, even delaying payments, until a couple had gone up in smoke. It was all because Malenkov had shouted his mouth off at a meeting of local businessmen during a government-organised trade fair some weeks earlier. He had even got a write-up, admittedly close to the back cover, in a prominent newspaper stating that the only way to deal with the increasing crime levels was to stand up and be counted.

Nine o'clock that night, Malenkov was working late in the small office at the back of the store. The day had ended well, and he wanted to ensure that all the paperwork had been dealt with and he had placed the orders for the following week's special offer. The office was modest; he had a better one at home, but it sufficed. He would, on most nights, have gone home and continued working from there. However, he decided to conclude at the shop, then go home and take his wife to a favourite restaurant for a celebration.

Oleg Yezhov only wanted to teach him a lesson. Accidentally or otherwise, killing someone was not ideal, especially in the protection racket. It only caused the police to become involved. Covering up a death cost more than getting the authorities to look the other way when it was arson, a bomb, or a petrol tank exploding.

The first rocket-propelled grenade pierced the shop's front window just after nine in the evening; the second followed thirty seconds later. Within two minutes, the shop was ablaze. Artur Malenkov had been trapped in his office. He died of smoke inhalation, his body almost reduced to ash by the intense heat.

His mysterious brother appeared the next day. He was indeed a big wheel in the government, a senior officer in the FSB who, by choice, kept a low profile and his name hidden from view as much as possible.

***

With the combined resources of the FSB, it was not long before Oleg, and his gang of protection racketeers were exposed. Three of them died in a shootout, and two disappeared, either courtesy of the FSB or simply of their own accord. Oleg gave everyone the slip and hurriedly departed the city of his birth. He could not claim his BMW M3 or even pick up some clothes from his apartment, where the lovely Natasha was waiting with a bottle of champagne and a soft bed.

Sensing no possibility of returning, he made a move as far away as possible, as quickly as he could.

His options were limited by his language skills – Russian, the only language he knew. He felt Moscow gave him the best opportunity, and it was relatively easy to get there. However, after a few weeks in the Russian capital, it was clear that the FSB were omnipresent, and although they were concerned about espionage, they were willing to make an exception in his case.

The move out of Moscow was urgent, although he did not know where. The West served no purpose; he had no contacts there and knew he would have been reduced to petty crime and hustling on the street. He saw himself as a better type of criminal than that. His only contact was in Tajikistan, suitably distant and remote. Pavel Suslov owed him a favour after rescuing him from a few tricky situations some years prior.

Suslov, the son of a police officer, had been incarcerated in the same rehabilitation centre as he had. He was an effeminate boy of thirteen when he had been locked up there, an effeminate man when he was released at eighteen. His crime had been to crack a glass bottle over the head of a sixteen-year-old in the school playground. The older boy had attempted to pull him around the back of the toilet block to rape him. It had been the same when locked up in a foreboding reform institution surrounded by young men in their sexual prime, frustrated in releasing that tension.

Many had tried to seduce him with sweet words and, failing that, by violence. Oleg had become his protector, although not out of any abiding affection for Suslov. He felt that Pavel Suslov was important to his future for some unexplained reason.

His intuition proved correct, and he realised Pavel was the person to contact. They had maintained contact over the years, email mainly, the phone sometimes, and there was an address in Dushanbe. It seemed far enough from the clutches of the FSB yet close enough in culture to be, at least, partly Russian.

***

The train trip out of Moscow had not been uncomfortable, apart from the tedious monotony of four days of continuous motion. When it pulled in at the railway station in Dushanbe, Tajikistan, the capital of the former satellite of the Soviet Union, Pavel Suslov was waiting on the platform. Then, Oleg decided he was a city person, and St. Petersburg was his kind of city. He had not heard from Natasha for some time and hoped she was well.

Initially, she had been just another lay. Over time, however, he had come to appreciate her homely manner, her welcoming dinner when he arrived at night, and her complete unwillingness to pry into the details of his business ventures.

Pavel Suslov had changed little. He was still effeminate, still openly homosexual. He greeted Oleg as a long-lost friend when they met.

'Oleg, it's good to see you.'

'And you, Pavel.'

'What brings you to this part of the world?'

'There was trouble back in St. Petersburg.'

'Trouble we can deal with. It seems to be our lot in life to be always moving from one disaster to another, interspersed with moments of pleasantness,' Pavel philosophised. He was a painfully thin man with fair-coloured hair and intense blue eyes. He spoke in the mincing tones of a homosexual, yet he was not promiscuous and only available to a select few.

Pavel was certainly of no interest to Oleg. He liked women; the more beautiful and sexually daring, the better. Since leaving St. Petersburg, he hadn't felt the warmth of a woman. He needed relief, although not with the man he had just met.

'What brought you here?' Oleg asked as they sat in a small café near the station.

'A lover, he was a Tajik.'

'And what of him now?' Oleg was neither shocked nor concerned by Pavel's statement.

'The way of all relationships, intense or otherwise. We drifted apart, no more than that.'

'Why did you not go back to Russia?' Oleg could not understand why anyone by choice would stay remote from the homeland.

'I just settled in here. I've got a good little number here, and life is agreeable, if not always good. Besides, I found myself another lover. Do I shock you with my talk of male lovers, Oleg?'

'No, of course not. What you do is your business if we remain friends separated by a handshake.'

'Enough of such talk. Oleg, what do you want from me? How can I help?'

'I took on the wrong person. I can't return to Russia. I need to stay here, make money, get myself some wheels.'

'Then I will vouch for you. There's a thriving industry here shipping heroin up from Afghanistan into Russia. I assume you're okay with that?'

'Pavel, that's great. Money is money. Where it comes from does not concern me.'

'Then your troubles are over. I am sure I can find you employment and something to drive.'

***

It soon proved clear to Oleg that Pavel's amenable and inoffensive nature had given him easy access to one of the most powerful men in Tajikistan.

Yusup Baroyev had been an amateur wrestler in his youth, a chess player of some note in his mid-twenties. He was approaching his mid-forties and prided himself on his physical prowess and sharp mind. Once a week, he would visit a wrestling academy just to keep his hand in. No one dared to beat him too convincingly or to throw him forcefully to the floor. It annoyed him, but he realised they saw him as a man of importance and a benefactor to many.

He headed up the largest drug smuggling ring in Tajikistan, and his network spread throughout the country and the region. He knew all the key players, the politicians, the police, the military, and if they were in his back pocket, they were fine. If not, they would be isolated or removed, peacefully or otherwise.

'Yusup's as tough as they come,' Pavel said.

'What's his history?' Oleg asked.

'He's a smart man, well-known in Tajikistan. Apart from that, I don't ask too many questions, and what I know I keep to myself.'

'How come you know him?'

'I came to Tajikistan with his brother.'

'And he didn't disapprove? I thought they were strict about that here?'

'They are, but he saw me as a calming influence on his brother, and with me, he has always been approachable and friendly. Even gave me a job. I still work for him. He'll find you something. He's that kind of person. Loyal to those loyal to him, ruthless beyond belief to anyone who crosses him.'

***

The trip to Baroyev's estate took thirty minutes down remarkably good roads. The entrance to the estate, a sprawling expanse of over one hundred hectares of mainly manicured gardens, was impressive. Security was tight, the door manned by men uniformly dressed in dark suits carrying pistols in holsters. Two men, one on either side of the gate they had entered, sat up high on observation posts holding AK-47s across their chests. To Oleg, they looked professional.

The mansion, set on a slight rise, shone in the setting sun of a late afternoon. Oleg could not help noticing the exquisite pool at the front of the main entrance with stunningly beautiful women sunbathing in skimpy swimwear. After his enforced celibacy, it was as if he had died and gone to heaven.

Yusup Baroyev, pleased to see Pavel, gave him the warmest of welcomes. He was dressed only in a pair of swimming shorts, blue in colour, with a large white towel draped around his neck. He quickly turned towards Oleg.

'Oleg, I'm told you're a good friend of Pavel's. Helped him out in the past.' Baroyev gave him the same warm welcome. He was a gregarious, extroverted man with a love of life, especially women, judging by the beauties hanging around his neck, aiming to pull him free and entice him out to the pool.

'What can I say? They love me,' Baroyev continued, increasingly distracted by the obvious charms of the women. 'Or maybe they love my money and the lifestyle I give them. If they weren't here, they'd be selling themselves on the street.'

'They're beautiful,' Oleg said. There was one down by the pool, dark-haired, buxom with a red bikini that had caught his eye.

'Oleg, tomorrow we will talk,' said Baroyev. 'Pavel's recommended you; that's good enough for me. I can always use a good man, but enough of business. Today is for pleasure, and if we can't have pleasure, what is the point of money?'

'Then we will see you tomorrow,' Pavel said.

'Nonsense, stay and enjoy the fun,' said Baroyev. 'Oleg, I assume you're not averse to some good drink, good food and the most beautiful women you'll find in Tajikistan?'

'Pavel's purely a friend, no more,' replied Oleg. 'If agreeable, I will stay and enjoy your hospitality.'

'Call me Yusup. And any woman except the blonde, she is mine. Pavel, you can watch television or sit by the pool. Oleg and I are going to get laid.'

'Thank you,' Oleg replied. 'I know which one I'm going to take.'

***

The next day, Oleg, still exhausted after the woman he had chosen, met with Yusup and Pavel in the main room of the mansion. He could not help but notice the original works of art on the wall, the fitted carpet of the best quality and a television screen that covered almost the entire width of one wall.

'Oleg, Pavel, yesterday was fun; today is business.' The gregarious man of the previous day was gone, replaced by another who was strictly business. His hair was combed and parted to one side. Oleg couldn't help but notice his manicured fingernails.

'Thank you for yesterday,' Oleg said.

'I'm glad you enjoyed it, but let me clarify. Do right by me, and there will be plenty more opportunities to enjoy my hospitality but cheat on me, and you're dead.'

'That's fine by me.' Oleg had been warned by Pavel that Yusup Baroyev was a ruthless man who did not tolerate disloyalty or incompetence.

'Pavel told you what we're involved with here?' Yusup asked.

'A broad overview only.'

'We're facilitators of a particular commodity. We move it from one place to another and profit substantially.'

'Heroin,' Oleg responded.

'Correct. How do you feel about that?'

'I've no problem, as long as the money is right.'

'Fine, then let's discuss business. You're a new broom, untainted by local corruption; I need someone I can trust. Pavel trusts you, and so will I until proven otherwise.'

'You can trust me.'

'Pavel is a good operative, but he'll never be a ruthless player. It's not in his makeup. Sorry about that, Pavel, but it's the truth.'

'That's fine, Yusup. Say it as it is,' said Pavel.

'Okay, let's continue,' said Yusup. 'I need someone to coordinate the shipments from the border and up through the country. I've got plenty of people, but they've become corrupt, think they can do side deals, and cheat on me. I've no problems with them being a little entrepreneurial, but some are now cheating big time, which annoys me. I've had a few liquidated, but some still remain.

'Firstly, I want you to follow the route from down south, up through Dushanbe and on into Russia. Secondly, ensure an unobstructed flow, and grease the palms of anyone who needs greasing. Thirdly, any person on my payroll who's causing trouble, impeding the operation, well… you can either call me, and I'll arrange it, or you can deal with it yourself.'

'That's okay by me,' Oleg replied. 'And if a few need to be removed, I'll let you know and get the all-clear from you.'

'That's fine. You'll need some spending money, somewhere to live and transport. Mercedes, alright by you?'

'Fine, thanks.'

'There's an apartment in town you can move into. I'll ensure the car is delivered tomorrow morning at the latest. You've got three days to settle in, then I expect you to be out here ready for instructions.'

'Sounds great.' Oleg was stunned by the generosity but realised that it came with great responsibility, and Yusup Baroyev wanted results, not excuses. He would not let him down.

'Asiya, the dark-haired woman you enjoyed at the party, will be yours for three days. After that, find your own women.'

***

The apartment in the new building, three floors up, had three bedrooms. It was expansive and luxurious. The Mercedes, two years old, was superb, and the woman was never-ending in her demands for sexual favours. He knew she had been paid, but she acted like she wanted to be there. He did not care but was glad for a rest at the end of the three days.

On the fourth day, Oleg made the trip out to the mansion. It was again down to business. No more pats on the back, friendly chats and harmless banter.

'I need you to get down to the border and check it out,' said Yusup. 'Find the weak spots and give yourself time to evaluate the situation. It's a wild place down there; a Russian will not be the most popular person near the Afghan border. One thing an Afghan does well is remember. To him, a Russian is only good if he's dead.

'Don't expect a favourable reception and five-star accommodation. You'll be lucky if you get a bed. There's a contact, Farrukh Bahori, a Tajik from Dushanbe. He's only one of many I have down there, but he's the most astute. I'm pretty certain he's involved in the occasional deal on the side, but let it go if it's in moderation.

'Otherwise, you can make your own decision. Just remember, if you decide to change anyone out, they'll need to be replaced, and close to the border, it's not easy. You'll hate the place, and the women down there are whores who have struck out here in Dushanbe. They'll be rough, so be careful. They're probably riddled with every kind of disease.

'Meet Farrukh, find out how it works and follow up from there and as far as Russia. Take your time; get it right. It's working well enough now; don't be rash.

'If you prove your worth, I'll consider letting you deal with the improvements, taking control of the whole transportation, but there's only one rule. You know what it is?'

'Don't cheat on you,' Oleg replied, although he saw there may be a possibility at some stage.

'That's right. Cheat on me, and you're dead.'

'I'll not cheat. It seems I've got a good deal here.'

'Oleg, remember it well. You're here in my country for a reason. You either cheated someone, or the authorities are after you, so don't give me any nonsense about being an honest man. None of that crap, please. It will only insult my intelligence. You're a villain, the same as I am. The only way we can work together is for me to be aware that your temptation to cheat will always surface, and yours is to know that you will be caught. And remember, I will ensure that, before you die, you will curse your mother for giving birth to you. Are you clear on this?'

'Yes, it's clear.'

'Good, and keep in contact. Updates every second day, or I start to get nervous.'

Chapter 4

It took a couple of days to get organised before Oleg left for the northern border of Afghanistan. He had hoped his favourable reception by Yusup Baroyev would have ensured a better job than checking transportation routes. Dushanbe was not St. Petersburg, but it was still civilisation, and the women were available and beautiful. Still, he reasoned, if he proved his worth, it wouldn't be too long before he'd be back in the capital of Tajikistan, enjoying the hospitality at his employer's mansion.

The distance to the border was not far, only one hundred and seventy kilometres, but the change in the surrounding environment was profound. The capital was modern and cosmopolitan, the countryside austere. The people he could see were becoming more conservative the further south he travelled. The ubiquitous burka the women in Afghanistan were known to wear was to be seen more often as he closed in on the border town. The drug smugglers avoided the main roads as much as possible, but he had come to meet with Farrukh Bahori, not to travel by four-wheel drive across the desert.

Bahori had clarified that a stranger in a drug smuggler's village would only raise questions. He had established his credentials; he didn't want them undermined. A Russian would cause concern, although some were in the area but never trusted and always watched.

Panj-e Payon, the main crossing point into northern Afghanistan, had been agreed upon as where they should meet. The Mercedes was back in the garage at his apartment. Oleg had swapped it for a cheap Toyota for the journey, although the road surface was sealed and in remarkably good condition. As Bahori had told him, a luxury Mercedes could be stolen and across the border into Afghanistan while they were having lunch.

***

Panj-e Payon was typical of border towns the world over. Full of trucks waiting to cross in each direction, customs inspectors aiming to look competent and incorruptible but were neither. The Tajikistan side of the border benefited from some semblance of civilization, whereas, as Farrukh Bahori had informed him when they met, the other side did not.

'It's a mongrel place over there,' Bahori had said, 'full of rabid Mullahs and vicious tribesmen. Cut your throat for the price of a bag of rice, and you would be strung up with your Russian clothes while they slowly remove your skin purely for entertainment.'

'They hate Russians that much?' Oleg asked.

Farrukh Bahori, a native of Tajikistan and avid admirer of the capital Dushanbe, looked more Afghan peasant than he did a cosmopolitan Tajikistan citizen. To Oleg, he appeared like those he had vehemently criticised. He was a youngish man, older than thirty, younger than forty, but it was hard to be certain as his face was covered with the substantial growth of an unkempt beard. His head was covered with what may have been a turban, although it looked as if he had just wrapped a piece of cloth around his head a few times, and the clothing – Oleg was unsure how to describe it.

'Apologies for the look.' Farrukh had noticed that Oleg had turned his nose up disparagingly when they first met. 'Down here, it's best to look inconspicuous. If you're trying to deal with the slime that comes across the border, then don't look as if you have money and don't look like an educated Tajik or a smart-arse Russian, which is what you look like now.

'There was a Russian in the village, he went by the name of Sidorenko, and he never learnt that lesson. He roughed up one of the younger whores and received a knife in the chest from her pimp. They dumped his body near the village for the dogs to eat.'

Oleg had no great love for mankind, but Farrukh's bitterness and hatred came as a surprise. Oleg only needed money in his pocket, plenty preferably, as many women as he wanted, and a decent set of wheels. The money was not as good as he had been making in St. Petersburg, but the woman, Asiya, was beautiful and willing as long as she was paid and the wheels were great.

'I was right to tell you not to bring the Mercedes. You'll be leaning against it one minute, and the next, when you turn around, you'll find they've replaced it with a donkey.'

'You sure hate them,' Oleg said.

'It's not hatred. It's bigotry I can't stand. They come across the border smuggling drugs, which is against their religion, and then they start pontificating about their piety, their God, and how it's all in a true and just cause. The moment they've finished attempting to cheat me, they're into the whisky and the whores with the scraps of heroin they managed to conceal.'

'But you dress like them?'

'Sure, what do you expect? Get down to one of the villages, more like camps where the drugs are bought and sold, and you'll understand why. It's best to blend in. Otherwise, you're likely to end up dead. Don't go there looking for a room with a view and a hot shower because neither exists. You'd be lucky to find a bed unless you give a whore enough to share hers for the night. Even then, you'll likely be sleeping with a few thousand fleas, and God knows how many diseases she's got.'

'It was a good idea we met here,' Oleg said. Farrukh had suggested meeting in the border town. He had agreed without hesitation. He had tried camping out as a child in a local Boy Scout troop in St. Petersburg.

'Good for the spirit, good for the soul,' his father had said, but the young Oleg had neither the spirit nor the soul, and the weather had been abysmal. It was not an experience he was anxious to repeat, even though the weather down where he had met Farrukh was neither cold nor wet. On the contrary, it was dry and too dusty for his liking.

'Farrukh, what's the set-up where you are? Yusup has asked me to check the operation from the border up to Russia.'

'Down here, it's fine. The Afghans process the drug on their side and then smuggle it across. There are other villages. I oversee them from my village and coordinate the transportation.

'The smugglers' routes vary, and the villages move every few months. The first we see of the Afghans is when they arrive in the villages, sometimes on a donkey, mostly on foot. They do the deal, get drunk, pray to Allah and spend time with the women.'

'The women, what are they like?' Oleg asked.

'They're not the smooth-skinned beauties you met up with in Dushanbe. Did you ever get an invite to one of Yusup's parties?'

'The first day.'

'Then just think the opposite of them. Most of the women in the village would have been beautiful, and some still show it; but once they're hooked on heroin, they're finished. To feed their habit in Dushanbe, they need to be beautiful and fresh to make money, but the drug withers them and hardens their features. Soon they can't get laid enough to buy sufficient heroin. Eventually, they end up at the border, where money is not the issue, only their ability to open their legs.'

Farrukh paused to take a drink of water from a water flask.

'Nozia, one of Yusup's women, is down here,' he continued. 'She was a knockout. I even tried her myself in the capital. If I feel the need for a woman, I pick her. I just hope I don't pick up too many diseases. As soon as I get the opportunity, I'll be in to the first clinic for a good check-up. Mind you, that's not too often. This is my first time out of the village in a month, and a clinic in this flea-bitten town won't be the most hygienic. More likely to catch something there than be cured of anything I might have picked up. I've got a nasty rash on, and the local experts, all amateurs, tell me it is "whore's balls". Too much screwing, not enough praying to Allah.'

'How do you deal with the smugglers?' Oleg enjoyed listening to Farrukh's honest and entertaining account of life in a drug smugglers' village.

'They'll come in with a couple of kilos, sometimes as much as five in a sack. It's top-grade and even comes with a quality stamp. They'll say a price, always too high, I'll counter with a ridiculous offer, and we'll meet somewhere in the middle. The final price varies, plus or minus ten per cent, depending on supply and demand. The demand has been high, and they have been getting a better price. After that, I figure out the best way to get it to Dushanbe. Once it's there, I don't follow through. In fact, I have no idea what happens after that.'

'What's the best way to get it through to the capital?' Oleg asked.

'Depends on who can be bribed.'

'You mean the police, the military?'

'That's it. You know how it works.'

'Farrukh, the whole world is corrupt. It's only the cost that varies.'

'Some are incorruptible. They believe it's their sworn duty to stamp out the pursuit of profit.'

'And what do you do about them?' Oleg asked.

'Set them up with a better class of whore to weaken their resolve, offer them a substantially higher bribe and occasionally threaten their family, although that's rare.'

'Why?'

'If we threaten, then we may need to follow up, which is not the issue, but the police or the military will need to mobilise in numbers and come down here and teach us a lesson. If we can't corrupt them with a woman or money, we normally bypass them., A senior officer can transfer them, and Yusup Baroyev has all of them in his pocket.'

'You send it by road up to Dushanbe?'

'That's the usual way. We will split the consignments, use several trucks, and ensure everyone on the way is suitably bribed in advance. Sometimes we lose some when it's found, but that's okay as it keeps the authorities off our back.'

'You set it up for them to find some?'

'Yes, why not? They can show their superiors that they're achieving results. We can then do a deal, buy it back at a discount rate from wherever it was confiscated, and return it on the next shipment. That way, everyone in the police and military is seen as honest and competent when nobody is. It's an ideal arrangement.'

'The bribes, substantial?' Oleg asked.

'Horrendous, but we still make plenty. What we pay an Afghan is a pittance compared to what a junkie spends on the streets in Moscow. Everyone wins, whether they are pretending to be an honest lawman or just a two-bit hoodlum living in a village full of whores and charlatans on the border with a country stuck in the dark ages.'

'You don't sound like a two-bit hoodlum to me,' Oleg admitted. He had warmed to Farrukh's endearing personality and comprehensive knowledge of how everything worked, at least in his neck of the woods.

'That's what I feel like down here. I was meant to be here for a couple of months, ensure everything was working and then back to Dushanbe. I hoped to try out a few more of the women Yusup has at his mansion.'

'I'll see what I can do,' Oleg said. 'I suppose the reality is that you're doing a good job down here and have made yourself indispensable.'

'Maybe I should make myself a little more dispensable. Stuff it up now and then.'

'Please, never do that. You know what will happen if you intentionally disturb the flow of drugs north.'

'Yes, of course. Yusup Baroyev, the affable and generous host and supplier of beautiful and exotic women, will have me strung upside down over a termites' nest with my balls dangling around my neck on a piece of string.'

'You understand as well as I do.' Oleg realised that Yusup Baroyev was the ideal boss. He was generous to a fault yet vicious without deviation if anything less than total loyalty was not forthcoming.

Oleg had been satisfied with Farrukh and his explanation of how the business worked. He realised he was probably involved in some fiddles, but who wouldn't? And unless they were severe, he would give a good report on him to Yusup the next time they met.

Asiya, the dark-haired beauty that Yusup had given him as a housewarming present for the first three days, had proved to be an exciting lay, but now he was paying, and she was expensive. Back in St. Petersburg, Natasha had been wild, and if he looked after her well, she was willing to stay. But she was far away, and the FSB was still sniffing around. They had even accosted her a few times and threatened her with unpleasant consequences if she withheld information regarding a known murderer.

No, there was no point in bringing her down to Dushanbe. And he knew that, in his business, tomorrow could not always be guaranteed.

***

On his return to Dushanbe, Oleg's meeting with Yusup to debrief him on operations down south did not go according to plan.

'You meet him in some border town, where he's not known, and then he spins you a story.' Yusup was dressed immaculately in a different suit from the last time they had met.

'I thought he was a decent man,' Oleg replied.

'Farrukh's a good operator, cheats a little, but not excessively. I'd bring him back here, but no one else could do the job as efficiently. If you come back here again with a placid, warm and fuzzy "he's doing a good job" report, you'll be down there doing his job.'

'I understand.' Oleg assumed it would have been a cordial discussion because it was a Saturday, and the girls were around the pool. He had dressed casually – open neck shirt, beige slacks and a pair of brown suede shoes.

'I hope you understand,' continued Yusup. 'Tomorrow, get back down to that village and find out what's happening. He didn't tell you someone is trying to muscle in on my business, did he?'

'No.'

'He may be trying to cut a deal with them, and you know what happens to people who do that.'

'Farrukh told me.'

'There's been a few who thought they were smart. I even used one as a frightener for a dozen others who were tempted. I made sure they sat through and watched his death while we all sat drinking beer. I don't want to use you or Farrukh as an exhibition, so you better find out who's muscling in and why he didn't tell you. And next time you come here, do not dress casually, assuming you'll get laid at my expense. And don't come with some wishy-washy report of what a lovely trip you've had. It's a no man's land down there, full of the most unscrupulous, foul-minded and devious people you'll find anywhere, and the Afghans are the worst of the lot.'

'I will return today. I'll need to phone Farrukh to guide me in.'

'Do it tomorrow.' Yusup Baroyev's manner changed abruptly. 'You're allowed one mistake; don't make it two. Is that clear?'

'It will not happen again.' Oleg Yezhov, a man who had killed and maimed, was frightened. He would be more diligent in future.

'Okay, get into some shorts, eat some food, down some good drinks and find yourself a woman. Remember, I get the first pick.'

'Don't worry, I'll check.'

'Don't mess up again.' Yusup smiled as he took off his jacket and loosened his tie.

***

The next day, Oleg made the trip south again. He phoned Farrukh in advance. He was neither affable nor welcoming.

'Yusup's seriously annoyed with me for not visiting you at your place of work.'

'There's nothing to be gained by you coming here,' replied Farrukh. 'Besides, a Russian in the village will only cause suspicion and distrust. I don't need you ruining my operation.'

His response concerned Oleg. *Is it because he has something to hide?* he thought.

Oleg decided to give Farrukh the benefit of the doubt. He understood the hatred felt by the Afghans towards the Russians; the same he felt towards them. Even the people in Tajikistan were not crazy about anyone from Russia. He had heard it mentioned a few times, mostly in jest, but he was never sure if there was still a deep-seated dislike. He had no issues with the people of Tajikistan, especially their women. The two at Yusup's party had been exceedingly beautiful and generous with their talents. He could only smile to himself on the trip south.

The instructions from Farrukh had been clear. 'Meet at the road junction, forty kilometres north of the border. You'll see a sign "Police post ahead. Prepare to stop". There's no police post, but it will tell you where to wait for someone to pick you up. It may be me; it may be someone else.'

Oleg had sensed an air of resignation in the Tajik's voice when he realised he had no option but to comply.

'I'll be there, twelve noon as agreed.'

'And don't come wearing a suit and try to look less Russian.'

'How do I do that?'

'Just look how the locals move. They saunter, not march as you do.'

'I'll practice,' Oleg replied, attempting to put some humour into their conversation.

'And keep quiet unless it's necessary. Don't get drunk down here and start singing Russian war songs. They'll have you strung up before you get to the first chorus – with me alongside if they think I'm with you.'

'I'll come as a teetotal mute. Is that okay with you?' Oleg responded, although this time with little humour. He didn't appreciate being lectured by an upstart such as Farrukh, whose only claim to fame was that he had gone native and was stuck out in the desert, being friendly with Islamic fundamentalists.

*****

An old Russian jeep picked him up; the driver was an unpleasant, unfriendly individual who did not want to communicate and only spoke Tajik.

After forty kilometres on tracks suitable for a goat, he had transferred to the back of a motorcycle. The village, forty minutes further, came into view as daylight was fading. It was remote and barren.

Village did not seem an apt title to Oleg. It was where a disparate group of individuals had gathered to conduct business, drink alcohol – whisky mainly, vodka sometimes – and spend time with the woman hawking their wares. There were plenty of them – not that any appealed to him. Those he saw from the back of the motorcycle looked of poor quality, and their finger gesturing, provocative lifting of skirts and pulling down of the tops of their blouses showed they retained none of the class of the women in the capital.

'You've made it,' Farrukh said as they met in the centre of the village. Oleg assumed it to be the centre as the village had no structure. There appeared to be no Mosque, no police – at least, none that he could see – and barely a shop, apart from one that seemed to be selling basic food items – wheat, corn, rice and chickens strung from a piece of rope. He hoped he was not staying long. He was used to fine dining, not eating in a shack that called itself a restaurant.

'It's a beautiful place you have here,' Oleg said, somewhat sarcastically.

'It's the arsehole of the world; you don't want to be here any more than I do. As bad as it had been when they had met at the border town, Oleg noted that Farrukh's appearance had taken a turn for the worse.

'It's necessary down here,' Farrukh said, again noting Oleg's disparaging eyes and nose twitching.

'Yes, you've certainly changed tailors since I last saw you,' said Oleg. 'And the smell… what's that?'

'If you want to do business down here, you've got to look the part,' said Farrukh. 'If you think I look and smell bad, wait until you meet up with the Afghans. How the whores can take them is beyond me, but they're so spaced out and desperate they probably barely notice.'

'I saw some on the way in. They looked rough.'

'You'll be glad of their company in a few weeks.'

'Thankfully, I'm only here for a few days. I'll hold out until I return to Dushanbe.'

'You better hope it's only a few days. Get on the wrong side of Yusup, and you'll be down here on a long-term assignment.'

'Is that what happened to you?'

'In part,' Farrukh said. 'I met up with one of his women, not as client and customer, just as friends. He didn't like it, never said anything, but then I'm down here and no way out.'

'You could just leave,' Oleg suggested.

'And go where?'

'Back to the capital, anywhere you want.'

'Yusup does not forgive or forget. He would regard that as disloyalty, dereliction of duty.'

'But you're a free agent. Do what you like if you don't angle in on his territory.'

'Yusup's territory? How big do you think his territory is?'

'Drugs running and peddling, keep clear of that at least.'

'Oleg, get real. The man has half the politicians in Tajikistan in his back pocket; the other half are too scared to do anything. There can't be more than a few police officers who aren't on the take.'

'He can't be that powerful,' said Oleg. 'You've just got a sense of the overdramatic from being too long in this place.'

'Do you know how long a man can live when looking at his balls dangling below him with the termites clambering up them?'

'No idea. A few hours?'

'Ten to fifteen, with the blood rushing to the brain, keeping him alive, conscious while the termites enter every orifice of his body, eating him from the inside out. I'll stay here until he forgives me or finds someone else to send down. This is a paradise compared to the alternative.'

'Okay,' Oleg resigned himself to Farrukh's explanation. 'What do we have here? How does it work?'

'Nothing complicated. The Afghans will come over most nights with sacks of heroin. We strike a deal, pay the money over to them, although they mostly don't want money, just guns.'

'Why guns?'

'Taliban, Islamic fundamentalists, and you ask why they want guns! They are raving mad. All they want to do is kill people, whether they agree with their distorted view of the world or not.'

'But money's easy to transport. They could buy guns when they get back over their side of the border.'

'You don't get it,' said Farrukh, astounded by the Russian's ignorance. 'Let me give a more detailed synopsis of our operation here.'

'Don't be patronising. I'm no dummy,' replied Oleg.

'Apologies. The smugglers buy a kilo of heroin in Afghanistan for about six hundred American dollars. We then pay close to two thousand.'

'That seems a high markup for them just to smuggle it across.'

'It's high, but a number get caught. The border guards, local military and local police, have to be paid off. It costs money, and everyone wants their fair share. It is only a fraction of what it will cost on the street in Moscow.'

'Moscow's not our concern. Focus on what we have here.'

'Why do they want a gun? That's your question?'

'Guns, yes,' Oleg replied.

'Yet again, it's simple. For each kilo they give to us, we provide them with an agreed number of weapons, usually AK-47s. A kilo is worth to us about two thousand dollars. We can sell an AK-47 to the Afghans for about sixty American dollars, so we will exchange thirty, maybe thirty-two, guns for a kilo.'

'And then?'

'The Afghan goes back over the border to his side and sells the guns for twice what he paid here. And by the time they get to the south, they've doubled yet again in value.'

'They're smuggling in both directions and making decent money?'

'There are some Afghans over there making fortunes, although we don't see them, don't even know who they are. And the donkeys they send over here have no idea, either.'

'The most the Afghans we see in the village are paid is probably no more than a hundred dollars American each trip. But if it's compared to what they'd get working in their own country, legit or otherwise, it's a fortune.'

'They think they're doing great,' Oleg said. 'But in reality, they're just the fools risking their neck for the fat cat, living in his fancy house, counting all his money.'

'What's the difference here?' Farrukh asked.

Farrukh had found himself a small hut, relatively clean, where Oleg bunked down for the night. The food at the restaurant, no more than a lean-to run by a Tajik peasant, was moderately clean – the beans and rice edible.

Lighting at night was by candles and gaslight, changing the village's appearance entirely. The only place with any activity appeared to be on the outskirts of the village, where the whores were entertaining. As he had been told, it was degenerate, and the women would commit to any perversion if it scored them heroin.

Farrukh went to partake. Oleg decided if he were there tomorrow night, he would see what all the fuss was about. He was still satisfied after the women at Yusup's mansion, but he'd be in need tomorrow.

***

The next day, Farrukh was up early, and Oleg had to admit the peace and tranquillity had ensured him a pleasant sleep, the best since he had left St. Petersburg.

Farrukh was all business. 'We need to go and strike some deals. Remember, play down the Russian. They would kill you if they caught you on your own outside the camp.'

'I'll keep a low profile.'

They walked the two hundred metres to an open compound, which had obviously been a pen for keeping cattle or goats in the past. The fences were no more than collected rocks piled on each other.

Farrukh explained that the village had only come into existence a few months previous; in the next few months, it would move again. They were only there for as long as they could keep paying the bribes to keep the authorities out. Once the village became known in the capital, the local authorities would be forced to close it down to show that Tajikistan was a law-abiding country determined to stamp out the scourge of drug addiction and drug smuggling.

He also explained that those who would come to close it down would be the same people who had accepted their bribes, and the village would get advance warning.

As they spoke, an Afghan tribesman approached, dirty and dusty from a long overnight trip from the porous border near Kunduz, in northern Afghanistan. He eyed Oleg suspiciously.

'Who's the person with you?' he asked Farrukh.

'He's a colleague. He can be trusted.'

'He doesn't look local. You know I do not like dealing with people I do not know or trust.'

'Najibullah, he is from the north of our country. They mainly speak Russian up there, but he is a Tajik.' Farrukh thought it a reasonable statement, and he assumed that an Afghan tribesman of limited education would not know that, in Tajikistan, the only people who spoke Russian were Russian.

'He looks Russian to me.'

'His mother was raped by a Russian soldier,' Farrukh said. Another lie, but he felt it was more acceptable to the Afghan than his previous statement.

'Then he has my apologies,' said the Afghan. 'We have had our share of Russians seeding their bastard children in our women.'

'Thank you,' Oleg said after Farrukh had translated for him.

'I have five kilos, the same rate as last week, is that agreed?' the Afghan asked.

He was a man in his late forties with dull, lifeless eyes, as though he had seen a lifetime of misery and despair, which Oleg assumed he had. His skin looked prematurely aged, yet he held his head high and firm. To Oleg, he seemed a seasoned fighter and would have been a young man fighting with his fellow citizens in the Russian people's Vietnam.

Oleg knew the history of his country, even if the history books in Russia tended to gloss over the facts – the retreat from Afghanistan had been far from honourable. The initial entry by the Russian military, a request from the Afghan government for support against the threat of Mujahideen rebels, was no more than a misnomer before the initial assistance became a full invasion.

Not many people in Russia believed what the books said, but the books were never revised. He could only assume the truth would be forgotten in another fifty or one hundred years.

The Russian retreat from Afghanistan had been a bloodbath, with atrocities committed on both sides. It was anything but noble, and ultimately it led to the collapse of the Soviet Union. Oleg did not concern himself with politics or history. The Afghan was not a person to like or hate, although his father had died at the hands of the Afghans during the retreat. But then, he could never be sure how much of that was true.

'Guns?' Farrukh asked of the Afghan.

'One hundred and fifty AK-47s in exchange for the heroin,' the Afghan replied.

'They'll be ready tomorrow. Will you stay the night?'

'Yes, of course.'

***

It was apparent to Oleg that Farrukh could maintain a cordial relationship with the Afghan, even though they were from different worlds. Farrukh was educated; the Afghan was not. Farrukh had no strong religious beliefs, whereas the Afghan would have been full of it, although it would not stop him from enjoying the women and sampling their wares. *He'll pray for forgiveness at a later date,* Oleg thought cynically.

With the negotiations concluded, Oleg, Farrukh and Najibullah retired to a corner of the compound to drink tea and discuss life in general.

Najibullah spoke about his children, Farrukh, about life in Dushanbe. Oleg kept quiet except when Najibullah pressed Farrukh to translate.

Oleg maintained his cover as the son of a raped mother, which continued to satisfy the Afghan. He resolved to intensify his study of the local language.

The Russian language – whereas many understood it, especially in the capital – did separate him from large sections of society. Many people could not forgive the Russians for their iron grip on Tajikistan at the height of the Soviet Union. The Union of Soviet Socialist Republics, of which Tajikistan had once been a part, had not been consulted if they wanted to join such an august grouping. If asked, they would have clearly said no, but they weren't, and the Russian Army had merely come in with force and crushed any dissent violently and without hesitation. Not that Oleg had anything to do with it, but he was assumed guilty by association.

He was unsure how long he was staying in the village, but Yusup was firm. Oleg was not to return until he found out what was happening at the border. This presented a dilemma. He had to rely on someone, namely Farrukh, to tell him the truth, but could he trust him? He may have been involved with the person or persons muscling in on Yusup's virtual monopoly, although somehow Oleg thought he was not. Farrukh seemed a weaker person than him, almost placid, and he could not imagine him willingly incurring the wrath of their boss back in Dushanbe.

Oleg thought someone tough in character, firm in voice and overbearing in nature would have been best to handle the Afghans, but maybe Yusup had been correct in his choice of Farrukh. How do you deal with an Afghan tribesman? Do you send someone tough to browbeat or someone with charm and wit to soothe?

The price for a kilo was set, and the variance from one week to the next was relatively constant. A poor harvest and the cost of the raw ingredient, opium, increased. A good crop, and it went down. However, as Farrukh had said when pressed, the prices were changing. Someone was buying heavy, and the quantities coming across at night were reducing. Farrukh said he did not know what was happening but thought it was temporary.

There was only one way to ascertain the truth, Oleg decided. He would have to ask him directly and threaten retribution if he procrastinated or aimed to change the subject.

It was late afternoon when they walked to where the women were. Oleg had felt the need badly the previous night. He would choose the best of them, although they all looked worn and haggard. But first, Farrukh needed to open up about the village and the drug smuggling.

'Yusup knows something is going on down here, but you clearly state that all is fine,' said Oleg.

'I don't know what he's talking about,' protested Farrukh. 'You have seen that business is progressing well. I can't see that he has any reason to complain.'

'He's not complaining but knows there is competition down here. It must be affecting the quantity and the price?'

'There's always competition, but we're still responsible for about eighty per cent of the drugs coming across. The others are small fry compared to us.'

'But your percentages are going down?' Oleg said.

'That's true, but it's not severe. I don't see anything to worry about yet. If the situation changes, I'll let you know.'

'I can't go back to Yusup with that. If you're playing for time, you're playing a dangerous game. You'll only lose.' Oleg's tone had become more threatening.

'Oleg, I'll give it to you straight. These are only rumours, but I believe the Russian mafia is trying to angle in on the action. They're not here in the village, but I've heard they've been seen. They even crossed into Afghanistan, and it must be serious for them to do that. They'd only go if a warlord, or someone influential, guaranteed them his personal assurances on security, and only then if serious numbers were mentioned about money.'

'Why didn't you tell me this before?' Oleg still maintained his threatening manner. Farrukh's statement had plausibility; however, before he returned to Dushanbe, he had to find out if the Russians were sniffing around, though it sounded like their style. Oleg had reasoned that they took control of the drugs once Yusup's people had transported them north to the border with Russia, although there was still transportation through Uzbekistan to be considered.

'It's only rumoured,' added Farrukh, 'and if I mentioned it before, it would have been left up to me to find the proof, and I just don't know how to go about it. I'm a good organiser, but chasing after the Russian mafia., that's not my forte. They scare me.'

'Okay, I'll accept your explanation for now,' replied Oleg. 'But you and I must work together to determine whether the rumours are true.'

'How? I don't know where to start. Ask too many questions, and you end up dead in a gutter with a bullet in the head or a knife to the throat, and I don't fancy either option.'

'Neither do I, but I'm not returning to Yusup with a statement that we *think* the Russian mafia is here. Tomorrow, you and I will spend time discussing our strategy. Tonight, bring on the women and let's try for the best lookers. We're about to put our lives on the line. I wouldn't want to think we had cheap-skated ourselves just before we ask too many questions and stick our noses in where they're not wanted.'

'Tomorrow. Agreed,' Farrukh said, hopeful that he had directed any concerns about his loyalty away from Oleg.

Chapter 5

Oleg had decided before arriving in the village not to become involved with the women. He still maintained a detached fondness for Natasha in St. Petersburg, although he thought he would not see her again. The woman in Dushanbe offered suitable compensation, but those he had seen on the trip into the village had filled him with no great desire. However, he had an overactive libido, and the need for a woman overrode his good common sense.

The woman sitting at what constituted a bar – although it was no more than a piece of old wood supported by a couple of trestles – enticed him. She had a look that appealed to him, even if her appearance portrayed the depth of depravity she had sunk to.

She said her name was Malika, although whether it was true did not concern him. Quick with her life story, she told him that she had come from Dushanbe and her life had been hard and tough. However, he was not a sentimentalist. Besides, he did not believe the story. Life was what you made of it. That was his motto. He hadn't chosen her to hear how life had been difficult, her father had abused her because she was the prettiest, or even how she wanted to be a model or an actress.

Why does every whore want to tell you their ambition was to be a model or an actress? he thought. *Why not a motor mechanic or a secretary?*

He had to admit she did not attempt to tell him about her desires or regrets, and her conversation was agreeable. She spoke passable Russian, and he found her increasingly desirable as they sat and talked. It was good that she had not stated her desire to be a model. Those he had seen, the truly successful, were rake-thin with small breasts and legs that looked barely capable of supporting them.

She was a pleasant-looking woman and probably had been beautiful in the past. The needle marks on her arms and the tattoos, apparently placed there by one of the other women during a lull in business, were of poor quality and barely understandable. One, the most recent, still showed signs of infection.

She reminded him of Natasha. Similar bone structure and hair colour, although Natasha's was natural, whereas Malika's was out of a bottle.

She had a rather pronounced nose which, on others, would have been off-putting, but it lent a certain allure to her. He felt confident he would choose her. Whether she was riddled with any diseases, he was not sure. If he had had a condom, he would have used it. He would take a chance, and once back in Dushanbe, he would check into a clinic for a full check-up.

The women at Yusup's parties came with a doctor's certificate giving the all-clear. As he had told Oleg, 'I don't want to be giving any of their diseases to my wife.'

It had come as a surprise to Oleg when he told him he had a wife. It was even a surprise to Pavel when Oleg told him later.

Only later would Oleg learn that the wife was willowy, blonde, and attractive. The two children, a daughter of nineteen and a son of fourteen lived with their mother in another mansion fifty kilometres north. Apparently, Yusup was devoted to all three, but he was larger than life, and gangster leaders are not satisfied with a wife to whom they go home at night and make small talk.

His wife accepted the fact as long as he visited twice a week, invariably by helicopter, mansion to mansion, spent time with the kids, laid her regularly and ensured her gold-plated credit cards had no limits.

She cost him a fortune, but the kids were strong and healthy, and he begrudged her nothing as long as she looked after them well and acted as the ideal hostess when he met and greeted politicians and honest business leaders alike.

Oleg, increasingly at ease with Malika in the village, eased his tensions, spent time with her, and even bought her a meal. She had proved to be a welcome distraction, well-skilled and made him feel as though it was he she wanted, not the heroin he supplied.

'You would not have been able to afford me two years ago,' she said during a brief interlude in proceedings while he gathered his strength.

'Why's that?' he asked.

'I had been a good student at school, full of ambition. I knew I could act, but that wasn't the driving force. My parents had struggled, pushed me to excel and made sure I wanted for nothing as long as my grades were good.'

Oleg sighed in exasperation but let it pass.

'And then what?'

'I could see that a professional career such as a school teacher or a doctor paid nothing,' continued Malika. 'I knew of the hardships my parents had gone through and vowed not to let it happen to me. I saw it as my responsibility to look after them as they got older. I had always participated in school plays at the end of the year, so I thought I'd try. Besides, the money's decent if you're reasonably successful.'

'And were you?'

'Oh, yes. I found a part in a weekly series on television. It was the life I sought, but then the series folded due to low ratings. The station found it cheaper to import from overseas and dub the voices.'

Her soft, dulcet tones reinvigorated him, and they made love again.

'I was out of work. My parents had become used to my monthly cheque. I did not want to disappoint them. I looked at the options.'

'More television?'

'That had dried up. The only job I could find was at a high-class strip joint.'

'Did you go there?'

'I had no option. But even though it was hands-off, with no grabbing, the sleazy men were in the front row. Soon I was asked to perform in private, where they expected my act to be more provocative.

'Not long after, I left and set myself up in business as a high-class escort. Some of the clientele had given me their business cards. They told me they would like to see me outside the club.'

'Business good?'

'The clients were gentlemen. Some even took me on business trips and paid me well. Two hundred American dollars for a few hours, one thousand for overnight. I couldn't believe my luck.'

'Then how did you get here?'

'Bad luck. One of the businessmen took me to a party in one of the top hotels. There was some cocaine. I couldn't say no to it without seeming to be critical of them.'

'Then what?'

'I liked it. I'd never been interested, never once took anything, barely a tablet for a headache, yet there I was, giddy-headed and looking for more. After that, the money I sent to my parents was spent on drugs. It was only a matter of time before I was hooked on heroin.'

Malika, as with Oleg, had not been entirely truthful in her explanation. The high-class escort had been true for a while, but not for long as the drugs affected her desirability. And, as for cocaine and barely a tablet for a headache, that was pure fabrication.

'You'd rather go back to the capital?' Oleg asked.

'Sure, but I'm a spaced-out junkie. It's not possible. I've got a habit to feed, and here's the only place to satisfy it.'

'But what if you could?'

'Anytime. But how could I break the habit?'

'With treatment, it should be possible.' Oleg weighed up the possibilities. He knew she would be loyal and honest with him and, without the drugs, beautiful and desirable. He planned to keep her for himself.

'I'll help you if you try to break the habit.'

'With your assistance, I will try,' she said.

***

The next day, feeling refreshed, Oleg revisited the question of the Russian mafia with Farrukh.

'What's the best way to find out about the Russians?'

Farrukh had spent time the previous night with Nozia, who undoubtedly had an equally harrowing tale as Malika. However, he merely satisfied his lust, paid her fee and left.

'That's the problem,' said Farrukh. 'They're not here in the village.'

'I contacted Yusup on a satellite phone this morning,' Oleg said. 'He's expecting results. We better deliver.'

'Assuming they crossed into Afghanistan, we should contact the border guards.'

'Anyone you trust?'

'There's one. He'll need money, plenty, probably. No one's going to tell tales on the Russians down here. As much as they hate them, they're scared of what they'll do to anyone who crosses them.'

'Then we'll go and see him.'

'The day after tomorrow, and then I can only afford a few days,' Farrukh said. 'There's a big shipment coming through.'

***

The following day, Farrukh confided in Oleg. 'There's a problem with the shipments I was waiting for from Afghanistan.'

'What problem?'

'I was led to believe that up to forty kilos would be coming. With the other villages, it should have amounted to close to one hundred and fifty, maybe a little more.'

'And what did you receive?' Oleg asked.

'No more than eleven here, and the other villages report similar numbers.'

'Problem?'

'It's the lowest I've seen it.'

'What do you think?'

'It may be circumstantial, but if the Russians are across the border, they may have made deals, figured out a different way to get the drugs out of the country.'

Farrukh was concerned. He knew that Yusup Baroyev would be nervous, even angry, and his anger, which was legendary, would be levelled at him, the innocent messenger of the bad news, not the perpetrator.

'Oleg, can you tell Yusup the situation down here? I don't think I can deal with his anger now.'

'Okay.'

Oleg took the opportunity later to make the phone call, uncertain of the reaction. He was as nervous as Farrukh had been earlier. A drug lord, especially Yusup Baroyev, did not want to hear about problems, only solutions and results.

'Yusup, there's a problem down here.'

'What problem?'

'The shipments coming across the border are less than normal.'

'Farrukh Bahori involved?'

'Not sure, but I don't think so. Not yet, anyway.'

'What's the plan?'

'We're going to meet with a border guard and find out where the Russians are.'

'Will he know?'

'Apparently, but he'll need plenty of persuading.'

'Do what is necessary and get someone across the border to find out what's happening. If it's the Russians, as Farrukh suspects, we've got big trouble. Those guys are dangerous; we could battle to control them.'

Yusup's reaction had come as a surprise to Oleg. He had expected him to be seething but remained almost too calm. Oleg had yet to learn that his boss was a rational man who dealt with facts, not hyperbole. He was letting Oleg run his race to see if he was worthy of a higher position in the organisation.

Farrukh was relieved when he was told of the reaction from Dushanbe.

'Okay, Yusup's fine,' Oleg said. 'It's up to us to find out what is going on. He said we must get someone across the border to follow up.'

'Count me out!' Farrukh exclaimed. 'I've seen enough of rabid Afghans over here. I may as well put a gun to my head now. Do you know what they do to people spying on them? Flay them alive.'

'That's what they did to my father, apparently.'

'And one of us is expected to go across? Count me out.'

'Let's talk with your border guard friend first.'

'He's no friend, just bleeds me for money every time I go near him.'

'Friend or otherwise, we need to talk to him,' Oleg said.

***

The following morning, Oleg and Farrukh left to meet with the border guard. They travelled in an old UAZ-469 Russian off-road vehicle. It was basic, grossly underpowered and uncomfortable but simple and easy to fix. Thousands were still around from the time of the Russian invasion of Afghanistan. It was ideal in a region with only badly trained motor mechanics.

Oleg missed the comfort of the Mercedes; Farrukh missed nothing. He delighted in the opportunity for a couple of days out of the godforsaken arsehole of a village.

The vehicle, nicknamed the 'Goat' by the Russian troops due to its ungainly appearance, bumped along the dusty track, its engine misfiring every couple of minutes due to the low-grade fuel in the region. The worn synchromesh on the gears complained every time Farrukh attempted to change gear.

'But out here,' he explained, 'it's the best vehicle there is. One thing the Russians do well is build vehicles fit for purpose.'

Upon reaching their destination, they headed off to meet with the border guard, an officer charged with stamping the passports and saying who would cross. He occupied a small brick building fifty metres from the Tajikistan-Afghanistan Bridge.

The bridge across the fast-flowing Panj River had been constructed by an Italian company and financed by the US Army Corps of Engineers. It was concrete, two-lane and of good quality.

Oleg could only think of the irony of how much contraband, bribery and corruption the US Government had, by default, been responsible for by financing its construction.

The bridge was making the border guard, Yuri Drygin, rich. The BMW parked to one side of Drygin's office, five years old at most, was not the mode of transport for an officer in the pay of his government, where the equivalent of five hundred American dollars a month would have been regarded as a good salary. Not that it concerned the government employee, but his ostentatious display of wealth should have raised questions about where he got the money. Oleg knew that nobody asked as long as palms were greased and money was in the hands of every grubby politician and greedy lawman.

***

'Yuri, I'm pleased to see you,' Farrukh said as they met with the border guard at a small tea house less than a kilometre from the bridge Drygin guarded zealously.

'Your friend is not from around here, is he?' Yuri Drygin asked.

A small man, he showed signs of ageing, with grey flecks starting to appear in his otherwise luxuriant head of hair. He wore the uniform that befitted his position. His trousers were resplendent with a vivid red stripe down the outside of each leg, clearly identifying him as an officer. His shirt was blue in colour, with epaulettes.

Oleg could not help but be bemused by the fact that, as much as the Tajiks professed dislike for the Russians, they still maintained the look of the Russian military. Nothing could achieve that aim more than a Russian military hat, which always looked two sizes too big for its wearer – the band above the brim, red to reinforce Drygin's official status. He was affable, especially when pressing Farrukh about his favourite subject.

'It's going to cost you,' Officer Drygin of the Tajikistan Border Service said.

'I haven't asked you for anything yet,' Farrukh replied.

'But you will. You wouldn't be here with me if it were only a social visit.'

'I need information about people who may have crossed the border here last week.'

'That's classified. Why do you want to know?'

'We like to know who our competitors are.'

'You still haven't mentioned who your friend is.'

'Oleg Yezhov.'

'Russian, am I correct?'

'Any problems with that?' Farrukh asked.

'Not at all, but if a Russian wants information, it can only mean one thing.'

'And what's that?'

'It's important, and it will affect the price.'

'Yuri, the price is reflected in the information you provide,' said Farrukh. 'It's supply and demand. You provide what we want, and then you can demand your price. It's as simple as that.'

'Oleg Yezhov.' The border guard purposely ignored Oleg's presence and leant over the table at Farrukh. 'Can he be trusted?'

'I vouch for him. He's one of us.'

'It is strange bedfellows we make,' Drygin mused out loud. 'One minute, we're at each other's throat, and then here we are drinking tea, old friends, almost.' Farrukh translated for Oleg's benefit.

'That was my father's generation, not mine,' Oleg said in Russian. He assumed the border guard did not understand. 'I've got no problems with anyone.'

'Farrukh,' Oleg addressed his associate in frustration, 'we've had enough of the niceties. It's time to find out who crossed the border, when and who they would meet.'

'Yuri, here's the deal,' Farrukh responded to Oleg's insistence. 'Did any Russians cross the border in the last ten to fourteen days?'

'You're asking too much.' Yuri Drygin was indignant and a little nervous.

'Why?' Farrukh asked.

'Turning a blind eye is one thing, but this is asking too much.'

'It's important.'

'My life is important as well. If I tell you anything, and it's traced back to me....'

'We'll guarantee your safety,' Farrukh replied. 'And besides, we're not telling anyone.'

'How can I believe you?' said Drygin. 'You'll report to someone in the capital, who'll tell someone else, who'll be bribed by someone else for information, and it will be me in a ditch with a bullet in the back of the head. Sorry, you ask too much of me this time.' It was clear that Drygin knew something, but fear had stilled his tongue. The only issue for Oleg was how to loosen it.

'Farrukh.' Oleg directed his conversation away from Drygin. 'How much do you typically pay him?'

'On average, about five hundred American dollars to look the other way.'

'Then tell him one thousand this time.'

'Your friend does not need to talk to me through you,' the border guard said. 'I understand Russian perfectly well.'

'You kept that secret from us,' Oleg replied.

'I saw no reason to let you know,' said Drygin. 'I still don't know if I can trust you. My family's experience with Russians has not been good.'

'And mine, with our friends across the border in Afghanistan, but that is past history,' said Oleg. 'We are of a different generation, a more forgiving generation.'

'Different generation, as you said, but more forgiving? I would not go so far as that. History repeats, and your fellow countrymen will be back here at some stage, with their military, aiming to subjugate and kill if we don't comply.'

'Unfortunately, you may be correct,' Oleg replied. It appeared to have some effect on Yuri Drygin.

'Some Russians crossed the border last month. Where to? I don't know.'

'Do you see many Russians crossing into Afghanistan?'

'In the past, never.'

'And now?'

'I've seen them cross two or three times in the last few months. They paid well to cross the border and for me to keep quiet. Russians are cruel people. If they knew I was talking to you, my fate would be sealed.'

'We'll not tell anyone,' Oleg assured him.

'Are you joking? This is a border town; even the walls have ears and eyes. Someone is watching us, even now, aiming to see if there's a financial gain.'

'You've started talking. You may as well continue,' Farrukh said.

'Two Russians crossed over recently, Viktor Gryzlov and Gennady Denikin.'

'How do you remember their names so well?' Oleg asked suspiciously.

'No reason. After fifteen years on the border, you develop an ability to remember details.'

'Describe them?'

'Viktor Gryzlov, a big beefy man, looked like he was into bodybuilding. Guttural voice, bad language, average intelligence.'

'And Gennady Denikin?'

'Different style of man. Looked like an accountant or a lawyer. Polished manners, very polite.'

'What do you reckon, Oleg?' Farrukh asked.

'I'd say Gryzlov is purely there as the bodyguard, and Denikin is the businessman, but from where and whom?' Oleg directed his conversation back to Drygin. 'Did they say where they were from or where they were going?'

'From, no, but they said they were selling tractors into Afghanistan and were looking for an agent to represent them.'

'Did you believe them?'

'Of course not.'

'Why?'

'Tractors in Afghanistan? They've got no money and, besides, how could you trust anyone there? They're all crooks. Send them a tractor, and they'll keep it, never pay, and Denikin did not look to be anyone's fool.'

'We need to find out what they were up to,' Oleg said, directing his conversation to Farrukh, hoping that Drygin would have some suggestions.

'Count me out,' Farrukh repeated his earlier comment on crossing the border.

'And me as well,' Drygin added. 'The halfway point on the bridge is far enough.'

'Someone's got to go,' said Oleg. 'I can't speak the local language.'

'I'm a border guard in the employ of the Tajikistan Government,' countered Drygin.

'And in the pay of whoever hands over the most money,' Oleg added scathingly. He knew Drygin was a villain, but his hypocrisy irritated him.

***

Oleg did not want to continue discussing the situation in the presence of Drygin. The meeting concluded with Drygin pressing for his money and Farrukh agreeing to process.

Oleg decided to contact Yusup. He seemed reasonable as long as he was informed of what was happening. The mobile phone network worked well enough in the border town. Oleg made the call.

'Someone's got to go. It obviously can't be you,' Yusup said. 'You'll stand out immediately. Besides, you need contacts over there. I don't give the person we send much of a chance to make it back, but we can't let the Russians muscle in on us.'

'Almost certainly,' replied Oleg.

'Why? Our relationship with them has always been excellent. We get the drugs to the border with Kazakhstan; they take it from there. We've always treated each other respectfully, and it's been highly profitable for both sides.'

'Maybe a breakaway group, aiming to take a piece of the action?' Oleg postulated.

'It's possible, but taking on the Russian mafia? That's a whole different ball game. They better know what they're doing, or else they're in trouble. We're in trouble if they know what we're doing. We need to find out what's happening; only one person qualified.'

'Farrukh?' Oleg said.

'There's no one else with the language, the contacts and the appearance.'

'What about the business with the smugglers?' Oleg asked the question. He was not looking forward to the answer.

'You'll have to deal with it. Farrukh shouldn't be gone for more than a few days, anyway.'

'I was afraid you'd say that.'

Yusup Baroyev laughed before hanging up.

Chapter 6

Farrukh and Oleg made their way back to the village. Oleg missed the capital of the country with its bright lights, the Mercedes in the garage and the spacious and elegant apartment. He realised it might be some time before he was back there.

Farrukh, for his part, said little on the return trip, his mind focussed on the journey into Afghanistan. He drove with his usual lack of care, nearly putting them off the track several times.

I may as well stick my head in the nearest termite's nest now, he thought, although he knew he wouldn't. He would do what was required, hopefully survive and then be rewarded with a return to Dushanbe. Oleg could stay in the village with his whore to keep him warm.

Farrukh's primary concern was whom he could trust. There was Najibullah, the most agreeable of the Afghans, but he wasn't sure whether he could trust him. They had learnt to be cordial with each other, even friendly, but where did his allegiances lie? He could be an advantage over the border. No doubt he was handy with a weapon, although whether that was good or bad, Farrukh couldn't be sure. There seemed to be no one else. He resolved to talk to the Afghan the next time he came to the village, maybe come up with a plausible story to tell him.

Oleg's concerns were more immediate. Upon his return, he quickly migrated over to Malika's area of the camp. She was showing the effects of withdrawal, but she had held on, waiting for his return. *What if I had not come back tonight?* he thought.

He had found some fondness for her but knew she was a junkie, and an addict would always do what was needed in desperation. He hoped he was wrong but realised his judgement may have been impaired.

Oleg, for his part, had found that his appearance had started to deteriorate. He had always prided himself each morning on being clean-shaven and freshly showered. Here, he imagined, he was beginning to smell of donkey rather than aftershave.

If he was to negotiate with the Afghans as they came over from the border, he thought he had better start to look the part. He should have been abhorred with the changes in him, but if Malika was there, he felt he could endure the compromise – if it were not for too long.

The clothes he bought from a local trader, brown in colour, allowed him to change his appearance, and the loose rag wrapped around his head suited him. Malika laughed when she first saw him, but, as he explained, he had to look the part, even if his language skills were limited. She offered to help with the transactions, but an Afghan tribesman would have rather communicated with a donkey than a woman. He had noticed that their treatment of the women was abysmal.

Once sated, they would blame the women for being wanton and agents of the devil.

On a previous occasion, Oleg had pulled an Afghan off one of the women as he held a knife to her throat. He had received a gash on the arm for his chivalry. It looked like a knife to the chest until Farrukh intervened and appeased the Afghan.

He later explained to Oleg he had told the Afghan that Oleg was also a junkie and a little soft in the head.

Oleg had initially been amused with Farrukh's definition of him, but later, in hindsight, he felt insulted that anybody, even an illiterate Afghan tribesman, could see him as soft in the head.

He noticed how the fresher-faced women coming into the village, there always seemed to be one or two a day, were treated much better, and the men protecting them were well-armed and not averse to using their weapons.

Malika had told him about the regular beatings, from the Afghans especially, and she had developed a detachment from their perverse and violent methods of sexual gratification. He vowed to protect her from further abuse.

Farrukh had given him a comprehensive run-through on how the operation worked. How the Afghans – there were forty or fifty, sometimes more – would cross the Panj River at different spots each night, depending on where the border guards were and who they could bribe. After crossing, they would travel to the villages by different routes. Dependent on the cloud cover, the weather and the border guards on the Tajikistan side, they would walk, ride on a donkey, and even use a motorbike to reach Farrukh. It was not far, but it would take them all night, and once they arrived in the camp, all they wanted to do was do the deal with Farrukh, aim to cheat him if they could, grab a quick feed and then get to the women.

As Farrukh had explained, they may not like Russians, but they would like Oleg's money and see him as easier to cheat, which was probably true. He would not notice them removing a little from the sack after he had carefully weighed it. Farrukh told him that it didn't matter too much, as the markup, as it transited Tajikistan and Uzbekistan before reaching Kazakhstan and ultimately into Russia, was sufficient to compensate for his inexperience.

If they thought they could cheat a bit more, it would be easier for him to be accepted. Malika had given him some instruction in the basics of the local language, Tajik, especially the numbers.

The transportation up to Dushanbe was a different matter. There were numerous police checkpoints, but the drivers knew who to pay and how much. Sometimes, a truck and a driver would be caught, but only because the police wished to be seen as incorruptible and diligent. Farrukh invariably had advance notice and subsequently reduced the truck's load.

The driver would receive a substantial bonus to compensate for his three months in prison, pending a trial, which would always be thrown out for lack of evidence. It was an annoyance, but Yusup controlled the authorities.

Yuri Drygin played his part. If the security on the bridge he guarded was lax, he would let a shipment through, but it put a dent in the margins. Still, it had advantages, as it simplified the whole operation, and larger quantities could be moved much faster.

He continued to supply information about the border patrols, changes in the senior officers and whether or not they could be bribed. Yusup would then ensure, through his contacts in Dushanbe, that the incorruptible was transferred – or, failing that, there would be an accident on the way home from work. There had been a couple of accidents, and the fatally wounded had been feted as pillars of society, shining examples of the modern police force and long would they be remembered.

Yusup thought they were bloody fools. However, as a prominent member of society, he regularly donated his time and money towards a more efficient police force.

***

Najibullah arrived in the camp the second night after Oleg and Farrukh's return from the border town.

'Oleg will be here for a few days, looking after operations,' Farrukh said.

'I don't like this,' the Afghan replied. It was the expected reaction. A smuggler, by definition, is a suspicious person and trust is built over time. Oleg was an unknown factor, and a smuggler risking his life did not want unknowns.

'I vouch for him,' Farrukh replied, attempting to calm the tribesman's fears.

'Are you sure he's not Russian?'

'I told you before. His mother had been raped by the Russians. You said you have some in Afghanistan.'

'That is true, but we can never trust them the same way we would a true Afghan.'

'Even if the children have committed no sin?'

'Their sin was to be born,' said the tribesman. 'I would never consent to sully my family's name by allowing one of my daughters to marry them.'

'I thought you did not care for your female children.'

'The dishonour of children conceived by the seed of an invader is. I would rather kill my daughters than allow their shame to besmirch my family.'

'Najibullah, will you accept Oleg at least for the next week or so?' Farrukh asked.

'If you guarantee him, then so will I.'

'And the others who come over at night?'

'I will ensure they accept him.'

Farrukh felt now was not the time to discuss the other issue: the visit across the border that he had feared but now offered some interest. He saw it as an adventure, albeit dangerous, but an adventure nonetheless.

Later that night, after Najibullah had spent time with one of the women and Farrukh had spent a short time with Nozia, they both sat down to talk.

'What would you say if I told you I wanted to go into Afghanistan?' Farrukh asked.

'I'd say you were mad.'

'It's important.'

'Nothing's that important. You'll not be welcome unless you know someone. Where will you go?'

'I know you?'

'I'm only a peasant trying to look after his family. Of what use would I be?'

'Someone's trying to take our business from us. You've seen that?'

'I know, but other people are always involved.'

'But this time, it's serious.'

'I have heard of another operation setting up,' Najibullah confided. 'But I am only the person who smuggles the drugs across the border. I do not listen to rumours. Besides, foolish talk can be fatal.'

'I need to know if it's true. It will be beneficial to both of us.'

'And deadly if we are caught.'

'Will you help me?'

'You would need to cross the border with me, and I'm not sure what can be achieved.'

'Tell me how you pick up the shipments?'

'It varies, but I often travel from my village to a nominated location. It changes from week to week. I am given the shipment and asked to take it across the river, as far as this place. That's all. I am paid on my return.'

'Do you see anyone when you pick up the shipment?' Farrukh continued to probe, but Najibullah continued to be reticent.

'No, but why are you asking me these questions?'

'Because, if you are agreeable, I will return with you.'

'I've not agreed.'

'I will pay you.'

'The return trip is not so easy. There are guns to carry, and the journey is more dangerous. A few kilos of heroin, I can hide under a rock. One or two hundred guns, I cannot.'

'Will you take me?' Farrukh asked.

'Why don't you just cross the border legally, and I'll meet you on the other side?'

To Farrukh, it seemed a reasonable solution. Oleg, however, had cautioned against it.

'What we don't want is for these Russians to know we're onto them,' he had said. 'It's best to keep it as secretive as possible. If your cover's broken, then run for the border the quickest way you can. If you can go with Najibullah, so much the better.'

***

Early the next day, Najibullah and Farrukh — with two donkeys to share the load of the semi-automatics — set off. Farrukh felt a rush of adrenalin; Najibullah just felt another slog back for a meagre financial return. He had heard of a Pashtun in the country's south making millions, but what could a peasant do? Life was hard enough without considering others, and Allah would always remember him when the day came to travel to Jannah, to Paradise.

The border was twenty kilometres away, and Najibullah kept to the valleys for the first fifteen. As the light dimmed and the border came closer, he became more willing to take the tracks leading up and over the hills on either side.

Farrukh had ceased to enjoy the adventure. He was now exhausted, and his feet ached. His calf muscles burnt as they breached every rise on the track. The Afghan appeared impervious to the privations and kept a relentless if tediously slow, pace. He had little sympathy for the pampered city man who accompanied him. He wasn't sure what the outcome would be, but he reasoned that he would either help him or sell him to those who would be very interested in why someone from Tajikistan was asking about the Russians.

He had heard the rumours, even gossiped about them, and it was clear that the Russians were, or had been, in Kunduz. He cared little who was running the drugs, only who was paying the most, and had heard it stated that the Russians would pay more.

His assistance to Farrukh, a man he cared little for, came at a price. He saw him as decadent; he knew the Tajik saw him as backwards and primitive. The relationship was financial, nothing more, nothing less. He had not told him that, and although he was barely literate, he came from an influential tribe in his region and knew who to contact for advice. His reluctant colleague slowed him down as they approached the river and the border guards.

'When the snow melts, the river is a raging torrent. Men have drowned on their way up to you,' Najibullah said.

He had been quiet for a couple of hours as he attempted to maintain a low profile. There had been reports of a new police commander on the Tajikistan side, stating how he would stamp out the drug trade once and for all.

The Afghan assumed it was just rhetoric, angling for a bigger bribe or aiming to impress his superiors, who were already on somebody's payroll.

'We've dealt with them,' Farrukh responded when Najibullah mentioned the reason for the enforced silence. He was glad of the opportunity to breathe freely again.

'Dealt with whom?' Najibullah asked.

'The guards, at least on this side of the border. I made a phone call up north. They fixed it so it would be quiet for us tonight. You don't think I'm going to take unnecessary risks?'

'It won't be so easy on the other side, and if they see me with you, they're bound to be hostile. If I give you the word, just get low, jump into a ditch. Whatever you do, don't come up until I give the all-clear.'

'I'll follow your lead,' Farrukh said. It had been an uneventful trip, apart from every muscle in his body aching. On the other side, it appeared that may not be the case. He had only ever seen Afghanistan across the river. This would be his first time there.

The river was wide and slow-moving, only waist-deep. It was easy to wade across, but it still maintained the ice-cold of the mountains. By the time they reached the other side, Farrukh was convinced he could go no further. Najibullah reminded him of the situation.

'Come daylight, there will be fisherman up here and a truck loaded with Afghan army conscripts. Do you want to stay here and explain to them why you are on their side of the river?'

'Let's move on.' Farrukh appeared to find a new lease on life, and within five minutes, he was moving just behind the Afghan, pace for pace. The river's cold had dulled his aching muscles; he felt sure he could make the drop-off point.

'It's another ten kilometres,' Najibullah said. 'When we are within two, I'll get you to duck off to the side. An old building there will provide respite from the cold, and no one will look inside for you.'

'Why?' Farrukh asked.

'It goes back to when the Taliban aimed to take control up here. The local warlord, who was against them, captured thirty and locked them in the building. Then he ordered some men from his private army to machine-gun them and set it on fire afterwards with a petrol bomb. The locals, even the Afghan army, see it as cursed.'

'And you?'

'I wouldn't go in there, even if a gun pointed at my head.'

'But you can ask me to,' Farrukh said.

'You're from Tajikistan, educated. You don't believe in such nonsense, am I right?'

'You're right, but it will give me the creeps thinking about it.'

'You'll survive. Give me two hours while I deliver the donkeys and the guns, and then we can go and find some hot food.'

***

It took another hour to reach the cursed hut. The invigorating effect of the cold river had worn off, and Farrukh's muscles ached as they had before. He was glad of the chance to rest his weary body, even if the building was as Najibullah had described. The signs of the carnage were all too apparent, with bones randomly scattered around. He could not tell whether they were human but assumed they were.

The intense cold, the wind whistling through the building and remembering Najibullah's story frightened him, even imagining that the building was cursed as others believed it to be.

He was glad two hours later when Najibullah returned. This time, he was without the donkeys and the guns.

'I've got some news for you,' he said.

'What's that?'

'Those that took the guns off me were talking about some Russians in Kunduz. They only wanted to string them up. They couldn't understand why they were being given preferential treatment.'

'We need to go to Kunduz then,' Farrukh said.

'We? You're presuming too much. If we go sneaking around, we're likely to get killed. I'm not doing that just because you have a problem with some Russians.'

'It's *our* problem. If they take my business, it may end your drug smuggling days.'

'I could always go and work for them.'

'They could pay enough to take it across by road at the legal border.'

'True, but I'm not going to get killed for you.'

'I've not come here to be killed, either. Let's find out what's being said on the street, and then we can decide what to do. With the money you can make helping me here, you will not need to make the drug run for at least a year.'

'How was it waiting for me in that building?'

'I swear I could hear voices screaming.'

'Probably the wind. We're a superstitious people.'

'It sounded like voices to me.' Farrukh was glad to be out and moving again.

Free of the donkeys and momentarily revived, Farrukh and Najibullah made the trek to the small village of Imam Sahib. Farrukh spoke Tajik but with a different accent, and as long as he kept his conversation limited, his voice low and let Najibullah do most of the talking, nobody would question him.

Farrukh could only reflect on the barrenness of the village. It barely had five thousand inhabitants, as many donkeys — many pulling carts — and a fair number of camels. By the time they reached the village, the early morning sun had risen sufficiently to allow its warm rays on their weary bodies. Even Najibullah admitted to being exhausted as they sat down for a meal of lamb kebabs with rice and the ubiquitous drink of green tea.

'Nothing saps your strength as much as complaining about the situation,' he said. 'How much energy have you lost?' Farrukh had to admit there was wisdom in what he said.

'Where do we go from here?' Farrukh asked.

'We'll take a bus into Kunduz.'

'Is it safe?'

'As long as you don't tell everyone on the bus how backwards we are.'

'I wouldn't do that.'

'It's what you think.'

'You are right,' said Farrukh. 'But then, maybe I complain too much.'

'We are backwards; I'm backwards,' replied Najibullah. 'There was never the chance of an education. We were either too poor, or there was a war, or someone had burnt down the school. I make sure my sons go to school. They can read and write, but it's too late for me.'

'Your daughters?'

'What value is education to them? They will learn everything from their mothers. They only need to know how to look after the house, cook and breed sons.'

Farrukh said nothing. He only thought about what Najibullah had just said and his apparent lack of concern for the females in his household.

***

With the meal finished, they boarded the bus. It was overloaded, cramped, and full of men in the front. The women, Farrukh noticed, were confined to the back in steerage. It slowly made its way to Kunduz, the major city in the region.

He virtually shared his seat with a goat while the women sat on luggage haphazardly stored in the rear. Nevertheless, he was enjoying himself, and, so far, the people had been courteous, although any attempt at familiarity with their women would have been tantamount to a death sentence. He hoped his time in the country would not be too long, and then he would report to Yusup Baroyev. Maybe even get an invite to one of his parties.

The thought brought a smile to his face, so much so that a stern-looking man, a Mullah judging by his clothes, looked over at him with a perplexed stare. *If only he knew that I was idly screwing one of the most beautiful prostitutes in Tajikistan. He'd probably have a heart attack on the spot*, Farrukh thought.

The distance to Kunduz was not far, about sixty kilometres, but it still took close to two hours, what with the loading and the off-loading of the baggage and everyone having to get off while the person in the back pushed his way to the front, and then everyone back on again.

Twenty kilometres west of Imam Sahib, they met up with the road from Panj-e Payon, the Tajikistan border town, down to Kunduz. The bus turned in a southerly direction for a relatively easy run into the city on a sealed road. After Imam Sahib, Kunduz looked like civilisation, although it was comparative. There were no street lights, most back roads were dusty tracks, and the few women he saw were concealed in Afghan burkas.

Most were in a colour that could only be described as 'Afghan Blue', although some were white. Farrukh had seen a few in Tajikistan, especially close to the border, but here they were everywhere, and he didn't like them. The men swaggered around, some carrying rifles, some with machetes, while the women in the taxis, old Russian Volgas – mainly yellow in colour – were confined to the boot, with one of the women holding the lid up with a stick. As befitted the society, the men sat inside, full of piety and smoking.

'What now?' Farrukh asked.

'We'll find accommodation, and then later we'll walk around, keep our eyes open and our ears pricked,' said Najibullah.

'That seems a random way to conduct an investigation.'

'What do you want me to do? Stand on a box and make a public announcement?'

'No, of course not.'

'Then leave it to me,' Najibullah replied. He hadn't figured out what to do regarding the Russians and Farrukh. He needed to talk to his cousin.

Najibullah visited his cousin with Farrukh ensconced in a guest house near the city centre. His cousin had found the drug smuggling job for him, and although it was dangerous, he was thankful.

Chapter 7

Ahmad Ghori benefited from a wealthy father. He had received a good education which, in time, rewarded him with the title of Chief Financial Officer, Kunduz Province. The title and the position afforded him great respect, easy access to the ear of the Governor of the Province, Ismail Samani, and a share in the lucrative drug trade that the country viewed as abhorrent but constituted almost half of its Gross Domestic Product.

Ismail Samani was a warlord with a private army numbering over ten thousand. He was a good man, steeped in the traditions of his people, who tried his best in a difficult situation. It had not stopped him from filling his pockets with ill-gotten gains and drug money, but to have not done so would have been stupid and naïve in a country where everyone else was doing the same.

Ahmad Ghori had fought with Samani, ensuring he was elected and looked after the province's finances, legitimate or otherwise. The otherwise was where the real money lay, although it remained largely undeclared and totally hidden from view.

As the most affluent of his extended family and his birth village, Ahmad Ghori was also their benefactor, a position he held with honour.

He was the protector and saviour of close to one thousand, and, whereas most were of limited intellect and talent, he always ensured a job – menial if necessary – and the food to look after their families. It had been to him Najibullah had turned when the poor crop he had been aiming to grow and sell in the bazaar had failed due to a severe frost. He had found Najibullah, a new occupation as a drug smuggler.

***

Ghori was a good-looking man with a luxuriant silver beard hanging halfway to his waist. He would dress for work in Kunduz in a suit of the finest cloth. At the weekend, he would retire to his country estate, don traditional clothing, administer and offer his opinions to those who came for his advice and assistance.

The wealth he had acquired afforded him the luxury of three wives. The first was old and respected. She was the mother of his eldest son, who had become – due to his spoilt upbringing – an adult of little worth and a great disappointment.

The second wife, a beautiful, beguiling creature twenty years younger when he married her at forty, had delighted him then as she did twenty years later. He felt a great fondness for her, a strange emotion for an Afghan warrior, but she suffered from premature arthritis and inflammation of the kidneys. It troubled him that she would not see her fiftieth year. She had provided him with two fine sons and three daughters. He treated them all equally, and all benefited from education in Dubai.

The third wife, he had married three years previous when he was close to fifty-seven, and she was a mere child of eighteen. It was a politically opportune move as she was the daughter of the Governor's brother, a wayward daydreaming man, and the marriage gave the brother importance, as the daughter was neither wayward nor dreamy. She was articulate, opinionated and, as the Governor had told his brother. *'Think of the sons the marriage will bring. A son with her common sense, her strength of character and Ahmad Ghori's intelligence. It is a formidable match, possibly a future president of our troubled country.'*

The Governor's brother could not complain as he was financially indebted to his brother. The young female, Hammasa, disappointed that she could not marry her second cousin, Nasir, relented and agreed.

The marriage had not been a great melding of the minds. Ahmad Ghori had, for a while, felt the reawakening in his loins, and she had been compliant. Viagra had ensured two pregnancies –both of which had resulted in sons.

Hammasa, her responsibilities completed, made it clear to her husband that there would be no more intimacy. A fact that did not concern him greatly as, combined with his age and a waning libido, he had ceased to have the overriding need to procreate or even make love.

He was free to give attention to his second wife, who relished his company, although her pain troubled him greatly. She never complained, never rejected his advances, even though they were few and increasingly far between.

***

The visitor to Ahmad Ghori's residence in Kunduz was unexpected.

'Najibullah, what brings you here?'

The reception room where they met was splendid in its decoration, with the finest wall hangings, exquisite carpets on the floor and the luxurious leather chairs where they both sat. A man such as Najibullah would not generally have been afforded such a privileged setting. Najibullah and Ahmad Ghori were first cousins, and although the hour was late, and Najibullah was still unwashed after several days of travelling, it was not enough to deter a welcome reception.

'Advice, confidential advice.'

'Anytime. Sit down and tell me your story.'

'I am not an educated man.' Najibullah knew humility was requisite for meeting with his influential cousin.

'Let me be your education,' Ahmad said.

'There are Russians in the city.'

'How do you know that?'

'Is it true?' Najibullah asked nervously.

'It is, but how do you know this? It is not common knowledge – or, at least, I hope it is not.'

'I have heard it mentioned several times.'

'Why should this concern you?'

'It does not, but others have asked me.'

'Who are these people?' Ahmad Ghori put his tea down and stopped eating the pistachio nuts he had picked from a silver bowl.

'I was asked in Tajikistan on my last trip there, and then I heard it mentioned when I dropped off the merchandise on my return.'

'It may be best if I meet with these people in Tajikistan who are so interested. It is a disturbing development,' Ahmad said.

'I brought one of them back with me.'

'Why did you do that?'

'I saw no reason to refuse. He was willing to pay me. I thought it may have been to our advantage.'

'Then you have done well. I will meet with him.'

'He will be reluctant. He wished to come here secretly, find out what he could and then go back.'

'His wishes are not my concern. Bring him to my estate tomorrow. We will talk there.'

Farrukh was initially angry at Najibullah for talking to his cousin but relented after phoning Baroyev.

'That's the situation. I can get the facts straight and then relay them to you.'

'Farrukh, you have done us proud. Oleg is doing fine as well.'

'No doubt he's with the woman every night.'

'He doesn't stand still for long when there's a woman around.'

'No, although I miss the clear-skinned beauties you have at your parties.'

'Farrukh, find out what's happening, then come up to Dushanbe. Oleg can hold the fort down on the border for the time being. The women will be here on your return. You have my word.'

***

The following day, the trip for Farrukh and Najibullah out to Ahmad Ghori's estate did not take long. It was located no more than fifteen kilometres from Imam Sahib. Najibullah had not mentioned before that this was where he came from. No more the old and decrepit bus for the return trip. This time, it was a Toyota Landcruiser with air-conditioning.

The estate was surrounded by a tall mud-brick wall. It was not an estate as in Europe. It was less impressive than Baroyev's; no swimming pool, and semi-naked women were prancing around. It was neat and tidy with the main house, a two-storey structure of indifferent construction. It showed the result of hastily constructed additions as Ghori's family had expanded. It looked neglected, with a dripping tap by the outhouse, a diesel generator that smoked and clanked, and the dissolute staff who slept in a corner until someone important appeared.

The exterior of the main building belied the interior, which was ornately decorated with velvet curtains and white marble floors. The sweeping staircase to the bedrooms was decorated with bannisters of the finest construction.

As Najibullah explained, 'That's not for us. That's for the master of the house and his family. We are located thirty metres away.'

It did not concern Farrukh unduly, as the room he had been given was fresh, with a functional air conditioner and a television with all the main satellite channels.

'Ahmad Ghori's coming later. We will meet him then,' Najibullah said.

'Fine, in the meantime, I'll take a rest. Try and catch up on some sleep.'

Before retiring, Farrukh took a shower. There was no hot water, but he did not complain. At this rate, he would return across the border before the week was out.

He rested peacefully for several hours and failed to hear the convoy of six vehicles enter the compound. As a senior government member, Ahmad Ghori was always a potential target, either for ransom or death. The extra vehicles were the protection he always travelled with.

***

It was two hours after Ahmad Ghori's arrival, in the very early hours of the morning, when Farrukh and Najibullah were summoned. Fresh clothes had been laid out for both. Farrukh was surprised that Najibullah had showered, trimmed his beard and displayed rugged good looks hidden beneath layers of built-up mud and grime.

'It's not often I get the chance of a clean bed and some fresh water to shower,' he explained.

They were ushered into the visitors' room. There they met Najibullah's cousin. As was customary, there was the usual social discourse about family, the economy and the weather.

It was twenty minutes before their host came to the point.

'Farrukh Bahori, what are you doing in my country? And please, no lies.' Ahmad Ghori's manner had changed. He was stern, unfriendly and with a pronounced frown that displayed his dislike of Farrukh.

'I represent a large company in Tajikistan, concerned that its interests are being usurped by a company in Russia.'

'Well put,' Ghori responded.

'Our shipments are reducing in quantity. We can only assume someone else is taking increasing supplies. We are also aware that production in Afghanistan is on the rise. I have been asked to come and investigate.'

'What a load of nonsense!' Ahmad Ghori banged his fist hard on the table, sending the various dishes of delicacies flying. 'If you wanted the truth, why didn't you come to my country openly and ask a direct question?'

'I was unaware that we have ever known who we were dealing with. We've always operated through middlemen.'

'And that's the way it should have stayed.' Ghori conceded Farrukh's answer was reasonable.

'The reduced quantities concern us.'

'I can see that,' said Ghori. 'But you've come across the border illegally, attempted to spy on us, and now you want me to sit here and be open with you?'

'Yes, that is what I am hoping for.'

'You have been honest. I will give you the benefit of the doubt and explain the situation.'

'Thank you. It is more than I could have hoped for,' said Farrukh, inwardly relieved.

'I will grant your courage in coming here. If you had not come, your quantities would have continued to reduce. There is now time for you to come in with a counterbid.'

'Then I will listen and relay back to my superiors. They will decide on how to proceed.'

'Superiors?' said Ghori. 'You only have one superior, Yusup Baroyev.'

'You have met him?'

'No, and I do not want to. He is a fornicator and a despicable person. He would not be welcome in my house.'

It surprised Farrukh that an Afghan could despise a man with loose morals and then indulge in an activity that forced people to commit a crime, even prostitute themselves to pay for the drug. He was hopeful that his time in Afghanistan would be short.

'Yusup Baroyev, that is true,' replied Farrukh. 'Does he know who he deals with over here?'

'No, and that is the way we wish it to remain. I am only speaking to you because of the seriousness of the matter, but you will meet no others. After this meeting, you will be driven to the border, cross the bridge back into your country, and never return. If you do, you will be killed. Is that understood?'

'Understood.'

'Farrukh Bahori, we have dealt with Yusup Baroyev because he has been the only person capable of taking the quantities we were shipping. We operate in a free market economy. When another operator capable of satisfying our requirements appears, we must consider them.'

'Is there another operator?' Farrukh asked.

'Yes, a consortium of Russian businessmen has approached us with a very lucrative offer. You should know that we have had a bumper crop and have expanded our planting areas exponentially per their requirements. They can take twice what Baroyev can and offer a premium price.'

'Have you finalised a deal with them?'

'We had until you appeared on the scene.'

'Will you allow us to make a counterbid?'

'We will consider it, but for now, we will honour our agreement with the Russians.'

'But you hate the Russians.'

'Yes, of course, but their money is fine.'

'Do you know which companies they represent?'

'Let's not be obtuse. Who else could it be?'

'The Russian mafia, the brotherhood,' Farrukh said.

'That is what we assumed, but we did not ask or care. Why should we?'

'We will need to set up a line of communication. How do you want to handle this?' Farrukh asked.

'After this meeting, you will be given two phone numbers and an email address. All communication will be through them. There will be no further face-to-face meetings.' Ahmad Ghori then concluded the meeting, shook hands with Farrukh, gave Najibullah a traditional hug and left the room.

As he exited the room, Ghori turned to his left and spoke to Ali Mowllah, who had remained hidden throughout the meeting.

'What did you think?'

'It will only complicate the matter,' Mowllah replied.

'It will mean increased profit for us,' Ahmad Ghori replied. 'Can you ensure we meet the production targets?'

'Ahmad Ghori, we will exceed as long as the demand remains.'

'The demand is enhanced with Baroyev and the Russian mafia competing.'

'It will be a bloodbath on their side of the border.'

'What do we care? Both their countries can go to hell,' Ahmad Ghori said as he left his secretive organiser alone and went to spend time with his family.

Chapter 8

Yusup Baroyev felt two emotions on receiving the phone call from Farrukh: delight, in that he had proved his worth, and concern that the Russian mafia was aiming to take his business. His relations with them had been cordial and professional apart from a skirmish close to the northern border of Tajikistan six months previous.

Before he fully debriefed Farrukh, he had one promise to honour. The pool was throbbing the day Farrukh arrived, still wearing the clothes Ahmad Ghori had provided. Ten hours earlier, his appearance on the Tajikistan side of the border had caused issues. He had not officially left the country and was looking to re-enter. A private word with Yuri Drygin, Tajikistan's finest customs official or its most corrupt, soon resolved the misunderstanding.

Thirty minutes after arriving at Yusup's estate, Farrukh had showered and shaved the hideous beard off after being informed he would not return to the village. He was too valuable now, and as he had met a senior figure in Afghanistan, he would be the ideal person to handle the discussions.

It had been almost nine months in the village. As exhausted as he was from the trip, his ardour for the women at Yusup's mansion could not be dissuaded.

He could only reflect that the trek across the border, the bus ride into Kunduz, and the meeting with Ahmad Ghori were justified if there would be such a party at the end. He knew it would be business tomorrow, and Yusup would be business-like and demanding. He resolved to get some sleep. He had been given Oleg's Mercedes and apartment while the previous recipient languished in the drug smugglers' village.

***

True to his word, the next morning at eight o'clock sharp, Yusup Baroyev was in his office, resplendent in a trademark suit.

Farrukh had also dressed for the occasion, wearing a beige-coloured jacket with open-necked shirt and dark trousers. A black leather belt of the finest quality complemented his ensemble. The Mercedes had purred on the trip up to the mansion, and he had discovered that Oleg's clothes fitted him just fine.

'Farrukh, update me.'

'The Russian mafia has struck a deal with the Afghans.'

'As you said, but do you have any details?'

'There are two issues to consider here. The size of the deal and how they intend to transport the drugs out of the country.'

'Specifics, I need specifics,' Yusup said.

'The offer from the Russians is for increased quantities at premium prices.'

'How can they do that?'

'Only by cutting out the middlemen,' Farrukh said.

'That's us.'

'I realise that, and if they intend to pay more, they'll not use the same route we do. They can only be planning to ship it direct by road across the border.'

'That would be horrendously expensive if they bribe every politician and policeman from here to Moscow,' Yusup said.

'Would that be possible?'

'It's almost impossible. I've tried it, and the cost just gets higher. The way we do it now has always been the best. We may lose some heroin on the way, but we're still profitable.'

'Oleg, is he staying down there?' Farrukh asked, anxious to ensure that his good luck and Oleg's car and apartment remained firmly with him.

'For the time being. I've had him on the phone already, moaning. I told him to shut up, consider it an apprenticeship, and get him out of there when possible.

'I bet he didn't like that.'

'What do I care? People do what they're told; they know the options if they don't like it.

'True.'

'Forget Oleg. Let's get on to how we should proceed.'

'I've got the contact details. It's best if we open a channel of communication.'

'Agreed. You'll be the primary contact. Find out what they want and what we must do to isolate the Russians.'

'It's going to get messy. The Russians will not let us interfere with their business plans.'

'So be it if we must fight fire with fire.

'We'll need to bring up some men with guns and few morals about using them,' Farrukh said.

'Let me worry about that. You just focus on the Afghan bastards who think they can take me out of the picture. They will rue the day they were born.' Yusup Baroyev was indignant and angry.

***

Dmitry Gubkin, located in Moscow, had managed to work with Stolypin while maintaining a discreet distance. It still concerned him that he was risking too much and that the reputation he had carefully nurtured over the years could be destroyed by one inappropriate action, one casual remark by Stolypin and his colleagues. He weighed up the situation. The agreement with the Afghans looked solid, but he did not trust them for one minute.

The reasons for agreeing to join with Grigory Stolypin were complex. Sure, there was a vast amount of money, but he already had more than he could hope to spend in several lifetimes, let alone one. Then there was the political and financial influence he would have. But mainly, it was the sense of a challenge.

White-collar crime, corporate crime, of which he was the acknowledged master, was cold and insular. Nothing more than decisions in a boardroom or behind a computer screen. With Stolypin, there was the chance of adventure and the allure of danger. For too long, he had been cautious, lurking in the shadows.

It was time to stand up, be counted, and be a man. To show his wife, Katerina, that although he may be in his sixties, he could still cut it with the younger men. She was still young, sexual, and willing, but he had sensed the change in him in the last year. The thought of sex still enticed him, but the physical act interested him less. He was a five-minute man now, but she wanted more. She wanted him to woo and caress, and he didn't have the time or the inclination. There were more important things to do than waste a few hours.

'Stolypin, how will this work? Give me the details about the people I'll be working with?' Dmitry had asked when they met for the second time.

'Currently, we pick up the drugs on the northern border of Tajikistan, from our contact to the south. We take responsibility for the distribution from there on.'

'Sounds a reasonable way to do business,' Gubkin said.

'It is, and it's worked well for some years.'

'So, why change?'

'A group of us….'

Dmitry interjected. 'A group of us? I thought you spoke for the Russian mafia.'

'Yes, we do.' Stolypin's reply was a little too hasty for Dmitry. He decided to let it pass.

'Continue.'

'We intend to bypass our contact in Tajikistan, maximise the profit margin and take the thirty per cent up to sixty per cent.'

'Let's go through what you just said.'

The gangster had not prepared for such an intensive meeting and was starting to feel out of his depth, but he reasoned this was why they wanted Gubkin. Not for his suave manners and debonair looks but for his impartial analysing and planning.

'Fine,' Stolypin replied, not sure if he had all the answers to hand.

'First question. Why do you want to remove your contact in Tajikistan if he's performing satisfactorily?'

'He has in the past,' replied Stolypin. 'No doubt he will in the future, but we can do a better job and get a better deal. Besides, we are Russian. Why should we let someone else take money that belongs to us?'

'Okay, I'll let that pass, but it hardly seems a good enough reason to take him out of the picture,' Dmitry said. *A patriotic gangster*, he thought. *How bizarre.*

Dmitry Gubkin was fiercely patriotic, but he didn't go killing his own people, which the Russian mafia habitually did with predictable regularity.

But isn't this what I'm doing now if I'm party to bringing drugs into Russia? he thought. He let it pass and focused on his second concern.

'Maximise the profit return. How do you intend to achieve this?' he asked.

'From Afghanistan and through Tajikistan and finally up to the Russian border,' replied Stolypin, 'there are middlemen, facilitators, corrupt policemen, army personnel, border guards and politicians to pay off. They all want a cut; it all adds up. Remove as many as you can, and there is another five per cent.'

'That seems reasonable. We'll discuss the transport route later. Thirdly, why take the thirty per cent of Afghanistan's output up to sixty per cent and how?'

'There are several components here,' Stolypin explained. 'We've already been in contact with the Afghans. They're ramping up production for us.'

'That explains the sixty per cent, but how do you distribute that much product?'

'Leave that to us.'

'I need to know,' Dmitry asked.

'We'll create the demand.'

'How?'

'We'll saturate the marketplace with a low-cost product for a few months and then jack the price up, standard business practice. If the demand is not there, we'll create it.'

'You intend to create thousands more heroin addicts?'

'Yes. Do you have a problem with that?' Stolypin asked. 'Enough to forego the money?'

'Not that much of a problem,' Dmitry replied.

***

Two weeks later, Dmitry Gubkin travelled the fifty kilometres north of Moscow to meet with Stolypin's associates. He had argued that he was to be known only to him, but Stolypin had insisted there needed to be a chain of command and backup if he was not unavailable. To the businessman, it sounded like a euphemism for being detained by the police or dead. He did not ask for a clearer understanding.

He agreed that he would meet the others this time, and from then on, it would only be face-to-face with Grigory Stolypin. The gangster agreed, as it also suited him.

Dmitry was not in a good mood on his arrival. His wife had insulted him, told him he was impotent, and she would find a man who could satisfy her. He knew she wouldn't; she was a trophy wife and only there because he was rich and she had been poor. He still loved her, but she cared little for him. He knew that if the money flowed and the overly-expensive trinkets were hers to have, she would stay.

Now in his sixties, it was true what she had said. He needed Viagra to keep the blood pumping, but there was a slight heart problem, so the dose was small. Hormonal replacement therapy, aiming to maintain his testosterone levels, had limited effect, and the tablets made him nauseous.

Grigory Stolypin arrived at the mansion on the outskirts with two other men. One was red in the face, bloated and wearing an ill-fitting suit that looked like he had slept in it. The other was solid and muscle-bound.

'Dmitry, allow me to introduce my colleagues. This is Boris Sobchak.'

The red-faced, bloated man put out his hand and gripped Dmitry's right hand firmly. He felt the bones in his hand were about to be broken. He would later discover that Boris 'the enforcer' Sobchak had earned the title by accepting no excuses from those who worked for him. His solution for disloyalty or incompetence was death.

Ivan Merestkov, the second of the introductions, was more agreeable; Dmitry warmed to him immediately. He was of average height, well-rounded, not fat and polite in manner and bearing.

'I used to be a weightlifter in my younger days,' said Merestkov. 'I represented Russia at the Olympics once. I still lift the weights, but my shoulders are not what they were.'

'Boris will ensure the men, Ivan, the marketing of the product, and I'll work with you, ensuring your plans are implemented,' said Stolypin. 'After today, you will only have contact with me.'

'So why has my cover been broken?' Dmitry reiterated his concerns when told he would need to meet with the two new men.

'We must pledge our loyalty to you,' replied Stolypin. 'There are three of us here, and two will always ensure the other one does not cheat or scheme against us.'

'Can that work?' Dmitry asked.

'Yes, all three of us know the consequences if we don't, and besides, you're going to make us wealthy beyond belief. Why would we cheat?'

'It is in your nature. You told me that before,' said Dmitry, reminding Stolypin of their previous meeting.

'You're right, but here we are, and here we stay, loyal to you.' Boris Sobchak and Ivan Merestkov acknowledged their agreement.

Dmitry realised he needed facts and time, but some concerns still needed to be addressed.

'The Afghans, do you trust them?'

'We have met with them,' Merestkov said.

'It was mentioned at my first meeting with Grigory, but do you trust them?' repeated Dmitry.

'Slit your throat as soon as look at you.

'They'll still aim to cut a deal with Baroyev,' Boris Sobchak said.

'That would be a logical assumption,' Dmitry said.

'Do we liquidate Yusup Baroyev now?' Grigory asked.

'He's safe until we've got the operation running successfully. Also, we need someone on the inside. Someone who feels they've been done an injustice, someone smart.'

'I'll work on it,' Boris said.

'The transportation routes, are they in place?'

'Another few weeks, and they will be,' said Ivan. 'We need to deal with politicians; their demands are proving difficult. Some may even be slated for removal.'

'Can you arrange that?' Dmitry asked.

'In time, we can. Time is not of the essence here. The demand is not going away, and the supply is intact.'

'We do this right,' Dmitry said. The other three acknowledged with a nod of the head.

'Is there any more to discuss for now?' Grigory asked.

'No,' said Dmitry. 'I will maintain contact with you and wish Sobchak and Merestkov a goodnight.' The meeting concluded with each man hugging the other as they left.

Chapter 9

In the six weeks since Farrukh had returned from Afghanistan, his position within Yusup's inner circle had continued to improve. He had also met Negareh, a beautiful and decent woman, and she had moved into the apartment with him.

Negareh's father, a prominent businessman, imported cars from the West and even imported the Mercedes that Farrukh continued to enjoy. Her father had disapproved of her actions when she had moved in, but she was independent of mind, and he had little to say on the matter. Farrukh was a known confidante of Yusup Baroyev, and that came with a certain respect and a great deal of fear.

Oleg, meanwhile, continued to fester down at the border. Malika kept him occupied, but he was tired of her. Her attempts at moderating her drug intake seemed in vain. She was a hopeless drug addict, and the belief that a good clinic in the capital could fix her appeared unlikely. And then there was the question of when he would get there. He had phoned and almost pleaded with Yusup the last time, but the answer was always the same.

'Not until we've resolved the issue with the Afghans. Farrukh's the only one who's had any personal contact. He's staying here, and you're staying there.'

Oleg realised his situation was not good and, whereas the money continued to come in, there was nowhere to spend it unless it was on vodka and food. Malika only needed heroin, and he could get that for free, although the number of smugglers from Afghanistan had continued to decline, and Najibullah, always so regular, had not been seen for a few weeks.

He had noticed that his personal hygiene and appearance continued to decline. Always so punctilious about his appearance, he now looked as Farrukh had. He dressed in trousers with a drawstring, a knee-length shirt, and a waistcoat, dirty after six days of use, complimented by a dark and wiry beard and an expanding girth. It raised him to anger, and only at the end of the day, when he was with Malika, was it moderated.

'You said you were going to take me to Dushanbe. Put me in a nice apartment, buy me nice clothes and drive me around in an expensive car, but it was all lies. You just wanted me to yourself,' she had screamed the night before.

It served no point to explain that life was not always straightforward. He could have told her he had a boss, a responsibility, and that the two days in the village had expanded to months, and he couldn't leave.

He told her to shut up and even hit her once.

He rarely left the village, apart from the trips to grease the palms of the border guards, Yuri Drygin included, along with the local police and the commander at the Army barracks not more than forty kilometres away.

'We're getting a better deal from the Russians,' Drygin said the last time they met.

Oleg could not help but like the man. Sure, he was a rogue pretending to be honest, but he could converse. More than could be said in the village, with its disparate collection of Afghan tribesman and Tajikistan rejects from the capital, scratching around, aiming to buy a few hundred grammes to sell on the streets of the capital. Most of the Tajiks seemed to give most of it to the whores in the village anyway.

It had even snowed once, and he was constantly cold. The intermittent electricity from a small and smelly generator allowed him to run a two-bar heater in the room that constituted his living quarters and office.

***

'Tell me about the Russians?' Oleg asked in the comfort of Yuri Drygin's office at the border crossing. He had to admit the customs official's surroundings were better than his own.

'Not much to say. They're paying someone very senior who orders us to stand down at certain times of the night. The gates are opened, and we look the other way.'

'How senior?'

'Government level,' Drygin replied.

'I thought we had them all sewn up.'

'Maybe you did, but someone's paying more. Does your boss know?'

'Which boss is that?' Oleg feigned ignorance.

'Yusup Baroyev.'

'How do you know his name?'

'We may be isolated from the city down here, but we're not stupid. I've always known who he was, and the Russians who went down through here some months ago mentioned his name.'

'They told you.'

'No, of course not. The pig-swilling son of a peasant bitch is what they called me when I questioned their dubious visas.'

'What did you do about the insult?'

'Nothing. On the one hand, they were slipping me five hundred American dollars in crisp new notes and, on the other, swearing about me in Russian. They assumed I was a pig-swilling son who only spoke Tajik. I would have killed them if they had said it elsewhere. Besides, what are a few insults? I've suffered worse in my life. I made sure a goat tied up at the back of the building urinated on their luggage before they left. It would have stunk after a couple of days.'

'You're letting them transport drugs through here unhindered?' Drygin's tale of the Russians had amused Oleg; he could only smile.

'Yes, that's the directive, although what they're carrying? Well, I don't know.'

'You know it's drugs.'

'Officially, no. Unofficially, what else could it be?'

'Why didn't you let us take drugs through?'

'I occasionally did, but it wasn't safe to do it more than a few times.'

'I'm stuck out at the arse-end of the world waiting for a few Afghan tribesmen while the Russians are coming through here in air-conditioned luxury?'

'Air-conditioned?' said Drygin. 'Judging by the vehicles, the only air-conditioning they would have is when they open their windows.'

The conversation continued, with Oleg progressively getting warmer and Yuri progressively richer. If Oleg wanted him to keep talking, he wanted more money.

'You never explained why we don't just transport the drugs across the border.' Oleg returned to the question that concerned him most.

'Basic economics, I would assume,' said Drygin. 'Paying off politicians and the law authorities in this country is expensive. It must be cheaper to buy it direct from the smugglers after they've crossed the river on foot.'

'But it's complicated, with so many people getting the merchandise to the capital. After there, I don't know what happens to it.'

'The Russians are getting a clear run. The roadblocks are letting them through.'

'They can't keep this quiet for long. Someone's bound to notice, and then the clamps will be applied?' Oleg posed a rhetorical question.

'Why?' replied Drygin. 'If the Russians are paying the right people, no questions will be asked. Anyone who sticks their head up will either have it shot off or they'll be paid to shut up. It seems foolproof to me.'

***

Oleg decided to spend the night in the border town. He found a cheap boarding house with a rudimentary shower, hot water, and a lady to wash his clothes.

In the relative luxury of his accommodation, he realised his time in the drug smugglers' village was ending. He would talk to Malika and see if she would go with him. First, he had to contact the Russians, although he was unsure how. He knew he would rot in the village, and Baroyev cared little about his fate. Farrukh was in his apartment, driving his car, wearing his clothes and screwing his women. He vowed to deal with that piece of slime at a later date.

He retired early for a good sleep in a clean bed, snug and warm. *No one with me, though*, he thought. *So much better for when I see Malika tomorrow.*

He had become adept at driving the 'Goat' –the old Russian jeep – and he now knew who to bribe as he took detour after detour to reach the village. He was feeling good, more confident than in a long time. He would honour his agreement with Malika. He was sure she was a good person, maybe even worthy of a longer commitment.

The Mercedes and the apartment still enticed him, and if Yusup Baroyev – high and mighty, omnipotent Yusup Baroyev – wouldn't give them to him, he'd find someone who would. Clearly, the Russians were the 'someone', and he spoke their language. They'd take him on board – a Russian who could speak Tajik. His success in learning the language had been astounding, and, apart from a few words, he considered himself almost fluent. He had to find the Russians, but how? The only person who would know was Najibullah, but he was across the border in Afghanistan, and there was no way he could contact him.

***

Oleg returned to the drug smugglers' village the next morning. It was a depressing sight as it came into view, covered with a thick blanket of snow. The track had been difficult, but he had managed – although he nearly ran off the track a couple of times – and, compared to Farrukh, he was a sedate driver.

He had been away for a couple of days, and he first intended to visit Malika to exercise his manly right to a quick cuddle and some serious sex. He had given her heroin to tide her over, not as much as usual, as she had convinced him that she was slowly cutting down. He hadn't been sure, but he had been pleased and had acceded to her request.

Her room, basic and invariably cold, apart from when he had been able to buy some wood from a passing farmer for the wood-burning stove, was at a distance from the track. It was a three-minute walk, two today, and he was in a good mood. He wanted her to hear of his plans first.

As he entered her room, he heard groaning. Malika, naked, was down on her knees giving a blowjob to an Afghan tribesman who, several days before, had sold him two kilos of heroin. Even by Afghan standards, the tribesman was an unsavoury character with no teeth, disgustingly old and smelly and breath that had forced Oleg to stand to one side when negotiating with him.

His breath reminded Oleg of the smell of the donkey dung that littered the village as it stewed in the midday sun, and here was the woman he cared for, aimed to rescue from her depravity, down on her knees. It was evident from the state of the cheaply-constructed bed and the green sheet and blanket that she had already screwed the man.

His anger rose to a level he did not know he was capable of. He always carried a knife as necessary protection and lurched at the Afghan with it. The Afghan suffered an immediate deflation of his erection, and Malika quickly retreated to the rear of the room, attempting to grab the blanket to wrap around her naked body. Oleg's first lunge with his knife missed its mark. The second did not, and the Afghan collapsed to the ground, with the knife firmly planted where his heart was. He was dead, and Malika was next.

'You whore! Why didn't you wait?' he screamed.

'I needed a fix. You didn't give me enough.'

'I gave you what you wanted.'

'It wasn't enough. I only gave a blowjob.'

'I had planned to take you away from here, but now I will kill you.'

With one leap across the room, he grabbed Malika by the hair, the blanket falling away to reveal her naked body. It was a body he had caressed many times, but now it was a body he would stick a knife into.

Oleg moved to grab the knife, now covered in blood, from the dead Afghan. Malika struggled and pulled away, attempting to get out of the room. He grabbed her again, pushed her to the floor, kicked her hard in the abdomen several times, and then hit her across the head with a piece of wood intended for the wood-burning stove. The beating continued for at least thirty seconds. To Oleg, it seemed like an instant. To Malika, it was as forever.

Her screaming and his shouting attracted the attention of other whores and their customers: one was Afghan, and the other was a Tajik. They quickly overpowered Oleg, beat him unconscious and hogtied him with a rope used to tie the donkeys to a post outside. The whores rushed to Malika, who was lifeless.

It would be two days before she regained consciousness and three before she realised that some of her ribs were broken and she had lost sight in one eye. The eye may have responded to medical care in a properly equipped hospital, but nothing could be done in the village.

She had been fond of Oleg, but the addiction had been overpowering, and she had succumbed to the only method of obtaining the hideous drug. That was how she saw it. During the convalescing period, she decided to leave the village. She would let her wounds heal and then go to Dushanbe, find her mother and make something of herself.

Oleg, meanwhile, was not having a good time. Hogtied, left to rot in his own urine and faeces and caked in blood, after every Afghan tribesman in the village came in to kick him some more and to threaten him with an unpleasant death.

***

Malika left the village on the tenth day after Oleg had killed the Afghan and almost beaten her to death. After the anger of the Afghans had subsided, he had been thrust into a corner of the room. He remained in his faeces and urine-laden clothes, but he was alive. One of the women had taken pity on him and hand-fed him a bowl of warm soup, some rice and a few pieces of chicken.

He felt shame at what he had done to Malika and wished he could have been more sympathetic to her plight. If he were to die here, then so be it.

On the fourteenth day, Najibullah unexpectedly turned up in the village. He had not come with any heroin.

'You have killed one of my tribe,' Najibullah said with little interest as he stood before the murdering Russian.

'I was angry. She was my woman.'

'A whore? How can you say such a thing?'

'I still liked her. She had a kind heart and a bright mind.'

'A woman is nothing. A donkey has more value.'

'I did not see her like that.'

'Why not? She was screwing anyone and everyone in this village. I even screwed her a few times.'

'What is it that you want, Najibullah? You've not come here to gloat.'

'Maybe I have come to kill you.'

'But why you?'

'He was a cousin, the man you killed.'

'Does that give you the right to kill me?'

'In my culture, it does, but maybe another solution exists.'

'What do you mean?' Oleg attempted to sit up and listen.

'A murderer can be slain in the same manner as the victim, or he can be forgiven by the murdered person's family.'

'Is that what you are offering?'

'Babak was not a good man. The shame of being killed in the company of a prostitute will only bring continued disgrace to his family. They wish to avoid that shame.'

'But he was in the company of a prostitute. How can you change that fact?'

'We will not mention the truth of it. We will say he died of an illness.'

'That's okay, but what do you want from me?' Oleg asked.

'You will need to be punished.'

'And this punishment?'

'I will tie you naked to a post and whip you until you are almost dead, then slit your throat. Or, you can pay his family for the life you have forfeited.'

'How much if I pay?'

'Five thousand American dollars.'

'I don't have that much money here.'

'Where do you have it?'

'In Dushanbe.'

'We will go there together, and you will give me the money. Remember, if you betray me, your death is certain. This is your only option.'

'You have entered illegally. How can you go to the capital?' Oleg asked.

'I am not carrying drugs. I entered Tajikistan legally at the border crossing in Panj-e Payon. We will leave for the capital tomorrow.'

Chapter 10

Oleg, released after satisfying the Afghan of his willingness to pay, felt much better after a wash, a change of clothes and some medicine. The sadness over Malika remained, and he had no idea what had become of her.

The trip to the capital of Tajikistan for Oleg and Najibullah was uneventful. Oleg imagined that Najibullah would have felt out of place in a city that looked more Western than Asian, but it was apparent he was not. Oleg suspected he had visited the city before but felt it was best not to ask.

'We will deal with the five thousand dollars that you owe Babak's family first,' the Afghan said. They had checked into a good hotel, some distance from the city centre – hopefully, far enough from Yusup Baroyev's prying eyes. Oleg guessed the events in the village, his dereliction of duty and the slaying of the Afghan would have impacted Yusup's business empire. He realised how the drug lord would have regarded that chain of events.

'And then, after the payment?' Oleg asked.

'You are free to go.'

'But where? My previous employer will not want me back. He will probably kill me if he knows I'm here.'

'What concern is this to me?' Najibullah attempted to walk away.

'You took Farrukh over to Afghanistan. Did you meet with the Russians?'

'That is not any of your concern.'

'I may be of some use to them.'

'I will enquire. If you are, I will let you know.'

'Thank you.'

After payment of the blood money and with time on his hands, Oleg checked out his old apartment from a vantage point on the other side of the road. He still looked like a tribesman – it provided a perfect disguise. He resolved to keep the beard and the overgrown shaggy hair, but there was no harm in a trim.

He resumed his position thirty minutes later, feeling better after a shampoo and a haircut. He did not have to wait long before he saw Farrukh, wearing the clothes from his wardrobe, driving his Mercedes with a beautiful woman in the passenger's seat. It could only be him, although now he was clean-shaven with short hair and the distinct look of affluence.

Oleg resolved to avenge himself on Farrukh for taking his apartment and his car.

Two hours later, Najibullah phoned. 'I have set up a meeting for you.'

'When?'

'Tomorrow. They will contact you.'

***

The man who phoned Oleg was the man who picked him up from a street corner close to the airport the following morning in a late model Mercedes. He was unfriendly.

'What can you do for us?' He was a quietly spoken man. The receding hairline was combed over to disguise the signs of premature baldness.

The man may have looked weak and retiring, but the other man sitting in the front of the car did not. He was big and strong and carrying a gun. The man speaking to Oleg appeared suspicious. He wanted answers. Oleg was certain they were the two Russians Yuri Drygin had mentioned.

'You were working for Yusup Baroyev?' the man asked.

'Yes.'

'Then, why do you want to work for us?'

'I killed a man.' Oleg realised that Najibullah had probably told him the full story.

'Why?'

'I caught him with my woman.'

'Was she worth it?'

'I thought she was, but maybe I was wrong.'

'We know the story. We also know you had an unfortunate run-in with the FSB.'

'How do you know that?'

'We have people inside that organisation.'

'It's true, an unfortunate accident. I was only aiming to force the man to comply. I didn't expect him to be in the shop.'

'That may be, but you have a history of unfortunate accidents. Assuming we wished to use you, of what advantage would you be?'

'I know these people. I've even learnt the language, and I'm Russian.'

'Russian or otherwise is of no concern to us, but your ability to speak Tajik may be of some interest. However, you can't stay here, or Baroyev will see you.'

'Thank you. Anywhere is fine.'

'We will send you somewhere you will be useful to us.'

'Anywhere is fine,' Oleg repeated.

'We will send you to Afghanistan. Is that acceptable?'

To Oleg, it was not the answer he wanted. He could not return to Russia, as the FSB would soon find him, and Andre Malenkov's brother would ensure he was dead. If he stayed in Dushanbe, it would be Yusup Baroyev, and he would not take kindly to him deserting his position, even if he had been hogtied for nearly two weeks. Then there was the disruption to business that he had caused. It was either a bullet in Russia, a termite's nest in Tajikistan, or living with savages in Afghanistan. He chose the latter.

'Afghanistan is fine.'

'That's good. Otherwise, we would have informed Baroyev that you had been speaking to the Russian mafia.'

'I'm screwed, whatever happens,' Oleg commented in a moment of indiscretion.

'Look on the bright side,' said the man. 'If you get down to Kabul, there may be Chinese whores. Every other Afghan with some money in his pocket would have been through them. I wouldn't fancy them, but you may after a few months in Kunduz. You stand a better chance of a little boy pulling you off there.' The man had a warped sense of humour, which Oleg did not appreciate.

The conversation with the man in the car had lasted no more than thirty minutes, yet he never said his name once. Najibullah met Oleg five minutes later, near where the vehicle had dropped him off. The Afghan had been waiting and watching for the appropriate signal from the car: two flashes of the headlights to indicate agreement, three to indicate failure.

The two flashes were clear and precise.

'It looks as if we are travelling companions to Kunduz,' Najibullah said.

'It looks that way,' the Russian said with a tone of resignation in his voice. It was not what he expected from the Russian mafia, but he was still alive and, with life, there was hope. At least, that was what he tried to convince himself, but for once, he was unsure.

***

Two days later, Oleg and Najibullah were back at the northern border of Afghanistan. Panj-e Payon had changed little since Oleg's last visit, and it retained the look of all border towns in Central Asia. The trucks stretched two hundred metres from the metal gate on the Tajikistan side. Stalls had been set up alongside the road, selling food and drinks and the women, also for sale, were only twenty metres distant. The drivers were either with the women or dealing with the customs fees and bribes. Yuri Drygin, the corrupt customs officer, was involved in the negotiations.

He offered no comment as Oleg presented his passport with two hundred American dollars secured inside the second page. The bridge, built with foreign aid money, was good and solid. Once across and into Afghanistan, the road rapidly deteriorated.

Oleg had thought the drug smugglers' village was unique in its desolation. Once in Afghanistan, he realised he had been wrong. The poverty was overwhelming, the decay and rotting excessive, and the women subjugated and covered.

The arrival in Kunduz, the main city in the region, had been delayed by the never-ending movement of vehicles, people and donkeys. It was apparent there were no road rules, apart from those who gesticulated with a brandished fist and beeped the horn on their vehicle. Najibullah organised a guest house close to the centre. It was the same guest house Farrukh had stayed in previously.

***

Najibullah left, promising to return in two hours, but it was closer to four before Oleg saw him again. He brought a man who instinctively did not like Oleg, not because of his look, but because Oleg was Russian and his family had suffered under the Russian invaders. Najibullah introduced him as Alam.

'Let me make it clear,' Alam said. 'I do not like or trust you. I will work with you, not because I want to, but because I must.' He was not an unpleasant-looking man, with a dark beard showing flecks of grey. He was freshly washed, and his sandals were open-toed.

His footwear surprised Oleg, as the ground outside was still frozen in places from the interminable, bone-gnawing cold. The sky was a dull, hazy blue, tinged with brown due to the smoke from the wood and charcoal-burning stoves in the city, which gave it an eerie, moonlike character.

'I appreciate your honesty.' Oleg was surprised at how competent his language skills had become. 'It will take time for us to adjust to each other.'

'I am to be your primary contact. I will assist you in any way possible and ensure that no harm befalls you,' the unfriendly Afghan replied.

'Then I thank you. I understand that my people, which I cannot be proud of, came here in a previous time and committed untold atrocities against the population of Afghanistan.' Oleg had come across this man's attitude before.

'They slaughtered my family.'

'It was not my generation. I have no issue with the Afghan people.'

'You are still the son of the invader,' Alam reiterated.

'And you are the son of the people who flayed my father,' Oleg rebuked.

'Then we are clear. I will work with you, assist you as I must, but do not assume we can share a friendship.'

'That is fine. Business and friendship are not two commodities exclusively aligned. We will focus on business, friendship maybe later.'

'Friendship, never!' the Afghan affirmed.

Despite the shaky first meeting, Oleg instinctively trusted the Afghan, who professed hatred and malice towards him. *An honest, plain-talking man, a man I can work with,* he thought, although he hoped it would not be for too long. His life had taken too many twists and turns, and this was one turn he did not appreciate.

Najibullah excused himself from the meeting and left. There was an uncomfortable silence before either Oleg or Alam needed to speak again.

'Why are you here?' Alam broke the silence.

'My position is unclear, but it appears I am the contact point for my people back in Russia.'

'Why you? What skills do you have?'

'Hopefully, my language skills and my knowledge of the industry.'

'It is a surprise you speak our language.'

'You seem to be an educated man,' Oleg said in return.

'Refugee camp in Pakistan. I had a few years at school, and I picked up the ability to speak English.'

'Unfortunately, I speak no English.'

'Then we can possibly agree to a mutually beneficial partnership.'

'I'm sure we can,' Oleg said.

***

The following morning, Oleg received a phone call from the man in the car who had assigned him the job in Kunduz.

'Have you met with your primary contact?' he asked.

'Yes, although he hates Russians,' Oleg replied as he cleared his eyes and coughed up the smoke in his lungs. The thick, slow-moving air in the city ensured the smell of embers remained long after daybreak. It was as if a brown fog had fallen over the city. It would take him some time to get used to it. His room had been adequate, the electricity intermittent, and the noise from the diesel generator, which started and stopped with annoying regularity, was overbearing.

'They all hate us, but they have no problems taking our money,' said the man. 'Never trust them for one minute. That's why you're there.'

'What am I here for?' Oleg asked.

'To ensure our interests are protected.'

'How do I do that? I don't even know your name.'

'You know my voice.'

'Yes.'

'Then why do you need my name?'

'It seems courteous to know who I'm dealing with,' Oleg said.

'Courtesy is for social occasions. Our relationship is purely business. I have no more interest in you than the Afghans. Do I make myself clear?'

'Crystal clear. Where do I start?'

'You need to visit the processing plants. Check their quality control and their methods of transportation. Ensure they're not cheating on quantity and never trust them for one minute.'

'This is dangerous. What protection do I have?'

'With the money, we're paying them? Or do you fancy your chances in Tajikistan or Russia?'

'I'll stay here for now.'

'Good, then move around. Find out what's going on. If you can meet with their leadership, go down to Kabul, and grease the politicians' palms if it helps. Yusup Baroyev knows you're in Afghanistan.'

'How does he know that?'

'The officer at the border, Drygin.'

'Will you remove Drygin for his disloyalty?'

'Why? He serves our purpose. He had been paid well enough to keep quiet but couldn't resist a little extra cash. We will remember. His day of reckoning will come soon enough.'

'And Baroyev?' Oleg asked.

'We are discussing with him to see if we can mutually agree to a deal. Until then, you are safe.'

'Then I must learn to love it or be dead.'

'Love? I'm not sure if anyone could love it there.'

'You've been?' Oleg asked.

'I've been. Found any little boys to suck your dick?' The man hung up on him.

***

He had a good night's sleep, even if slightly troubled by events, and he had woken up needing a woman. There must be women here somewhere, he thought. Prostitution is universal. It can't be stamped out because a Mullah says it is wrong. Men need to screw, and women, especially here, must need money. He promised himself to ask Najibullah the next time he saw him. Alam, he could not entirely trust yet.

'We've found you a house not far from here,' Alam said when he arrived mid-morning. 'There's a guard who can be trusted and someone to clean the house and provide you with meals.'

'The guest house is fine.'

'Do you trust everyone who comes here to accept a Russian in their midst?'

'No, I suppose not.'

'I have been charged with keeping you safe and alive. If you are harmed or killed, the same fate will befall me.'

'Rough justice,' Oleg commented.

'It's the only justice here.'

'What are we doing today?'

'We will discuss the transportation of the merchandise.'

'Here in Kunduz?'

'No, it is a short distance to the north.'

'Then let us go.' Oleg was anxious to do something.

'We will wait until it is clear.'

'Why?'

'The merchandise has to be dispatched before you arrive. There are too many suspicious people involved. The local police will not take kindly to a Russian nearby while they're receiving their payoffs.'

***

It was two o'clock in the afternoon before they left for the forty-five-minute drive north, Alam and Oleg in the lead vehicle, a Toyota Landcruiser in an agreeably good condition. To the driver's right sat a guard with an AK-47 strapped to his chest. To the rear of the Landcruiser, a pickup truck followed with two men standing precariously in the back, holding on to a roof bar mounted on the cab. They both held on with one hand while clutching weapons in the other. A machine gun mounted on the roof of the pickup truck's cabin completed their weaponry.

'Are we expecting trouble?' Oleg asked.

'Normal precautions. Bandits and rival gangs.'

'I assumed your people had the market sewn up.'

'We are the only ones transporting in any quantity into Tajikistan.'

'Others are aiming to take over the business?' Oleg asked.

'This is not Russia or the West. Friendly takeovers, agreements in boardrooms, transference of shares is not what occurs here.'

'Kill the key people and take it for yourself,' Oleg observed.

'Exactly.'

'It also happens in Russia, but it's not often reported. If you want ruthless, then try the Russian mafia.'

'Yusup Baroyev can also be exceedingly violent,' Alam said.

'What do you know about him?'

'The fornicator?'

'Why do you call him the fornicator?' Oleg asked.

'We are aware of his parties and the promiscuous women. It is an insult to Allah, and he, a Muslim.'

'But I have seen Afghans with the women in the village.'

'We are all made of flesh. We have our weaknesses, but we recognise them and ask Allah for his forgiveness. Yusup Baroyev does not.'

'He would appreciate the title.'

'You have been to his parties, lain with his women?'

'The truth?' Oleg asked.

'I know you for a Russian heathen. You would have no guilt.'

'Yes, on several occasions.'

'I would sin for them,' the Afghan said in a moment of weakness. It was the first civil word he had said in their time together.

The conversation was cut short as the compound came into view. It was isolated from the next place of habitation by at least a kilometre of open land. Guards, poorly dressed for the weather, walked slowly around the perimeter holding AK47s at precariously dangerous angles. He had seen it many times, how the untrained and the uneducated held the barrel pointing at their feet. It made no sense; he imagined it was laziness.

The gate opened with two beeps on the horn from the lead vehicle. Normally, that would have been all required for the gate to open. Not this time. On the other side of the gate, blocking their passage, was a Toyota pickup truck with two men propped up high, aiming a machine gun at Alam and Oleg. The men in the truck looked professional. The men outside did not.

Another man left the compound and walked towards the Landcruiser. He was wearing a bulletproof vest and accompanied by another two men carrying Kalashnikovs, this time, held correctly. Alam spoke to the man in Tajik and, at his command, the truck blocking their passage pulled back.

Inside the compound, the main building was mud brick. Hastily constructed huts were off to one side, aluminium from what Oleg could see, while a noisy diesel generator, puffing smoke, supplied electricity. Oleg had noticed the searchlights mounted around the compound on high poles from the outside. Once inside, he saw that, at strategic positions on the parapet of the walls, additional men watched out in crouched positions.

'We're serious about security here,' Alam said nonchalantly.

'Who's likely to attack this place?' Oleg asked. He knew the compound represented danger, and he was danger-averse. He was following up per his new job description, but being out here and exposed was not where he wanted to be; he had already experienced animosity about his being Russian back in Kunduz.

Everyone seemed to have had a relative or a tribal member or had been in a village that had felt the heavy hand of the Russian war machine. His protection had been fine in Kunduz, but he was not so sure out here. There were at least twenty of the most vicious men holding weapons. He wasn't sure if the guards they had brought up from Kunduz could dissuade any of them from putting a bullet through his head.

Life takes many turns, he thought to himself. *It's best to get on with the job and not worry too much about my fate.*

Alam explained that this was their main distribution warehouse, although it had only been in operation for a couple of months. Within another month, it would be closed, and they would relocate. Oleg asked why.

'It's clear. We can't protect it indefinitely.'

'Who would be able to take this place down?'

'Rival warlords, local military. Plenty of people want a piece of the action.'

'I thought your people had it under control.'

'Yes, it's under control, but sometimes there's upwards of three to four hundred kilos of merchandise here. That's a lot of money for Afghanistan.'

'Is there anyone in this country capable of taking you on?'

'Oleg, we are a violent people. There is always someone who believes he is capable. And would your people care who was sending the merchandise, as long as it arrived on time?' It was the first time Alam had referred to him by name.

'Probably not, but the deals would need to be renegotiated.'

'They will, anyway.'

'What do you mean?'

'Do you think a cast-iron agreement between the Russian mafia and an Afghan is a binding contract?'

'I would have thought it would have held up for some time. It is to both parties' mutual interest,' Oleg replied.

'The heroin leaves Afghanistan for no more than six or seven hundred American dollars a kilo. By the time it reaches the streets of Russia, its value has multiplied a hundred-fold or more. Do you think that is equitable? Believe me, there will be renegotiations, or else Yusup Baroyev will again become our primary customer.'

'What you say disturbs me. What do you think my people will do if presented with this situation?'

'What will they do?' Alam exclaimed. 'They'll accept it, or else.'

'They would feel the need to respond.'

'How? Send the Russian military in here again? I don't think so. You are here, we will honour our agreement for now, and if there is to be a change, we will let you bid against Yusup Baroyev, against Farrukh.'

'Farrukh? You know Farrukh?'

'Of course, we do. He was here, almost got himself killed for his impertinence, but we trust him more than you. His people did not come here and slaughter us.'

'The hatred runs deep. I understand that, but I was not here.'

'Your father was.'

'And you flayed him, by all accounts,' Oleg replied angrily.

'The stories of the skinning of Russian soldiers have been greatly exaggerated. We killed Russian captives. But flaying? Not often, if at all.'

Alam was equally angry. It was a painful subject for him. His father had been butchered by the Russians when the crops had failed, and he was looking for assistance from the conquerors. In desperation, he had rushed forward and jostled with a young Russian soldier, who had promptly shot him through the head with his pistol. Alam hated the Russians, although he had not learnt to hate Oleg.

The visit to the compound lasted thirty minutes. Oleg spoke to no one apart from Alam. He was shown where the heroin came in, stored, weighed, and ultimately shipped out. He noted that there were two distinct areas for dispatch, one larger than the other.

'Why the two?' Oleg asked, pointing to the confined areas in the corner of the main building.

'One is for your Russian friends; the other is for Baroyev.'

'Which is which?' Oleg asked.

'Which do you think is for Baroyev?'

'I'd say the smaller,' Oleg replied. By his calculation, the Russian mafia received nearly ten times as much as Baroyev. Assuming the Tajikistan gangster received twenty kilos daily, the Russians received up to two hundred. He calculated, in total, a wholesale value in Moscow of over six million American dollars. No wonder the Afghans would be looking for a better deal.

***

The return to the city took less than the outward journey. It was his first time at the house Alam's people had secured for him. Oleg was pleasantly surprised, as it was a two-storey house painted a dull blue on the outside. There were three bedrooms and a spacious sitting room. The main living area had heavy curtains, dark green in colour, three comfortable chairs and a settee. On the floor was a carpet of the finest quality. Alam told him later that it was Bukhara and very valuable. The kitchen appeared clean, although he did not look too closely. There were servants to deal with whatever went on there, Alam explained.

The wood-burning stoves in the main rooms kept the house immensely warm, too warm for Oleg, but their regulation was limited. It was either sauna-like heat or freeze. He chose the sauna.

The grass at the back was reasonably short, and there were the signs of flowers, although the weather was too cold, and the few remaining stalks were frozen hard in the morning. Overall, Oleg was pleased, and his first few days in the city had not been as bad as he had expected, but he still needed a woman; it was starting to worry him. He would talk to Alam the next day and see what he could do for him.

***

The next morning after an agreeable but solitary breakfast at a table designed for twelve, he met with Alam again. The Afghan was agitated: there had been a development.

'What's the problem?' Oleg asked.

'It's not your concern,' Alam replied.

'It is if it affects the shipments.'

'It will if it is not resolved.'

'Then tell me the details.'

'There is a viable threat that the Afghan army will close down our entire operation.'

'Why don't you pay them off?'

'We pay everyone, but sometimes it is not enough. They were calm if we only supplied Baroyev, but now the quantities we are shipping are much larger.'

'Can't you pay them more?' Oleg saw no problem. Enough money was moving around to pay everyone some extra.

'It's not that simple,' said Alam.

'Why?'

'They feel that the best deal is struck if they push us to the brink, show us that we are not immune.'

'But why destroy your operation and then ask for more money?'

'It is how it works here. Power is everything, especially when negotiating. Whatever happens, they know we will rebuild. Besides, the government must show those supplying aid money to Afghanistan that they are serious about stamping out the illicit drug trade.'

'Who are "they", and are they serious?' asked Oleg.

'The government, the politicians, that's who.'

'I assumed that. Are they serious?'

'Most do very well out of the drug trade, either by direct involvement or bribes. They don't want it to stop, but the aid money is all important, and the donor countries, mainly America, make it a condition that Afghanistan reduces its output of drugs.'

'Russians have no more love for the Americans than the Afghans,' Oleg said.

'That may be, but we still accept their money and smile as they hand it to us. Or, at least, hand it over to the politicians.'

'You are critical of your politicians?' Oleg asked.

'How much of the aid money reaches the people?' said Alam. 'It's not a lot, and the Americans know that. To them, it's just a game they play with the Russians, with us in the middle.'

'What do we do about the army?'

'We need to stop them.'
'How?'
'We need to go to Kabul,' Alam said.

Chapter 11

Malika made the trip back to Dushanbe in the company of Rena, the prostitute who had told her that her mother was alive and well. All of the women had taken turns to care for her in the village after the savage beating from Oleg, but it was Rena who had been adamant that it was her responsibility to ensure her friend was reunited with her mother and that she received proper medical care. Her pimp had complained, but he was not violent and acquiesced when she told him she would return at the earliest opportunity. Something she had no intention of doing.

They found Malika's mother on their first day back in the city. It had been joyous, tinged with sorrow. Her mother had found a job working in a hospital as a nursing assistant, and Malika was confined there for six weeks. The wounds healed quickly, although one eye would never give more than a blurred vision.

With the help of her mother, she finally shook off the addiction that had plagued her life. Rena, meanwhile, had returned to the streets of Dushanbe. She deserved better, but she was doomed. Sadly, it was evident to Malika that it was only a matter of time before Rena would return to the village.

'It is behind us now,' her mother said, although Malika could see the sadness on her face.

'I have come to rebuild my life.'

'We will rebuild it together, my daughter.'

In the weeks since reuniting, they discussed their lives at length. Her mother had wandered lost for months until she found a refuge for single women. There, she found herself and worked as a seamstress until the opportunity to work at the hospital became available. It had not paid much, but it was peace, all she wanted, apart from her daughter.

Malika opened up slowly about the degradation of her life as it spiralled downwards out of control. She told her mother about selling herself on the street. Her mother cried profusely, but Malika consoled and told her it was in the past. Her mother came to accept the inevitability of a drug addict.

She told her about the drug smugglers' village and the people she had met there, some good, some bad. She felt it wise not to go into detail about the Afghans and their perverted demands, the violent beatings she had suffered, and how she came to be so severely bruised and battered, with one eye that would always be impaired.

She would never tell her mother of the hatred she felt for a man she had cared for, and thought had cared for her. He had been intolerant and angry when he should have been sympathetic and forgiving. She hated him and what he had done to her, and she knew that one day, somehow, she would have her revenge.

Her condition continued to improve. After years of selling herself, the bruising and the scarring on her body ceased to be visible. The addiction continued to trouble her, but she resolved not to be tempted, and with her mother by her side, the guilt was acceptable.

Her father had been a good but weak man, and throwing himself under a bus was a sign of that weakness. It was what her mother would always say, but Malika wasn't sure if it was for her benefit or her own or even true.

The tattoos, unpleasant as they had been in the village, mellowed in their intensity and, with minimal make-up and a long-sleeved blouse, were barely visible.

Malika quickly found a position at the hospital, but it offered little interest. She tried other jobs but with the same indifference. She had one skill, and with the months passing and her beauty re-emerging, she felt there was no reason she should not become an escort of a wealthy man or two. *I had been one of the highest paid in the city; why not again?* she thought.

At several of the jobs she had tried, she had been propositioned. At one interview, she recognised an old client sitting across the solid wooden desk, asking about her typing skills, clerical abilities and what experience she could bring to the position. He knew full well what her experience was, but he was seated next to his wife, a stern, bitter-looking woman with the figure of a melon and the face of a pig.

She failed to get the job, as the ugly wife saw competition. Besides, she didn't want him attempting to plant his unsheathed penis into her mouth while she was trying to reorganise the filing cabinet.

***

Her mother had been distraught initially when Malika outlined her plan for the future.

'Mother, it's what I'm good at. If I keep away from drugs, I'll be fine.'

'It is a sin.'

'It is a sin I have committed many times, and I will look after you.'

Malika knew her mother would never accept, but she saw no option. She phoned the managing director with the ugly wife and offered her services to him at a reasonable price, more out of charity than anything else. As she explained to him later, as they both lay naked on the queen-size bed in the upmarket apartment she had rented, 'If you have to go home and sleep with her, the best I can do is offer you a special rate as my first customer on my return.'

'Sleep with her? Fat chance there is of that,' he said. He was a decent man who treated Malika well, even if worn down by life.

The customers came fast, mainly from referrals. The majority that visited were decent, hard-working and successful men with stressful jobs and non-caring wives.

She always made it a condition to meet a potential client at a restaurant. He would be disqualified if he burped, passed wind, or scoffed his food down. Her standards were high, her skills at satisfying her clientele immeasurable and within six months of taking the apartment, she was at the height of her profession and commanding a substantial fee.

Some of the men came only for companionship, the opportunity for conversation and a pleasant diversion from their normal stresses. Most came for sex, but they all treated her well.

*****

Her mother grudgingly accepted the situation and sometimes assisted in vetting the men, although she would not visit the apartment. Life had been hard enough for both women, and, as her mother rationalised, her daughter was coming to no harm.

Malika, to the world, seemed a balanced and successful woman. There was a decent car in the garage, a small Audi, plenty of clothes in the wardrobe and a fridge full of food. There was only one chink in the armour, her hatred for Oleg.

She maintained a passive approach to her clientele, who she saw as friends. The latest man came as a surprise. He picked her up some distance from the apartment. She kept the address secret until she was certain the man was worthy. The green, chauffeur-driven Bentley was like no other car she had been in.

The black leather, wooden trim and drinks cabinet in the back made her feel like royalty. She reflected on the difference between the village and the car as they drove to the restaurant thirty minutes away.

The man, who sat to one side of her in the rear seat, was distinguished and handsome with the first signs of ageing. He knew he would need to pass a test to be allowed into the inner sanctum of her apartment.

She knew him by reputation, although he had not given his full name. He said his name was Yusup. She knew it was Oleg's boss, Yusup Baroyev.

There was no question of relaxing her demanding standards, even for a chance to exact her revenge, but arriving with a Bentley, transporting her in resplendent luxury to the best restaurant and buying the best champagne, Dom Pérignon, was an almost automatic acceptance. His manners were exceptional, his conversation enlightening, and his etiquette superb. She arranged to meet him again on the following Wednesday.

***

Dmitry Gubkin enjoyed the opera that night in Moscow. The performances had been excellent, and his wife had been in a good mood for once. His latest corporate takeover had been a dazzling success, netting him a few million dollars more, but the money and the challenge were small-fry to what he was now involved in. The elite of Moscow society congratulated him on his business acumen and the beautiful wife on his arm.

She had come courtesy of another successful man whose business he had crushed. Dmitry knew the moment he showed failure, she would wiggle her arse to another man. He suspected she was having an affair with a much younger and more virile man. He could have employed a private investigator to check. He certainly had the money to hire the best, but he didn't want to know. Not yet, anyway.

The thrill of working with Grigory Stolypin had given him a new lease on life. It wasn't what he had imagined when he first agreed to work with him and his colleagues. He still suspected that, somehow, Stolypin was working outside the code of the brotherhood, but he had neither the proof nor the inclination to enquire further. The amounts transporting up through Tajikistan were stable and showed promise for a substantial increase. The money was flowing in, and the number of addicts continued to rise.

He ensured to be elected to the government committee attempting to control drug addiction. He knew it was a contradiction and smiled inwardly each time the committee met.

True to his word, Grigory Stolypin had kept him isolated. The only communication they would commit to was by email and phone. It was proving to be an ideal arrangement.

During the final thirty minutes of Verdi's 'A Masked Ball', Dmitry received a text message on his mobile. He had muted it as demanded, not switched it off as required.

Afghans giving trouble. Demanding a better deal. We need to talk.

He had learnt that an urgent message did not require an immediate response. Invariably, the problems were easily dealt with if careful consideration was given. It would wait until he arrived back at the substantial house he owned. He would wait until Katerina had gone to bed, although the tablets the doctor had given him were working wonders, and he could have easily visited her in her bed and seduced her for the second time that day. However, business was business; she would be there later, whereas the Afghans may not.

'Grigory, what's the problem?' he asked over the phone from his office.

'They want a better deal, and now the Afghan army is sniffing around. We need to do something fast.'

'I don't work like that. That's why you asked me to lead here,' Dmitry reminded him.

'Fine, but what do we do?' Grigory sounded edgy.

'Let's deal with each item separately,' said Dmitry. 'The most pressing issue is the Afghan army.'

'Why do you say that?'

'We have less control over them. The Afghans' money demands we can deal with. They were always bound to renege on the initial agreement. We all knew that.'

'The Afghan army is threatening to close down the operation over their side of the border.'

'Why?' Dmitry asked.

'The usual reasons: abhorrent trade, show the world they're serious, increased aid money.'

'So, it's just rhetoric.'

'Maybe, but they'll do it anyway.'

'There are two options. We either pay them or someone to stop it or offer a token compromise.'

'What do you mean?' Grigory asked.

'Someone needs bribing, but the Afghan army and their government want to show they're serious.'

'How can they do that without closing us down?'

'We get our Afghan colleagues to offer them an alternative target, ensure they find drugs. It will slow down the operation for a few weeks while they take the accolades. Let them grab the aid money, then we ramp up to cover the lost time.'

'Can we do that?' Grigory asked.

'We have no option. Who do you have in Afghanistan?'

'Oleg Yezhov?'

'Do you trust him?'

'Not really, but he's an opportunist. He'll do what he's told.'

'Otherwise?' Dmitry asked.

'Otherwise, we'll hand him over to the Afghans. Tell them he was cheating.'

'Okay, gangster's justice. Get Yezhov on a phone conference. Don't use my name.'

***

It was two o'clock when Oleg was awakened from a deep slumber. It had been a long day, and he was glad of the rest. His dream, rudely interrupted, was the same as usual: a woman, exceptionally long-legged and sexually demanding.

'Who the hell is phoning at this godforsaken hour?' Oleg shouted to an empty room.

He turned on the bedside lamp and picked up his mobile.

'What do you want?' he bellowed, not caring who was on the other end.

'Oleg Yezhov, we need to talk to you,' Dmitry said.

'And who are you?'

'I am the person coordinating this operation.'

Oleg realised his previous outburst had been inappropriate. 'My apologies. It's early morning. I just woke up.'

'Apology accepted. You are aware of developments?'

'Yes, it was me who passed them on.'

'And what are you planning to do about it?' Dmitry asked.

'Firstly, we're planning to go to Kabul to see how we can resolve the bribe situation.'

'That's fine, but it won't stop the Afghan army from attacking our operation.'

'It will if we talk to the right people down there,' Oleg said, still anxious to go. Alam had told him about the Chinese prostitutes, and he wasn't sure how long he could go without a woman.

'We need an agreement with whoever is responsible for the attack. Can that be arranged?'

'Our Afghan colleagues are planning to do that anyway. They will let the Afghan army show everyone they're competent and determined, then carry on as normal afterwards.'

'Just make sure it happens,' Dmitry said.

'And their demands for the extra money? The people we're dealing with, I mean?' Oleg asked.

'We'll deal with that later. First, stop the army interfering.'

With that, Dmitry and Grigory Stolypin, who had been listening to the call, hung up.

'Dmitry, what do you reckon?' said Stolypin.

'If he can pull this off, he will have our trust. Maybe bring him in closer to the operation, maybe into Dushanbe.'

'That's fine by me,' Grigory said.

Oleg attempted to return to his sleep, but it was impossible. A bleary-eyed Russian greeted Alam on his early morning arrival at the guest house.

'The flight is at nine,' said Alam. 'We'll need to get to the airport early to avoid the chaos.'

***

There must be something worse than an internal flight in Afghanistan aboard a fifty-year-old Russian twin-engined turboprop aeroplane, Oleg thought, but he did not want to experience it. Not only did it spew oil out from the engine casings on the ground and in flight, but it rattled incessantly, and the seat in front of him was either fully upright or collapsed almost onto his lap. The cabin smelled of burnt oil, and the people, crushed in tight, were uncommunicative.

He sat quietly, said little and breathed a sigh of relief when the plane finally touched down in Kabul with a bone-shattering thud.

After that episode, he vowed 'never again'. However, as Alam explained later, the other option was multiple hours traversing the Salang Pass, risking the bandits, the Taliban, and the lunatic drivers. Better your life in the hands of whatever God you pray to for an hour or two than fifteen, possibly twenty, but no less dangerous.

The guest house in Wazir Akbar Khan, the diplomatic area of Kabul, was reasonable, although his place in Kunduz was better. Although Oleg felt comfortable, relaxed and at ease, it would not last long. There were people to meet, palms to grease, deals to be made, and plans to be formed. The pressing issue was how to defer the impending attack on their operation by the Afghan army.

'Why do I need to be here, Alam? Surely your people could have dealt with this.'

'You are right, but who can you trust? With you, there will be a degree of honesty. Credibility is paramount, and no Afghan will openly admit to being corrupt, especially in front of a fellow Afghan, if a foreigner is present.'

'Why?'

'It's cultural. In the north, they are Tajiks. Down here, they are mainly Pashtun.'

'Is that a problem?'

'It's not a big problem. Your presence will ensure the corruption is moderated, not eliminated.'

'Okay, so who are we going to meet first?'
'The Minister of Defence.'
'Why him?'
'He controls the army.'

***

At ten o'clock the following morning, Oleg and Alam presented themselves to the Minister. A little man with greying hair and a ruddy complexion, he was hardly Oleg's idea of a senior politician. It mattered little as the man was affable, polite and spoke good Russian.

'I went to school during the occupation,' said the Minister. 'If you wanted to do business Russian was vital. Nowadays, it is English. The invaders change, but life goes on.'

'Thank you for seeing us,' Oleg said.

'It is my pleasure to assist our Russian brothers.'

'It is good to meet someone who does not openly despise me.'

'I am a pragmatist. The Russians were not good people, but time moves on. Dwelling on past events does not help anyone, and we Afghans are regrettably too good at remembering the past.'

'It must have been difficult,' Oleg said.

'Yes, but my family prospered. We kept the Russian army fed; they paid us well. Sometimes, the quality was not so good, but they still paid.'

'We have a problem in the north.'

'Yes, I know commerce is impeded between Afghanistan and Russia. This concerns me greatly. We are a poor country, and interfering with commercial ventures is non-productive. What can I do to help?'

Minister Nazif Arsala, the son of a Pashtun father and a Tajik mother, had been born in Kabul. An educated man, he realised that a commodity he should condemn was also responsible for a significant proportion of his country's wealth.

He could stamp out the trade, let it flourish, or compromise. He chose to compromise, not only because it was better for his country but because it was profitable to him.

He had no great affection for the Russians, no great animosity either. They had been cruel and heartless and had attempted to subjugate his people. He also recognised that the Afghans were cruel and, with the Taliban gaining in influence, it was better to ensure his family's well-being if they needed to retreat to a more peaceful country.

Foreign Aid money was all very well, but there was only so much that a politician could syphon off, even a politician as skilled as he was. If he had been questioned whether it was right or wrong that taxpayers' money, mainly Westerner taxpayers' money, was being diverted to his and his cronies' pockets, he would have replied that it was only fair.

Afghanistan had not asked foreign invaders to come to the country to loot, plunder, and wage war, but they came anyway. If they wanted to hand out compensation to ease their consciences, then it was not for him to criticise. He would have told them that life was tough and taking a little off the top for expenses was neither criminal nor corrupt. It was how it had always been. Those who had not learnt that lesson were looking for a handout on the street. Let the foreigners deal with them; he had a family to provide for, and they were more important.

'Can you ensure the impact on our business will be minimal?' Oleg asked.

'I cannot see how. I am aware there are activities in the north of my country, which are abhorrent,' the Minister said. Oleg recognised a lie when he heard it.

'Sometimes, it is necessary to bend a little. Afghanistan is an impoverished country. My people only aim to alleviate your suffering.' Pure rhetoric, Oleg realised, it was no different from the rhetoric he had used in St. Petersburg. There, it had been to convince a reluctant businessman that he was better off paying for his protection than running the risk. Here, to convince a wily politician to take the money and turn a blind eye.

'Our Western cousins require us to be resolute in stamping out this trade,' said the Minister.

'And what gain will there be to your country? Additional funds to allow them to remain longer, to take further business interests from you? To plunder your mineral wealth and to give you a pittance in return?' Oleg, who knew little about such matters, had been sufficiently coached from Moscow by Dmitry Gubkin, who maintained his distance from the office in a government building in Kabul. Oleg thought it smelled vaguely of mothballs.

'Your answering is convincing, but we must shut down your operations. We cannot ignore the directive. Additional aid money is critical to rebuilding my country,' the minister said.

'Are you able to assist?' Oleg asked.

'We are not foolish people,' replied the Minister. 'We do not want to bring undue hardship to the poor people of Afghanistan by depriving them of income, no matter how meagre.'

'That is what will happen.'

'Of course. It is not for us to act irrationally. Our response will be measured. I will let Alam know when and where we will focus our activities.'

'I thank you.'

As the meeting concluded, with Oleg on the other side of a closed door, the Minister pulled Alam over to one side and spoke to him quietly.

'You will ensure my assistance will be compensated?' he said.

'Yes, of course.'

***

Alam was in a good mood as they left the Minister's office.

'There are other people to see, but that will wait for tomorrow. Tonight, we celebrate,' he said.

Oleg had to acknowledge that his initial impressions of Alam had been wrong. He had proved himself educated, logical and accomplished in a country where all three were not always obvious.

'Alam, I met you in Kunduz, but I assume other people are involved.'

'You will meet them in due course. When they are confident that you can be trusted.'

'Have I not proven my trust?'

'You have worked with Yusup Baroyev, a man of questionable morals. You have killed one of our people. Trust is earned, not given. It will be some time before we are willing to accept you.'

'Is that how you see Baroyev?'

'Some deride his shameful habit of fornicating with numerous women, but I cannot judge him. A woman's pleasure is to be savoured; if he can afford many, that is to his advantage.'

'It has been some time since I have been with a woman,' Oleg admitted.

'Yes, I know. That is the celebration for tonight, assuming you have enough money and stamina.'

'Money, yes. Stamina, we shall see.'

It had been true what Oleg had been told. There were Chinese prostitutes in Kabul. Their presence was well-concealed, but those with money knew where they were.

They drove to a house close to Wazir Akbar Khan, well-protected and surrounded by guards who were a cut above the rest. Entry was purely on an invite, yet Alam had managed to secure one with little difficulty. Inside, behind dark curtains, was an alien world. Exquisitely-dressed Chinese women s moved freely around the rooms.

The bar in the corner maintained a frantic pace supplying the male patrons, Afghan and Western. The prices were exorbitant, whether for the girls or the drinks. It was good that Oleg had brought close to two thousand dollars. Tonight he was going to spend it all. Not just on himself but Alam as well, who was consuming more than his fair share of Johnnie Walker Black Label.

Oleg had a more pressing need. He had chosen the girl with the flower in her hair the moment he walked through the door. She was slim and tender with pert breasts.

Once she was free of a drunken American who only wanted to kiss her, too drunk to take her, he moved close to her.

'Hello,' he said in Russian. He tried Tajik, but no response.

'Fucky,' she said in heavily-accented English.

One word they both understood sealed the deal. The bedrooms were up a spiral staircase. It was pay-as-you-go. He handed over five hundred American dollars to a stern-faced, middle-aged woman at the bottom of the stairs before he was allowed to proceed. He wasn't sure if he had paid for an hour of the young Chinese girl's time or a night, but he accepted the price. In the village, it had only cost a few grammes of heroin.

The Chinese brothel was neither the time nor the place to argue the price. Besides, only Alam would understand what he was saying and judging by his appearance, he was already virtually incapable of speech.

The room where Liu practised her trade was small and ornately styled with Chinese lanterns and fairy lights. She was an attractive woman, probably not more than twenty or twenty-one. She was not to the standard of Malika, but after so long, he was pleased.

Clearly, the five hundred dollars entitled him to more than one hour of her time. She had been insistent on his showering first, and she had joined him there, applied the soap and lathered him down, ensuring that she made the briefest of touches on his erect penis. She teased and delighted while holding him at a distance. Once showered and on the bed, she massaged him with fragrant-smelling oil.

It seemed like an eternity, but eventually, she relented. It was a process that was to repeat itself until the early morning.

The next day, she bade him farewell with a fond embrace. She then went into the house; he did not see her again. Alam was waiting outside in the vehicle.

'Are you better?' he asked.

'Yes, much better. And you?'

'A dreadful headache, but I have sinned. It is just that I suffer now.'

'You are a man. You did not sin. Men need to drink and make love to beautiful women. It's only natural.'

'That may be, but the Mullah at my Mosque would not agree with you.'

'Maybe you should bring him here,' Oleg joked.

'If the Taliban knew of this place, they would slit the throats of every whore there, including the one you spent the night with.'

'Then we had better not let them know. What is the agenda for today?'

'We will meet another person.'

Oleg had failed the night before to phone his contact in Tajikistan. He took the opportunity as they proceeded back to the guest house.

'Are you certain we will receive a warning of the army's pending attacks,' the nameless man asked. 'Can you be sure?'

'In Afghanistan, what can you be sure of? It's the best information we have,' Oleg replied.

'Then, when you return to Kunduz, I want you to meet one of the Afghan smugglers' senior people.'

'Alam said I would only meet him when they trusted me.'

'It is already arranged,' the man said.

As dusk approached, Alam and Oleg drove to a large house on the city's outskirts. Alam said it was the road to Jalalabad, but Oleg soon lost his bearings as the vehicle deviated in and out of the traffic; the lack of street lights and road signs made it difficult to understand where they were. It was a busy, chaotic city, and although he could not say he liked it, he had to admit it had a charm.

'The person we are about to meet,' Alam said. 'He is a man who prefers to remain hidden. Don't ask who he is or where he is from. He will ask you questions; you will answer. My people place great faith in his wisdom.'

Chapter 12

Ali Mowllah spoke Russian with limited fluency. He had taken the opportunity to meet the Russian mafia's representative before a more formal meeting in Kunduz, to the north. Oleg thought he was a splendid-looking man, and it was clear from his speech that he was educated.

'We have met because we have mutual issues to discuss and resolve,' Mowllah said.

He sat cross-legged on a carpet. There were comfortable chairs, but it seemed apparent to Oleg that adopting a similar position on the floor was preferable. Alam easily assumed the position, Oleg with difficulty. He had spent enough time in the country to manage it for a short period, but he had been troubled by a cramp a couple of times. He hoped it would not happen this time.

'What is it that you wish to discuss?'

'The partnership we are involved in.'

'Am I the right person to discuss this with?' Oleg asked. 'I am here as a representative of my organisation, but I am not within its senior echelons.'

'I wish to discuss the inequitable arrangement that currently exists.'

'I am told that this agreement was made recently. A contract signed to that effect,' Oleg said.

'That is true, but the situation has changed.'

'You are referring to the impending action of the Afghan army?'

Ali Mowllah moved in his seat. He stood up and looked away from Oleg.

'The Afghan army presents complications. What I am referring to is more serious.'

'Please continue.' Oleg felt that the man was showing him disrespect.

'We have honoured our side of the agreement and raised our production levels significantly.'

'This I understand.'

'Yet, we see little return.'

'I thought that the money was flowing into your bank accounts.' Oleg was not fully cognisant of the present arrangement, but he had been forewarned that they would be looking for a better deal.

'We can supply more, but we will want a better return,' said Mowllah. 'The costs to defuse our government's interest will be more than expected. You must make up the shortfall in our profit margin.'

'I can only be the messenger here,' Oleg replied. 'Any final decisions would need to be made by others.'

'It may well be that those who came here initially need to return. Otherwise, we will need to deal with your opponent.'

'My people do not respond well to threats, regardless of how carefully they are worded.'

'Threats!' the Afghan replied with feigned indignation. 'You do not know the meaning of the word.'

'The Russian mafia does not appreciate being told what they must do. Surely, you must realise that.' Oleg stood up, glad of the opportunity, as he could feel a cramp coming on.

'I am not telling anyone what they must do,' said Mowllah. 'I am purely stating the situation. Another party we have had good dealings with will be in Kunduz within the next few weeks.'

'Does this party have a name?' Oleg assumed it was Yusup.

'You know who I mean.'

'Yusup Baroyev.'

'Yes.'

'He will not be able to move the quantities my people can.'

'He assures us that he can. We trust him. He is a brother, a fellow Tajik, although his behaviour is not something we can countenance.'

'I know him well. He cannot give you as much business as we can.'

'We shall see. He is sending a representative in fourteen days once we have dealt with the army.'

'Baroyev's representative, did he give a name of who he would send?' Oleg asked.

'The person we met before, Farrukh Bahori. Do you know him?'

'Yes, I know him,' Oleg replied. He knew exactly what he intended to do when they met again.

The meeting had not taken long, but the message was clear. Oleg realised his time in Afghanistan was likely to be prolonged. In Kabul, there were Chinese prostitutes. In Kunduz, he would need to ask Alam.

***

A late afternoon flight the next day to Kunduz, in the same plane that had brought them down, returned Oleg safely to his guest house. It was warm and well-equipped, with at least a hundred channels on the television courtesy of the satellite dish on the roof. He could not complain about his comfort, but to be without a woman indefinitely gave him concern. He now had the added complication of a visit from Farrukh, the same Farrukh who had taken his apartment, clothes, and car. Without the demands of a woman, he mulled over Farrukh's fate.

As Alam explained the next day, the compound they had visited was being readied as the intended location for the Afghan army to attack. The bribes had been paid, and the date and time agreed upon.

'What about business?' Oleg asked.

'We will move to another compound,' replied Alam. 'It is of little concern.'

'And what will they find at the present compound?'

'It will give the appearance of being in use. There will be a few kilos of heroin, armed men and a suitably impressive security system. The spotlights will be on; we will ensure there are savage dogs to complete the subterfuge.'

'Will the army believe that it is the primary distribution point?'

'Those present will. There will be a battle, men will die, and heroin will be found. They will claim a great victory, tell the world they have smashed a major drug operation, and then everyone will return to their regular business.'

'And what of the men killed?'

'What about them?' said Alam. 'They will not be our people, just peasants with guns who have been paid well enough to believe that we care about them.'

'You will condemn them to maintain the subterfuge?'

'What do you want us to do? Let the army close us down?'

'No, of course not.'

'My friend, life is cheap, and nowhere is it cheaper than in Afghanistan. Have you not killed innocent men before?'

'They have not always been innocent,' said Oleg. 'But yes, I have killed.'

'I know that. You killed my cousin.'

'Your cousin?'

'The one you pulled off the whore in the village.'

'I am sorry. I was angry. I cared for the woman, but her addiction was too strong. She could not resist the need for a fix, even when she had said she was fine until I returned.'

'There is no need to apologise,' said Alam. 'You have paid the money to his family. The matter is closed. We will talk no more of it.'

***

The Afghan army's offensive against the compound was planned for one hour after dusk on Tuesday. Alam suggested they go and watch from the safety of a nearby hill, not more than four hundred metres away. Oleg could see from his vantage point that the military was planning a massive show of force. He calculated there were at least three hundred troops with armoured vehicles. Helicopters circled in the distance, waiting to arrive at the appropriate command. The guards in the compound continued to doze, unaware of their impending fate.

A flare shot up into the night sky, signalling it was time to move in. The drug smugglers had chosen the compound because there was open land on all four sides, which provided good security. If twenty or so men had aimed to attack, which would have been the case with a rival gang, the security would have been fine, but with three hundred, it offered little protection.

The Afghan army infantry was well-armed, well-disciplined, and moved in formation. The return fire from the compound was uncoordinated. It was clear that those inside the compound, the defenders, were not of the same calibre that Oleg had seen on a previous visit. They were shooting wildly without a clear target. He had not had the discipline of military training, but it seemed clear to him that you did not waste a bullet if you did not have an intended and viable target. The army maintained a distance, allowing those inside to continue wasting ammunition.

Once the shooting lessened – a clear indication ammunition was running low – the army moved forward again. The four armoured cars, one to each wall, slowly moved over the frost-hardened ground, the soldiers keeping to the rear of the vehicles, apart from the brave and foolhardy fools who felt the need to show off to their colleagues. Those in the compound could not miss them. They suffered some casualties.

Faiz and Wais, two of those inside – peasant farmers at any other time – were brave, even diligent in the face of overwhelming odds. They saw the situation as futile and that they had been set up. A hastily constructed white flag made of an old piece of fabric had little effect when Wais attempted to wave it

144

vigorously in front of the advancing troops. It had cost him his life, as he was cut down by a bullet from an American M16 assault rifle that one of the soldiers carried. The battalion commander had made it clear – no prisoners, no surrender. It was a clear signal to those who dealt with drugs that their form of trade would not be tolerated, and to the world, the Afghan army was competent and incorruptible.

The battle lasted no more than sixty minutes. Of those in the compound, none survived. Twenty of the Afghan army had died, and another fifteen were injured. The government in Kabul was quick to announce to the world that a major drug-smuggling ring in northern Afghanistan had been crushed by its military's prompt and efficient action.

Also, Minister Nazif Arsala had made another substantial payment on the three-bedroom apartment he had bought for himself in Dubai. It had been a good result for all. The drop in merchandise leaving the country had only taken a momentary dip.

***

On the return trip to Kunduz, Oleg asked Alam about a subject that worried him.

'What do you do for women?'

'This is not Kabul,' replied Alam. 'There are no Chinese women in Kunduz.'

'I realise that, but men are men.'

'I am not sure if I should tell you.'

'I would appreciate it if you could.'

'There are local women, abandoned wives, young girls who do what is necessary to survive.'

'Can I meet them, or are they shunned in society?'

'I will see what I can do for you.'

Satisfied with Alam's answer, Oleg returned to the primary reason for being in Afghanistan.

'When will I meet with the chief person in Kunduz?' His only contact had been Alam and, briefly, Ali Mowllah in Kabul.

However, although Alam had been accommodating, almost friendly, it was clear that he served as a dependable lieutenant, no more.'

'Soon. Baroyev's representative is coming here in the next week.'

***

With time to spare before Farrukh's arrival, Oleg and Alam checked the bill of quantities for the merchandise leaving the country and ensured they aligned with the recorded amounts in Dushanbe. Oleg had to admit that, as chaotic as it looked, the Afghan side of the operation proved to be efficient.

'They run a tight operation down here,' Oleg told his contact in Dushanbe.

'We thought they did. Has the issue with the army been resolved?'

'Yes.'

'Good. I assume it cost a substantial amount,' the man in Dushanbe asked.

'That would be the case.'

'What's next?'

'Baroyev's representative is coming down soon.'

'We're aware of that. He's trying to re-establish himself, take our share of the business.'

'We're not going to let him, are we?' Oleg asked.

'Not at all.'

'I will represent our side?'

'Yes, unless something unforeseen comes up, you can deal with it.'

'And if it gets complicated?'

'I'll come down, but it's an arsehole of a place. It's yours for the time being.'

'Thank you. How much longer do I have to stay here?'

'Until we trust you.'

'I can be trusted,' Oleg said. There was a glimmer that he could get out and back to civilisation.

'That may be the case, but you worked for Baroyev. How do we know you are not in contact with him?'

'Baroyev would have me killed if given the opportunity,' said Oleg.

'Maybe, but we'll deal with Baroyev when the time is right,' said the man. 'Do you understand his operation?'

'Not totally, but I've a fair idea,' Oleg replied.

'That may be advantageous. We may have a place up here for you. Fix up the situation with the Afghans and then come back to Dushanbe.'

The conversation with Oleg in Kunduz was quickly relayed to Dmitry Gubkin via Grigory Stolypin. He agreed with what had been discussed.

'Oleg Yezhov may be to our advantage,' said Dmitry. 'We only need to remove Baroyev, and then we will have no competition – or, at least, no viable competition.'

'Are we discussing liquidating Yusup Baroyev?' said Stolypin.

'Any problems from your side?' Dmitry asked.

'Not from my side, but taking out a prominent member of Tajik society may cause some issues.'

'I'll think that through,' Dmitry said. 'We may have to discredit him first.'

***

The situation in Kunduz had become tense. What had been started by the Afghans to put pressure on the Russians was complicated by Yusup Baroyev.

Ahmad Ghori, the local government minister in Kunduz, was reluctant initially, but he could see the wisdom of playing the Russians and the Tajik drug lord against each other. He would have preferred not to have become directly involved in the discussions, as he was still a senior politician in the region and a possible future key player within the central government in Kabul.

Outwardly, he portrayed a competent and incorruptible leader while secretly acting as the senior member of an Afghan consortium trading in heroin. It was a knife edge, and he was not pleased, but there was no alternative. He had to take control. Otherwise, Noorzai, the Taliban leader, would assert his aggressive manner in the proceedings and, without a doubt, ruin all the good work he had done.

Farrukh arrived in the city and stayed in a hotel close to the centre. He did not want to be there. His apartment, the car, and the woman suited him fine, and the occasional party at Yusup's mansion pleased him no end.

His boss had been insistent on his crossing the border.

'Get down there and find out what is going on. We cannot let the Russians march in and take our livelihood.'

'But what can we do?' Farrukh had said. 'The quantities they are moving are much larger than we've been able to sell.'

'Find out what's going on,' Yusup had said. 'Isolate the Russians, and then we'll strike a deal with them to move it to the border with Kazakhstan, as we did before.'

'Is that possible?'

'How the hell should I know? We can't just sit here and watch our business go down the drain.'

Reluctantly, Farrukh headed down to Kunduz. He decided to take the Mercedes. The Afghans had agreed to a vehicle to always follow him and to protect it with their lives.

'The Russians have someone down there in Kunduz. It could be Oleg,' Farrukh had reminded Yusup.

'If you don't fix this up, you'll be down there permanently with him. If it is Yezhov, you can also deal with him.'

Yusup Baroyev's concerns were all too real. After the events of Oleg and the killing of the Afghan over the whore, operations in the drug smugglers' village had virtually come to a standstill until a replacement had been found. He had proved to be not as good as Farrukh, not even as good as Oleg, and the

148

Tajik drug lord was starting to feel minor constraints on his lifestyle.

He had not forgiven Oleg for abandoning his position, and an excuse such as *detained due to killing someone* held no weight with him. To a wayward employee, he was the devil incarnate, and Oleg had committed an error of judgement, which had left him exposed.

***

Ahmad Ghori occupied a large two-storey building close to the centre of Kunduz. It had been built in the last few years and, whereas not as impressive as his country estate, it was impressive nonetheless.

Farrukh's welcome was in stark contrast to the first time he had met the prominent Afghan. Then, he had been in fear for his life, but now – it was as if he were a long-lost relative returning.

Najibullah met Farrukh on his arrival in the city and had taken personal responsibility to look after him and the magnificent car parked outside, with a guard holding a loaded rifle at each corner. It wasn't the first Mercedes to be seen in Kunduz, but it was certainly the most impressive, and the guards were fully occupied keeping the people and their hands off it. They had even been forced to slap a few hard around the face, but no one had been killed. Farrukh regretted bringing it, but it was too late now.

'Farrukh, we have a problem for which I hope you have a solution,' Ahmad Ghori said, reclining in an immensely plush black leather chair.

'It is disturbing that our business has suffered.' Farrukh had chosen to wear traditional clothing. Ahmad Ghori wore a navy suit, white shirt, and black tie.

'It is your business that has suffered, not ours,' Ghori said.

'That is true. I only hope we can realign our interests.'

'So do I, but it is us who hold the strength. I am not sure you can compete with the Russians, but I will let you try.'

Ghori puffed on a large cigar. He was a man who felt comfortable with himself and his position in the government and the community. He felt even more comfortable that two criminal organisations were vying for his business. He knew someone would pay well, probably both.

'Why do you deal with the invaders? We are brothers. It is us you should deal with,' Farrukh said. As an opening ploy, he knew it was weak, but it was all he had. He was at a disadvantage until he saw the Russians' man.

'Farrukh, your argument is valid, but you know my reply.'

'That business is business. Politics and history are another matter.'

'Of course.'

'Tonight, I will lay on a banquet. You will be present, as will the Russian representative.'

'Have you met him?' Farrukh asked.

'Not yet, but I am told he is competent. We will meet him together. It may be possible that the two of you can come to an agreement beneficial to all parties.'

'I see that as unlikely, but I will meet with him as you have requested,' Farrukh said.

Chapter 13

Yusup Baroyev had satisfied Malika's requirements. He had found her delightful; she thought him magnificent. Their second meeting allowed him to visit her apartment.

It was an unlikely pairing, a former whore from a drug smugglers' village and an urbane businessman.

He arrived at the apartment, not in the Bentley, but in a more modest car, almost inconspicuous. The bodyguard he usually travelled with maintained a cautionary distance, watching for any sign of trouble. Two assassination attempts at the last count and a bullet wound in the arm from a rival he had put out of business.

Tonight, it was clear to the guard that all was calm.

Malika had dressed elegantly in a long gown made of silk, a pearl necklace around her neck. The tattoos, abhorrent to Oleg, were barely visible. The complexion, hard and blotched in the village due to the drugs and the infrequent intake of any quality food, had blossomed, and she showed the look of the healthy, vibrant person she had become. Her legs were long and slim, and her hair flowing and lustrous. She had made a special effort for this customer, a man she genuinely liked.

Her mother, now reluctantly accustomed to her daughter's unusual lifestyle, had decorated the apartment with flowers and ensured the kitchen was well-stocked with the best food money could buy.

It was fortunate that Malika could afford what she wanted, and she rarely thought back to that night when the mad Russian had killed another man and almost killed her. She did not know what had become of him, nor did she care. The eye patch she wore, one of several, was made by a man close to the centre of the town. It had become a fashion statement to her and not an encumbrance. Her damaged eye tended to look off-centre, and people felt uncomfortable looking her straight in the face without staring.

Her neighbours in the apartment block, successful business leaders and their wives, did not notice the men entering her apartment, or if they did, they did not comment. No one asked, and no one pried. She had even spent a pleasant evening in the next-door neighbour's apartment, discussing history with him and pottery with his wife. Her past was never raised, although the wife asked about the tattoos.

'A moment of wildness in my youth,' Malika had said, and the subject was left to rest.

***

Yusup knocked on the door at the agreed time. Malika hesitated to rush and open it. He had brought her flowers, a bottle of the finest champagne and a selection of wines from his extensive cellar. The dining room table had been laid, and a meal was in the oven. She wasn't sure if it was appropriate, but he said he appreciated the thought.

He spoke of his childhood. She talked about her parents. Neither spoke in detail of their subsequent lives.

He told her how he had risen from obscurity. She never mentioned her time in a drug smugglers' village or how she came to lose an eye other than to say it was an accident. They spoke of life, love, history and many other things, but he did not attempt to touch her. He had held her hand and gently kissed her but never once indicated a move to the bedroom.

It was early the next day when he left. The champagne he had brought had been consumed. As he left, he gave her a long and lingering passionate kiss, the first sign of overt sexual emotion during the night.

She had found a man who had treated her like no other, a man she was drawn to both sexually and emotionally. He felt a calmness with her that he had not felt for many years. Yusup realised on leaving that his wife was a fine woman, but she had become cold and indifferent. The women at his parties were fun, but conversationally they were bereft. He was not sure why he did not make love to Malika. She was available and paid for, but he was glad he had not.

They agreed to meet at a restaurant near her apartment the following week. They both saw it as a date, but he would still ensure she received her money.

***

Dmitry Gubkin was a worried man. The meeting was in Kunduz; he was in Moscow, relying on people he did not know. He was unsure the Afghans could be trusted, although he knew of Oleg Yezhov and his history: the extortion in St. Petersburg and the issue with the FSB. He also knew he had previously worked for Yusup Baroyev, the gangster in Tajikistan. It was hardly a glowing reference for someone entrusted with such responsibility.

Grigory Stolypin had been right in that Dmitry Gubkin's vanity would force him to join with his mafia brethren. He had not told Dmitry they did not have clear authority from their senior leadership. They were running a risk that, ultimately, he hoped Dmitry would be able to resolve.

Dmitry saw a dangerous precedent was being set in Kunduz, where Baroyev's man would meet with their man in what appeared increasingly to be an auction. One would win, and the other would probably die before the full details were revealed to the losing party. He had to ensure his man won. He could not go to Kunduz; there was no advantage if he did. But one way or the other, he needed to control the outcome.

He phoned Stolypin. 'Grigory, this is not going well.'

'Dmitry, I realise that. The Afghans would always trouble us, and now Baroyev is breathing down our necks. What do we do?'

'We stack the odds in our favour.'

'But how? We're not down there. It's up to Yezhov.'

'Can Baroyev's man seriously impact what we've set up?' Dmitry asked.

'It seems unlikely, although he is known to the Afghans.'

'Will they be swayed by a friendly relationship?'

'Probably not, but it will help,' Grigory replied.

'How can Baroyev offer them the same money? He was only shipping small quantities compared to us.'

'That's true, but he could reclaim the transportation to Kazakhstan and force us to deal with him.'

'It's what I'd suggest if I were Baroyev's man.' Dmitry agreed with the wisdom of Grigory's statement. 'One thing's certain,' he added. 'His man must never return to Tajikistan.'

'What are you saying?'

'Oleg Yezhov must kill him.'

'The Afghans will string Oleg up if they know.'

'Then, they must never know. Tell Yezhov the situation.'

It had not been necessary for anyone to inform Oleg what was required of him. As he arrived for the banquet, albeit reluctantly, he saw the Mercedes – *his* Mercedes – parked outside with a disruptive group of men aiming to stretch their necks to peer inside. He resolved that the car would have a different driver on the return trip to Tajikistan.

***

'Oleg, I did not expect to see you,' Farrukh said when they first met.

'Still driving my car?' Oleg replied sarcastically.

It was not a good start to the evening for either of the two men at the function organised in their honour.

Ahmad Ghori was seated at the head of the table. It was the first time meeting him for Oleg, the third for Farrukh.

'Farrukh, it is good to see you again. I hope we can see more of you while you are here in our country.' Ahmad Ghori's welcome seemed disproportionate to Oleg, considering the reduced amount of business directed Yusup Baroyev's way. Oleg assumed it was a ploy by Ghori to disarm the Russians, especially him, into thinking that Farrukh and his people were welcome bidders.

'Oleg Yezhov, this is our first meeting,' said Ghori. 'I hope your stay in our country has been to your liking.' Ghori was more formal with him. Oleg was not sure if it was a typical response or whether it had been planned. Regardless, he resolved to enjoy the evening and, if possible, talk cordially to Farrukh, who he blamed for his current predicament.

It was to be some hours before the opportunity presented itself.

'How long have you been in the country?' Farrukh asked.

'A few weeks,' Oleg replied.

'You are working for the Russian mafia now?'

'It appears that way, yes.'

'Business good?' Farrukh asked.

'Yes, how about you?'

'It's fine, about to get better.'

'It would be best to work together on this,' Oleg said.

'I'm not sure how we can. Besides, Yusup will be displeased to see you here.'

'It's a free country. I can choose where I want to be.'

'In Tajikistan, that would not be true. Free is not the word I would use in this godforsaken place, and surely you don't want to stay here. I assume Ahmad Ghori does not throw parties as Yusup does.'

The conversation was not going well. Oleg excused himself and went to talk to Alam. Farrukh sent an SMS to Yusup Baroyev.

Oleg Yezhov is the Russian mafia's representative in Kunduz.

The response was predictable.

Ensure he does not leave Afghanistan.

The message was confusing. *Have I been given carte blanche to kill him? How will the Afghans react?* Farrukh thought. *Will they let me go free and thank me for removing one more Russian from their country? His people are providing them with serious money.* He resolved to talk to Yusup further once he had ascertained how the negotiating was to progress.

The banquet was long and tiring, and Oleg was glad to go back to his home. Ten minutes after he arrived, a knock on the gate that secured the house from the outside world. Farrukh stood there, hoping to gain entry.

'What do you want?' Oleg asked in a curt, offhand manner.

'We need to talk.'

'I don't see there is much for us to talk about. You are up in Dushanbe, living in my apartment, driving my car and no doubt screwing my women.'

'None of them are yours. They all belong to Yusup.'

'What are you here for then?'

'I can remember being stuck in that village with no hope of reprieve,' said Farrukh. 'I know you spoke to Yusup and argued my case for me to relocate to Dushanbe. I have no bitterness towards you.'

'That may well be, but now we are on opposite sides.'

'It appears we've been given a rough deal, although mine is immeasurably improved,' said Farrukh. 'It is, however, still dependent on the caprice of Yusup Baroyev. I could be hanging over a termite nest tomorrow, and so could you. Let us keep our apparent animosity in check until we conclude our negotiations with Ahmad Ghori. Then we can meet and see if there is any mutually beneficial common ground.' It had been a good speech. Farrukh hoped that Oleg had been convinced of his goodwill, insincere as it was.

The men parted on good terms. Oleg had not believed a word of what he had said. He still intended to take his car back. As to Farrukh, he could go to hell.

***

Ahmad Ghori was direct when he met with Oleg the next day.

'We are taking all the risk, yet you are taking all the money.'

'My understanding is that there was a contract signed.'

'What is the worth of a contract when your people did not tell us all the facts?'

'What facts are these that you mention?'

'We were unaware of the massive profits you are making once our product reaches Russia – and now, we are led to believe, into Europe. It may be best to strike a deal with Farrukh, who we know and trust.'

Ghori did not trust Farrukh and Yusup Baroyev any more than the Russians. It was purely the opening salvo in a drawn-out and lengthy negotiation.

'You dealt with Baroyev before. You know he cannot move the quantity,' said Oleg.

'He assures us he can.'

'But how? Have you asked him for details? I know his operation. I know he cannot do what he says.'

'He can take the quantity from us and sell it to you.'

'We would not buy.'

'Oleg Yezhov, do not treat me like a fool. Russians see us as ignorant savages, but we know you well. We have had the experience of Russians in the past. Baroyev and his people have never slaughtered our men and raped our women.'

'That is not my generation,' Oleg protested.

'What does it matter? Russians do not change.'

The meeting had not gone well. Ghori had been dismissive, almost rude, yet he had not explained the compromises he sought.

***

Dmitry Gubkin was equally baffled when Oleg relayed the details to him.

'But what does he hope to gain?' asked Dmitry. 'We're giving them plenty of money.'

'It is unclear,' Oleg replied. 'I came here to ensure the merchandise was being shipped and that quality was maintained, not to enter into commercial discussions with the Afghans.'

'That is true, but it would not be useful for anyone else to come down there.'

'I will continue with the discussions and update you. They may want more money, and Baroyev will never be able to match us in quantity shipped.'

'It's probably no more than that,' said Dmitry. 'And remember, Baroyev is to be taught a lesson.'

'I will deal with his representative.'

Dmitry Gubkin's statement that he would not come to Afghanistan was obvious. His name was known to Grigory Stolypin and a few others. He had been behind the scenes setting up the deal with the Afghans, and he knew they were treacherous and not to be trusted. The drugs flowing into Russia in greater quantities aligned with Stolypin's initial premise, and with the special rates on heroin, the number of addicts in the country that Gubkin felt great patriotism for continued to rise.

'Once hooked,' Stolypin had said, 'we raise the price.'

Shipments onward from Russia and into Eastern Europe and even further west showed a steady increase. Dmitry saw the challenge and the money and embraced both with ardour. It was clear that the risk to his person and his reputation was also exacerbated. Entering an auction with the Afghans, maybe even the Taliban, dramatically enhanced the likelihood of exposure.

*****

After the phone conversation with Afghanistan concluded, Dmitry Gubkin focused on another issue that troubled him greatly.

It had been at a visit to the Bolshoi Ballet, a performance of 'Swan Lake', that he had seen the first signs. He had always known that Katerina, his wife, was an adornment. She was there to make him look good, and he was to make her rich. It was an arrangement that had served him well for five years. He had often suspected her of a younger lover, but he had never taken the time to pursue a resolution. With his business-related activities to deal with and sitting on the board of several leading companies in the country, he had let his suspicions pass. Then there was the patronage of several well-known charities to consider. He was a busy man; a wayward wife was a distraction he did not want to consider.

Anton Davydov, a family friend of long standing, was twenty years younger than Dmitry and in his late thirties. He had become recently widowed after his wife, Maria, had succumbed to a long-fought battle with cancer. He was attractive, almost as tall as Dmitry, and possessed great wealth. He was old money and generous to a fault. Dmitry liked him immensely, and judging by the touching hands during a break in the ballet, so did Katerina. The hand touching, the smiling and the glancing eyes were clearly not those of friends.

He suspected they were lovers. He was almost sure of it, as she had been late home one night from a friend's house, supposedly, and he had seen her exit Davydov's car. She had brushed it off, said he had just popped up at the friend's door, and she had taken the opportunity to accept a lift home. At the time, he had accepted her statement. Anton was a decent man, a friend; Katerina, a woman he had bought but somehow trusted.

It weighed heavily on his mind, and he knew that, in business, a clear mind was paramount. He needed to ask her, although he did not want to. An answer in the affirmative would have troubled him greatly.

***

Farrukh's meeting with Ahmad Ghori had not gone as well as expected. The Afghan had been direct with him, as he had been with Oleg.

'The Russians take a considerable quantity,' he said.

'We will match them.' Farrukh was surprised to see the man so unpleasant when he had been hospitable and friendly at the banquet.

'That's impossible,' said Ghori. 'You have neither the distribution channels nor the money.'

'Yusup Baroyev assures me we have.'

'I will need a firm proposal of how you intend to achieve this and who your customers will be.'

'Our customers are confidential.'

'Do not treat me like a fool as the Russians do,' Ghori replied angrily.

'Yes, of course,' replied Farrukh. 'But even I am unaware of what happens to the merchandise after it leaves Tajikistan.'

'Then let me tell you.' Ahmad Ghori straightened himself from the reclining, disinterested position he had previously adopted. 'You sell it to other members of the Russian mafia.'

'That is what I suspected.'

'What is the point of talking to you?'

'We are of the same blood. We are Tajiks.'

'This is business we are talking about here, not tribal issues and certainly not family.'

'The Russians are our enemy,' Farrukh said.

'I would kill them with pleasure,' Ghori replied, 'but they have the money, and we need it.'

Farrukh's meeting had not gone any better than Oleg's. Yusup Baroyev spoke in detail about his plan when Farrukh phoned to update.

'He is right, of course. Our only customer is the Russian mafia,' said Yusup.

'But they will not deal with us. They have cut us out so far,' replied Farrukh.

'Why not?'

'They have the business sewn up.'

'Why do you say this? You spent too much time in that village. You are out of touch with reality.'

'Are you saying, if I manage to secure a deal, the Russian mafia will be forced to make another deal with us?' asked Farrukh.

'Precisely. I am already in initial discussions. We are not finished yet. You conclude a deal, and then we are back in business, even bigger than before. We will have a party to celebrate unless you've fallen in love with the woman you're living with.'

'Love, yes, but one of your parties? I will be available.' Farrukh said.

Chapter 14

Yusup Baroyev's mood was upbeat. The second meeting at Malika's apartment had gone well, and they had slept together. They complemented each other's personalities and needs. It would not be long before she became his mistress. Her mother was pleased and sad at the same time. She was no longer selling herself as a common prostitute but was unmarried and committing sin with a known gangster and married man.

Malika had told her this was an ideal arrangement, and she was fond of the man. He enjoyed her company, and, on occasions, they would not have sex but talk and laugh and discuss current affairs and art. With time on her hands, she took the time to revitalise her education. A bright, above-average student in her youth, it had taken time for her brain to kick into gear. Yusup paid all the bills and ensured she was picked up and dropped off at the college whenever she wanted.

It had been a few weeks into their relationship when, in a particularly candid moment for both, she told him all about her past, the successful life as an escort, the drop into despair and how she ended up in a drug smugglers' village. She told him how she knew Oleg Yezhov. She mentioned her previous fondness for him and how he had reacted when he found her with another man. She told him of the killing and the beating she received, and the eye he had destroyed.

Yusup had known how Oleg Yezhov had killed an Afghan and that his weakness had cost him a considerable amount in lost revenue. He had not known the woman and had assumed she was just another whore of no consequence. He was initially shocked when she told him.

She explained how her fondness had turned to hatred, which forced her to leave the village to find her mother and finally rid herself of drugs.

'He saved me,' she said, 'but I hate him. I wish him dead.'

Yusup Baroyev had already decided, before her telling him the story, that Oleg Yezhov was a dead man walking. He would now kill him for her as well. He had not known where he was until Farrukh had told him.

He would need to contact Farrukh and countermand his instructions. He, Yusup Baroyev, would personally deal with Oleg Yezhov's death.

***

Trade resumed after the Afghan army raid, and the post-raid levels were even higher. Grigory Stolypin was pleased with how seamlessly it worked. The Afghans were loading at the new compound, the packages concealed in a shipment of minerals from a copper mine in the north of the country, or a sheep container strapped to the soft underbelly of a sheep, carefully located in the most inaccessible part of the truck's restraining pen.

The animals were left in the sun for a few days with adequate food. The smell of urine and faeces was overpowering. Only the most ardent of border guards and customs officials would have investigated with any zeal, and none had that virtue, although a few had crisp American dollars for their negligence.

Bandits had attempted an attack on a truck moving up to the border on the Afghan side. They had waited, hidden behind rocks on a rising bend, when the truck, labouring as they always did due to poor maintenance and chronic overloading, was at its slowest, no more than a walking pace.

They had come out, fast and determined, brandishing rifles and making threatening noises. They had failed to notice the two men sitting in the truck's cabin, armed and professional, compared to the bandits. The bandits' bravado soon dissipated when the first and, apparently, the bravest or the most foolhardy, was cut down with a burst of rapid fire from the AK-47 that

Ashkan, a former Afghan army conscript and subsequent deserter, carried.

Sensing the situation was precarious and no other being brave or foolhardy, the remaining bandits, six in total, made a dash down the sloping ridge the truck was crawling up, attempting to get away. One did; another five did not.

After the incident, the number of bandit attacks reduced dramatically. Sometimes, the trucks even dispensed with the guards after Alam, on instruction from Ahmad Ghori, had made a deal with the largest bandit gang.

'You protect our convoys. We will pay you a retainer,' he had said to Azad, a fierce-looking man who claimed to be their leader. He was a rogue who professed piety to his God, yet that did not prevent him from abusing his children, especially his teenage daughters, and hitting his two wives at the slightest provocation. He was illiterate, uncouth and a loudmouth who bragged about his exploits fighting the invaders, Russian and American, and how many he had killed in single combat.

Alam knew him for what he was and would have been no more than ten years of age when the last Russian had retreated across the border to their north. Those he bragged to either did not know that he consistently lied or, as was more likely, did not care. The abuser of little children – girls mainly – and hitter of women still provided for an extended group of one hundred people if the bandits' families were included.

He provided meagre assistance, but in a country where one dollar American was regarded as an average daily wage, even if there was work, the three to four that he managed to provide seemed like a fortune. The bandit leader received one hundred a day to protect the convoys. After giving five a day to each of his ten bandits, that still left fifty for him. He was illiterate, but the trucks were making him rich. In another six months, he could see an extended house, another wife and two hundred more goats that would give milk and feed his family.

***

Once the border into Tajikistan was crossed, the trucks moved north along a good and sealed road. One incident occurred when a policeman checked for contraband but failed to receive his regular payment for not finding any.

The truck drivers carried no money for bribes, and the policeman had been difficult until a phone call to the police commissioner in Dushanbe, who phoned his commander down where the incident occurred. Then, the commander's phone call to the policeman told him to stop causing trouble, or he'd be confined somewhere so remote he would wonder which country he was in. Typically, the police went through the motions, looked official, occasionally asked a few questions, and then waved the vehicle through.

After reaching Dushanbe, several different transportation methods were utilised. A truck up to Kazakhstan and then through Uzbekistan into Russia, or sometimes a train. Commercial flights were occasionally used if the airport and airline officials were corrupt and open to a bribe.

Intelligence gathering was vital, and, in Russia, there was barely a problem, but Kazakhstan could be difficult. Eighty-five to ninety per cent of all shipments were making it through to market, and, considering the quantity of the freight, it was a good result. Any shortfalls in revenue would be made up by the end-user, the drug addict, who would find the extra money, one way or the other.

To Grigory and his mafia brethren, where they obtained the money did not concern them.

However, it still concerned Dmitry Gubkin, the Chairman of the Committee for the Rehabilitation of Former Drug Addicts in Moscow. The contradiction was so extreme that he had learnt long ago to separate his public persona from his criminal bent.

He would espouse abhorrence at the demon drug in a meeting or when making a speech. 'The scourge of our young people...' Then, five minutes later, he would be on the phone with Grigory questioning why shipments were down, the current rate on the street for a gramme of heroin and what he was doing to bring the price up.

Gubkin was a complicated man who felt he was losing his edge. The situation with his wife continued to trouble him. Finally, she admitted that she was in love with Anton Davydov and intended to leave and marry her younger lover, who could give her children while he, Dmitry Gubkin, was impotent. He decided to talk to Grigory for a solution.

*****

With negotiations stalled in Kunduz and Ahmad Ghori unavailable, Oleg took the opportunity to visit a processing plant where the raw opium was converted into heroin. It took Alam and Oleg four hours to reach the factory along dirt tracks. The four-wheel drive Toyota struggled for the last few kilometres. Alam explained the factory was one of many, and as soon as one was discovered by the authorities, the production at the others was ramped up to compensate.

Latif, the head of the heroin processing facilities, attempted to explain the manufacturing process to Oleg, who had little interest in the subject.

'It's a simple process,' said Latif. 'It was developed by an English scientist.'

'What was?' Oleg replied.

'Heroin, diamorphine.'

'Diamorphine, what's that?' Oleg did not care to listen to a man whose voice grated on the ear.

'That's the medical term for heroin,' said Latif. 'He developed it as a non-additive form of morphine. It's still used today in hospitals.' It was clear that Latif, an eager little man with eyes that seemed too close together, was knowledgeable. Oleg, however, was not interested in how it was produced, only in how his people could make more money.

'Very interesting.' Oleg attempted to be polite, but Alam had received word that Ahmad Ghori was back in Kunduz, and he was not alone. A significant person in the Afghan drug smuggling industry was with him. He knew Farrukh would be sniffing around at the first opportunity, and they needed to be back as soon as possible.

Farrukh continued to irritate Oleg with his ingratiating to every politician and corrupt official he could find. Diplomacy was not Oleg's strong point. He recognised that. He did not have his opponent's innate charm or easy way with words. He had the Russian stance of being blunt, direct to the point, and offending when no offence was intended.

The Afghans responded to Farrukh's approach more than his, but he had money, and the size of the Russian mafia's business was on his side. He only hoped it was enough.

'Latif, our time is limited,' Alam said.

'Then it's a quick tour you want?' Latif finally sensed his visitors were not staying long.

Oleg did not see a factory, more a varied array of plastic bins, 44-gallon drums, and bags of chemicals. It did not impress him, and how quality could be assured, he did not know. He realised the quality received in Russia had never been substandard. On the contrary, it had been excellent and commanded a premium price on the street.

'We scrape the poppies. From every ten kilos of poppies, we get about one kilo of opium which we roll into balls and place in barrels of hot water,' Latif said.

'And then what?'

'We add a diluted solution of lime until the pH is high enough.'

'What's pH?' Oleg asked.

'It's a measure to determine whether it is acid or alkaline.'

'And you want alkaline?'

'Correct. Once the pH is high enough, we leave it overnight to allow the oils and resins to float to the surface.'

Oleg was not enjoying his education, but the Afghan with the irritating voice would not stop.

'We then syphon out the morphine,' continued Latif.

'Our time is limited.' Alam attempted to speed him up.

'We then precipitate it by adding ammonium chloride to solidify the opium. Then we add acetic anhydride.'

'Carry on.' Oleg and Alam gave up. It was best just to let him get on with it. Besides, Alam had received an update. No one would get in that day to meet with Ahmad Ghori and his associate. Time was no longer of the essence.

'We pour the mixture in warm water and filter it,' said Latif. 'Then we add bicarbonate of soda to release carbon dioxide gas and lower the acidity.'

'Is that it?'

'Not yet. It's heroin but a brownish colour. The white that you are used to requires some additional steps. It's then diluted in a solution of hydrochloric acid.'

'How's the quality controlled?' Oleg asked.

'Constant filtering at every stage and watching the pH. The final process is when we evaporate the liquid. What remains is the heroin we send to you with a quality stamp.'

'The facilities seem basic here,' Oleg commented.

'We need to be able to move quickly, so if the facility is destroyed, we can set up again.'

Oleg did not like the factory, peopled as it was by drug-addicted workers, but he saw no reason to complain, and the Afghan production manager seemed competent, if tiresome. He would give a good report to his people in Tajikistan and Russia.

***

Dmitry Gubkin was a man who valued his assets, whether they were artistic, motorised or female. He would not allow the disgrace of a wife, who he was sure would tell the world — or, at least, the world he circulated in — that he was a lousy husband, an even worse lover and that he had treated her abysmally, none of which were true. But he realised that truth is not the reality. It is the perception people want to hear, the salacious gossip, the innuendo and the downright absurd.

He had carefully garnered his reputation; he was unwilling to allow a spoilt, vain and increasingly vacuous woman to destroy what he had fought for.

He phoned Grigory. 'I have a problem.'

'Dmitry, your problem is my problem.'

'There is a person who troubles me.'

'And you want someone to deal with him?' Grigory asked.

'Yes, and it's a "she".'

'It makes no difference.'

Dmitry explained the situation, who he wanted to be removed and why, although he left out the part about his being a lousy lover.

'What you ask is not impossible, but are you sure?' Grigory asked.

'I am sure.'

'She is a beautiful woman. Can't you plead with her to stay?'

'Her lover is wealthier than I am,' said Dmitry. 'She sees love, but she is mercenary. Love with her comes with an inexhaustible credit card and whatever she wants. I have shown her every indulgence, yet she chooses another. My mind is firm.'

'You will be a party to a criminal act,' replied Grigory. He had no issues with ordering the liquidation of anyone. He had done so many times, but Katerina, Dmitry's wife, was beautiful and young.

'It is to be an accident,' said Dmitry. 'I must be devastated and show the appropriate remorse. No blame must fall on me. Is that clear?'

'We are good at accidents,' Grigory bragged.

***

Yusup Baroyev had other problems to deal with. The smuggling village, where most of his income had come from, was virtually deserted. The last three weeks had only seen one Afghan peasant make the dangerous night-time trek from his side of the border, and then it had only been two kilos, which Farshad, Oleg's replacement, had discarded as inferior quality.

Ahmad Ghori's organisation was the main supplier of drugs across the border, but it was not the only one. There were freelance operators, but they were infrequent and unreliable. If discovered, Ghori's people would visit, threaten and allow them to join the cooperative at a much lower rate than they would otherwise have expected. It was a persuasive argument: join us, or you're dead. Most joined without reservation, but some, misjudging their predicament, had refused. None resisted for long, and some had died.

The organisation, of which Ghori had become the de facto mouthpiece, was not his alone. Its tentacles stretched far throughout Afghanistan. There were others in the senior hierarchy. Ali Mowllah was the organiser; Ashraf Ghilzai, the heroic former Taliban commander, now responsible for the heroin production, whose loyalty to his previous colleagues was being questioned; and Arif Noorzai, the determined senior Taliban in Kandahar, who saw the drug money as vital to his plans to reinvigorate the Islamic fundamentalists.

Along with Ahmad Ghori, the respectable face of the group, the four were brothers in business, partners out of necessity, but never friends. Ali Mowllah was a businessman interested in profit while feigning an interest in fundamentalism. Ahmad Ghori, the politician, was interested in power and money, but primarily power.

Ashraf Ghilzai, however, had seen through the Taliban and what it had become. It mouthed Sharia and piety yet dealt with the misery and despair of drugs. He had no illusions. He intended to make himself rich and to hell with anyone else. He was a bad man in a country full of bad men.

It was a country where an agreement in writing, or only spoken, was valid until a better deal could be renegotiated. Regardless of their protestations, affirmations and goodwill statements, none trusted the other and continually looked for the upper hand.

Unbeknown to Farrukh and Oleg, all four had come together in Kunduz to discuss. While they debated, the two protagonists from the north waited. During the seven days of enforced idleness, they followed their separate paths, sometimes overlapping. Farrukh would attempt to curry favour with the local politicians and men of influence to impress them with the car he drove.

'You could have one of these,' he would say.

Oleg overheard him making the statement to a local businessman. *I will. Yours!* he thought.

Oleg spent time with Alam and met with Najibullah, who was exceedingly hospitable. Alam had been questioned enough by Oleg regarding women.

'There are women,' Alam finally admitted.

'Then organise one for me,' Oleg said.

'This is not Kabul.'

'Then who are these women?'

'They are not easily found.'

'Then find one for me.'

'I will get you a phone number. You can make the arrangements.'

'Very well,' Oleg said.

***

With the phone number supplied, Oleg was quickly on the phone. The woman at the other end of the line spoke pleasantly, and his Tajik was suitably fluent. It was a short conversation, setting up the time and place.

Farhana elaborated on her life the second time they spoke. On that occasion, it had been face-to-face – or, more correctly, face-to-veil, as she was enclosed in a burka.

'I came back from Iran, where I had spent many years as a refugee, to a country that does not respect women.'

Once the burka was removed, she was a pretty twenty-two-year-old with a slender face and an olive complexion. Their initial meeting was at a remote farmhouse on the city's outskirts, which Alam had arranged. He either did not approve or was afraid, but he drove her there and waited outside while Oleg and Farhana concluded their business. He said he would wait and drive her back afterwards.

'I had received a good education, but no one would employ me,' she continued. 'I worked for a foreign charity for a while, but they have since left the city.'

'Are you not worried about doing this?' Oleg asked. He found her pleasant to look at and interesting to talk to. He could not understand a male-dominated society where the men seemed to revel in each other's company. Why men would hold hands, kiss each other on the cheek and hug and sit close to one another, legs sometimes intertwined, made no sense to him. A man should hold a woman's hand, kiss her, sit close and make love to her as often as possible.

Alam told him it was their culture. The men did appreciate the benefit of a warm woman in a warm bed, but they would not openly admit to it. Oleg did not understand; however, it was the least of his concerns with Farhana in that small, unpleasant farmhouse with its open fire in one corner, a couple of chairs, and an uncomfortable bed.

'You do this for money?' Oleg asked.

'That is all,' she replied.

'And if you are caught?'

'My father would bury me alive for the shame I have brought on our family.'

'Is it worth the risk?'

'What else do I have? I must live, and my father has no money.'

'He would rather you starved than sell yourself?'

'Yes.'

'I will support you; your secret is safe with me.'

'Thank you.'

She was surprisingly easy to undress for a woman who had arrived covered in the ultimate demeaning feminine attire.

Underneath the burka, she wore a long-sleeved white blouse and a pair of designer jeans, good quality but probably fake.

She responded to his touch and even appeared genuine, although his hands were hard and rough and her skin pallid and smooth. She wore no bra, and her nipples were firm and erect, her breasts small and upright. It was not long before she stood before him naked. The bed was small, and both held the headrest to stop falling out onto the dirt floor, which was frozen hard. She was warm to the touch, and she pleased him.

She did not have Malika's skills or Natasha's roundness, and he would have described her as passive. Later, Alam drove her back to the city and left her at a remote corner near her house. She left the vehicle and quickly disappeared down a side alley.

'Was it worth it?' Alam asked the next day.

'You know it was,' Oleg said with a smile.

'If the Taliban catch her, you know what they'll do?'

'I assume they'll kill her,' Oleg replied.

'Stone her to death.'

'It's either a burial from her father or a stoning from the Taliban.'

'What else can she do?' Alam said. It was a remarkable admission.

Chapter 15

The Afghan four rarely met as a group. The seriousness of the situation decreed that they made an exception this time.

Ahmad Ghori had assumed leadership of the meeting.

'We need to decide on a strategy. Do we go with the Russians or our friends in Tajikistan?'

Ali Mowllah, the businessman, saw it clearly.

'The Russians,' he said. To him, profit was the defining factor, and the current arrangement rewarded him financially.

Arif Noorzai, the Islamic fundamentalist, decided by considering other criteria.

'The people in Tajikistan are Muslims,' he said. 'The Russians are infidels and former invaders. We should not forget the atrocities they committed against our people.'

Ashraf Ghilzai, a former Taliban and now responsible for the heroin factories in Badakhshan to the east of Kunduz, took a more pragmatic view.

'Whoever pays the most.'

Ahmad Ghori summed up the mood of the meeting.

'We need to hear the presentations from both sides. The arrangement with Russia is working well, although it is only a matter of time before Baroyev attempts to interfere with the operation in Tajikistan.'

'Then we kill him,' Arif Noorzai said. It was the typical response of the Taliban. To them, death was an easier solution than negotiating.

'Arif, are you forgetting that he is in Tajikistan?' said Ahmad Ghori. 'Not all their police and military can be bribed. Some of their politicians are even honest and incorruptible.'

Arif Noorzai had not travelled, and he did not believe in the concept of an honest politician.

There were certainly none in Afghanistan that he knew of apart from Abdul Sarabi, but he had been Hazara and a Shia, and to a Sunni Taliban, a heretic. A car bomb, as he left his compound in Kabul, had dealt with him. He had been the most prominent politician in Kabul for his people. His heritage stretched back eight hundred years to when the Mongol Emperor, Babur, a descendant of Genghis Khan, had marched through their known world.

Sarabi's distinctive features, more Chinese than Asian, had long isolated his people in Afghanistan. It was only in a new, enlightened Afghanistan that the fledgeling political process had allowed him to attain a position of importance. It would not have been possible in his childhood. His father, a local magistrate in Hesa Awal Behsood District to the West of Kabul, in Wardak Province, had been a prominent man in his region but derided by the Pashtuns in Kabul.

Abdul Sarabi's initial presence in Kabul, after he had been elected to Parliament, had caused consternation – even rioting – due to his being Shia Muslim rather than Sunni, as were the majority of the population. But, over a few years, he had shown himself incorruptible and genuine. He had personally overseen the removal of a notorious gangster in Paghman Province, who had been terrorising the local people. He had even arrested some of his fellow parliamentarians and had them thrown in jail for taking bribes. He was a marked man, even before the Taliban dealt with him.

'What has the killing of Baroyev got to do with honest politicians and policemen?' Noorzai asked.

'They will investigate and set up a commission of inquiry,' replied Ghori. 'They will stop every truck on the road.'

'Then we pay those we bribed more to let the trucks through.'

Ali Mowllah entered the conversation. 'Those who have been paid off will aim to distance themselves from wrongdoing. Suddenly, those we know are on the take will be standing and arguing for restoring law and order.'

'What do we do if we can't kill them?' Noorzai asked.

'We neutralise,' Mowllah said.

'And what does that mean?' Noorzai asked.

He was not an intelligent man. He saw life along fundamentalist lines. If you were with him, then fine. If not, you either changed sides or you were dead. It was a philosophy that had served him well and had made his transition to Taliban easy and his rise to a senior position rapid. An outer suburb of Kandahar had been his birthplace forty years prior. The exact date of his birth, even the year, was unknown, but it mattered little to him.

An aggressive, angry man, Noorzai had never been averse to violence as a solution, and he saw no reason to change. He hated the Russians for what they had done to his country and his family. His father had died enslaved in a labour camp, making concrete bricks for the extensive building programme they had embarked on when they occupied the country. They had starved him to death, worked him until he could stand up no more and beat him as he lay on the ground. The ardent Taliban could not tolerate the Russians, and he was certain his reaction to their mafia's representative would be hostile.

He had a vision of re-energising the fundamentalist organisation and retaking Kabul, but that needed lots of money, and the Russian mafia had plenty of it. If he had to deal with the devil, he would.

Arif Noorzai hated Ashraf Ghilzai. To him, he was a traitor. Ashraf Ghilzai had been a senior Taliban, a colleague of Arif Noorzai, and even a friend, but he had become disillusioned. The Taliban had been about religious purity and a better world based on the tenets of the Koran. It had not been about overt violence and personal wealth.

It was not that Ashraf Ghilzai had any issues with either, but to preach one and practise another was contrary to his Islamic belief, and he saw himself as a good Muslim.

He saw Arif Noorzai and his cohorts as no longer pure. He well-remembered the days of the Mujahedeen when they were fighting the Russian invaders, later the Americans. And then there had been the march into Kabul when they grabbed the Russian puppet ex-president, who had been hiding out in the United Nations compound and dragged him around the city attached to the rear of a truck, minus his genitals.

Ghilzai knew that some of the leadership in Kandahar were living in luxury, and, in Karachi, they were driving around in armour-plated Mercedes cars and living in two, three-storey monoliths with their expensive fittings and Italian marble floors. There was even one he had heard of that boasted an indoor swimming pool, where the Russian whores out of the Cyclone Club in Dubai would come for a week or two while people starved in the street.

It was an enviable lifestyle, which Ghilzai wished to emulate. But he would not be standing outside of the house preaching to his humble lieutenants to maintain the holy fight when not more than ten metres away, behind a couple of hefty wooden doors, were a couple of prostitutes.

He had been placed on a Taliban list for summary execution after he had absconded from Kandahar and relocated to a remote village in the Hindu Kush. His execution had only been delayed while he was of some use. Ghilzai had been the provider of the best-quality heroin in Afghanistan, and it was only the best that the Russians wanted.

Noorzai was determined that one day, Ghilzai would be held accountable for his crimes. Ghilzai was sure he would have a Karachi-style mansion, only his would be in Dubai.

Ali Mowllah was neither Taliban nor violent. He was a businessman who looked for profit. He knew the four of them were the best in the country. Noorzai, for his ability to maximise the opium poppies under cultivation; Ashraf Ghilzai, for transforming it into heroin; and Ahmad Ghori, for dealing with the logistics of moving it across the border into Tajikistan and dealing with all the bribes and corruption required.

Ali Mowllah's skills were clearly acknowledged. He was the clear analytical brain, the adviser. He did not know the

Russians had a detached, unemotional counterpart, equally capable, but Dmitry Gubkin in Moscow had women trouble, whereas he was perfectly content with his two wives, who had given him strong and healthy sons. His women were both easy to the eye, pleasant in bed, and they never refused him.

***

Katerina Gubkin's day had started well. There had been shopping, expensive as usual, but she neither looked at the price nor the dent it made in her husband's bank account.

A couple of deals in Moscow had gone sour for her husband, although the money from his arrangement with Grigory Stolypin compensated him financially.

For Dmitry, however, it was not the same. He received accolades for the deals in Moscow when they went right, brickbats when they did not, and now they were going wrong. His wealth was unaffected, but no one praised him for shipping another two or three hundred kilos of heroin up to Russia, and he missed the acclaim.

He knew what the problem was. It was his wife. She was putting him off his game, and her impending accident weighed heavily on his mind. Her indiscretions were becoming more apparent. A celebrity photographer had even snapped her kissing Anton Davydov at a restaurant the previous week, and it had been printed in full colour on the front cover of the most scandalous magazine devoted to trivial matters. Dmitry realised he could no longer wait.

Grigory had counselled great care and told him that these things tend to backfire when you least expect, but Dmitry was firm. It would cost him well over a quarter of a million dollars, but it was a meagre amount to what it would cost if she took him to court and claimed half his assets. He could have fought her, but the resultant publicity would have put a chink in the impenetrable armour of his reputation and respect in the community.

As she drove away from her final shop for the day, Katarina did not notice the two cars following her, one a BMW, the other a Toyota. She took a left turn as she moved down Kuznetsky Most Street, just behind the Bolshoi Theatre and the home of some of the most fashionable shops in Moscow. It was only a ten-minute drive, and the traffic was relatively light.

Her day's shopping had been delightful but exceedingly expensive. A pair of red shoes had set Dmitry back a thousand dollars in the American equivalent; a blouse, close to that amount and a handbag, Gucci and leather, well over four thousand. She had not looked at the price – the style was all that was important, and if a man could not afford such necessities, he was not the man for her. She was in a good mood; that night, she intended to dedicate herself to her husband.

Anton Davydov had been a great lover, a frivolous interlude in a seemingly sterile and dull marriage, but Dmitry was stable, generous, trustworthy and, above all, devoted to her.

She had discovered the night before, after a passionate session of unbridled sex, that her younger lover possessed few of Dmitry's meritorious traits. The waiter at the hotel had been late bringing the champagne, and Anton had shouted at him, demanding a refund. Later, while he was sleeping, exhausted, she saw the SMS on his phone. The message meant two things to her: the first, that he had another woman and, second, that they intended to meet later that night after he had got rid of her in the nicest possible way.

It should have upset her, but it did not. For once, she had seen the reality. She had been the mistress of several prominent men before she met Dmitry, but he was the only one who had wanted to marry her. He had told her he did not care about her past if she was with him.

As she approached the house, she avoided the drop down to a lower road fifteen metres below. The safety barriers had been removed for repair, and the road was rough. She failed to notice the large, four-wheel drive Toyota that came alongside her and bumped her towards the large drop. She instinctively braked, but the second car, the BMW, had positioned itself close to her rear.

Her car plunged down the almost sheer embankment, rolling as it went down. At the bottom, it came to rest on its roof. Katerina Gubkin was dead. Her husband would never know that she intended to return to him. The negligee she had planned to wear to bed that night, to entice him to make love to her, was strewn across the road.

The newspapers' society pages were dedicated to Dmitry Gubkin, the grieving widower, and his stoic manner in the days following the tragedy. The funeral entourage numbered over five hundred. The elite of society, senior politicians and business leaders attended. It would be weeks before Gubkin would re-enter Moscow society and weeks before he would be useful to Grigory Stolypin.

They were the weeks when his absence would cause the most difficulty.

***

Apart from Grigory Stolypin, Dmitry Gubkin had met two other men – Boris 'the enforcer' Sobchak and Ivan Merestkov. True to their word, neither Sobchak nor Merestkov attempted to contact him after the initial meeting, where they had sworn fealty to him.

During Dmitry's absence, a situation developed that required his advice. It had become apparent that somebody was double-dealing, giving information to the competitor, to Yusup Baroyev.

Baroyev's knowledge of shipments could have only come from one source, and the successful hijacking of a couple of trucks close to the northern border of Tajikistan was too predictable to be a random event.

Only one person could have given the information; only one had detailed knowledge of the trucks and where their illegal contraband was located. The vehicles had been found later, parked fifty kilometres up a forestry track – the merchandise removed, clearly the work of amateurs. They knew what they were after, and Grigory knew full well that Boris Sobchak was the informer and Yusup Baroyev the recipient of the drugs.

It was not the conclusion worthy of a Sherlock Holmes or a master detective. Sobchak controlled the movement of the merchandise, and only Baroyev had the infrastructure to sell it.

Grigory Stolypin had brought in Dmitry to advise on such situations, and he was unavailable. He had tried phoning him, but all he received were disinterested replies. He knew that it was up to him to make a decision.

His first decision was to liquidate Boris Sobchak; his second was to entrust Oleg Yezhov if he could extricate himself from the Afghans.

Oleg was delighted when told the news of his impending elevation and return to Tajikistan, although Yusup Baroyev still concerned him.

'Don't worry, we'll protect you,' Stolypin said, although Oleg wasn't sure if anybody could protect him if Baroyev were intent on killing him.

Oleg realised that a return to Tajikistan came with benefits and risks. He deemed the risks acceptable. The only outstanding issue was how to speed up the Afghans, who continued to debate and procrastinate.

For their part, it was a case of weakening the bargaining position of Farrukh and Oleg, and for Oleg, it had the necessary result. Farrukh, a more balanced individual, was okay to wait, but Oleg was not, and his meetings with Farhana were too far apart and difficult to arrange.

***

It was late at night when Farhana phoned him. She needed money, something to do with new clothes. He made a fateful mistake and brought her to his house in the boot of his car. No one had seen her come in, and she quickly went to his bedroom on the second floor. He had ensured the staff was absent. The guards at the gate were invariably asleep, although they jumped to attention when he had beeped the horn for entry. He knew that, within five minutes after they had closed the gate, they would be huddled up in their guard hut, heater on, fast asleep.

She had been more willing that night, comfortably encased in a warm, luxurious bed instead of a cold, flea-ridden one out at the farmhouse.

'Do I not please you?' she asked.

'Yes, of course.'

'When you go to Tajikistan, will you take me?'

It seemed a reasonable request, but how and was it advisable? He did not see a long-term future with her, but if he could help, he saw no reason not to try. He felt guilt over Malika, and assisting the young Afghan prostitute seemed like redemption. He had destroyed the life of one; saving the life of another made sense. He would try, although how he could drive her across the border, he didn't know. It seemed impossible. He would ask Alam.

His life improved immeasurably. He had a woman, and there had been no issues, coupled with the bonus Grigory Stolypin had offered him a job back in Tajikistan for a week. Russia was still out of the question, as the FSB had not given up on him entirely. An email from Natasha in St. Petersburg confirmed she was sure her phone was being bugged.

Doesn't she realise they're tapping her Internet connection? he thought. But, apart from that, he gave it little concern, although he did worry about her. He felt completely safe; the FSB were not about to come to Tajikistan, let alone Afghanistan. He had, however, underestimated the resolve of Artur Malenkov's brother.

It had been close to four weeks before the four Afghans were ready to talk again. They had weighed up the options, deliberated on who offered the best possibility and achieved in frustrating Farrukh and Oleg.

Chapter 16

The four Afghans continued to debate, even though they had asked Oleg and Farrukh to present their submissions. They did not like the Russians, but how they could avoid dealing with them seemed unclear. Farrukh persisted in trying to see them, so much so that they had to tell him to keep his distance until called for.

Oleg, in the meantime, busied himself with understanding how the business worked, the potential money involved and the quantity of heroin required.

Farrukh may have the charm, but Oleg would have the knowledge. He assumed the Afghans would be more interested in business and potential money than charm.

'Don't do it, don't even consider it,' Alam said when Oleg suggested a different place to meet with Farhana. 'Just be glad she is available. You do not want to be responsible for her death, do you?' Oleg did not let on that she had been making regular visits to the house, and he had just been attempting to bring Alam into her transportation.

Oleg was aware of how much a kilo of heroin cost when it reached the drug smugglers' village; in Afghanistan, however, he did not know how much profit the smugglers' leadership was making. Alam proved of limited value apart from some vague figures. The smartest man he had met was Latif, the heroin production manager. Oleg suggested a return visit. Alam was initially reluctant. He did not want the guided tour again, but in the end, he relented.

The trip the next day took less time than the previous one. It was obvious that a grader had smoothed out the road.

'How much do you pay?' Latif asked.

'When smuggled across to the village?' Oleg asked.

'Yes.'

'Close to two thousand American dollars a kilo for the best quality.'

'I only supply the best quality,' Latif proudly said.

'I realise that, but others are not as diligent as you are in their production.'

'Then I hope you reject it.'

'In the past, yes, but supply was not always regular. I couldn't always be so discerning.'

'Others could answer as to the reason.'

'I know the reason now,' replied Oleg. 'The Russian mafia has been bypassing Baroyev.'

'But you are now with the Russians, so it no longer concerns you,' said Latif.

'As you say, I am now with the Russians. The reason is no longer my concern, although your people in Kunduz are attempting to raise the price, maybe strike a deal with the Tajikistan gangsters.'

'Isn't that supply and demand?'

'You are right, but I cannot afford to fail.'

'I can only give you some guidelines on the costs involved,' said Latif. 'It was sold to you in the village for two thousand American dollars, and we had sold it previously to the smuggler – or, at least, his boss – for six hundred American. Our production costs are relatively low, maybe two hundred American a kilo, by the time we've paid for all the chemicals and the facilities around the region. Then there are the bribes to be paid.'

'What about the farmer who grows the poppies, the men working in the factories?' Oleg asked.

'The farmers, maybe thirty dollars a kilo,' said Latif. 'And the factory workers, lucky to receive more than two dollars a day, only spend it on heroin.'

'Who's making big money?' Oleg asked.

'Maybe you should ask the people in Kunduz that question. I make sufficient to send my sons to school. That is all I need.'

Alam said little at the meeting with Latif, although he proved more communicative on returning to Kunduz.

'What did you gain from that?' Alam asked.

'Just a little more background information,' said Oleg. 'Now that your leaders are more communicative, I'll need to be able to counter any offers from Baroyev through Farrukh.'

'What about his car?' Alam asked. He had been one of the admirers of the beautiful Mercedes that Farrukh drove with pride around the dusty city.

'His car? It's mine, as is the apartment he lives in. I intend to take it back before he leaves.'

'Be careful, very careful. If you offend the hospitality and protection he has been given here, it will not be Farrukh you will have to worry about.'

'I would have thought it was between him and me.'

'You would be wrong. I would not want you killed over a matter of a car, no matter how good it is.'

'I will check with you first.'

'Good,' Alam said.

Ahmad Ghori was affable the next day when he met with Oleg. He was not alone.

'Oleg, I have asked my colleagues to join me. For our initial meeting, I will not refer to them by name.' One was instantly recognisable to Oleg as the man he had met in Kabul.

'I am pleased to see them here,' Oleg replied, confident there would be serious discussions and he could return to Dushanbe.

Farhana, the local woman, he was not sure about. It seemed an unnecessary complication to take her back with him. The quality of the women was immeasurably improved there, and, with a key position within the Russian organisation, he could afford the best. An Afghan prostitute of limited skills was not the person for him to be squiring around the capital. He would have to dump her on the street or pay her upkeep. No, he had decided to give her some money, wish her well and leave her in Kunduz.

***

The decision regarding Farhana mattered little in the end. Two days after the return from Latif's production facility, and the day after he had spent the night with her at his house, she had been waylaid by a group of black-turbaned men.

'You have shamed your family and Allah,' they said.

It was a trial and sentencing by a mob, with no representation of defence. Farhana was convicted of riding in a car with a man who was not a family member and behaving promiscuously. The indiscretions she had committed with Oleg were not known by the mob, which was just as well, for he would have suffered a similar fate if they had been known.

It was equally fortuitous that the unruly and boisterous mob, who could not resist the urge to grab her breasts and paw her, did not know that she had just spent two hours with Ali Mowllah.

A man, especially one of prominent as Mowllah, was above derision and contempt. In that sad society, it was always the woman who was the temptress, who caused the man to weaken and deviate from the path of Islam and Allah.

The open ground, not far from where she had been cornered, was soon awash with the illiterate, the intolerant and the curious. It was an all-male gathering with one woman, Farhana, the centre of attention. Her father, a humble man who had despaired of his daughter's longing for expensive clothes and Western fashion magazines, was forced to throw the first stone. His aim was poor, the stone small, and if Farhana had looked, she would have seen a tear in his left eye. It would never be known if he had agreed with what they were doing.

It would have made little difference if he had failed to denounce his wayward and dissolute daughter in front of the rabble. He would only have suffered the same fate, and his family would have been fatherless. Without financial support, they would have quickly been begging on the street. His younger daughters, even his wife, would have been reduced to selling

186

themselves, not for the expensive clothes Farhana had seen as so important, but just to put food on the table and a roof over their heads. They would have been lepers in a backwards society. Their only hope of restitution lay in the hands of the mob.

After the first stone had been thrown by her father, the black-turbaned men took their turn. Their stones were much bigger, and their aim more accurate. After the fourth or fifth stone, she collapsed to the ground, blood oozing through the blue burka which covered her. With that, the mob of several hundred men surged forward, hurling stones, beating the body with sticks and kicking indiscriminately.

How long she lasted was unknown, but at the end, all that remained was an indistinct mass covered in blue, tinged with red. The body was left until dusk to show her shame and to let the people know that the Taliban did not tolerate disobedience or any insult to Allah.

Her father came back later as the light faded and retrieved her body. He placed it with care in an open grave he had crudely outside the city and covered it with soil the best way he could.

Oleg was visibly shocked when Alam told him of her fate.

'But why?' Oleg asked.

'I told you the danger of associating with her.'

'I know, but stoning her to death. What crime had she committed?'

'It matters little. Those who condemned her make up the rules.'

'And no doubt sleep with her if they could afford her price.'

'Of course, but this is not a just society.'

'It is barbaric,' Oleg said, realising that he may have offended Alam, a member of that society.

'Barbaric, yes, but I must survive here, as you must. I hope that you will keep your urges in check from now on.'

'I will.' Oleg had forgotten the savage beating he had given Malika. While he spoke of Farhana, it caused him to reflect on what he had done to her. He knew he could not stay in Afghanistan.

***

Ahmad Ghori was succinct the day he and the other three met with Oleg and Farrukh. A wily individual, he saw that discussions needed to be protracted and flexible and that a final decision would only be reached after all options had been evaluated and thought through.

'What's the consensus here?' he asked those assembled. Drug smuggling was occurring throughout the country, and a significant amount of heroin left the country through Pakistan and a smaller amount through Iran, but the route north into Tajikistan and out into the heartland of Russia and then on to Western Europe was predominant. Ghori intended to ensure his group remained in control of the northern route.

'Why don't we play them off against each other?' Arif Noorzai said.

It was not due to lack of money, as the Taliban and now the drugs had rewarded him with a comfortable income to secure four wives – none he had any great affection for – although the last one had proved satisfactory. They were there to breed him sons, seven at the last count – although one was born with an addled brain and another had an extra digit on each hand. Of the seven, two had been killed in the struggle.

One of the two, the eldest and apparently the bravest, had blown himself up while planting an improvised explosive device (IED). In his enthusiasm, he had inadvertently caught the trip wire and ensured martyrdom and the eternal thanks and praises of his Taliban brothers, although six months after his death, his name had been long forgotten.

The son with the addled brain – of considerable embarrassment to the hero Taliban commander – was kept out of sight and stayed with the women. Arif Noorzai did not want to be associated with weakness and infirmity, especially within his family. Ghori promised that one day, he would solve the problem, take the boy out into the desert, and assure him of a martyr's death by putting a gun to his head and pulling the trigger.

'Arif, this is what we do,' said Ghori as he attempted to propose an alternative. He was not to be given the opportunity. He should have been shocked by Noorzai's naivety, but he was not. He knew the calibre of the man. Ghori was a politician, and a politician evaluates, considers, and debates before making rash statements.

'I agree with Arif,' Ashraf Ghilzai said. Ghori was shocked by his outburst. He had seen him as a smarter man. He had been smart enough to escape the fundamentalists near Kandahar in the south and take responsibility for heroin production, which was now running at record levels.

'You are both missing the point,' Ghori countered. 'Baroyev cannot take the quantities the Russian mafia does. He may be more palatable ideologically. He is, after all, a Muslim and not one of the invaders, but he cannot operate at the same level.'

'Then what can we do to assist him?' Ali Mowllah asked. He did not like the Russians, either.

'Ali, how can we assist, and why should we?' asked Ghori.

'Do we trust the Russians?' replied Mowllah.

'We know of your hatred.'

'My hatred is not the issue, but they are Russians. They hate us as much as we hate them. Once the opportunity to cheat us arises, they will.'

'Ali is right,' Ghilzai said.

'I agree.' Noorzai savoured the moment of all three taking a united stand against Ahmad Ghori, the smug and sanctimonious politician who acted as though he was the leader of the assembled group.

'If, as you say, the Russians will cheat us,' said Ghori, seeing that it was opportune to go with the majority, 'then what do you suggest we do?'

Ali Mowllah was the smartest of the disparate grouping that had made a stand against Ahmad Ghori. He was the first to speak. 'We encourage the Russians, maybe try to squeeze a higher price per kilo. But apart from that, we do no more.'

'Why?' Noorzai snapped.

'Arif, my friend, you do not understand,' Mowllah replied in a gentle, condescending manner, hoping to appease the anger of the Taliban commander. It did not.

'Don't take that tone with me,' shouted Noorzai. 'I'm not some fool you can charm with eloquent manners and regal clothes.'

'I apologise,' replied Mowllah. 'Let me continue.'

'I will accept your apology. Continue,' Noorzai said, although he was a hard man who did not forgive easily and never forgot.

'The Russians are putting plenty of money into our accounts,' Mowllah explained. 'We stay with the Russians. We tell them they are our preferred option.'

'And then what?' Noorzai interjected.

'We enter into discussions with Baroyev.'

'Ahmad is correct,' said Ghilzai. 'He is incapable of moving the quantities.' He felt the need to enter the conversation. He did not want production to go down dramatically.

'What I am saying is,' Mowllah felt the need to clarify his position, 'Baroyev cannot take the quantities now, but with our assistance, he may be able to.'

'Are you saying we get involved in the transportation through Tajikistan and the distribution into Russia?' Ghori asked.

'Who are the Russians?' Mowllah asked.

'The Russian mafia,' Ghori replied.

'Are you saying they represent the entire Russian mafia?'

'That is what we assumed.'

'Then what if we are wrong?' What if they only represent a small part of the organisation, and those we are dealing with are a splinter group operating independently?'

'Are they?' Ghilzai asked.

'It's possible.'

'How will we find this out?' Ghori asked.

'Baroyev is our best bet. He will be able to find out.'

'So how do we make contact with him?' Ahmad Ghori asked.

'His representative is here.' Ali Mowllah had momentarily taken the lead position of the four assembled Afghans. 'Let us meet with him and discuss. First, we must speak to the Russians' agent and send him back to Tajikistan.'

'I am in agreement with Mowllah's suggestion,' Noorzai said. Ashraf Ghilzai nodded his head in compliance.

'And after he has gone?' Ghori asked.

'I will travel to meet with Baroyev,' Mowllah said.

'And I will go with you,' Ghori added.

***

The subsequent meeting with Oleg was shorter than expected and to the point.

'We will maintain the agreement with your people, subject to certain conditions,' Ahmad Ghori said.

'And those conditions?' Oleg replied, sceptical that such an easy resolution was possible. The Afghans had been anything but conciliatory down at the smugglers' village. They were always bargaining for that little bit extra, a sweetener, an enticement for them to continue to do business with him.

He knew their ploy. It was no different from what he had used when he had been a standover man in St. Petersburg, but there he had real leverage. The Afghan smugglers in the village, degenerate as they were, could hardly have burnt his premises down – he had nothing other than a wooden hut. And there was no one else trustworthy in the village they could have dealt with – Baroyev had dealt with that by scaring off anyone muscling in on his business.

'We require an increase in the price,' Ghori said.

'My people will not be very responsive to this.' The reply that Oleg gave surprised even him, diplomatic as it was. He would have preferred to tell them to keep their unreasonable and offensive demand, and he would go somewhere else; but here, as in the drug smugglers' village, there was nowhere else to go. Those sitting in front of him knew that all too well.

'There are no options,' Ali Mowllah said.

Ashraf Ghilzai, silent until now, offered a comment. 'Our costs of manufacture are rising now that the Afghan army is increasing its presence in the region. They are backed up by American satellite surveillance and drones.'

Oleg could feel his blood boiling. He knew when he was being fed a line. The Afghan army was only vigilant when Ghilzai did not keep up with his bribes to the senior men in their military, but he supposed their demands could be rising. If there was one business where greed rose to dominance, it was crime – especially when that crime came with a surfeit of money, and here the surfeit was astronomical.

Oleg knew his greed was equal to theirs, but his new best friend, the Russian mafia, had sent him down to negotiate a more equitable deal, not to be asked to pay more. He knew their nature, and they would be hostile to him, maybe even jeopardise his return to Dushanbe. He had still not given up on returning to Russia once his pockets were full of ill-gotten gains.

'I can understand your wish to maximise your returns,' said Oleg. 'However, everyone is looking for a bit extra in Tajikistan. If we agree to an extra payment to you, then everyone else will want a similar increase. We would then be forced to look for another supplier.'

'There is no other supplier,' Noorzai brusquely summed up the situation. A Taliban commander was not known for subtlety, only for total obedience or death to those who got between him and his desired objective. He had little time for a Russian, even if the one in front of him was palatable to the sight and reasonably refined in his manners. Noorzai had heard the rumours surrounding the Russian negotiator, including his involvement with the whore his men had stoned to death.

'There is always another supplier,' Oleg said, although he knew that he had probably made a statement based on nothing but air.

'You insult us with arrogance and intransigence,' Ali Mowllah retorted. 'We have treated you with respect, a person from a country that caused great suffering to the people of Afghanistan, and here you mouth words which you know to be untrue.'

'With respect,' replied Oleg. He was careful not to show his anger. He could feel his body's nervousness as the increased adrenaline levels surged through him. 'Your people killed my father, and with a level of barbarity which can only be the mark of an uncivilised people.'

All in the meeting were on their feet. Arif Noorzai's men, standing just outside the room, burst in at a command from their leader and grabbed Oleg firmly from either side. They were about to beat him until Ahmad Ghori intervened.

'This is not how a meeting should be conducted. We are all businessmen here. The history of the past must remain in the past. Even amongst ourselves, there is derision, even hatred, but we have a common cause – the pursuit of money to serve our needs and the needs of our people.'

***

It would be another couple of hours for the tempers to calm before the meeting could resume. Oleg had taken the opportunity to contact his superiors and give them an update. Surprisingly, they were pleased that it was only five per cent, but they were insistent – do not come back until you get it down to two and a half, three at the most.

He was determined to secure a deal and leave the country. Farrukh could have his car as far as he was concerned. He would soon get another one in Dushanbe.

'Let us resume,' Ghori said. It still irked Noorzai that he acted as the leader of their group. But, after the unpleasantness of earlier, he, like Oleg, decided to remain calm, whatever the provocation. He would have easily had the Russian shot and thrown to the dogs; he would still do so if the opportunity arose.

'I have spoken to my people,' Oleg said. 'They are agreeable to two per cent.'

'We want a five per cent increase,' Ali Mowllah said with little conviction. 'Our costs are escalating. Two per cent is not sufficient.'

'My people will not agree to five.' Oleg remained calm.

'Then your people can go to hell,' Noorzai shouted. He was still tense, although Ghori and Mowllah had spoken to him earlier and reminded him that the Russians were giving him the money he needed to further his fundamentalist cause. The group had also offered him a five per cent increase for the opium poppies he produced and sold to Ghilzai and a higher percentage return on the money the Russians were paying. He knew a good deal when it was thrust in his face, and it justified his earlier outburst, although it did not temper his wish to have the Russian killed – in fact, *any* Russian if he could get his hands on them.

'Then let us agree on three per cent,' Oleg said. The day was drawing to a close, and he was certain the border would close at dusk. He did not want to spend another night in that dreary city, which had been his home for too long. Alam had also told him earlier that the men with Noorzai were almost certainly present when Farhana, the fashion-loving prostitute, had been cornered and stoned.

Oleg could be a brave man. He had been at times, especially when Malenkov's brother, the FSB operative, had been on his trail and anxious to kill him. But with Noorzai and his group of hardened Taliban fighters and a city which was pitch black once the sun went down, lit only by the headlights of the cars and trucks as they hurtled around the city – that was something different. It would be stupid for him to stay, and he was afraid and not unwilling to admit it. *If they go for the three per cent, I'm out of here*, he thought.

It still took another two hours and endless cups of tea and pistachio nuts before an agreement was reached – three per cent. Oleg was pleased, Ahmad Ghori and Ali Mowllah were delighted, and Ashraf Ghilzai was complacent.

Arif Noorzai, however, was livid. He was livid on two counts. The first was that any agreement with a Russian was not what he wanted and, at a lower rate, was obscene. The second annoyed him more than the first – he had been forced to give an assurance that the Russian mafia's man was to be left alone, even escorted to the border. The money and the business were more important than the hatred of a Russian.

***

As Oleg made the trip to the border in the company of Alam, still driving the old Toyota that he had come in, not the black Mercedes he had promised himself, his conversation turned to what had transpired.

'Alam, what is going on? They have agreed to three per cent, far too quickly for my liking.'

'This is Afghanistan,' Alam replied. 'You have only set in place the possibilities for further discussions.'

'I should not be overly elated?'

'Elated? You should be ecstatic.'

'Why?' Oleg asked.

'You have reached an agreement. And you are still alive and going back to Tajikistan.'

'I must be grateful for that, I suppose.' Oleg could see sense in what Alam was saying, but he was unsure that his visit to the country and the people who had slaughtered his father, and thousands of other Russians had been an unmitigated success.

'As I said, you're still alive.' Alam sounded almost philosophical.

'Is that all I achieved?'

'Considering the circumstances, I would say that was a significant achievement.'

'Why do you think that?'

'On the one hand, you insulted Arif Noorzai, a man who has good reason to hate Russians. And then you were having sex with the prostitute, even took her to your house a few times.'

'I thought nobody knew about that.'

'I overheard two of Noorzai's men; they knew.'

'But how?' Oleg asked.

'Do you think a Russian could pick up an Afghan woman, put her in the boot of his car, then drive to his house past guards and expect not to have been seen?'

'I suppose not,' said Oleg pensively. 'But when they killed Farhana, why was I left alone?'

'Ahmad Ghori protected you.'

Chapter 17

It was dark when Oleg said farewell to Alam. As the old Toyota rattled its way across the bridge into Tajikistan, Farrukh began meeting with the group in Kunduz that had given him such a hard time earlier.

This time, the meeting was more cordial; Farrukh was a fellow Muslim. The Russian mafia – or, at least, Oleg's Russian mafia – were in the bag. Now was the time to see if a better deal could be struck with the Tajikistan gangster, Baroyev.

Ali Mowllah had seen the possibility but not the solution. Farrukh was the man they wanted to talk to.

'Farrukh, we have sent your friend back to Tajikistan with an answer,' Ahmad Ghori led off.

'May I ask what that answer was?' Farrukh realised he was in safe territory here, and his manner with the four was relaxed.

'Farrukh,' Mowllah said, 'we have agreed to continue with the present arrangement.'

'With the Russians?' Farrukh had assumed they would supply him with good news. They were, but not the news he was expecting.

'Yes, with the Russians,' Noorzai, the Taliban Warlord, said bitterly.

'It is for us to explain our position.' Ghori sensed the disappointment in Farrukh's body language, with his arms folded and no longer leaning forward earnestly. He now slouched, leaning backwards in a defensive manner. 'The Russians can take the quantities you and your people cannot. This you cannot deny.'

'But we are brothers. The Russians are the invaders.' Farrukh certainly understood the logic – it would have been the decision he would have made, but he could not accept defeat without putting forward a vigorous rebuttal. He had taken the opportunity to contact Yusup before the meeting.

It annoyed him that it had come to nought after so many weeks of endlessly floating around in Kunduz without a woman.

He had kept himself in check, often by some excessive praying at the Mosque. He hoped for a quick exit across the border, a fast run in the Mercedes to the capital he loved. The apartment, however, was empty. Negareh, the live-in girlfriend, had departed after his enforced stay in Afghanistan at her father's insistence.

'You deserve an explanation and a solution,' Ghori said.

'A solution?' Farrukh had seen a closed door. Now there seemed to be an opening.

'First, the explanation,' the Afghan continued. 'Business needs to be maintained, and, as much as we hate and distrust the Russians, they take the quantity and pay us well. As a business arrangement, it is admirable. But, as you say, they are Russians.'

'Does that mean you wish to still deal with us?' Farrukh asked.

'Smuggling across the border in the dead of night, with a local tribesman carrying a few kilos of heroin, no longer interests us,' replied Ghori. 'But that is all you can offer us at this present moment. Am I correct?'

'Correct in what?' replied Farrukh. Ghori's question had proved to be a little obscure.

'Baroyev cannot set up an organisation to compete with the Russian mafia.'

'In the past, he would have been responsible for transporting up to the Russian border and then on-selling it to the Russian mafia. It was an arrangement that worked well. Why do you want to change it?' Farrukh asked somewhat naively, overstepping the space between cordiality and rudeness. He sensed that his question may have been a little too direct.

'Farrukh,' Ghori felt obliged to rebut him, 'we have been lenient with you. It would be wise to think before you speak and to allow us to state our position.'

'I apologise, but naturally, I am disappointed. To go back to Yusup Baroyev and tell him I have not been successful....'

'What makes you say that?' Mowllah said. So far, Noorzai and Ghilzai had said little. Noorzai busied himself with the spread of food laid out before them. Ghilzai considered how to achieve next month's production target. The climate in the main growing regions had not been ideal for the optimum crop; there had been too much rain, and he had had to order extra chemicals to extract the required quality.

'I am not going back without a secured deal,' Farrukh replied. It wasn't only the deal that concerned Farrukh. Yusup had promised him a welcoming back party if he came back with good news, and here he was, returning with nothing but a few words of appeasement from his Afghan hosts.

'Then you are wrong. You are going back with more than that,' Ghori said.

'Am I?'

'Yes, of course. You are going back with our support. We need the Russians, we all do, including Baroyev, but not necessarily those we are currently dealing with.'

'I don't understand,' Farrukh said.

'Let me explain,' Mowllah said. As the master organiser, it was for him to detail the plan. 'The Russian mafia we know here is only a part of a much larger organisation.'

'They are not the people that Yusup used to deal with,' Farrukh replied.

'Then,' Mowllah continued, 'what if we meet with Baroyev? See how we can assist him in the transportation up through Tajikistan and Kazakhstan to the Russian border?'

'But why would you want to do that?'

'For financial gain, what else?'

'The idea is fine,' said Farrukh. 'But wouldn't this create open warfare between the factions within the Russian mafia and with the organisation I represent?'

'The Russian mafia, what do we care?' replied Mowllah. 'As for Baroyev and your people, we will protect them.'

'Why would you protect Yusup Baroyev? You have not shown any fondness for him.'

'You are right,' Ghori said. 'He is, however, a Muslim and a Tajik. And, regardless of his habit of consorting with prostitutes, which we find distasteful, he is still one of us, a fellow brother.'

Ali Mowllah sheepishly grabbed a handful of a savoury dish as Ghori commented about prostitutes. He had been the last man to have had sexual intercourse with the hapless Farhana before her stoning. He relished the opportunity of an invite to one of Baroyev's legendary parties. Taking Ahmad Ghori along with him to Dushanbe concerned him. It was bound to cramp his style.

Mowllah had considered himself exceptionally lucky with the prostitute in Kunduz and, whereas he had snuck her into his room at the back of the house he occupied in Kunduz, he had nearly been caught. He had almost tripped over a guard at the house, who should have been awake, but was not. Upon his return from dropping her off down a desolate and darkened street several blocks from the house, he returned and chastised the guard, even had him beaten the next morning, for his failure to stay awake.

'We will return with you to Dushanbe and meet with Baroyev,' Mowllah said. This both pleased and disappointed Farrukh, who realised his visit to a woman on the Tajikistan border would not happen. But then, if he brought two senior Afghan drug lords, he would have at least come back with a better-than-expected result. It would still be seen that he had had a successful trip to Afghanistan. Yusup would throw him the party he wanted.

***

Two days later, Farrukh arrived back in Dushanbe to a welcome from Baroyev.

'I am pleased to see you,' Yusup said. 'And what of our esteemed guests?'

'They are comfortably settled in the guest house you provided for them.'

The guest house, located five kilometres from the main residence where the parties were held, was sufficiently close if the visitors wanted to attend and sufficiently distant if they did not.

The downturn in the drug trade was impacting Yusup's cash flow. While his other activities would ensure no curtailing of his lifestyle, at least in the short term, he did not want it to continue indefinitely. The Russians were poaching on his turf; he wanted them out. If showing the Afghans hospitality was necessary, he had no trouble with it.

'Have you got yourself laid since you got back?' Baroyev focused on the necessities first.

'As soon as I offloaded the Afghans,' Farrukh replied.

'And the apartment?'

'It's great, just lonely.'

'I'll send you someone for a couple of days. But remember, you must be fired up on the weekend.'

'I'll be ready.'

'No women in Afghanistan?' Yusup seemed not to want to talk about business. Farrukh was quite comfortable indulging in small talk.

'There are, but it is too dangerous. They will likely beat you to a pulp and take off your balls if caught with one. Yezhov was nearly caught. He was lucky and got away with it.'

'He will not be so lucky here. I still have a score to settle with him.' The Tajik drug lord saw Oleg as a traitor, and, as such, he needed a traitor's death. And then there was Malika, who had suffered at his hands.

The relationship between her and the gangster leader remained resilient, so much so that his wife complained of neglect.

He reasoned that all he needed to do was to pack her off with the children to somewhere warm in Europe, equip her with a credit card and let her spend to her heart's delight. She would stop complaining or be out on the street with barely enough money to survive.

Not that he wanted to do that, but there was only so much complaining one man could take. If any of his men had dared to speak to him in the manner she had, they would be dead.

Ahmad Ghori had been to Dushanbe before, but Ali Mowllah had not. To Ghori, it represented decadence, and whereas it remained a Muslim city, the Russian influence still tainted the city with its austere concrete buildings. Even the police and military looked as if they had just flown in from Russia, and the senior military, especially the officers, continued to wear the same mildly absurd officers' caps with their wide rims and peaks.

He wanted to conclude business as soon as possible and return to where he belonged, the bear pit of local politics. He also wanted to ensure his burgeoning wealth due to drugs in main and local corruption, in part, which was endemic, did not falter.

Ali Mowllah saw something different. He had experienced many years in the sprawling megalopolis of Karachi, in the far south of Pakistan, and the capital of Tajikistan excited him. He had no issue with the decadence, and if Baroyev's parties were as he had heard, he was determined to get an invite.

***

For two days, the Afghans enjoyed the luxury of the house provided. It boasted five bedrooms, five bathrooms and a swimming pool in the manicured grounds – heated as befitted a climate that ranged from freezing in winter to boiling in summer.

Ali Mowllah had learnt to swim in the freezing waters, as a child, in his home city of Sarobi, but Ahmad Ghori had not. He sat to one side, studying the Koran, but not failing to notice the appealing features of the two female housekeepers who dressed in a provocative, Western style, showing too much leg and cleavage. One had bent over to pick up a glass on a small table to his right, and he had not resisted the opportunity to look down the front of her blouse to her exposed breasts and erect nipples. She wore no bra.

Mowllah had noticed his leering but made no comment. He had made an inappropriate gesture to the most becoming of the two women when she came to make his bed and received a disdainful look for his efforts and a slap to the face. He realised they dressed provocatively, promiscuously even, but they were neither, and he conditioned himself to no longer assume that the women were available, even if they looked as if they were.

Farrukh took the two days to spend time with the woman Yusup had supplied. At the end of his time with her, he wasn't sure he would be ready for the weekend party. But then, he reasoned, he had spent too long in Afghanistan being chaste. He would find the energy.

***

The long-awaited meeting between Ali Mowllah, Ahmad Ghori and Yusup Baroyev convened at the Afghans' guest house. Yusup arrived in the green Bentley. He thought it sufficiently prestigious, not overtly ostentatious. Ali Mowllah was overawed with the car and managed to talk Yusup into letting him have a drive of it in the next few days. Ahmad Ghori was taken aback by its opulence.

The room where they met, to the left-hand side of the sweeping semi-circular staircase, was decorated in a neoclassic style. The statues, one in every corner, as Ahmad Ghori noted, were reproductions of Greek classical nude females; he was neither excited nor offended by them.

Yusup Baroyev was proud to tell them that the room had cost over a quarter of a million American dollars and considered it well spent.

The conversation soon turned to business.

'You have told Farrukh that you wish to work with us. Is this correct?' Yusup asked.

'We wish to investigate the possibility,' Ghori said. He was still overawed by the mansion's luxury and enjoying it too much.

He was a wealthy man in his society but a modest man by nature. He saw wealth as support for his family, not something to be thrown around in a bragging manner as Baroyev had done.

Ghori took the lead role in the discussions. He and Baroyev spoke Tajik, whereas Mowllah did not, not with the necessary fluency. Ali Mowllah could follow the conversation, but the nuances of the language were beyond him.

'That's an ambiguous statement,' Baroyev said.

'It must be. The Russians are making us wealthy, whereas you cannot.' Ghori was blunt in his reply.

'Then why did you want to come here and meet with me?'

'Because we want you to make us wealthy, not them,' Ghori said.

'But how can I? The Russians throw money around like it was confetti at a wedding. I cannot compete; it would be open warfare if I tried. My life would be threatened. I treasure my life too much to be open to such a situation.'

'Are you a coward?' Ahmad Ghori pointed an index finger at Yusup Baroyev.

'You insult me.'

'It is not an insult. It is a question. We can only help if we believe the person we are dealing with is worthy of our assistance. Are you worthy?'

'To take on the Russians needs a firm plan,' Baroyev retorted. 'Not some ideological stand based on a deep-rooted hatred or religious fervour.'

'And now you insult us,' said Ghori. 'We are not obliged towards the Russians, and believe me when I say that we do indeed hate them.' He banged his fist on the table. 'We are businessmen, not religious ideologues. We came here to help, to form an alliance and to see if you were worthy.'

'What is your evaluation?' Baroyev asked.

'We know of your reputation.'

'My reputation, good or bad?'

'Confused would be the best description.'

'Why do you say that?'

204

'We trust you, whereas we do not trust the Russians,' said Ghori. 'And that is nothing to do with hatred.'

'You are right not to trust them,' Baroyev replied. 'Those you are dealing with are not the people I have dealt with in the past.'

'Then who are they?' Ali Mowllah listened intently and managed to pick up some conversation. He found Baroyev's accent clearer and more precise than Ghori's. Tajik and Pashtun were related languages; the common words and sayings outweighed the unusual ones.

'They are either a renegade offshoot of the Russian mafia, the Bratva or aligned with the political leadership in Russia.' Baroyev was reasonably sure of the truth but chose not to reveal it. The Afghans had a fearsome reputation for treachery and double-dealing.

He would keep his counsel until he was sure of the two sitting comfortably in his antique chairs.

He liked the look of Ali Mowllah, who he judged to be in his fifties, an open man, both in his nature and his religion. Yusup had laughed outrageously when told of his amateurish attempt at seduction of one of the housekeepers. Supplying them both with women would not have concerned him, but Ahmad Ghori did not look like a man who would accept.

He would endeavour to find out what their preferences were. There was one thing Yusup Baroyev had learnt: a man without vices is not a man to be trusted. Besides, he needed an edge that he could hold against them if they decided to cheat on him later, and he knew an Afghan always would. They saw it as the natural condition of doing business.

'How do we find out who we are dealing with?' Ahmad Ghori returned to the reason they were in the country.

Baroyev could not help but smile inwardly when one of the housekeepers brought in some tea. He noticed Ghori glaring at the tight dress clinging to the woman, showing the prominence of her breasts and the curve of her thighs. Ali Mowllah, he had noticed, had crossed his legs to conceal a growing erection. He would come to Farrukh's party, but how to get him away from Ghori? Maybe he would come if his presence was kept discreet.

'I will conduct an investigation,' said Baroyev. 'It may take a few days, but please feel free to stay here and enjoy my hospitality. I will ensure the Bentley will be here at your convenience, with a driver on call. I am having a get-together at the main house to celebrate Farrukh's return. You are both welcome.'

'Will this be one of those parties we have heard about?' Ahmad Ghori asked seriously, with no sign of any humour.

'I am not sure what parties you have heard about,' said Baroyev, 'but it is a party as befits a senior businessman here in the capital. It serves many purposes: it is good for business, entertainment and fun and cements my position as an important man in this city.'

'It did until the Russians elbowed in,' Ghori responded sarcastically.

'Yes, as you say, but we agree. We will work together to ensure my position is restored. You will receive a more equitable financial deal with a fellow Muslim instead of with the invader. We suffered under the Russians, although not as much as you. We trust them no more than you do. Hopefully, we can formulate a plan to rid ourselves of them and make more money for ourselves.'

'Then we agree on that issue,' Ghori said.

'So do I,' Ali Mowllah said, 'and I will accept your invitation. It will be a means of cementing our newfound friendship.'

'It is not a friendship yet, but hopefully, we can agree,' Ghori acknowledged.

'Will you come as well? As a sign of friendship,' Baroyev asked, noting that Ahmad Ghori had become increasingly more agreeable.

'I will not associate with the women.'

'That is fine. It is a big house. There are plenty of places where you will not be disturbed.'

'Then I will accept your hospitality as befits our newfound friendship, although I believe that Ali will not be keeping me company,' said Ahmad Ghori, smiling.

Chapter 18

Oleg's return to the capital of Tajikistan had given him great relief. There may have been guards to protect him in Afghanistan, but they had not liked him any more than the general populace. It surprised him how deep the hatred remained after so many years since the Soviet military had exited their country. The people in Afghanistan were haters and hated him more than any other. The Americans had come after the Russians but did not hate them, only despised them.

The televisions beaming CNN, or a dreary and inane soap opera, suitably subtitled, seemed to amuse them immensely, while the bazaars were stocked with cheap tee shirts emblazoned with 'USA' and 'New York'.

He had even seen an old Chevrolet Camaro driving around the city; the owner, a young man with a wisp of a beard, proudly showing off to his friends. He never saw anyone driving an old Russian car other than the ubiquitous Volga, and they were left for taxi duties. The men in the car, the women in the boot.

He realised that apart from Farhana — the now dead prostitute — and the Chinese woman in Kabul, he had spoken to no other female from when he crossed the border into Afghanistan until he returned across it.

Not encumbered with transporting two Afghan men as Farrukh had been, Oleg had sought out the services of a woman at the Tajik border town as soon as he had crossed over the bridge separating the two countries. It had been a two-minute affair, a darkened room around the back of a fabric shop, trousers around his ankles, skirt hitched above her waist, and both standing up with her voluminous arse banging against the side of the wooden walls. It had cost him the equivalent of twenty American dollars. If the urge had not been so great, he would have bargained the price down to ten.

He had left satisfied, hopefully disease-free, as he had not bothered with a condom – he did not have one, and neither did the woman, who was probably teeming with pubic lice. He promised to get himself checked out once he reached the capital, which he did; however, apart from a nasty rash, which some cream would deal with, he was fine.

His new bosses had organised accommodation for him, not as good as Yusup had provided, but it was adequate. He knew it would not be long before he would live as well as before. It was two blocks from his old apartment, and, in the weeks to come, he would often see Farrukh wafting around at the wheel of his Mercedes with one or another quality woman sitting in the passenger's seat.

For him, there were women, not so many and not as beautiful as Farrukh's, but then it was up to him to pay for them now, even seduce them if cost became an issue. After time in Afghanistan, he had to admit he did not look as presentable as before. The complexion of his skin was blotchy, no doubt due to a lack of the appropriate vitamins. The vegetables and fruit had not suited his palate, and he had avoided them as much as possible. The enforced diet of chicken and rice, adequate if basic, had sustained him, but it was not balanced.

He also noticed his previously firm physique was becoming flabby. It was clear that wooing any woman would require him to get in better physical shape. One thing the Russian mafia insisted on was a smartly-dressed individual, even for their killers, although he hoped his killing days were behind him. For Farrukh, he would make an exception, but that was personal.

***

It came as a surprise to Oleg when he saw Malika. It was on one of the days that he attended the gym. He had lost five kilos and was looking a lot better. She was coming in as he was going out. It was fortunate she was looking the other way.

He had to admit she looked well and fit and happy. Even the tattoos, so badly gouged into the skin of a pallid and dissolute whore in a drug smugglers' village, as she had been, looked acceptable on her skin, now silky smooth and lightly tanned.

'Who's the classy-looking woman?' Oleg asked the attendant at the exit door of the gym.

He had not forgotten her, still regretted what he had done and hoped that, maybe, there was a chance of forgiveness, perhaps even the rekindling of a romance. Two lost souls down on their luck, reborn. It seemed clichéd, but maybe it could be true for them. His idle speculation did not last long.

The attendant, an effeminate-voiced man with bulging muscles and barely any neck, after numerous push-ups with weights too heavy and an unhealthy addiction to under-the-counter steroids, regarded gossip as more important than reality.

'Her? The stunner?' the attendant asked. *Maybe the effeminate-voiced man still fancied women?* Oleg thought. *But then, the steroids would have shrunk his testicles. He was probably impotent, as well. Fancy them he may, but there would be nothing he could do about it.*

'Yes, the stunner,' Oleg responded.

'Keep away from her unless you want to sing soprano.'

'What do you mean?' Oleg asked.

'She's Yusup Baroyev's woman. You know who he is?'

Oleg was visibly shocked, which caused the attendant to ask more questions than he would otherwise have.

'You know him?' the attendant badgered, anxious to glean any information to gossip around the gym.

'No, who's he?' replied Oleg.

The attendant could smell a lie. Everyone knew who Yusup Baroyev was, rich or poor, honest or dishonest. A denial was tantamount to hidden secrets; he would endeavour to pull them out of Oleg.

'She's his mistress. His wife was raising complaints, so he shipped her off to Europe. He won't be too far behind if his woman is here.'

'What about his parties?' Oleg realised that he had let slip that he knew of Yusup Baroyev. The attendant, who said his name was Tolib, had asked too many questions. He was bound to say something to Malika, perhaps even Baroyev, if the opportunity arose.

'Are you free for lunch?' Oleg casually asked.

'I was just about to go now. What do you have in mind?' Tolib asked.

'Somewhere local where we can talk. I'm interested to hear more about who's who in this city.' Oleg thought his response was suitably obtuse and enticing for the attendant to agree. He was proven correct in his assumption.

'There's somewhere not far from here,' said Tolib. 'A small restaurant, it does an excellent line in home-cooked food. It's a bit expensive for me, but if you're paying….'

'I'm paying,' Oleg said.

***

The restaurant was expensive, but Oleg regarded it as money well spent.

'Tell me,' he said, 'what you know about the woman.'

'Malika,' replied Tolib. 'She apparently had a rough time when she was younger but now very cosy with Baroyev.'

'And what about Yusup Baroyev?'

'What's to tell? He's a big man in the drug business, which makes him a big man in Dushanbe.'

'Why do you say that?' Oleg asked, suitably naïve.

'Money,' said Tolib. 'It's all to do with money, and he's got more than anyone else.'

'The parties, do they still happen?'

'Oleg…' It was the first time the attendant had ventured to address him by name. 'What do you know about him, and why did you pretend not to know him?'

'I did not want to be too open with you. Baroyev's a dangerous man, and I need to meet up with him, but not before I know the lay of the land, so to speak.'

'You can trust my discretion,' the gym attendant said. Oleg knew he could not.

'The parties, what about the parties?' Oleg continued.

'They continue. I've never been, but I've heard they are something special. Plenty of women, best-quality that money can buy and as much drink and food as you can consume.'

'Does the stunner go?'

'I'm told she turns a blind eye and keeps well away when they're on.'

At the end of the meal – and with Tolib consuming the best part of a couple of bottles of wine and three stiff shots of whisky, they left the restaurant, ostensibly heading back to the gym.

Not that the attendant was in any fit state to work. Once in the comfortable seat of Oleg's car, with the heater turned to warm, he drifted off into a deep sleep.

Oleg turned away from the direct route back to the gym and headed down a side track hidden from the main road, not more than three hundred metres distant. A disused quarry, open-cut and flooded after years of abandonment, proved the ideal place.

The gym attendant, semi-conscious after the effects of the alcohol had lessened, did not see the thick handle of the wheel brace as it came crashing down on his head. Oleg then applied a firm lock on his head and around his neck and twisted with force until an audible crack could be heard. Tolib's neck was broken; he was dead.

A rope in the car's boot allowed Oleg to attach the overly curious gym attendant's body to an iron beam, evidently belonging to a crane's infrastructure in the past when it had been an operating quarry. Then, he threw the body over the cliff into the murky water below. The only witnesses were a couple of ducks startled by the body hitting the water. They flew off to the other side of the lake.

Oleg had not wanted to kill, had vowed not to, but Malika with Baroyev presented a complication he had not foreseen. He had been discreet at the gym, careful to avoid the direct gaze of the waiters at the restaurant.

What to do about Malika, he was not sure, but he did not want to kill her. Quite the opposite, in fact, but there was Baroyev to consider. If she had told him about the incident at the smugglers' village, his life would be in jeopardy, more than it already was, and his life was more precious than hers.

Oleg's day had not turned out as he had hoped, and that night, he took solace in a bottle of whisky. He saw that Dushanbe was not a place for him to remain for too long, and an immediate return to Russia was needed. However, there was still the issue of the FSB man, who was determined to avenge the death of his brother.

He did not understand why, as he had a brother and did not care whether he lived or died. The brother, Arkady, was five years older than him, a bully as a boy and a thug as an adult. He was now in Kresty Prison in St. Petersburg.

Oleg had not seen him for ten years and had no intention of paying him a brotherly visit, even if the chance arose.

***

Oleg's primary contact, Gennady Denikin, had been more forthcoming on his return. Before his trip to Afghanistan, Denikin had been nameless. Oleg did not like him particularly. He was always accompanied by his protector, Viktor Gryzlov.

Denikin, the gentleman gangster, was how Oleg saw him. A precise little man who fidgeted excessively whenever he sat for more than five minutes. He had the mind of an accountant, which he had been before he had been struck off for fiddling the books of the government department he had worked for in

Moscow. It had cost him five years in a particularly unpleasant prison.

Valentina Brezhnev, no relative to a previous President of Russia, had seduced him one night late after work when he was drunk, and she needed another benefactor. Her last paramour, a middle-ranking civil servant, could no longer keep her in the manner she required, which was expensive.

A shampoo for her beloved poodle cost two hundred American dollars. The apartment where she lived and regularly serviced the middle-ranking civil servant cost more than three thousand dollars a month in hard currency, cash on the table. And then there were the designer clothes and the trips to Paris during fashion week. Somebody had to pay.

The civil servant's name was unimportant, only his ability to corrupt the money out of the department he worked for. He was adept at issuing lucrative contracts to companies which did not deserve them but paid him plenty to ensure they did. Or payments for ignoring the shoddy work delivered afterwards and issuing compliance certificates.

The civil servant had been of a similar temperament to Denikin. An overactive mind, continually doing the figures in his head and a similar taste in women: voluptuous, with bouffant hairdos, overly red lipstick and prominent bosoms. Valentina Brezhnev had satisfied on all counts.

She had spent the first sixteen years of her life struggling with a father who abused her physically and sexually as a teenager. And that by the age of seventeen, she knew how to work the system. If they wanted something, she wanted something in return. A phone when she was a teenager, a car later, maybe a trip somewhere, but her father took her for free.

It was not a good upbringing, and at eighteen, Valentina left the house and married a foolish man of nineteen who genuinely loved her.

For fifteen years, she laboured for him, bearing him two children – a daughter, bright and precocious, and a son, the spitting image of her father, and there was every indication he would grow up to be an abuser of his own children, especially the females. She tried to love him as a son but could not. The daughter she took from the family house one day after finding the son attempting to force himself onto the daughter. They never returned, and whereas she had struggled for some years, she never regretted the decision.

There had been a few men before the civil servant of varying wealth and means, and her daughter had wanted for nothing. At the age of twenty, her daughter had married a good and honest businessman who treated her well and for whom she felt great affection.

The son, she knew little of, other than he had become involved with crime and was in and out of jail with alarming regularity.

The civil servant had been suitable, but her demands and his new boss, a boorish man with old-fashioned ideas of honesty and fair dealing, had squeezed his skilful ability to extract the necessary corrupt amounts of money to satisfy her.

He had informed her one summer's day when she had just returned from giving her poodle a walk in the park that he could no longer afford her and that it was over. The rent on the apartment was due in two weeks, and he was not going to pay. Indignant at his affront, she hit him squarely between the eyes with a jewel-encrusted hand and kicked him out of the apartment.

***

Desperation forced Valentina to the bar to find someone else. The accountant had seemed ideal. He had been pleased with her company, enamoured that someone so beautiful could appreciate his limited conversation, focused as it was on money and taxation laws. His wife did not understand him. *They all say that*, she thought.

She seduced him that night at her apartment. The rent was paid the next week, and Gennady Denikin was hooked.

He was to have a similar problem as the civil servant. Her demands were to escalate; the previously luxurious apartment was no longer luxurious enough, the poodle needed a companion, and there was another round of fashion events for her to attend in another exorbitantly expensive capital city in Europe, and he would have to pay.

Adept at maintaining two sets of books – or two sets of databases, as they were stored on a computer – he had managed to syphon off the necessary money to keep her passionate and willing. The poodle sitting at the end of the bed did nothing for his performance, complicated by Valentina and her obligatory sounds of orgasmic joy. He was not sure they were genuine.

Denikin soon came to see it as a farce, but his wife, purse-lipped and stringent with her sexual favours, had given him no option. It was either Valentina, with her excessive financial demands, or a tart on a street corner, but he had never felt the inclination or the courage to approach them and ask how much.

Unable to double-dip the accounts at work or at least as much as was necessary, he became careless. An independent financial audit of his department's accounts showed his guilt with no hope of a mistake on their part. At the resultant trial, embarrassing in the extreme, his wife, in desperation, had stood up and announced to the assembled throng that Gennady Denikin was a waster and wanted no more of him. She made it clear at the divorce that if he wanted to see his two children, she would fight him through the courts to stop him.

Ten years in prison, but out in five for good behaviour, he looked to be a hopeless case. He soon drifted into petty crime, handling the books for an illegal gambling operation in Moscow. His skill soon elevated him from petty to minor to major until Grigory Stolypin recognised his talents and brought him on board.

Denikin's redemption with Stolypin and the mafia had been swift. Whereas he may have cheated others once, he would not cheat them.

***

'It's not safe here in Dushanbe for me,' Oleg told Denikin at one of their regular meetings.

Viktor Gryzlov, Denikin's bodyguard, stood close – too close for Oleg's liking. Gryzlov was a bear of a man; the sleeves of his suit looked as though they would split when he flexed his muscles, as he was apt to do. He had an annoying habit of cracking his fingers and neck joints. Oleg saw it as intimidation. He had known some tough men, but this one stood out from the majority.

To see Denikin and Gryzlov from the rear was akin to a silent movie, with Denikin not even reaching the shoulders of his permanent shadow, and then the hat that Gryzlov never took off added another fifteen centimetres to his height. Gryzlov said little, Denikin said plenty.

'You wanted to come here,' Denikin reminded Oleg.

'That was before I knew that Baroyev was after me.' Oleg had purposefully kept quiet about Malika.

'Did you expect him to welcome you back with roses after you swapped sides?'

'No, of course not.'

'Then stop complaining and get on with your job. We will deal with Yusup Baroyev at some point. When the time comes, you can have that pleasure.'

Gryzlov nodded approval of violence in the future.

'Okay, then what do you want from me?' asked Oleg.

'We want you to ensure the goods are transferred through the region. That's not too difficult, is it?'

'No, but you must update me on the details.'

'I'll ensure they are given to you.'

'And then?'

'I will go back to Russia.'

'I wish I could go,' Oleg said.

'Will you ever stop moaning?' Viktor Gryzlov rarely spoke, but when he did, at least to Oleg, it was direct and unpleasant. Oleg felt it appropriate to stop discussing his woes and focus on business.

'Who do I need to meet to ensure the business flows freely?' he asked.

'Just about every damn politician, senior military man and senior policeman,' Denikin replied.

'That will take forever.'

'I was talking figuratively. We need to ensure they hold to their side of the agreement.'

'And if it doesn't?'

'We will either make them see the error of their ways, or we'll arrange an accident.'

'Do you expect many of them?'

'There will be some, already have been.'

'You're not expecting me to be responsible for the accident?' Oleg asked. He had killed too often, and he said it would be the last each time. But then again, someone inquisitive, someone in the wrong place at the wrong time and another death. The gym attendant had not concerned him greatly. He just hoped he had not been seen.

'If needed, you either do it or get someone else. Do you see any problems?' Denikin asked.

'No, that's fine.'

***

The party at Yusup's mansion, the highlight of Farrukh's week, was as promised. It was a rip-roaring affair of exceedingly beautiful and compliant women, a smattering of politicians – – and a cross-section of the most successful businessmen in Tajikistan. There was only one rule: no business was to be discussed.

Yusup had been annoyed that Ahmad Ghori, who sat in a room away from the entertainment at the pool, had attempted to discuss plans formulating in his mind. However, he was put in his place very quickly.

Yusup had judged Ghori correctly. Twenty-something with firm breasts, tight arse and a flat stomach was not for him. Instead, a mature woman in her early forties, with a good intellect and a voluptuous body. The woman Yusup had considered suitable came into the room where the Afghan had been sitting, a little bored.

'I see that you are alone,' she said. 'My name is Nilufar.'

'I am Ahmad,' he replied sheepishly. He was not used to being addressed by a woman who treated him as an equal. A woman in his society was subservient; the only women he would talk to regularly were his wives, though they would only speak after he had first addressed them. It felt wrong to him that this woman should sit across from him, her face uncovered, the cleavage of her bosom visible and feel no shame.

Before coming to the party, he had decided to bring no preconceptions or prejudices. Knowing how Baroyev's society behaved was important if he and Ali Mowllah were to help the man. It would not be possible to assist by applying Afghan values and behaviour patterns in a society that acted and moved differently.

He spoke to the woman calmly and agreeably. He was not unattractive, his beard too long for Nilufar, but she could see herself seducing him.

'I am not used to this society,' he said.

'You mean the openness of the women?'

'Yes, I suppose that is what I am referring to.'

'Does it disturb you that I am dressed in a manner that must be provocative, distasteful even to you?'

'In Afghanistan, yes, but here it troubles me little. You would be shamed in my country, stoned for dressing in the clothes you are now wearing.'

'I grew up in a small village near the border with Afghanistan. I understand the situation there.'

'Then what brought you to the capital?'

'My father was a politician in the region. He was elected to represent them here in the capital.' Nilufar had spoken the truth. She was a virtuous woman, not a pay-by-the-hour tart. In Ancient Greece, she would have been regarded honourably as a concubine, an intelligent woman who could mix in male society and dispense her pleasures as she saw fit.

For her to be with an Afghan did not cause her concern. As to whether she would sleep with him or not, that depended on her discretion. Yusup had agreed without hesitation. He knew the Afghan would weaken in the presence of an articulate and beautiful woman.

Yusup had used her occasionally, with an older politician no longer up to threesomes or wanting to prove how many women he could seduce in a night. With her, it was the full package, the elegant dining, the enlightened conversation, the gentle massage, the hot tub and, possibly, the sex. She saw Ahmad Ghori as worthy of the full treatment.

They talked for several hours about regional politics, the issues in Afghanistan, and the increasing intolerance and extremism in society, all the while becoming friendlier, eventually sharing the same leather sofa. She held his hand, stroked his face, and he felt at ease.

Neither remembered which of them first suggested the bedroom, but eventually, long after the sun had gone down, that was where they had ended up. Ahmad Ghori had forgotten who he was and the society he belonged to. With him, Nilufar felt no inhibitions or need to complete their lovemaking and dash off. They were content and stayed in the room until the next morning, when Ali Mowllah, with a grin stretching from ear to ear, knocked on the door to remind him it was time to return to their guest house.

Nilufar, for her part, stated that she would visit Ahmad at his guest house the next day.

Ali Mowllah had been a major hit, frolicking in the pool with the girls and seducing them, either in the pool when the light went down or in the many bedrooms to the side of the pool.

Farrukh's initial disappointment when he first espied Ghori and Mowllah at the mansion quickly dissipated, and he regarded the party as living up to what he had expected. How Mowllah, an older man, had seduced more women than he had caused concern. But then, he thought, an Afghan would not get a lot of practice back in his home country, and he was only blowing off pent-up frustration.

Chapter 19

With the party behind him, Yusup reverted into business mode. His approach at the guest house the next day was more formal, although Ahmad Ghori looked a little sheepish. Ali Mowllah's ribbing did not help, though even he was looking every one of his fifty-something years, plus a few more. Yusup was not surprised, judging by his enthusiasm at the party.

'Let's get back to how you can help,' Yusup started, although one of the maids came in abruptly and began to place cups of tea in front of them. He was annoyed but let it pass.

'You cannot compete with the current situation. The Russians are taking much larger quantities, and the risk to us is infinitely reduced,' Ahmad said.

'That's already been stated enough times, but what's your idea?' replied Yusup. 'I do not want my business to suffer because of opportunistic Russian gangsters muscling in on my territory, but you are right. I cannot take the quantity.'

'Who do they bribe to get the drugs through Tajikistan and up to Russia?' Ali asked.

'The same people I bribed in the past. Still do, for the meagre amounts that I can transport now.'

'Then why don't you emulate what the Russians are doing?' Ahmad continued. His focus had suffered since the night before. Five minutes before the meeting, Nilufar phoned to tell him she was coming over that night. Her casualness in inviting herself to the house had thrown him, but he had said nothing. He was quietly pleased.

'It's the scale firstly and, whereas we could ramp up to compete, even take higher quantities, I would still need to find the market in Russia to sell to,' said Yusup.

'But you've indicated that the Russians down here are not the same as you used to deal with,' Ali said.

'That is correct. The only one that I know is Oleg Yezhov, but he is not important, just a late blow-in after he ran out on me. He killed one of your fellow countrymen and almost killed a woman.'

'We know about that,' Ahmad said. 'Nearly got himself killed in Afghanistan, messing around with a local woman.'

'Can you mess around with the women there?'

'Depends on whether you have an affinity for rocks being thrown at you,' Ali said casually.

'Our society is not perfect,' Ahmad said. 'Oleg Yezhov found one woman. She was stoned to death for her crime.'

Ali Mowllah sat still, hoping he would not be dragged into the conversation.

'She was stoned because she was with Yezhov?' Yusup asked.

'For being with someone else,' Ahmad said. 'The Taliban knew that Yezhov had been taking her back to his house, but I paid them to leave him alone. It wouldn't help our relationship with the Russians if their man were killed while he was our guest.'

'If I had been there, I would have paid them to kill him,' Yusup said.

'That may be, but he was our guest. It was our duty to protect him, regardless of whether he deserved to be punished or not. What you do with him over here is no concern to us.'

'I will do nothing until the appropriate time.'

'Getting back to the subject,' Ahmad said. 'Is it possible that the people we are dealing with are not sanctioned by their senior executive in Moscow?'

'It is possible,' Yusup acknowledged. 'Why are you concerned? You are making plenty of money.'

'It is because we do not trust them and want you to take more.'

'More? How can I?' asked Yusup. 'I do not have access to the sellers on the streets in Russia. That is all sewn up by the mafia, and I do not have access to their senior leadership. I do not know who they are and how they operate.'

'Then it would be best if you made their acquaintance. Pull in some favours, talk to the Russians you have dealt with in the past,' Ahmad said.

'Yes, I can do that, but I need a few days.'

'That is fine,' Ali replied. 'We will wait here for an update.'

Yusup resolved to get Ali Mowllah, a female companion. Ahmad Ghori said he was fine. Yusup left the guest house determined to find a solution. He was a Tajik, and a Tajik would never let a Russian take control in his country.

***

Andre Malenkov's obsession with Oleg had caused a reprimand on one occasion and the threat of disciplinary action on another. He had been told explicitly to stop using government money and resources to conduct an investigation that was clearly personal and unrelated to the country's security.

He had acquiesced, apologised profusely, and said it would not happen again. For some time, that had been the case – except that he had never issued a countermanding order to stop monitoring the emails of Yezhov's girlfriend in St. Petersburg.

It was a cursory glance late one Friday afternoon when he had settled at his desk at the Lubyanka Building headquarters on Lubyanka Square. Reclining in the chair, the front two legs just raised off the ground, the rear two taking his weight, the back of the chair just touching the top of the radiator behind him. Almost teetotal, he sipped on a glass of vodka, although his consumption in the past had been prolific. He had nearly been killed when a CIA agent had managed to take secrets out of a government department, and he had been told to deal with the situation.

It was before the days of encrypted emails and instant communications, and the CIA man was on his way to the railway station and on an overnight trip to the border. Malenkov had cornered him two blocks from the station, went to pull out his gun, fumbled the safety and received a bullet from a standard-issue CIA pistol in his left shoulder.

He spent two weeks in hospital, another three on light duties and received a severe reprimand from his superior officer, who had the temerity to accuse him of being drunk on duty. It was ironic when the whole department knew the superior officer was intoxicated from walking in the door at nine in the morning until leaving at night.

Malenkov did not need the reprimand. However, he needed vodka occasionally and, over time, moderated his drinking to one or two glasses every night.

The email, sender unknown, had been received ten days previous by Natasha, the girlfriend who was back on the game and selling her favours to the more affluent of St. Petersburg. *More affluent than me, anyway*, Malenkov thought.

He remembered her as an exceptionally attractive woman with pale skin, long dark hair almost down to her waist, and a figure to die for. Andre Malenkov, a reformed alcoholic avenging his brother's senseless murder, would have taken her. He digressed into daydreaming as he read the email.

'Back in Dushanbe, all well.'

He knew he would follow through, even if it meant possible suspension. He put the flight on his government-issued credit card. He would deal with the flack on his return.

***

Oleg, back in Tajikistan, was not feeling as comfortable as he should have been. Malika was visible in the places he would usually have frequented. He also assumed Yusup Baroyev was looking for him, no doubt for more than a chat. And then there was Farrukh, not more than two blocks from where he was staying, irritating him immensely with the black Mercedes. He thought the situation could not worsen; he was to be proven wrong.

Two days prior, he had seen the two men in the four-wheel drive Toyota aimlessly sitting for a couple of hours on the corner, fifty metres from the two-bedroom apartment he leased. The previous one on a lower floor had been adequate, but this was a penthouse, and, with the advance payment that Denikin had given him, he could afford it. It gave him a good view of the surrounding area, and the blue Toyota initially gave him little concern. He had not done anything wrong in Tajikistan, or at least nothing anyone knew about. The gym attendant, he had found out, was transient, going from one gym to another until he was ejected for sticking his nose in where it was not required — invariably a female changing room. He was not missed, and no one had raised the alarm.

The vehicle, at odd hours, day and night, caused him concern after the third day. It may have been there before, but he would not have noticed it, the view obstructed by a building to the right.

He did not know what he could do about it. Gennady Denikin would have cared little for his problems. He had no one he trusted that he could turn to.

The best thing he could do was to get out of town for a while and check on the route from the border with Afghanistan and up through Tajikistan. Denikin had told him not to worry after it had crossed the northern border of Tajikistan, as they had other people dealing with that part of the route.

Oleg could not see sense in checking something that was already working well, and he knew they would be after more money if anyone discovered he represented the Russian mafia. He held firmly to the principle of *if it isn't broke, don't fix it*, but Denikin was an accountant with an accountant's fastidious mind, always looking to improve.

To Oleg, that was fine if the drugs arrived in Kazakhstan with sufficient margin. Why become further involved? At least, his theory had worked well enough in St. Petersburg until the unfortunate incident with Artur Malenkov.

***

Unbeknown to Oleg, his nemesis, one week earlier, had been sitting on an uncomfortable chair at the State Committee for National Security headquarters, the FSB's equivalent in Tajikistan.

The one thing Oleg did not realise was that the secret services of any country were more closely aligned with their foreign counterparts, regardless of ideology and government directives, than they were with their own countrymen. They were a club of secretive and devious individuals, mainly men, who wallowed in the cesspit of espionage. The cold war of forty years previous had been between governments, not between rival security services. They exchanged information and people as required, killing each other when necessary, but they followed the rules, not always Queensberry or Geneva Convention, but rules nonetheless.

Malenkov knew this, and he knew the Tajikistan State Committee for National Security's name belied their vicious nature.

'Yezhov, it's personal,' Andre Malenkov had said as he sat in a charmless room that his Tajikistan counterpart considered perfectly acceptable, bare apart from a small desk with two chairs. The desk was augmented with a computer screen, which appeared, to Malenkov, to be at least five years out of date, but he was no expert on such matters. The FSB's equipment was always up to date.

A forlorn flowering shrub, planted in a large metal pot close to a small and dirty window, clutched for the meagre sunlight which attempted to stream into the room.

Malenkov did not like his counterpart very much, but he needed him. He would be polite and endearing, obsequious if that were necessary. They had done business before, mainly following up on fundamentalists and villains who may have had a grievance against Russia and a means to make it known.

The man behind the desk pretended to check his emails. He affected an air of indifference. He was of medium height and slim with a healthy glow to his face. He looked as if he exercised regularly. The collar on his shirt was frayed, and his suit jacket was dusty and faded.

The man spoke. 'We're not here to deal with personal matters.'

'I realise this,' replied Malenkov, 'but I said that to ensure further cooperation from you. I assumed you would understand that this is a matter of family honour.'

Yudik Khujandi, the man, continued to speak. His previously fluent Russian, from when the Soviet Union had held his country in an iron grip, had lost its edge. He cared more for intrigue than national or international borders. Selling secrets to the Russians, selling back secrets to the Tajik government, and even assassination caused him few sleepless nights or guilt trips.

He was a solitary man with no time for a woman, which was just as well as they would not have found him attractive, with the pronounced mole just below his left nostril, a scar on his chin and an irritating habit of cleaning his nose with one of the fingers of his right hand. Andre Malenkov had not wanted to shake his hand and would not have done had the meeting not been so important. Once the initial greeting was over, he excused himself for an urgent call of nature and rushed to the bathroom to scrub the mucus from his hand.

Yudik Khujandi continued to procrastinate, although there was no doubt that he would help, personal or otherwise. There was always a villain, a double-dealing agent or someone waylaid by one side or the other for suspected espionage activities, mainly an attaché who worked at the other's embassy in Moscow or Dushanbe. They rarely met, but Malenkov did not forget favours given and received. He would remind Khujandi if necessary.

***

Yudik Khujandi had relented and assigned two men to conduct surveillance activities. Oleg Yezhov had not been difficult to find. His association with Yusup Baroyev had been recorded, and the Tajikistan Secret Service noted his new position with the Russian mafia. The criminal activities of the Russian mafia did not concern Khujandi and his people, the police could deal with that, but the Russian mafia sometimes became involved in espionage and selling secrets. It was not often, but there had been instances when the money had been sufficient and the risk acceptable.

Andre Malenkov had his man, but Khujandi had made it blatantly clear.

'He's your problem, not ours. If you want to liquidate him, do it in your own country, or else you will have committed a crime, and I'll make sure the police deal with you. Is that clear?'

'That is clear,' Malenkov said, although it presented a complication. His boss, the vodka-swilling superior, had asked questions about where he was and what he was spending FSB money on. One of his associates had given him the update, and he wasn't sure what to do. Knowing where Oleg Yezhov lived served little purpose if he could not liquidate him, and the State Committee for National Security wouldn't do it for him.

Malenkov had done them enough favours in the past, even liquidated a renegade Tajikistan national before he had had a chance to fly out of Russia, intent on killing the President of Khujandi's country. Not that he didn't deserve killing, corrupt and evil, but he was friendly to Russia, and one thing any country's government does is look after their friends, whether good, bad, indifferent, competent or worthless. The president he had saved had long fallen foul of a coup d'etat, and he could now be found in a dacha, a country mansion close to the Black Sea on the Russian side, enjoying life immensely. According to reports, the deposed president was surrounded by a twenty-four hour guard, electric security fences and a bevvy of women.

Why is it, Andre Malenkov had thought when he had heard of the ex-president's fate, *that I, a hard-working patriot of Russia, have to suffice with a squint-faced woman at home? All she does is complain that I don't make enough money, that I've missed the endless opportunities in life, and that she struggles to put food on the table.*

She was right, of course, but he never said so. He could not change the situation. History was history, long past and buried, and now his requirements in life were modest, and for peace of mind, he chose not to respond to her endless mouthing. He felt like hitting her sometimes but never did. He was not a violent man, though he could be. He had killed in his time but had seen them as worthy of death.

His wife could sometimes do with being told to shut up. Maybe he would one day, but then he knew the outcome. She would be out the door, straight down to the government department that deals with such matters, and he would find an automatic debit on his salary, meagre as it was.

He knew why he had not risen the slippery pole to an executive position and a well-appointed office. It was because he was comfortable in his job, good at what he did and enjoyed it.

Sometimes, he would speculate whether he had chosen the right vocation, especially after seeing Oleg Yezhov's girlfriend. He realised she was out of his league – or, at least, his pay scale – whereas a grubby gangster could afford her. It irked him, but he dealt with it by turning a blind eye and busying himself with work.

He missed the good old days when the Tajikistan and Russian Security services were not accountable to bureaucrats and open government. Then it was easy, grab Yezhov late at night, swift stiletto knife in the back and a quick and decisive cutting of the throat, no questions asked, no case investigated.

***

Seven days after Khujandi had agreed to his request, Andre Malenkov's supervisor, Mikhail Kandinsky, phoned him.

'What are you doing down there?' he asked impolitely.

'I'm following up on some leads.' It was a lame reason, often used, seldom believed, and not going to work this time.

'Don't give me that hogwash. You are down there checking up on Yezhov, and don't lie.'

He saw no reason to lie. If he was suspended, so be it. He was tired of the bellicose supervisor slurring his words, although he sounded remarkably coherent this time.

'What if I am?' He had taken the bait and responded in a manner that he had somehow restrained before.

'Look here, Malenkov, I'm not concerned about why you're there, but for once, you're in the right place at the right time.'

'What do you mean?'

'Something big is going down, and we are being pulled in to help. More of a police matter, if you ask me, but we know they haven't got a clue what they're doing. We'll fix it up, and they'll take all the credit.'

It was verbose, which irked Malenkov. How many times had he saved the department's reputation? How many times had Supervisor Mikhail Kandinsky taken the credit?

'What's so big that the police need our help?' Malenkov asked. 'Normally, they avoid us like the plague.'

'Bratva, the Russian mafia.'

'Why are they our concern? They're criminal?'

'Andre….' The supervisor had never used Malenkov's Christian name before. He recognised a favour being asked. 'There's a war brewing.' Kandinsky continued in a remarkably affable tone.

'Between Russia and Tajikistan?' Malenkov failed to understand what Kandinsky was saying.

'Indirectly. The Russian mafia fighting it out with their equivalent in Tajikistan,' said Kandinsky. 'And then there's the added complication of splinter groups here in Russia fighting against each other.'

'It still sounds criminal.'

'Andre, you are right, of course. But this can bring down governments.'

'Senior politicians?' asked Malenkov. 'What is the issue? If it's criminal, what has that got to do with the politicians, senior or otherwise?'

'Are you naïve, or are you just trying to wind me up?'

'Not at all. It just seemed a valid question.'

'Valid, maybe,' said Kandinsky. 'We have politicians in Russia and Tajikistan standing up and spouting their determination to stamp out organised crime. How many do you think are in the pay of the criminal organisations? This, unchecked, could bring down important people.'

'Is that our concern?'

'Not directly, but we are a government organisation. Our function is to follow the government's directive and prevent the impending war from escalating. Information is what we want.'

'We'll end up protecting politicians who should be locked up in a prison cell, you know that?' Malenkov said.

'Yes, of course,' replied Kandinsky, 'but we've always been doing that one way or the other. We serve; that's our function.'

'What do you want me to do down here?'

'Keep your eyes peeled, follow up on leads and understand how the society works down there. Who the major criminals are, corrupt politicians, that sort of thing.'

'Yudik Khujandi, my counterpart down here?'

'He'll be brought up to speed.'

'What's the war about?' asked Malenkov. 'You never said.'

'Heroin and it's coming over from Afghanistan in ever-increasing quantities. The amounts of money are enough to turn anyone's head, even yours and mine.'

'Don't worry about me,' Malenkov said. 'I'm incorruptible, stupidly incorruptible.'

'So am I. At least, we sleep with an easy conscience,' Kandinsky replied.

Andre Malenkov thought a restful sleep was hardly compensation for his inability to afford Oleg's girlfriend in St. Petersburg or to drive around town in a Bentley, as Yusup Baroyev did in Dushanbe. He realised he was not as incorruptible as he had previously thought. There was only one further statement from Kandinsky before the phone call concluded.

'Lay off Oleg Yezhov for now. He's involved, in the thick of it and until the situation is clear. We need him; you need him.'

Chapter 20

Dmitry Gubkin maintained a detached indifference to the problems coming up from Tajikistan. He made it clear to Stolypin when he became involved with the Russian mafia that he was a white-collar criminal, above suspicion and wanted it to stay that way.

It was not progressing as well as he had hoped. Firstly, there were aspersions over the death of his wife. It had been some time since her death, and he had dutifully mourned her. Especially when he discovered Katerina had ended the romance with her younger lover. He was unsure of the truth, but the lingerie was strewn across the road after Stolypin's men had driven her off the embankment, crushing her skull as the upturned vehicle impacted with the street below. The shop assistant where Katerina had bought the lingerie said it was a special treat for her husband that night.

He had learnt to deal with the guilt in the ensuing months, but he could never be sure. He had moved on, found another trophy woman, a girlfriend this time, and she was less demanding, more dependable, and less interested in spending his wealth. He hoped that was true, but once he married her....

He regretted agreeing to become involved with the Russian mafia. Stolypin had reminded, too rudely for his liking, that he came in of his own free will. It was also on record that he had been the driving force behind his wife's murder, and they had obliged as a favour. If they were going down, he was going down with them. He could see no way out.

The opera patronage, the visits to the ballet and the social functions continued with another woman on his arm. He was eloquent, educated, dispensing wisdom, listening to the old women with their plastic surgery while they told him about their decadent lives.

He would reflect in the quiet of his office and in his house. However, he was not a man to dwell on the past, and issues required his attention.

***

Oleg Yezhov's last communication had troubled Dmitry Gubkin. *Why would the two Afghans be guests of Yusup Baroyev?* he thought. To him, it seemed illogical.

He had initially passed it off as two Afghan rogues attempting to play the field to see if more money could be made, but now he wasn't so sure.

Yusup Baroyev's transport route through Kazakhstan and Russia was broken; Grigory Stolypin had seen to that. He said he had killed a few, but Dmitry had not asked too many questions.

'Grigory, the Afghans with Baroyev, what do we know?' Dmitry asked over the phone. He did not like to be seen associating with criminals, and he liked Grigory Stolypin no more than when they had first met, and he didn't like him much then. He appreciated his honesty, saying he was a criminal with a criminal's mind and was neither proud nor ashamed to say it. How many white-collar criminals, himself included, professed honesty while at the same time circumventing the corporate and financial laws in the country to achieve their aims, then hiring the very best legal teams to defend their position afterwards?

'Not much,' Grigory replied. 'They are staying at his guesthouse, even been to one of his parties. Apart from that, there is little more information.'

'Then you'd better find some,' said Dmitry. 'I cannot sit at the end of a telephone imparting wisdom when I don't have all the facts. Who have you got down there?'

'Oleg Yezhov's our main man now.'

'What happened to Gennady Denikin?' Gubkin asked.

'We sent him up to Kazakhstan to check for any problems.'

'Are there?'

'None that we can see.'

'What do we know about Yezhov? What is his history?'

'Came out of St. Petersburg, did a runner when the FSB was after him.'

'Espionage?'

'He was running an extortion business, inadvertently killing an FSB operative's brother. The brother took it personally and put the resources of the FSB behind him.'

'And he's still alive?' Dmitry said.

'Yes,' replied Grigory. 'He high-tailed it to Tajikistan and ingratiated himself to Yusup Baroyev, who then shipped him off to the Afghan border. Supposedly killed an Afghan over a whore, then switched sides and joined us.'

'I hope that's not a reference on his résumé?' Dmitry was used to an assorted bunch of nefarious characters in the mafia, but Oleg Yezhov seemed to take the cake.

'He was in Kunduz the same time as Baroyev's man, but then I told you that,' said Grigory. 'You even spoke to him.'

'I know, but I need to know if we can trust Yezhov. What do you reckon?'

'Too early to say. He did alright in Afghanistan; he's out now checking on the transportation of the goods. But whether we can trust him, only time will tell.'

'We don't have time and need to know what Baroyev's up to. Can we get someone in on the inside?'

'Unlikely in the short term. He's a shrewd character. His trust does not come easily. If we managed to put someone there, he'd come to an unpleasant end if he were found out.'

'Unpleasant?' Gubkin said.

'Baroyev's speciality, upside down over a termite nest, minus your balls,' replied Grigory. Dmitry cringed at the thought of it and crossed his legs.

'Can we get Yezhov in there?'

'Not a chance. Baroyev would string him up at first sight.'

'That much bad blood?'

'Apparently, and it's complicated by Yezhov having put Baroyev's mistress in intensive care sometime in the past.'

'Gennady Denikin, what about him?' asked Dmitry.

'Infiltration is impossible, but he could meet with Baroyev and sound him out. It can't do any harm. He may be able to figure out what's going on.'

'Set it up.' Dmitry put the phone down and went to see what his girlfriend was up to and whether she was in an amorous mood.

***

Gennady Denikin had done a decent job in Kazakhstan. It was another of the former Soviet Union satellite countries that stood between Tajikistan and Russia but had never given the same level of problems. Russian migration, forcible in the early days, had ensured a high percentage of people in Kazakhstan claimed Russian heritage. The Russian mafia was well-established, and transportation caused relatively minor issues.

He had not needed to go but had taken the opportunity to get out of Dushanbe and let Oleg get on with it. He still had serious doubts about Oleg. He seemed to come with too much baggage, and trouble seemed to gravitate towards him. The phone call from Stolypin came as a surprise. The request concerned him.

'We need you back in Dushanbe.'

'What for?' Denikin asked.

'We need you to meet with Yusup Baroyev.'

'Are you serious? That man does not appreciate intrusions lightly, and we've been taking his business.'

'Yes, we know about him and how he deals with people who cross him,' said Stolypin. 'But setting up a meeting carries little risk.'

'Three days, okay?'

'Three days is fine. What's the situation where you are?' Stolypin asked.

'Fine,' Denikin replied. With little to do apart from meeting up with the mafia leadership in Kazakhstan, he had taken himself down to a brothel, where he had been wiling away his time. The women were not as demanding financially as the woman who had inadvertently put him in prison, not as sour-faced and whining as his wife had been. A hundred American dollars a night, and they were fine.

He had hoped to head north into Russia, not south as Stolypin requested, but it made little difference. He would follow through on the request, maybe even get an invite to one of Baroyev's legendary parties.

***

Engaging with Yusup Baroyev on his return had not been as difficult as Gennady Denikin had imagined. He had merely phoned Farrukh Bahori, whose phone number he had obtained from Oleg. He was not pleased that his immediate superior wanted to meet with the one man who wanted him dead, even more than Andre Malenkov.

'Oleg, it's business. It may even help you,' he said, although he cared little for his well-being.

Oleg, back in the capital, was maintaining a low profile. He wanted to be out and about making money and picking up women. The Russians did not pay as well as Baroyev, not yet anyway, and quality women were expensive. Natasha kept in contact, but what could he say and do? He assumed she was selling herself. It was what she had been doing before he had set her up in a nice apartment and told her to be available for him and no others. It had been an excellent arrangement, but he wasn't there. The bills still needed to be paid, and he knew she had kept the apartment.

Denikin's return to Dushanbe had one more disturbing component. It came with an additional piece of information.

'Your man's in town.'

'Which man? Baroyev?' Oleg responded.

'No, the FSB man who's after you.'

'Malenkov?'

'Yes. He's with the local equivalent of the FSB.'

Oleg's fears had been confirmed. Here he was, with Yusup Baroyev on the hunt for him, although he must have known he was in town. And there was Andre Malenkov, which explained the four-wheel drive. Malika was moving around freely, and lately, the two Afghans, Ali Mowllah and Ahmad Ghori.

If he had been a superstitious man, he would have thought the cards were stacked against him and that he was doomed.

With so much against him, he reminisced back to northern Afghanistan and the obliging, if vain, Farhana, but she was dead. She had been undemanding, uncomplicated, and, for the price of a new top or a pair of jeans, she would spend as long as he wanted satisfying his every whim. She had been a limited lover, devoid of the consummate skills of a Natasha, the wild animal movements of a Malika, or the infinite beauty of one of Baroyev's whores. But, with her, it was less complicated. He would have swapped his present predicament for a simple life back in Kunduz if he could; but it was just an illusion, a momentary reflection brought on by the current situation.

He needed to talk to Gennady Denikin, sound him out and get him to agree to move him somewhere else soon. Sitting in his apartment, not free to move, was no better than a prison, which he had managed to avoid over the years. His only relief was the occasional woman he could phone, who would come over and deal with his frustrations, but even that was being affected by the worry of the tenuous situation he found himself in.

***

'I can't stay here,' Oleg said. Gennady Denikin agreed to meet with Oleg in a café on the city's outskirts, somewhere he felt safe.

'What is it? Yezhov?' Denikin did not appreciate the meeting at short notice. His shadow, Viktor Gryzlov, was at his back. He looked menacing. He glared intensely at Oleg.

'It's just too dangerous for me here.'

'What do you want?' replied Denikin. 'We bring you here; saw you as a good risk, an asset to the operation. So far, all you've done is moan and groan, and your complaining has taken on epic proportions. Maybe it's best to let Baroyev know where you are and let him deal with you.'

Denikin was in no mood for small talk, although he neither wanted Oleg dead nor to tell Baroyev where he was. He assumed he knew anyway. He still wanted to return to Russia. Without Oleg, he would be stuck back in Tajikistan for the foreseeable future.

As far as Gennady Denikin was concerned, the only good news was that Yusup Baroyev had invited him to the mansion for one of his parties on the coming Saturday.

'I'll have a talk to Baroyev when I meet up with him,' he said. 'I'll also look into the matter of Malenkov. There's not much we can do about him, but maybe Baroyev will have some ideas. Perhaps he will be able to pull some strings.'

'But why would he want to help me?' Oleg failed to understand.

'You work for us.'

'And that will work in my favour?'

'Why not? Baroyev's a businessman. Personal animosities and hatred will not get in the way of money, at least not the money we can put his way.'

'But you've cut him out of the loop.'

'That's true, but we can always bring him back somehow. Maybe we'll get him involved or pay him to keep out of our way. Who knows? It's all to do with the percentages.'

'Do you think he'll go for that?'

'No idea, but it is worth a try. We don't want a war down here between his people and ours, and then there's the possibility of war up in Russia.'

'Is there?'

Gennady Denikin had said too much to a man who may be more indiscreet than necessary. 'You focus on down here. Ensure the business keeps operating. Just maintain the margins, make sure the wheels are greased, and money where needed, but don't let any of those thieving bureaucrats and petty officials get the upper hand. They are all too greedy for my liking. If any issues need resolving, I'll leave it up to you.'

***

Malenkov was to become the least of Oleg's worries. On his return from the café, he noticed that the four-wheel drive had disappeared. Two days later, it was still not there. He did not know what to make of the situation other than to feel relief.

His fears soon resurrected when, late one night, with a knock on his door. The woman had just left. He assumed she had forgotten her handbag or phone. Certainly not her money. He had never known one who failed to secure that tight on their person. Half asleep and, without thinking, he opened the door – the safety chain not in place.

'Oleg Yezhov, we meet at last,' said a tall, red-faced man, puffing from walking up several flights of stairs. The lift wasn't working due to the electricity failing yet again, as it seemed to every other night; something to do with load-shedding or low water levels in the dams.

The man stood firm. He was wearing a dark suit, Russian-made. He was slightly overweight, with a pronounced chin and a hairstyle parted in the middle. He was not an unattractive man – although, to Oleg Yezhov, he was the most evil man in the world. He was Andre Malenkov.

'May I come in?' he said.

'I don't see how I can stop you,' Oleg said, looking down at the standard, FSB-issue Makarov pistol firmly pointed at his chest. 'Have you come here to kill me?'

'Personally, I would. Professionally, I am here to offer you a chance of redemption.'

'Do you need the gun?'

'We shall see. It depends on your reaction to my proposal.'

Oleg saw no option but to invite him in and make him welcome. He had a gun hidden in his bedroom but wished it was closer. If he were to be killed, he would endeavour to, at least, take Malenkov with him as well.

'We shall talk then,' Oleg said. 'It appears I have no option.'

'That is correct,' replied Malenkov. 'No option.'

Oleg made some strong coffee and placed the two mugs and some biscuits on the coffee table in the middle of the room. Malenkov continued to hold the gun, although his grip had weakened, and he no longer kept his gun finger on the trigger.

'I did not mean to kill your brother,' Oleg said by way of an apology.

'Yezhov,' said Malenkov, 'you are a small-time hoodlum who has found himself in the middle of a war. My government has ordered me to make you an offer.'

'And you? Will you still kill me, given the opportunity?'

'Given the opportunity.'

'Is there no hope?'

'There is always hope, but not yet. It depends on your reaction tonight.'

'My reaction to what?'

'I am to make you an offer which you should consider.'

'If I consider the offer and reject it, then what?'

'My instructions are clear. If what I tell you does not ensure complete and unequivocal agreement on your part to work with us, then I am to kill you. That will not be a personal action, but an action sanctioned by the Russian government.'

'What is to stop me from killing you and making my escape?'

'It is not possible.'

'Why?'

'I came into your apartment alone. That does not mean I am. Six men from the Tajikistan State Committee for National Security are on the street. They will ensure you will die if you leave this building before me.

'Maybe I could avoid them.'

'Impossible. They have been trained by the FSB. You will not escape.'

'Then it may be best if you put the gun down,'

'And it may be best if you prepare another pot of coffee, this time without any sedatives.'

Oleg made a fresh brew of coffee.

'Here's the situation,' Andre Malenkov said as he sipped his coffee. 'There's a war developing.'

'I have heard it mentioned, but I know little of the details,' Oleg replied, more relaxed than before when the gun had been pointed at him.

He looked out the window and saw the four-wheel drives. Either he agreed with Malenkov, or he would be killed. If he could get to the bedroom, second drawer, bedside table and then run for it.… But run where? His opportunities were limited. Gennady Denikin would do little for him, Russia was out of the question, and Dushanbe offered no possibilities. Afghanistan, maybe, but what was he to do there? A Russian in that country with no benefactor and no one looking out for him was as good as dead.

'You're tied in with the Russian mafia, correct?' Malenkov asked.

'Yes.' There seemed no point in denying the fact.

'Before that, you were with Yusup Baroyev, but you fell foul of him.'

'There's no point denying what you already seem to know.'

'Precisely.'

'Then why don't you get to the point.'

'Baroyev is being squeezed,' replied Malenkov. 'His business empire is crumbling. The Russians, your people, are trying to cut him out entirely or make a compromise agreement. That is why Denikin is meeting up with him. Then two Afghans here have supposedly stitched up a deal with the Russians. According to reports, they are also friendly with Baroyev, staying at one of his houses. Then there is the senior mafia executive in Russia, asking questions as to who sanctioned all these deals and whether they are receiving their full financial returns. There is a war coming, criminal in the main, but this is a war across countries, and the politicians will be dragged in, whether they like it or not. There is too much money involved.'

'What do you want from me?'

'Initially, information as to what's happening, key players.'

Oleg saw no reason to refuse. 'Okay, I've got no issues, but I need your commitment.'

'You want me to agree to not kill you, is that it?'

'Yes.'

'Okay, you have got my word. I will not kill you. In fact, I need to ensure your safety from now on.'

The meeting concluded. Oleg had failed to secure his gun, though he would not have needed it. He slept soundly that night, at least for the three hours before the sun rose.

With Malenkov no longer posing a threat, Oleg turned his mind to the other problems in Dushanbe. There was still Malika and her lover, Baroyev, as well as Farrukh. He had not forgiven him for taking his apartment and the Mercedes. The Audi he was driving was fine, but the Mercedes was better. He needed more money, and he needed it fast. If Malenkov were off his back, possibly forever, if he just fed him information, he could consider returning to St. Petersburg and Natasha. He emailed her.

'All looking good. Hope to see you soon.'

Andre Malenkov received a copy of the email directly to his laptop. *You're not off the hook yet*, he thought.

***

Yusup Baroyev and Gennady Denikin were to meet the day before the party. There were matters to discuss, and neither, primarily Baroyev, wanted the following day's entertainment compromised with the need to talk business.

Baroyev was concerned about his declining profits. However, it was not apparent to the visitors at the mansion, to the women who still commanded premium rates, not even to the politicians with their greedy snouts in the trough, bleeding him for all they could while taking money from the Russians at the same time.

Malika still spent his money as she wanted, but she was not an extravagant woman. All she needed was the latest fashion, the best hairdresser and an apartment, but only sufficient to sustain the lifestyle that befitted a woman in her position. She was the mistress of a drug lord, a former drug addict and a prostitute, but the society matrons easily adopted her. They were fickle and cared little about where she had come from or her background as long as Yusup Baroyev was her lover.

With funds slowing dramatically, Baroyev needed to make a deal with someone as soon as possible. He preferred the Afghans, but that was long-term, and he could not see how they could help him with the movement into Russia and the distribution channels. So far, they had only managed to enjoy his hospitality and take advantage of the women he had put their way.

***

The mansion was devoid of females the day Gennady Denikin arrived. Strict instructions had been given, no need to bring security. Viktor Gryzlov, the permanent shadow, was aggrieved at the rejection and found solace in a bottle of local vodka.

Denikin arrived at the mansion in a Rolls Royce reserved for special guests. He was suitably impressed. Baroyev was charming, eloquently dressed as usual and straight down to business.

'You're causing me great concern,' he said.

'It is not our intention to cause anyone concern,' Denikin replied.

'If you had come to me, I could have handled the Tajikistan side of the business. It would have been a much easier arrangement for you.'

'In hindsight, maybe you're right.' Denikin saw it as a possibility to defuse the situation. Elements in the Russian mafia, especially in Moscow, were rallying for war, and he had received explicit instructions to come to an agreement.

One war in Russia between rival mafia enclaves was enough. They did not want another in Tajikistan. If it spilt over into Afghanistan, it could become political, and the militaries would become involved. Not that Denikin cared, not even Stolypin, but Dmitry Gubkin did. His previously unassailable position in Moscow society was threatened by continuing articles in some of the most scurrilous newspapers questioning who Dmitry Gubkin was.

Was he the master businessman? Or the master gangster, as they would allude indirectly. If they had made a clear statement, he would have sued them.

Even the ballet had declined his patronage for the first time in ten years, and no amount of money would make them change their mind. The stupid bitch girlfriend was giving him aggravation, nagging him as to when he would make an honest woman of her, and then there were the increasing amounts of money she was spending on silly nonsense.

He could see that he would have to get rid of her eventually. Maybe put her back on the street – or, at least, a street corner where she could sell herself to some drunk. But she had heard things, knew things, and if she talked to the police – or, more importantly, the media –placing him in an embarrassing position, being asked questions for which he had no answer.

***

Yusup Baroyev set aside most of the day for Denikin. A sumptuous meal, with the best of wines, had not helped Denikin in his deliberations. He instinctively liked the Tajik gangster when he was meant to be impartial, even a little hostile.

'What do you reckon we can do to redress the imbalance?' Denikin asked.

'Give me control of the transportation up through my country,' Baroyev replied.

'That presents complications. It's all working well, and then you have the Afghans up here trying to set up another deal to put us out of the picture. You know what will happen if that occurs?'

'It will get violent.' Baroyev was no fool. He saw where this was heading. Violence was not the issue, but the scale of it may be. Once the politicians and the police began to get scared and unwilling to accept bribes, the whole trade would grind to a halt, possibly going back through the drug smuggling villages. That had been fine in the past, but now....

No, he reasoned. The Russians were doing a decent job, making plenty of money. It was just that he wanted some of it, and if he could somehow make a deal with the Afghans, then maybe it would all work out without violence and in a spirit of harmony. There was still one issue to resolve.

'Yezhov, he's working for you?' he asked.

'That's correct,' said Denikin. 'You've got some issues with him, so I'm led to believe.'

'He's a dead man if I take him.'

'That is what he said. What has he done to incur your hatred?' Denikin asked.

'It's professional and personal, that's all.'

'It must be serious, though?'

'It is, but let us not talk about him,' said Baroyev. 'I know where he is. At this present moment, I have left him alone.'

'Why?'

'Until I had met with you, I felt it was best. If I had liquidated him, it would have been seen as pre-emptive violence that could have ignited a war between our two groups. I did not want to be the person to start it.'

'You were correct; for now, he mustn't be harmed.'

'For now,' replied Baroyev. 'He is safe for the foreseeable future, even welcome at my house. But he must never go near my woman. Is that clear?'

'That's clear, and tomorrow?'

'Bring him.'

'I will respect your confidence. He will not know of our agreement. Personally, I care little for him. Trouble gravitates towards him; the sooner I am free of him, the better.'

Gennady Denikin saw a possible deal that would satisfy all parties, although not Oleg. Once his usefulness had ended, he would be thrown to the wolves – or, in this case, *the wolf*, Yusup Baroyev.

There had been no time to discuss financial details, and Baroyev had been clear with Denikin that he still needed to talk to the Afghans. He saw no advantage in revealing that he was communicating with another arm of the Russian mafia, and he intended to travel to Moscow to meet with one of their people.

Chapter 21

Oleg was pleased when Gennady Denikin phoned him on his return from meeting with Yusup Baroyev.

'It's all squared,' said Denikin. 'He will leave you alone. He'll even forgive you if you work for us.'

'And if I'm not working with you?'

'For now, you're safe.'

'That's fine.'

'The FSB, what about them?'

'The cars have disappeared, must have been a false alarm,' Oleg said, almost as a throw-away line, which concerned Denikin.

'Just one other thing. Keep away from his woman.'

'Which one?' Oleg asked obtusely.

'The one he's keen on. The one you spent time with.'

Oleg agreed. *But how, when she was visible too often, and he did want to talk to her?* he thought. He saw no problems phoning Andre Malenkov with a précised version of what Denikin had told him. He still saw Malenkov as critical if he wanted to return to St. Petersburg.

Life had taken a turn for the better, and Oleg felt freer than he had for the last few weeks. There was a party to go to – Denikin had given him the invite courtesy of Yusup – and the transportation of the drugs up through the country was going well.

In fact, he seemed to have perilously little to do, and he wondered what his function was. He could not openly meet with the politicians to grease their palms. Someone else must do that. The police did not want to meet or talk to him at the roadblocks, as they took their directives from police headquarters. It seemed to him an unusual arrangement. For the present, however, he would wait and see where it headed.

If he played it straight with Malenkov for a little while, he would ask for written proof that his return to St. Petersburg was possible. Natasha had contacted him and said she was willing.

He could go back to the old business of extortion, but trading in drugs seemed a better prospect, and with the contacts, he was forming, it was possible. One day before the party, he felt the need for a woman. He knew of one, and her price was reasonable.

She could come and keep him company, but tomorrow was Baroyev's party, and he needed to be fresh and fit. Maybe he would run around the block before the drive up to the mansion to get the blood pumping.

***

Yusup Baroyev was exceptionally cordial on meeting Oleg at the mansion.

'Welcome to my house. It is good to see you.' It was unexpected, and Oleg could not be sure whether it was feigned or genuine. He suspected the former.

There was no reason for Yusup to feel any great warmth for him, and Denikin had confirmed that suspicion the previous day. He had caused the local drug lord a substantial loss of money due to his enforced absence. Dereliction of duty would have been Yusup Baroyev's opinion. The fact that he had been tied to a post after he had killed the Afghan would not have been a sufficient excuse.

There was also the matter of Malika, now firmly established as Yusup's mistress, and she must have told her story to him. Oleg could see no reason for the friendly welcome.

Regardless of his misgivings, he was determined to enjoy himself at the party. He was concerned when he saw Farrukh there as well, but even he had been cordial. Ali Mowllah, one of the Afghans from Kunduz, was already in the pool cavorting with the women. Ahmad Ghori was absent as he stayed at his guesthouse with another woman.

Later that night, Farrukh drove the Mercedes back to his apartment, whereas Oleg drove back in his Audi to an empty apartment, but it concerned him little.

***

Denikin phoned Oleg late the following morning. 'What do we know about the Afghans? Can we trust them?' he asked.

'Afghans, never, but then you should know that,' replied Oleg. 'You met them in Afghanistan before I went there.'

'That's what I think, but what can they be planning with Baroyev? They can't impact our business and set up a rival transportation route – or can they?'

'Certainly not up through Tajikistan,' said Oleg. 'At least, I wouldn't have thought so. But the Afghans are resourceful people. If there is an angle, they'll find it. We need to find that angle first and close it.'

'Agreed, but where do we start?'

'That's the problem. I've no idea.'

'We're paying you good money,' replied Denikin. 'Figure it out and get back to me before the day ends.' He slammed down the phone.

Oleg's contacts were not many in Tajikistan. The only one he could think of and trust was Pavel Suslov, the effeminate homosexual he regarded as a friend as long as he kept his hands to himself. He phoned him.

'Pavel, good to speak to you. How are you?' Oleg said over the phone.

'Fine, long time. Let's catch up.'

Feeling freer than he had for several months, Oleg took Pavel to a restaurant close to the city centre. It was the same restaurant he had taken Tolib, the over-inquisitive gym attendant, before his untimely demise.

Pavel appreciated the chance of a good feed as life had not been good to him. He was now reduced to running a few men selling drugs on shady streets around the city. The money was sufficient if meagre. His latest lover had just moved out, taken his stereo and left him with a black eye.

Oleg promised to deal with him. Pavel said not to bother and that it was an occupational hazard for an effeminate queer. A black eye and a few electronic goods were minor compared to what had happened in the past. Oleg did not ask him to elaborate.

'What's the problem?' Pavel asked.

'I'm not with Yusup.'

'That's what I heard.'

'You know this country better than me.'

'Not a lot. I've barely been out of Dushanbe,' Pavel replied. Oleg could see that life had not been good for him, as he ate disproportionate portions compared to his size. It was as if he hadn't eaten a proper meal in days.

'Is there any other way to transport the drugs from Afghanistan?'

'Not to my knowledge. The main transport route from Kunduz is across the border at Panj-e Payon and then up to here. There are other crossings, but the roads are not so good, not to mention a new setup of bribing and corruption would be needed to put it in place.

'That's what I thought. I need someone to accompany me and prowl down by the border. Are you up to it?'

'I'm a city person,' said Pavel. 'Down there will scare me.'

'We need to know what's going on and whether any plans are in place for a rival operation. Pays well, and you look like you need money.'

'The money will come in handy. I will go with you,' Pavel said.

Oleg had an answer and a plan for Denikin. He hoped it was enough.

Early the next morning, Oleg and Pavel made the trip back to the border town. Oleg hoped he would not have to cross the border again. Pavel hoped his time out of the city was minimal, but the money was good, and he knew there would be no black eyes with Oleg, which suited him fine.

***

The Tajik Air flight to Moscow was full, although Yusup Baroyev, up in First Class, cared little. Malika was seated alongside; his wife spending his money at an escalating rate somewhere in France and pleading to come home.

His affections had firmly been transplanted to Malika, and she was regarded as his wife in Dushanbe. His wife had, in the past, turned a blind eye to his women, but the reports on the current one troubled her. Whereas she missed her husband, she knew that part of his legitimate business was in her name and she would be financially well provided.

Firuza loved Yusup Baroyev – though less than when they first met in college. He was majoring in business studies, and she was in social studies. They were both in their teens, idealistic and innocent. Pregnant in her early twenties, they had beaten her father to the wedding ceremony a couple of weeks before the bulge had become obvious.

Her father had blown his top, and her mother had gone into hysterics at the shame of a daughter of theirs getting married when she was already pregnant.

It concerned her new husband that he could not provide his wife with the lifestyle she was accustomed to. She had come from money, the daughter of a banking executive, and her home had been a large house in a tree-lined suburb with sufficient staff to look after the place.

With Yusup, it was a small apartment in an old Soviet-era apartment block. Not that Firuza complained, but he did. He was the assistant financial manager in a small textile factory and could provide no more, but he was ambitious and determined.

The first foray into crime came from a silly, sanctimonious friend Yusup liked, but his wife did not.

'I need someone to deal with the money,' Iskandar said as he and Yusup rested after the tennis they played on a Thursday night after work.

'What kind of help?' Yusup asked. Iskandar, the son of the textile company's owner, seemed to have no issues with money. He drove a good car, got around with classy-looking women and always dressed well – too well, considering he was meant to be the maintenance manager. But then, he never got his hands dirty.

'It's a sideline,' said Iskandar. 'I'm tired of sponging off my father. Besides, he's keeping most of it for himself. A regular Scrooge, if you ask me. I'm worth more than the miserable allowance he gives me.' He was sanctimonious. Yusup's wife, Firuza, was right in that estimation, but Iskandar made him laugh, and he was always good company.

'What sort of sideline? I am always looking for ways to make more money.'

'Supply and demand,' Iskandar said.

'That's a little vague.'

'It's not strictly legal.'

'Nor is the tax dodging that I'm fiddling on behalf of your father. But I am there, doing it for him.'

'I buy drugs and sell them for a profit. It's a cash economy, very profitable.'

'Okay, by me. What help do you want? What are the risks?'

'The risks are minimal, but the rewards could be substantial with someone smart like you doing the numbers and figuring out the percentages.'

Six months later, Yusup had supplanted Iskandar in the business, made his first serious stack of money and bought his wife a house several blocks from where her parents lived.

Iskandar had been looking for a few hundred American dollars on every trade. To him, it was fun; extra money for a better car and woman. He wanted to party every night, and, as the son of a wealthy man, he knew the money was coming his way. His father wouldn't live forever, not with how he worked, worried and smoked – cigars, mainly – to compensate for the stress.

Yusup had no such father or inheritance to look forward to. His father had laboured all his life in a junior administrative role in the nondescript office of a minor government department. An honest man, salt of the earth, they said, when he suddenly died at the age of fifty-two. Yusup had listened intently to the eulogising of his father and felt sadness at his demise. He was determined not to follow a similar path.

The textile company was the best he could do. It was not what he wanted, but Firuza was pregnant. Her father was adamant that she was his responsibility as Yusup had got his daughter pregnant. He was a hard but caring man. As soon as the baby entered the world, he was there, lathering kisses and presents on the infant.

The relationship between Firuza's father and Yusup would always be tenuous. Neither liked the other very much, but they remained civil.

Yusup had seen the potential in Iskandar's enterprise. It concerned the textile factory owner's son little when he had been sidelined. There was an agreement he would receive five per cent of any business going forward, which seemed insignificant

'Don't worry about it. It's not important,' Iskandar had said, but Yusup honoured the agreement right up to the current day when that five per cent had become substantial and worth millions of American dollars.

It was just as well due to an unforeseen recession and the textile company going into liquidation. Iskandar's inheritance became Iskandar's burden. When Iskandar's father passed away, the creditors knocked on his door. They always bought someone solid and physically threatening to deal with his constant denials that he was only the son, not the father, and he was not responsible.

*****

Over the years, Yusup had transformed a small sideline of Iskandar's into a major business, growing at a staggering rate. The mansion had been a gift to his wife at the end of the third year, but she neither liked the place nor the excessive security.

A necessary part of the business, he would say, when quizzed.

'Maybe,' she said, 'but I do not want the children growing up in such an environment. You provide for us, but I prefer not to know the details.'

Within two months, Firuza had returned to the old house while Yusup remained at the mansion. It was an arrangement that had served them well in the intervening years. He was free to focus on his business interests, which included serious entertainment, and a drug lord's entertaining entailed women and plenty of them.

At first, he had declined to partake, only supplying for others, but it looked suspicious with him drinking and every other man, politician, police official and drug runner cavorting with them. It raised questions about whether he was homosexual – although not to his face, which was just as well. He used violence sparingly as a tool but with great vindictiveness when required.

His enforced celibacy lasted six weeks before he took one of the women for himself. He had always been a one-woman man, but Firuza was comfortable. The children were fine, and as long as she saw him at regular intervals, no questions were asked on her part, and no reasons were given on his.

He had reasoned that she must have known what was happening, but she turned a blind eye to it.

'I don't want to know what and how you conduct your business,' she had said.

'It is best you do not know,' he had replied. 'I must maintain a certain lifestyle. It goes with the image and the business.'

'From what I've heard, you work incredibly hard at your image.'

It was the only time Firuza ever alluded to the fact that she knew of the parties, but then everyone knew of Yusup Baroyev and his lifestyle, even at the children's school as they got older. Sometimes, they would come home upset that someone had said something which wasn't very nice. Their mother would tell them other people were jealous of their father's success.

Firuza knew that the wealth did not come from running a corner store or a small business, but she had made an agreement and would keep to it. Sometimes, she wished they could live as an ordinary family, but she realised that would never be possible.

Her husband was too far entrenched in the business and controlled it with an iron rod. There were no deputies, natural successors, or reliable lieutenants he could trust implicitly.

Iskandar remained Yusup's friend, but he had been the son of a wealthy man, and, with such people, they are either driven to continue in their father's footsteps or not to care. He proved to be the latter. The debts, the heavies, and the threatening letters after the failure of his father's business were dealt with by Yusup.

'Refer them to me,' Yusup had said.

It was the least he could do. It had been Iskandar who had set him on the road to salvation. The debtors came, often with their heavies, but Yusup's heavies were heavier, and a solution was soon arranged. Most had gone away empty-handed; some had received a fraction of what they demanded. Some had left the mansion, never to be seen again.

Iskandar continued the life of frivolity and irrelevance, although it came with a luxury motor cruiser in the Mediterranean and a crew of young women. Yusup paid for it all and occasionally visited, although Iskandar had become corpulent and an alcoholic. The women stayed because of Yusup's money, but they never cared or asked where it came from.

***

Heroin addiction, especially in Moscow and St. Petersburg, had been escalating exponentially since the collapse of the Soviet Union.

It had been Yusup who had seen the potential for increased sales into Russia. He had been ambitious and saw himself as a businessman aiming to turn a profit. Plenty in the government and the military were willing to go along with his plan as long as they were financially rewarded.

Tajikistan had been awash with crime, corruption and bribery. So much so that it formed the larger part of the impoverished country's economy. Yusup knew he was just taking advantage of the situation and making the best of it, though better than anyone else, as it turned out. He was a smart man who knew how to turn a profit, make the percentages and keep those on the take out of sight. Although some were now openly disregarding him for the Russians. He knew who they were. When the time was right, he would deal with them.

Feliks Kalinin had been his primary contact with the Russian mafia. They had met fifteen years earlier to discuss expanding operations through Tajikistan and into Russia. He had proved to be a good man. He was a criminal but honest. An oxymoron, although Feliks, once he had set a deal in place, honoured that deal. The one he had presented to Yusup had been good and solid. It had served both them and Feliks' superiors well over the years. Yusup regarded him as a friend, and he was now a friend in trouble.

Questions were being asked of Feliks by his superiors. A graph showing the amount of heroin up into Russia and the price on the street showed a steady upward trend, but the Bratva, the name the Russian mafia preferred, was not seeing the full returns.

Mafia had connotations of greasy Italians with moustaches or Al Capone and machine-gun killings in the street. The Bratva was more structured, and greasy moustaches and machine guns were not their modus operandi. They ran more as a multi-national business, and the senior executive, under the leadership of the Pakhan – the godfather – understood graphs and charts and, as long as the right numbers moved in the right direction, they were fine.

The meeting of Bratva's senior group had raised concern at a meeting some weeks earlier. Feliks Kalinin had been called in at short notice. He had been with his mistress; she had been none too pleased.

The business had been running well for many years, almost like clockwork. He had taken his eye off the game. He had seen the healthy trade in heroin on the streets and assumed it was coming up through Yusup, and he had been left out of the loop. Not that it had worried him unduly, as he was still making plenty of money. He had been lucky to get off with a severe warning when meeting his superiors. Forced to confront Yusup soon after, he found out that the Tajikistan drug lord had played square with him, and he was not responsible for the current situation. Feliks realised he would not leave alive the next time the Bratva's senior executive met.

***

Feliks was waiting at Domodedovo Airport in Moscow early in the morning to meet the flight from Tajikistan. Yusup left the plane first, followed closely by Malika on her first visit.

Feliks was a worried man, and his greeting to Malika was brusque. Yusup understood and told her that matters were serious and that he and Feliks needed to sit down and talk as soon as possible. She acknowledged the situation and left them for the hotel. Feliks had organised a car for her. She checked into the penthouse suite, and then, after a suitable period to freshen up, she hit the shops, although not with the vengeance of Firuza, Yusup's wife, or Dmitry Gubkin's, Katerina.

The range of goods from every part of the world left her speechless. She had travelled little, other than the occasional trip to Uzbekistan, but Dushanbe had been her home, and before becoming the mistress to one of the most influential men in Tajikistan, she had never considered travelling as part of her life's experiences. Her life had been tainted by drugs and violent men; however, now that she was with Baroyev, she felt she was finally at peace. Her mother was comfortable and complacent and had even found herself another man, the owner of a small car hire company.

It would not be until later that night that Yusup returned to the hotel. She was anxious to show him everything she had bought; he was slightly drunk and ready to sleep. She let it pass and put him to bed. He had never been a heavy drinker, but Feliks Kalinin was, and the next day, Yusup apologised. He said it was necessary; Feliks was in trouble, the Russian mafia was in turmoil, and it would get nasty.

It was the most he had ever spoken to her about his business when they had been together, and the tension showed on his face. Unable to spend time with her, he wished her well. She booked herself on a tourist bus to see the sights of Moscow from the comfort of a double-decker bus. She would have sat on the open top, but the climate was colder than she was used to.

***

Feliks and Yusup met the next day at ten in the morning. Feliks arrived wearing a suit, an open-neck shirt and black leather shoes. Yusup, as usual, was impeccably dressed in a suit of the best quality.

Feliks was a dependable man but short on attention span. At least, that had been Yusup's impression the first time he had met him. That was why it was only now he realised the seriousness of the situation. Yusup had contacted him several times in the last few months.

'Keep your eye on the business. Find out what's going on,' he had said, but to no avail.

'It's all fine,' was all Feliks had said until the wake-up call from the Russian mafia's senior members.

Yusup was pleased that he was finally taking notice. He had come up from Dushanbe, where he felt comfortable and safe. Nobody would touch him down there for fear of what would have happened if he had survived; it was not so certain in Moscow.

Feliks had provided the security, but they looked indolent; Yusup had little faith in them. He had agreed to give Feliks two days of his time to give him some ideas and find out what was going on, and then he would head back to where he felt safe.

Gennady Denikin was also hanging around in Dushanbe, so maybe he could sort out a deal with him, although he would have to leave Oleg Yezhov alone – for the time being – and he hadn't told Malika that he was back in town yet. The Afghans were still unknown, although there were possibilities there to perhaps set up a rival operation and maybe include Feliks, or maybe not.

'Feliks, you know this part of the world,' said Yusup. 'What do you know about Gennady Denikin?'

'Minor player. Seems to have landed on his feet.'

'Who is he reporting to? Have you managed to find that out?'

'The best I can figure is Grigory Stolypin,' Feliks replied.

Feliks was a slight man with small bones and was slightly shorter than the average man in the street. He was not impressive; his diction was poor, and he limped slightly on his left leg – which, he told Yusup, he had been born with, and his head tended to jiggle on his shoulders as he spoke. He wore heavy-rimmed spectacles. He did not look like a gangster, but he had been one of the most vicious in his younger days.

'Grigory Stolypin, who's he?' Yusup asked.

'He's a senior figure in Bratva. Although, if it's him, he should have been conducting the operation with the full authority of the Pakhan, the godfather.'

'And he's not?'

'Apparently, otherwise, the money would appear on the accounts.'

'If it's not, does that mean he's gone renegade?'

'That appears to be the case, but how to prove it?' Feliks said.

'Do you need to prove it?'

'I can't tell them of my suspicions about Stolypin without proof.'

'What proof do you need?'

'I'm not sure. We need to connect him to the operation and show that he's taking the money. But he's a gangster, not an organiser – not at this level, anyway.'

'There's someone else behind the scenes?'

'I would have thought so, but whom? It's hard to imagine anyone would be so foolish to act against the interests of the godfather. They're signing their death warrant if they're caught. They must know that.'

'How do you find out?'

'That's the difficulty. Ask too many questions, and you end up dead.'

Yusup sensed he was getting nowhere with Feliks, and, besides, what happened in Russia concerned him little. What happened in Tajikistan did, and there, he had problems.

***

Malika was pleased to be going back. Two days had been enough for her, although there would be excess baggage to pay for all she had bought, even with the increased allowance in first class. Feliks dropped them off at the airport, unaware that they had been followed at a discreet distance by a black, late-model Volvo.

After leaving the airport, Feliks drove back into the centre of Moscow. Taking a detour down a back street to avoid the traffic, which was building up as the day drew to a close, he found himself boxed in by the Volvo at his rear and a BMW 7 series at his front. Unable to get out due to the width of the road and the cars parked on either side, he was trapped.

He had dismissed the security at the airport except for one, the most reliable of those who provided him with security –

this was his city, and he felt safe. The pistol in the glove compartment served no use, as the rear doors of both vehicles opened and a man from each vehicle exited, the AK-47s they carried on rapid fire. Feliks and his security were dead within fifteen seconds, although the weapons continued for ten more. The assailants then left the scene, the Volvo backing up the narrow street, the BMW accelerating away to the front.

Yusup received the news on landing at the airport in Dushanbe. One of the supposed security guards had phoned him. He was glad to be back on home territory. He did not tell Malika what had happened. She would have only worried, not fully understanding how dangerous the situation had become.

Chapter 22

Yusup Baroyev was not the only one who took the news of Feliks Kalinin's death hard. Dmitry Gubkin's attempts at orchestrating the drug smuggling operation out of Afghanistan were unravelling. He was being drawn inexorably into the open. The aspersions about his criminal activities, no longer scurrilous gossip, were now receiving media coverage in the major newspapers, and some of the readers were his former social peers.

His ostracising from the polite society of the city continued unabated. They had suspected what he was before the press did, but the good society people did not care as long as no one else knew, and now it was being blasted across the pages of every newspaper.

The new girlfriend was gone, a victim of the bad press, but there were other men, ageing and aiming to relive their youth with a much younger woman. Gubkin felt trapped, and Stolypin was doing nothing to help. The assassination of Feliks Kalinin, without checking with him, was counter-productive. There was an element of risk which he saw as unacceptably high.

Stolypin saw the assassination differently. He felt it sent the right signal – deal with us or nobody else. Gubkin had judged Baroyev as a man who did not respond to threats.

He reminded Stolypin, who became exceedingly angry, of their initial agreement.

Firstly, he would be kept out of sight, which was not the case anymore. Secondly, he was to be the brains behind the scenes. Gubkin further reminded him that he had clearly said he was a gangster with a gangster's mind, and they needed someone impartial in control.

Stolypin, in turn, reminded Gubkin that he was now part of the organisation and hiding in some fancy house, pretending to be a good and honest citizen, no longer held any weight. He would be contacted when needed unless he came up with constructive assistance.

Dmitry had missed one other factor, mainly because he was unaware of the situation, and Stolypin had failed to realise the repercussions it was to have.

The senior executive of Bratva became aware of the assassination of Feliks Kalinin within six hours of it occurring. They had previously received a cursory communication from Kalinin telling them that he was aware of another offshoot of the mafia muscling in on his business. Details were scarce, as he had little or no proof and had not mentioned any names, only intimating that Grigory Stolypin was involved.

Kalinin's death was clearly suspicious. If Dmitry had known, he would have advised caution and attempted to explain it to Stolypin.

Stolypin became aware of the recklessness of his actions within a week. The senior executive of the mafia intended to investigate certain names, Stolypin initially and then his associates, Gennady Denikin included.

Stolypin's travels down to Tajikistan were thought to be suspicious. His further incursion into Afghanistan put the executive on edge. Instead of Feliks Kalinin being asked to explain where the money was, Grigory Stolypin was summoned.

***

Feeling suitably concerned that he did not have the answers, Stolypin phoned the one man who could extricate him from the current situation.

Dmitry was not affable and became downright cold and unpleasant. He was being subjected to a tax audit, and the accountants and lawyers, who would have been at his place for the substantial money he would pay them, were nowhere to be seen and unavailable every time he phoned. He had never been subjected to an official enquiry into his business dealings. He had always paid someone suitable money to make it go away.

'Look here, Dmitry,' Stolypin went on the offensive. 'If I'm going down, you are coming down with me.'

'Don't threaten me,' replied Dmitry angrily. 'Who do you think you are? You are nothing but a two-bit hoodlum who thinks he is a master gangster.'

'Watch what you say. From what I hear, you are no longer the darling of the social set. A pariah, as they see it. Whether you like it or not does not concern me. We need each other now, so we may as well be civil.'

Dmitry realised that Stolypin had spoken the truth. He would never survive a tax investigation, and his previous corporate takeovers, daring as they had been, had come about in part due to industrial espionage and a team of lawyers, who would as quickly become witnesses for the prosecution, saying they had acted on written instructions. He was cornered, and his life, good as it had been, was over. His only hope of redemption or a life of quiet solace lay with the man at the other end of the phone line.

'Grigory, you are right. We may not like the situation, but we are tied to each other. We must plan our strategy – and please, this time, leave the thinking to me.'

'Dmitry, maybe I was wrong having Kalinin killed.'

***

Dmitry saw that he had less than two weeks before the shutters came down. He gave himself five days to secure his money. There were eighty million American dollars in a bank account in Switzerland and another twenty-five million in an offshore bank in Cyprus. He would need to delete all the passwords from his computer. He had four houses aside from the Moscow mansion, but they were owned through a complex structured offshore company and trust setup. Whatever happened, they would be secured, although selling them may prove difficult.

The money in his Moscow bank accounts amounted to several million American dollars. He moved quickly to move the majority out of the country. A couple of million he kept as travelling money. Where to, he did not know, but if his cover was blown, he may as well become a gangster. He liked the style of Yusup Baroyev. He had never met him, but he seemed to be his kind of person.

Maybe he could fix up a deal with the senior executive and regain the upper hand in the drug trade. He needed Stolypin, as there would be dirty work to be done, people to be pressured, people to be assassinated, people to be removed, politely or otherwise. Stolypin could deal with that if he followed instructions.

Instead of a man in despair, Gubkin was excited. He had spent too much time sitting in an office working the numbers, squeezing the lawyers and the accountants to fudge the figures up or down until they came up with the right result. There would be no more pretending to the pompous arses with their society airs and graces, who at the first hint of scandal had dumped him, and no more frivolous women bleeding him dry financially. He would become a gangster and get himself a gangster's moll. He looked forward to the future, but first, he had to get Grigory Stolypin out of trouble.

***

Dmitry and Stolypin met two days later. There seemed little reason for subterfuge anymore, and they met in a good restaurant in a good part of town. His ex-girlfriend sat in the far corner, draped over a man who must have been in his eighties. Dmitry had no animosity, but he kept his gaze averted from her as she did from him. She had been fun for a while and had fuelled his ego, but she was forgotten. Grigory Stolypin interested him more now than she did.

Society matrons sat at a table to one side as he entered, pretending to be deep in conversation and not notice him.

However, they were all eyes when Stolypin sat in the chair opposite Dmitry.

'Fancy joint,' Grigory said.

'It seemed appropriate to celebrate our renewed friendship,' Dmitry replied.

'Yes, sure, whatever you say.' Stolypin shifted uncomfortably on the chair, not used to ingratiating compliments.

'Where's the money gone?' Dmitry asked.

'Why ask me? You received all the financial statements.'

'My question was rhetorical. If we are to get you off, we must devise an answer that will satisfy.'

'Okay, I see what you're trying to do. You are attempting to shift the blame onto someone else.' Stolypin sat upright in his chair, pulled in his chest, which still hung over the white tablecloth like a lump of white lard, as his white shirt was immaculate, along with the rest of his clothes.

'What are we doing?' asked Dmitry. 'Was it ever sanctioned by the mafia's senior executive?'

'We never officially told them.'

'We can't just offer to pay them what's owed and hope for forgiveness, I suppose?' Dmitry knew the answer. He immediately regretted its naivety.

'Not with these guys. An admission of guilt is a death sentence unless you can convince them to leave us alone. Make them an offer they cannot refuse, so to speak.'

'Any idea what Baroyev and the Afghans are planning?'

'Denikin's trying to find out,' replied Grigory. 'They'll need someone in Russia to deal with the distribution and selling.'

'Sanctioned by the senior executive?'

'It's possible, but no proof either way. Denikin's meeting up with Baroyev.'

'Baroyev's not going to be too pleased with him after you killed his contact in Russia.'

'Okay, it was a mistake,' said Grigory. 'Besides, we're not sure if Baroyev knows the truth.'

'Maybe he doesn't, but he will be suspicious.'

268

'Everyone's suspicious. What's new in that?'

'Let's get back to getting you, us, off the hook.'

The discussion had not dampened the appetite of either man, who ate the expansive array of food– three courses with wine, dessert and even a cheese plate. The ex-girlfriend had left, smiling Dmitry's way as she walked past his table, which he returned. The society matrons lingered over their desserts, taking in the body language between their former friend and the big, well-built man with the greased-up hair and the small moustache.

'What do you reckon?' Grigory asked.

'We need someone to take the blame. Then we need to work out a deal with the mafia leadership.'

'They'll bleed us for at least twenty per cent.'

'Okay, they'll bleed us. We'll just have to up the quantities or the price to compensate, that's all.'

'I'll take your advice. You run it the way you want.'

'What about the other men you brought to the meeting last time we met?'

'Boris Sobchak and Ivan Merestkov?' asked Grigory.

'Can we place the blame on them? Are either of them suitable?'

'They've not done much, left it to me mainly. Take your pick if it is going to save our skins.'

'Which one would be the most plausible?' Dmitry asked.

'Boris, for not telling the executive, and I am certain he's been talking to Baroyev. There were a couple of trucks hijacked. It could only have been him. Ivan is the most likely candidate for taking the money.'

'Can we pin it on both of them?'

'Ivan's done a fair job with the marketing, but Boris is not really needed. I would go for Boris, but we better be quick. At least, before he finds out we have put the blame on him, or else he'll have us killed.'

'We better take them both out,' Dmitry said.

'Okay, if you think that's best,' replied Grigory. 'The marketing, I suppose I can deal with that.'

***

Life should have been good in Dushanbe for Baroyev. Malika was happy, and even his wife was not pestering him to return anytime soon. The children had been enrolled in good schools in France. *No doubt expensive*, he thought, but it concerned him little.

The death of Feliks Kalinin had shaken him more than it should have. It was not a situation that he would allow to continue. It was unclear who was involved, although he assumed the Russians were taking his business and Gennady Denikin was with the Russians, as was Oleg Yezhov, and he still had a score to settle with him.

Gennady Denikin's scheduled visit to the mansion was not pleasant.

'Denikin.' The tone of Yusup Baroyev's voice gave him some reason to worry. 'Who killed Kalinin, do you know?'

'I've no idea,' Denikin replied truthfully. He had not been told anything, although he had his suspicions. He realised that Grigory Stolypin was being implicated and was fighting for his life in Moscow.

Kalanin's death had been as much a surprise to him as it had been to the man who stared at him across the table in the mansion. He had no answers, and without clear instructions, he wasn't sure where the conversation with the drug lord was heading. He had been told to make contact, sound him out and see if a deal could be structured, but what deal? The business from the Afghan border was running fine, and Oleg was down there seeing who else, possibly Baroyev and the Afghans, was attempting to muscle in on the business.

'It could only be your people,' Yusup said.

'Why would they do that? They ask me to meet you to set up a deal, and then they kill your man in Russia? It doesn't make sense.'

'Sense? the Russian mafia is not known for that, killing maybe.'

'I'll check,' Denikin conceded.

'Fine, let's move on. What deal are you offering?'

Gennady Denikin was out of his depth. He had not signed on to deal with the senior gangster in the country. He was a facilitator who ensured the operation flowed smoothly once someone else had set it up. He had been in Afghanistan and handled that well, but dealing with a smooth operator like Baroyev was different. In Afghanistan, there were the regular phone calls back to Moscow, Stolypin, and the nameless voice who had told him what to say and do.

Neither of the two back in Russia answered the phone, and he needed advice. He could see no reason for prolonging the meeting at the mansion.

'A percentage to stand aside and let us run the operation, or else you could take over the transportation here in the country,' said Denikin, although only a couple of ideas came to mind.

'Either may be acceptable,' replied Yusup. 'Why are you here offering, anyway?'

'We would rather have you with us.'

'So, when there is a fight amongst your mafia friends, I'll be on your side, not theirs.'

'That sounds about right.'

'I need to see concrete facts before agreeing to any deal. And, if it's going to get violent, then I need to know what to expect.'

Gennady Denikin left the mansion soon after. It had not been a good meeting from his point of view. Yusup Baroyev saw it differently. If the Russians were in trouble, he could strike a deal or take the business from them. However, his distribution channel, Feliks Kalinin, was dead, and he wasn't sure who else he could trust.

***

Back at his house, Denikin had two phone calls to make – one to Oleg, the other to Stolypin, if only he would answer.

Oleg was easier to get hold of. He was down at the border town with Pavel Suslov, fishing around, aiming to find out if anyone was talking to anyone about increased business or different distribution routes. Pavel did not like it down there. Oleg did not like it much, either, but he was out of harm's way, and regardless of how agreeable Yusup Baroyev had been, he didn't feel comfortable in his presence. A few days away would do no harm.

Yuri Drygin, the border guard, was making himself rich by taking money from everyone. He was the best lead for knowledge of what was going on. He was not happy to see Oleg initially, reticent to even talk to him. Oleg was suspicious. The Russians were his chief benefactor now, and Oleg was with the Russians.

Oleg was determined to find out. He had ensured the payments Drygin received were paid promptly, and there had been no disruptions in the shipments coming through. Friction in Russia, apparently within the Russian mafia and disputes with Yusup Baroyev in Tajikistan had little effect on the flow of the heroin, still carefully concealed in the myriad of vehicles crossing the concrete bridge from Afghanistan.

Drygin had been thorough in his duties, caught a few attempting to hide drugs in hidden compartments in fuel tanks, strapped to a sheep's underbelly, or wrapped around the waist of a peasant coming over the border. Due to the new bridge, the peasants came for casual work in the shops that had sprung up in the border town. The Friendship Bridge, they had called it, when the Presidents of both countries had made the speeches, patted each other on the back and pronounced that it signalled a new beginning between their two great nations.

Yuri Drygin only knew that the friendship began with his bank account, which looked very friendly. As to the friendship between the two great nations, there was nothing there unless it came with a suitable bribe – in his case, large.

The new player in town was talking of more friendship and money, and Oleg Yezhov was not the person he wanted to see.

***

'Drygin, why are you avoiding me?'

Oleg waylaid the border official at the restaurant where they had dined on a previous visit when he had been checking out Farrukh at the smugglers' village. It was just before he had caught Malika with the Afghan, just before he had put her in intensive care and the Afghan in an early grave.

'Oleg Yezhov.' Drygin approached him, gave him a firm embrace and acted like an old friend. 'Nothing of the sort.'

Oleg saw no reason to be belligerent towards the man. He let Drygin's comment pass. He had served the mafia well and ensured that he had a relatively untroubled life in Dushanbe.

Others up the road, towards the capital and the border with Uzbekistan, had not been as accomplished in the task the bribes were supposed to have ensured. A minor police official, fifty kilometres north from where Oleg and Yuri Drygin amiably sat, had attempted to garner a little extra for his goodwill. He had stopped a couple of trucks, found some drugs, put the drivers in prison and taken a payment hastily organised by Oleg to release them. The third time he tried, it was his last. Viktor Gryzlov had visited him and ensured that a bridge in construction over a slow-flowing river had some additional reinforcement, namely the police official, who was now residing inside one of the concrete supports.

Further up, close to the Uzbek border, a customs official, similar in stature and position to Yuri Drygin, attempted a similar trick. Once again, Viktor Gryzlov and a local Tajik man paid him a midnight visit. His office was empty the next day, and no amount of complaining and crying by his wife would bring him back.

'So, who else is paying you money down here?' Oleg asked.

'Why would I take money from anyone else?' replied Drygin. 'You pay me well enough.'

'Look here, Yuri.' Oleg tried another method to obtain his cooperation. 'It's only normal that others would want a piece of the action. If I were in their position, I'd be doing the same. You must know something.'

'I have been approached, but I've done nothing about it. Besides, I don't think they've attempted to ship anything yet.'

'Who is it?'

'They paid me to keep quiet. If I tell you, they may come down here and have me eliminated. My word is my bond.'

'And if you don't tell me, I may have some of my people come here and save them a trip. The choice is yours.'

'Okay, okay.' Drygin saw that he had no option. 'Another Russian syndicate, that's all I know.'

'But who did you speak to?'

'Someone from Dushanbe.'

'Russian or Tajik?'

'Tajik.'

'Name?' Oleg asked.

'Rasul Dostiev. He told me that there were some other Russians. Apart from that, I know no more.'

Chapter 23

It was evident to Oleg that he would get no more from Yuri Drygin. He and Pavel left for the capital within the hour. Pavel had achieved little; his trip down had been wasted, but Oleg had another job for him – find Rasul Dostiev.

Gennady Denikin, meanwhile, had eventually been able to contact Grigory Stolypin, who was preparing his defence for the meeting with the senior members of Bratva. Dmitry Gubkin, effectively isolated from the upper echelons of Moscow society, spent increasing amounts of time with him, mentoring him on conducting his defence.

'Gennady, I'm busy up here,' said Stolypin. 'What do you want?' The upcoming meeting was playing on Stolypin's nerves; he was not handling the situation well. He knew the wrong answers with a poorly planned defence, and he and Denikin would be convicted and sentenced with no chance of appeal. The executive's decision was final, and the sentence would be carried out immediately.

'Baroyev, what's the deal with him? What can I offer?' Denikin asked.

'What does he want? What have you offered?' Stolypin was not focused on the conversation.

'I offered him a percentage and the option to take over the movement of merchandise through his country.'

'Did he go for it?'

'He's interested, but he's playing all sides. He will not come to a decision quickly.'

'Neither will we. Just ensure that the merchandise gets through while this is happening.'

'There's been an approach by a rival organisation, apparently Russian, down at the Afghan border,' Denikin said.

'Any details?'

'Oleg has a name. I'll follow up and keep you posted.'

'Fine. Now let me get on with what I've got to do here.' Stolypin hung up the phone.

'What was all that about?' Dmitry asked.

It was the first time for Stolypin in Gubkin's country house. He was staggered by its beauty.

'Dennikin,' replied Stolypin. 'He's met with Baroyev. Yezhov has been down on the border. He's confirmed that someone else, probably Russian, aims to muscle in on our business.'

'Who?'

'He doesn't know.'

'It may be significant,' replied Dmitry. 'We need to know if they are coming through the senior members of Bratva, whether they are sanctioned or freelance. It may help with the defence.'

***

Rasul Dostiev proved to be elusive. Pavel tried all the clubs, ferreted in the city's underbelly and paid money out in his hunt for the man. Eventually, he traced him hanging out in a den of inequity in a suburb north of the city, a low-life place frequented by drug addicts, pimps and prostitutes. It was Dostiev's kind of place.

Pavel was uncertain how to approach him, as he was surrounded by a group of men. Shady was how he described them to Oleg, who told him to back off and that they would pick him up later that night.

It was midnight when Dostiev left the club. He was drunk, staggering down the street, oblivious to his surroundings. He took off down a side road where the street lights did not work.

Oleg was out of the car – Pavel was driving – and over to the man. He hit him across the back of the head with a baton he kept in the vehicle, just in case it was ever needed. It had been needed that night, and soon Rasul Dostiev was gagged and bound and in the car's boot, heading to a place where everyone could have a cosy chat.

Oleg had resumed driving as Pavel was a poor driver, too nervous, and the last thing Oleg wanted was an accident, or to be pulled over for failing to observe the traffic lights, or because the car was wandering on both sides of the road. The trip to a remote location previously picked out by Oleg was isolated and out of sight.

The old barn was warm, although the smell was not pleasant. Ravel Dostiev moaned as he slowly regained consciousness. He failed to understand the seriousness of the situation.

His hands were shackled with rope, his ankles firmly secured. Oleg judged him to be about forty-five years of age and not in good shape. He had attempted to delay baldness by combing his hair over the top of his bald patch. He wore prescription spectacles. He reeked of vodka, which he had apparently consumed with relish that night – and probably most nights previous, as his complexion was blotchy, his nose ruddy and his eyes bloodshot.

His attempts at standing up were ridiculous and hilarious. Each attempt would cause him to collapse as if in slow motion. The bindings, especially on his ankles, were too tight, and as he straightened, they twisted and caused him to lose balance. He would have realised the pain if sober, but he was still powerfully drunk even after a thirty-minute drive.

Oleg did not have time for the niceties; he needed answers and fast. Stolypin was becoming increasingly nervous and had been on the phone every couple of hours for the last couple of days, and it was starting to irritate him. The sooner he could give some information, the better it would be for all concerned.

'Dostiev, wake up!' Oleg firmly hit him on the shoulder, aiming to revive his prisoner.

'What do you want? Leave me alone.' Dostiev seemed unaware of his circumstances.

'You've been on the border with Afghanistan.'

'Who are you? What do you want, and why am I here?' Dostiev said. His accent was coarse and slurred. Oleg struggled to understand him, but Pavel had no trouble.

'Who sent you to the border?' Oleg persisted.

'Nobody sent me. I just fancied a drive.' Rasul Dostiev was not proving to be an ideal witness. He was either too drunk or too stupid. Pavel thought he was both.

Oleg found a bucket which he filled with water from a rain tank. He threw the water over Dostiev. It had the desired effect, and the prisoner regained full consciousness.

'Dostiev, who told you to go to the border?' Oleg asked again.

'Nobody did. I told you that,' said Dostiev. 'What do you want me for? I'm just a harmless drunk.'

'Harmless and drunk, I don't care. I do care about why you went to the border and why the Russians are using you?'

'Russians? I don't deal with any Russians. I spent ten lousy years in Moscow, working as a security guard. The pay and the weather were lousy, and the people were pigs.'

'You speak Russian?'

'After ten years, what do you think?' Oleg realised one of the reasons they were using him. He spoke their language.

'Who was your contact?' Oleg reverted to his mother tongue.

'You're Russian,' Dostiev replied. His Russian was more understandable than his Tajik, at least to Oleg.

'Who are the Russians?' Oleg asked. He was getting tired of the procrastination.

'I don't know any Russians.'

Oleg hit the man firmly in the chest with the end of the baton. Pavel looked away.

'Who are the Russians you have been speaking to?'

'I don't know any Russians.'

This time, Oleg hit him across the face. There was a sound of cracking bone or breaking teeth. Pavel went outside and vomited.

It was a couple of minutes before Rasul Dostiev could speak again. The blood streamed from his mouth. His speech was barely audible.

'Who are the Russians?' repeated Oleg.

'Don't hit me. I'll tell you all I know.'

'Then be quick, or I'll be forced to hit you again.'

'Don't, I'll talk.' Dostiev gulped and took a drink of water that Pavel held to his mouth. 'I don't know their names.'

'You've spoken to more than one?' Oleg asked.

'Only on the phone, and I don't know their names.'

'You've said that already. Tell me about them.' Oleg sat on an old wooden crate, the baton on the floor at his side.

'They asked me to go to the border, talk to the border guard there.'

'And what else?'

'Nothing else. They told me they were taking over the operation and wanted me to be their man in Tajikistan.'

'And that's it?'

'I heard them speaking in the background. One was called Boris. They said they were tired of playing second fiddle to Stolypin. That's all, I swear it. Please, let me go.'

It was clear to Oleg what he had heard. It was the information that Grigory Stolypin needed. He phoned him immediately. Stolypin said to leave no loose ends. Oleg told Pavel to go and sit in the car.

Thirty seconds later, Rasul Dostiev was dead. Oleg Yezhov, the reluctant killer, had killed again. He buried the body under a pile of compost in another corner of the barn, knowing full well that all that would remain in time would be bones.

Pavel said nothing as they drove back to the city. He did not want to know what had happened to Dostiev.

***

With the information from Oleg, who had finally proved his worth, Stolypin and Dmitry Gubkin considered the situation. Stolypin was for slash and burn. Gubkin needed time to consider.

'It seems we have a chance to get you off the hook. All we need to do is state the facts,' Dmitry said.

'But where's the proof?' Grigory replied. It was a fair question.

'What sort of proof do you need?'

'Iron cast,' said Grigory. 'Otherwise, it's my word against them, and Ivan Merestkov is no fool. We have one shot at this. If we can't convince the executive of their guilt, Boris will go into full war mode, and you and I will be seriously inconvenienced.'

'Seriously inconvenienced?' Dmitry questioned.

'Dead. How else do you want me to say it? Boris and Ivan's best hope will be to lay the blame on us, and that won't be difficult. The executive will assume that Boris doesn't have the brains, and Ivan doesn't have the guts or the skills.'

'Does Merestkov have the necessary skills to run an operation of this size?' Dmitry asked.

'Hypothetically, yes,' said Grigory. 'If you and I are dead, we'll never know. You're the brains; think of something.'

'Grigory, give me time. Ten minutes' peace and quiet while I mull over the situation.'

Dmitry moved over to his favourite seat, poured himself a glass of vintage sherry and closed his eyes. To Grigory Stolypin, it looked as if he had fallen asleep; for Dmitry, however, he could look out the box, see the problem from all sides, and see the actions and counter-actions, the possible scenarios. It had served him well during corporate takeovers. He hoped it would serve him well now.

The ten minutes stretched to fifteen, and still, Grigory waited. Dmitry barely sipped on the sherry, just held it firmly by the base. Grigory was ready to interrupt, but he stayed calm. Eighteen minutes later, almost to the second, Dmitry opened his eyes, stood up, drank his sherry and spoke.

'We need to separate Boris Sobchak and Ivan Merestkov,' he said.

'Where's the gain in that?' Grigory asked, perplexed.

'If you go in there and have to stand up to arguments from Boris and Ivan, you'll lose. You tried to play it smart with them. They know this. They will corroborate each other's statements, leaving you out on a limb.'

'Okay, then, how do we separate them?'

'You've got to kill Boris Sobchak.'.

'Hold on, I'm not a killer,' replied Grigory angrily.

'Then find someone who is.'

***

Gennady Denikin was not pleased that Oleg Yezhov and Stolypin were talking or that Yezhov had, by default, become Stolypin's favourite man down in Dushanbe. He had been working with Yusup Baroyev and not achieving a lot.

Baroyev was playing hard to get and spending time with the Afghans. Denikin was even more displeased when Stolypin told him to send Viktor Gryzlov on the next plane to Moscow. He had no option but to comply, and early the next day, Gryzlov arrived in the Russian capital on what was to prove to be a cold and overcast day. The snow clouds had been forming, and the forecast was for an early start to the cold season, not that it was ever very warm. Gryzlov turned up the collar on his fur-lined jacket and hailed a taxi.

Freed of any immediate responsibilities, Oleg took the time to enjoy himself. He rejoined the gym, where he had nearly bumped into Malika. She hadn't been there for some time, so he thought it was safe. The new attendant, a muscle-bound individual with a T-shirt designed to show his physique, said little when Oleg casually asked what had happened to the previous attendant.

'Just didn't turn up for work one morning,' he said.

Oleg thought it best not to tell him that he was resting at the bottom of a lake in the quarry on the outskirts of town. How many people had he killed now when he had wanted to kill no one? How many would he have to kill before this was over and he was back in St. Petersburg with Natasha? He thought he may even make an honest woman of her, marry her, have children, and get a legitimate business. But he realised that it was probably a daydream. His life revolved around crime and violence. It was all he knew.

***

Viktor Gryzlov was unhappy with the news when he met up with Stolypin. They were casual acquaintances, having only met when Gennady Denikin had been around. Gryzlov respected and trusted Denikin, but his feelings towards Stolypin were ambivalent, and here he was, asking him to assassinate someone. He was unsure he wanted to be involved and less sure how to get out of it.

'Viktor, it's one death, and then you can return to Dushanbe.'

'But why me? Can't you get someone else?'

'This is important. If I go down, then so does Gennady. It's that simple.'

The delegated assassin had no option but to comply. It was what he was paid for, what he was good at. But Boris Sobchak? He knew him by reputation, and if it went wrong, his retribution was too frightful to consider.

Stolypin laid out the plan. 'Every Wednesday, he visits the same restaurant. All you need to do is position yourself somewhere nearby, a rooftop maybe. Then, when he exits, you shoot him and get out of there quickly.'

'It sounds too simple to me,' Gryzlov replied. He was not a man of many words.

'Choose any weapon you like, and I'll arrange it. Just check out the place and be ready.' Gryzlov did not like simple plans, especially for the assassination of a prominent member of the Russian mafia. It was bound to have repercussions. Even he could see that.

He saw Stolypin as a desperate man, but then they were all desperate, at least by association. If Stolypin were found guilty and subsequently liquidated, there would be a call to find all those associated with him, find them all guilty on the flimsiest evidence, and dispose of them. He did not want to kill and even phoned Gennady, but he said Stolypin was right and there was no other option.

***

Boris Sobchak was passionate about pasta, especially homemade, and his favourite Italian restaurant made the best. Each Wednesday, without fail, when he was in town, he would come down with a group of people. There would be a few men, possibly even more women and bodyguards, four at least, who would stay outside in the cars or on the street.

Viktor Gryzlov reasoned that his only chance was to get one clean shot at the restaurant as the target entered. A rooftop on the other side of the road seemed suitable. The building was three storeys; the ground floor, a florist, and the upper two floors, good quality apartments. He had paced out his escape route. He calculated that thirty seconds after firing the shot, he would be down the stairs, over the back fence at the rear of the building, into his car, and away. The timing was tight, but he could not risk any more.

As the first shot pierced into Boris Sobchak's chest, two or three of the bodyguards would be moving in the direction of the bullet – the angle of trajectory easily calculated by the angle of entry, based on the position he had been standing when he had been hit. Gryzlov did not want to be caught by them as they would torture him until he told them all he knew. He had used torture before and knew everyone has a breaking point.

Grigory Stolypin had supplied him with a semi-automatic Dragunov sniper rifle with a silencer, as requested. Gryzlov had used them before, and it was the best, the only weapon of choice for the serious marksman.

Wednesday evening came, and he was on the roof. He had managed to conceal himself early before the people in the apartments had come home from work. If the stairs proved too difficult to negotiate, there was a metal ladder fitted at the rear as a fire escape. It was the least favourable option, as it would be slippery due to the steady rain, and there was no light to show him the rungs if he clambered down. He discounted it as it would have taken at least forty seconds longer than the stairs, and he wouldn't have the time.

The rain was annoying, the cold was already becoming a nuisance, and he still had two hours to wait. Sobchak, a stickler for punctuality, usually arrived at 8 pm sharp but was thirty minutes late. Gryzlov was feeling excessively cold, and his legs were starting to cramp. He couldn't jump on the spot to warm up, as the occupants of the apartment below would have heard him. He had been on stakeouts in Chechnya, but it had not been as cold there, and he had been a younger man.

Boris Sobchak and his entourage arrived: three men in a good mood, laughing, and four attractive women in ankle-length fur coats. The men grabbed the women, putting their arms around them and joking, the women letting them do what they wanted. To Gryzlov, they looked bought. Not that he cared. All he needed was a clear shot. The temperature had dropped to close to freezing, the falling sleet distorting his visibility. He knew he would not get a clear shot as they entered the building. He would have to wait until they left the restaurant.

It was another two hours before the group left. The snow had eased, and the target was clearly in his sights when Gryzlov pulled the trigger, a perfect shot. He was up on his feet and moving towards the stairs and the rear exit when his left leg folded under him. The cold temperature and sitting for a prolonged period had caused his leg to go to sleep. Under normal circumstances, it would have been a minor issue. He would have just hobbled around for a couple of minutes until the leg received warmth and circulation, and then he would have been fine. Here, he did not have a few minutes or seconds as two bodyguards were coming his way.

Two had stayed with Boris Sobchak, but that served no point. He was dead before he hit the floor. The women were screaming; the men were shouting instructions at the bodyguards. Viktor Gryzlov heard nothing up on the roof. His problems were more immediate. Hobbling, he made the top of the stairs, inadvertently dropping the weapon. Cursing his stupidity at losing his only protection, he continued down one flight, then two. He should have been down four in the time the first two had taken and closing in on his car, but he wasn't.

The first guard was already on the first floor of the apartment block, and he had the assassin in his sights. He took a shot but missed. His balance had been thrown by the uneven flooring in the building. The second guard further down steadied himself and took a shot. He hit Gryzlov in the shoulder. Still upright, he moved on down, catching the first guard a glancing blow with his fist and knocking him over the balustrade. The man hit the tiled floor three metres below, cracking tiles and breaking a leg.

The second guard, now the only obstacle between Viktor Gryzlov and escape, took aim again. He hit him with a clean shot in the stomach. Bent over in agony and bleeding, Gryzlov continued moving down until blood loss weakened his strength. The third shot from the guard to the head killed him.

'You fool,' another guard shouted as he rushed through the door at ground level. 'Now, we'll never know who he was or who sent him.'

The second guard answered back. 'Viktor Gryzlov, that's his name. He worked for Grigory Stolypin.'

***

Ivan Merestkov was the first to hear of his partner's death. Personally, he cared little either way. He had not liked Boris Sobchak any more than Sobchak had liked him, but their attempt to wrest control from Stolypin and Gubkin was thrown into confusion at a time when confusion was not needed.

The negotiations with various people in Tajikistan, the impending approach to Yusup Baroyev and a representation to the Afghans were thrown to the wind with this one death. The disappearance of Rasul Dostiev also caused concern. That was the reason for Sobchak's lateness at the restaurant. They had been on the phone discussing his disappearance, which could only be seen as suspicious. Dostiev was an unpleasant weasel of a man, but with the money they were willing to pay him, they were convinced he hadn't just failed to pick up the phone.

It had to be Stolypin, on instructions from Gubkin, who was organising everything behind the scenes. And then, there was the impending meeting with the senior members of the mafia, and without Boris to back up his story, there was a possibility that Stolypin, with Gubkin's coaching, may have been able to talk his way out of it.

Merestkov was a worried man, and, as with all men in such situations, they act irrationally and out of character.

He was not alone. He was a serious player in organised crime and had his trusted lieutenants, foot soldiers, thugs and villains. He saw the need for retribution and knew who the enemy was and where he was hiding. Without the reasoned advice of a Gubkin and the cunning of a Baroyev, he was to make the wrong decision.

Stolypin was protected well enough for the present, and after the assassination of Sobchak, his security was tighter than ever. Gubkin would be equally well-protected, but he wasn't mafia, just an adviser. He saw Stolypin's people down in Tajikistan as possible, but how and who could he use?

***

Gennady Denikin learnt of Viktor Gryzlov's death soon after Merestkov. Denikin was sad at the news. He and Viktor had formed a good team and had been through tough scrapes together. He trusted him more than any other man.

Grigory Stolypin had phoned to tell him the good news about Sobchak and to express remorse over Viktor.

It took time to digest the news and the best part of a bottle of vodka that night before Gennady Denikin fell into a restless sleep.

Stolypin's instructions had been clear. 'Continue discussions with Baroyev, intimate that a possible other player is out of the game.'

'Is he?' Denikin had asked.

'Merestkov can't do anything on his own. He'll soon be pushing up daisies,' replied Stolypin.

Dmitry had given Grigory a plan to handle the upcoming meeting that concerned them both. It looked good, and he was convinced that, in two weeks, it would be business as usual, and Baroyev would either agree to the deal or he would not. Personally, he felt sure he would.

'We need Baroyev to deal with the transportation,' Stolypin said the next day when Denikin had woken up.

'Why?' he asked.

'Pure logistics. We've set up the trade route, put the plan in place and shown that we don't need him. Now we offer him a piece of the action to keep him off our back. Besides, it was always the plan to bring him back in. It's a nightmare dealing with all the payments to every two-bit official down there, and Baroyev can handle them better than we can. He can have his piece of silver if we take the gold.'

Chapter 24

Ivan Merestkov had not slept well. One assassination required another, and turning up at the meeting with the Russian mafia's senior executive without Boris Sobchak's support would weaken his case against Stolypin. He realised that Boris Sobchak's death would need to be avenged. Someone had to die, and soon. That someone had been chosen. The only issue was to whom to entrust the task.

Rasul Dostiev was gone – assumed dead, but then he would have been useless as an assassin.

Khasan Boqiev had been taken on by Merestkov at the same time as Dostiev. Boris had interviewed them and recommended them both as suitable, at least in the short term. Dostiev was an organiser, but not a very good one, judging by the dismal results he had achieved. He had spent plenty of money, but the results and the information supplied had been limited.

Khasan Boqiev had not been employed for his organisational skills, although he could not have done a worse job than Dostiev. Boqiev was a physically tough man. He made a reasonable living as a bouncer at some of the more boisterous clubs in Dushanbe, where the music was too loud, the alcohol flowed too freely, and the drugs were too readily available. He supplemented that meagre income with the occasional murder to order. He was not as sophisticated in his technique as Viktor Gryzlov had been, but Ivan Merestkov judged him adequate for the task.

'I want someone dead,' he said on the phone to Boqiev, a man with a distinctive Asian appearance and eyes that looked strange. Cross-eyed was how Boris had described him. He dressed poorly, his clothes invariably two sizes too small, which made his muscles look more than they were. He had few friends and many enemies.

'It will cost.' Boqiev's standard reply.

'How much?'

'Two thousand American dollars.'

To Merestkov, it sounded a bargain. In Russia, death would have cost five thousand. He agreed.

'Who do you want to take out?' Boqiev said.

'Gennady Denikin. Do you know him?'

'Sobchak sent me a picture. He told me to keep a watch on him. He didn't say why.'

'It has to be today.'

'Any problems where or how?' Boqiev asked.

'That's up to you. Just phone and let me know when it's done.'

***

Gennady Denikin prepared for the day. He still felt a throbbing headache from the vodka he had drunk the night before. The meeting with Yusup Baroyev was scheduled for two in the afternoon. He had time to catch up with Oleg, give him an update and see that all was okay. He saw the day as not too strenuous, and, hopefully, that night, he would catch up with a lady he had met not far from the house he occupied, who was both pleasant and available. He was surprised at how quickly he had dealt with losing his colleague.

For Denikin, security had never been a major issue in Dushanbe, and Viktor Gryzlov had not only been a bodyguard but a companion and loyal friend. He had no plans to replace Viktor in the short term, and the trip to Oleg's apartment was no more than a two-minute drive in the BMW he had purchased. It was only two years old and in fine condition. He enjoyed driving the car and took every opportunity to give it a spin around the block. Khasan Boqiev also knew the car, having observed his target in it on several occasions.

At the first intersection after leaving his house, Gennady Denikin braked, obeying the stop sign displayed to his right. He always followed the rules when many just sped across with barely a glance to their left or right. As Dennikin stopped, Boqiev approached the vehicle and stood in front of the car.

Denikin beeped the horn on the car, the road was clear, and he was ready to drive forward. At the second beep, longer than the first, Boqiev raised his right arm and levelled the pistol he carried, a Russian-made MP-443 Grach. He pulled the trigger twice.

Gennady Denikin slumped over the steering wheel, firmly pressing on the horn, which continued to sound. The motorbike standing to one side with its motor running provided the perfect getaway for the assassin, who quickly disappeared. The stolen motorcycle would be discovered, a burnt-out wreck, sometime later.

Boqiev phoned Merestkov. 'Two thousand dollars, and make sure it's in my account today.'

***

Oleg had been quick on the scene. He saw the car, the slumped body, and the local police hovering. He did not stay long enough to check who the body was, but he knew the car.

He phoned Grigory Stolypin, who was thrown into panic mode. He made it clear to Oleg that he was to take Denikin's place and get out to Yusup Baroyev's mansion for the arranged meeting. Oleg was not pleased with his request.

He knew that, during the week, Malika would often be there, and so far, he had managed to avoid her. How she would react at seeing him was still unknown, although he imagined it would not be favourable.

Stolypin quickly passed the message to Dmitry, who expressed dismay and wondered why he had ever become involved with gangsters, murderers and thieves in the first place. However, it was too late for him to back out now.

For Dmitry, corporate crime, bankrupting a competitor and instigating a fraudulent tax investigation against them to make them more conducive to his offer, did not come with murder. Sure, there were occasionally a few deaths, but they were suicides when the people and the companies couldn't take the heat, and some had taken the easy way out. That was how he saw it, and there was no way he, Dmitry Gubkin, would take that option.

Evgeni Ovechin, a successful corporate raider, had built up a sprawling empire of interlinked companies, elaborate tax avoidance schemes and an impressive portfolio of prime real estate in the post-Soviet era. He had fallen foul of Dmitry Gubkin's aggressive takeover tactics. The tax audit, the criminal trial for tax evasion and the subsequent ten years of hard labour without remission, courtesy of a group of Gubkin operatives manipulating, pulling in favours and bribing officials.

Ovechin had lasted six months in jail before hanging himself from the security bars welded into his cell window, using a piece of rope purloined from the prison stores. Long before his death, Dmitry Gubkin had purchased the bankrupt assets, including the substantial real estate portfolio. He had made fifteen million dollars on the deal. Ovechin's premature death caused him little concern.

Alex Plushenko, a successful entrepreneur with several department stores, was a similar story. A corporate raid, scurrilous rumours and a subsequent criminal investigation into how he was importing so much into the country and he was gone. The Russian train system provided the solution, as he threw himself in front of an express train passing at speed through the station near where he lived.

There had been others, but Dmitry had been little affected. But now? It was too real for him, and he worried for his well-being.

'Is this a gang war?' he asked.

'Probably,' Grigory replied.

'You seem very casual about the situation.'

'What do you want me to be? It's happened. We just have to deal with it.'

'So, what do you suggest?' asked Dmitry. The situation had changed. Grigory Stolypin had become the adviser.

'We're targets, that's certain, but we should be safe until after the meeting with the senior executive.'

'We? Doesn't you mean you?'

'Ivan Merestkov would see you as a liability,' replied Grigory, 'and liabilities are not what he requires now.'

'My life is in danger. Is that what you are saying?'

'Yes.'

'Maybe it's best if I disappear for a while.'

'Maybe, but where? I still need you for my defence.'

'Your defence doesn't come at the cost of my life.'

'If I lose, what do you think will happen to you?' asked Grigory.

'You tell me,' Dmitry countered.

'They'll come for you.'

'You approached me,' said Dmitry angrily. 'How did I know you were cheating the Bratva out of their money?'

'Do you think they will be interested in your protestations? It's not a court of law.'

'What do we do?' Dmitry accepted the situation. He had to help Grigory, and he had to stay alive.

The moving of his money from one bank to another was complete. Passwords were changed and encrypted, cash was stored in various locations worldwide, and backpacks with cash in railway station lockers around Moscow. He was ready to move, although he still wrestled with the problem as to why he had become involved, but it was history now. Better just to get on with it and see where it leads.

Grigory suggested that Dmitry vacate his house and move to a secure location he had in the country – Dmitry agreed. Grigory also phoned Oleg for an update.

Oleg informed him that he had spoken to Baroyev and the meeting was going ahead. The news of Gennady Denikin's slaying was common knowledge, and Baroyev regretted the death.

Grigory knew that Baroyev would not have been concerned and that it was just a courtesy he had shown. Oleg went over the deal and how far he could go. He asked whether he should phone from the mansion if there were any issues.

Grigory had told him just to make a deal. If it needed fine-tuning, he would come down to Dushanbe and sort it out, once he was clear of his current problem. Oleg had no issues with pressing forward.

Oleg's drive out to the mansion in his new Mercedes was pleasant. The weather was balmy for the time of the year, and the windows were down. He had no issues with Denikin, although, with his demise, his escalation within the organisation looked more certain, as long as he could agree with Baroyev and ensure Merestkov's alternate drug smuggling operation was scuttled.

*****

Yusup Baroyev was magnanimous and exceedingly polite when Oleg arrived. Malika was not present, not that he could see.

He did not know that Baroyev had told her the man who had beaten her severely and permanently damaged one of her eyes was meeting with him.

She had been angry, but he had told her it was only a temporary arrangement and that his fate was sealed, just delayed. She accepted his statement and left the mansion early.

With Oleg Yezhov present in the circle where she and Yusup moved in, Malika was uncertain how she would react if she encountered him face to face. She admired Yusup's ability to act like a friend when the person was anything but. She was not confident she could emulate him, especially with Oleg, who had treated her well initially and then treated her badly. She determined that, whatever happened, she would remain calm as long as Yusup honoured his agreement to deal with him when the time was right.

'Oleg, I am so sorry about Gennady.' Baroyev shook his hand vigorously, put his other hand on Oleg's shoulder and escorted him into the mansion. The table before them was adequately supplied with tea, coffee, and savouries. Oleg declined, apart from tea with no milk.

'He was a good man,' Oleg said.

'Gennady spoke about a deal last time he was here,' said Yusup. 'Has his death affected our arrangement, or should I look for another business partner?'

'Nothing has changed. It is just an unfortunate aspect of the Russian mafia that occasionally people die before their time.'

'It happens here, my friend.' Oleg found Baroyev's over-friendly manner disconcerting. He did not succumb to it for one moment.

The discussion went well. Oleg offered Yusup full control of the transportation through Tajikistan and for him to facilitate the movement up through Uzbekistan and Kazakhstan. The contacts in those two countries were the same as when Oleg had been working for Yusup. Yusup, for his part, promised to not look for any other deals with any Russians. Besides, he had no one reliable after the death of Feliks Kalinin.

The transportation of goods through Tajikistan had become a profitable nuisance. A Russian aiming to deal with the intricacies, the bribing, and the issues that invariably come from bribing were difficult even in Russia. In Tajikistan, they were more so, and Oleg was hopeful he could pass it over to Baroyev.

He had failed to mention the percentages, but he thought Grigory would be the best person to deal with that. He could see himself stuck indefinitely in Tajikistan and was still anxious to return to Russia and Natasha, whom he was now supporting. She was enrolled at a local business college. He assumed she was no longer prostituting herself.

***

Later that day, Oleg received his regular daily phone call from Andre Malenkov, his former nemesis, now his protector.

'Oleg, what's the latest?'

'I met with Baroyev.' Oleg did not want to talk to him as he still did not trust him, but he had no option. Malenkov was his passport back to Russia.

'I know that. What did he have to say?'

'Normal discussions regarding business, nothing more.'

'Don't hide facts from me,' said Malenkov. 'I am only interested when it affects the stability of the state. The assassinations in Russia and here are potentially destabilising.'

'You heard about Gennady Denikin?' Oleg thought that not revealing the truth would only hamper his relationship with Malenkov, and he still needed written proof that he would be free to move back to St. Petersburg.

'Not only Denikin but there's also Boris Sobchak and Viktor Gryzlov,' replied Malenkov, 'and they worry the department more than the assassination of a gangster here. Are they related?'

Oleg decided to tell all the facts as he knew them. 'Boris Sobchak was aiming to take over the current operation. Viktor Gryzlov was his assassin, although how he came to be killed is unclear. Gennady Denikin, I would assume, was payback.'

'Payback by whom?' Malenkov asked.

'I don't know all the details.'

'It was Grigory Stolypin who had Sobchak killed, wasn't it?'

'Officially, I've not been told,' Oleg said. 'Unofficially, it seems likely.'

'Coming back to Boris Sobchak,' said Andre Malenkov. 'He wasn't the smartest man. He couldn't have set up a takeover on this scale. Who was backing him?'

'I don't know,' Oleg said.

'Ivan Merestkov, have you heard of him?' Malenkov asked.

'No,' replied Oleg.

'Boris Sobchak and Ivan Merestkov are, or were, closely associated. If anyone was behind Sobchak, it would be Merestkov, and he is certainly smart enough to set up such a deal.'

He paused for a moment. 'Yusup Baroyev, what's the situation with him?'

'He says he is willing to work with the Russian mafia and take a percentage for his efforts.'

'Do you believe him?'

'I have no reason to believe him for one minute,' Oleg said.

'Why is that?'

'If he can pretend to me that I am his long-lost friend, then he can certainly say anything to anyone as necessary while setting up another deal.'

'*That friendly?*'

'That friendly,' Oleg replied.

'Is he setting up another deal?'

'I've no idea, but I wouldn't be surprised to learn that he is up to something with someone else.'

***

Besides a trip back to Afghanistan, Ali Mowllah and Ahmad Ghori remained at the guest house.

Ahmad had been driven down, and Ali had flown, as Kabul was more distant, and he needed to get down to Sarobi. Poppy production was slipping, requiring him to clarify that production was not to falter. If they could not make the quota, the farmers would need to allocate more land. They had complained and said that their families would starve.

Ali had been unmoved by their complaints and informed them that either they made the quota or he would bring in others who would. They understood what he meant. He was not a difficult man, but the farmers were either lazy or stupid and, in many cases, both.

If they cannot afford to feed their children, why were they so keen on breeding them? Ali Mowllah thought.

'Allah commands us,' they would always say.

He was a good Muslim, always praying as required and committed himself to the Haj, the pilgrimage to Mecca, as required by all devout adherents, but he was also a realist. He saw that the Koran, the holy book, was there to guide, and those who bred mouths they could not feed were not following it correctly. But then, most could neither read nor write and only followed the dictates of others who could.

Satisfied that all was in order and the quotas would be met, Mowllah returned to Dushanbe and the sexually charged life he was leading there. He did not know that their host was tired of supplying women, and unless he and Ahmad Ghori came up with solutions, he would send them back with their tails between their legs.

Ahmad Ghori had returned to Kunduz to deal with various issues for the provincial government. His appearance had changed in the weeks he had been away, raising comments. He was cleaner-looking with a trimmed beard, and his clothing and the sandals on his feet were new and clean. His almost live-in woman, Nilufar, had been gently altering his look and approach to life.

After two days back in Kunduz, he realised the city and the people were too provincial, too staid and too dull for him to consider staying indefinitely. He could see himself moving to Dushanbe on a longer-term basis.

Noorzai, the Taliban commander down in Helmand Province, was enjoying a bumper crop of opium poppies; the previously rainy weather had moderated, and he was looking at how to ship more of the product. Iran was a possibility, but the money was better up through Kunduz. He didn't like doing business with the Shia Iranians, as they were ideologically unsound and religiously heretical. If Mowllah and Ghori couldn't find a solution to the quantities he had, after Ghilzai had processed the raw opium into heroin, he would go with the Iranians.

Ashraf Ghilzai maintained production. He did not want to raise heroin production but would do so if the money was right.

***

Ali Mowllah and Ahmad Ghori felt the pressure keenly at their next meeting with Yusup Baroyev, who was uncomfortable with the recent spate of assassinations. Feliks Kalinin had been a possibility for another avenue of sales, but Stolypin had assassinated him, regardless of what Yezhov had said, and he was ready to accept a deal with the treacherous Russian.

Malika refused to come to the mansion during the week due to Oleg possibly being there. She never came at the weekend. She knew about the parties and the women, but she knew that her lover was a powerful man with a powerful ego and friends, which was what powerful men did. Yusup could not always get down to visit her during the week, and her lack of affection was starting to affect his mood. The two Afghans were to feel the brunt of his frustration.

'How much longer before you come up with an offer?' Yusup shouted. The two Afghans were startled by the change in his manner. He had always been cordial in the past. They did not know what to say.

'We are suggesting a different route, where we will supply you only,' Ahmad blustered. The pleasant time in Baroyev's guest house had dimmed their attempts at a solution. The Russians were making them plenty of money, although they were concerned about the assassination of Gennady Denikin. His replacement, Oleg Yezhov, they did not see as up to the task.

'Is that all you've got?' Yusup was not appeased.

'The options are limited,' Ali said. 'The current arrangements that we have with the Russians must look suspect. You would agree with that?'

'If they continue to kill each other, then maybe it is,' Yusup agreed.

298

'We must assume that will be the case, which will not suit us well,' Ahmad said.

Yusup Baroyev saw that his options were limited. His distribution channel, virtually useless after the death of Feliks Kalinin and the agreement that Oleg Yezhov had put forward, was conditional on Stolypin maintaining control.

Knowing they could not deal with such a complex operation, he could see no advantage with the Afghans.

He resolved to let the Afghans stay where they were. He decided to talk directly to Grigory Stolypin.

***

Ali Mowllah and Ahmad Ghori left soon after and returned to the guest house. They noticed they had not received an invite to that weekend's party. Oleg had, and he was delighted, but he had grave misgivings about how long this would last.

Oleg continued running the business for Grigory Stolypin, who was remote and uncommunicative whenever he spoke to him. Grigory was feeling less secure by the day.

Ivan Merestkov, disturbed as he was over the death of his colleague, Sobchak, and worried in case he was next on the list, had commenced a campaign to discredit Grigory and Dmitry Gubkin. It was, by all accounts, successful.

He had clearly shown to the senior figures in the mafia – even the godfather – that Stolypin was the group's leader and that he and Sobchak had delegated all managerial decisions to him, including informing the senior executive. It was a lie, but, proven or unproven, it had the desired effect and the meeting, where both sides put their case, had been brought forward.

Secondly, Stolypin had brought in an outsider, namely Dmitry Gubkin, when it was clear they should have been consulted. Thirdly, the funds had found their way into Stolypin and Gubkin's accounts – falsified bank statements provided. Fourthly, the death of Boris Sobchak by one of Stolypin's men was a clear indication of guilt on Stolypin's part.

Ivan Merestkov felt he had sewn up the deal and would be able to take over the operation unchallenged, with the full blessing of his superiors. This time, he would keep them informed and give them their percentage, which they didn't deserve. He had the advantage of not having to share his cut with Sobchak, Stolypin or Gubkin.

He felt the need to talk to Yusup Baroyev. He realised that transporting the goods was a job best left to locals.

***

Yusup was pleased with the call when it was received. It was the first time that he and Merestkov had spoken.

'I'm offering you a percentage as long as you deal with the transportation,' Ivan Merestkov said over the phone.

'Stolypin has offered me that already.'

'You're assuming he is in a position to uphold such an offer.'

'Why shouldn't he be?' Yusup knew that Stolypin's position was precarious, and if Merestkov took over, it would make no difference to him. Stolypin had killed Feliks Kalinin. *Maybe Merestkov was better?* he thought.

'He may not last,' said Merestkov.

'It concerns me little. If he survives, I deal with him. If he doesn't, then I deal with you. It seems an ideal solution to me.' Yusup also reasoned, although he didn't say it, that if Stolypin was out of the picture, Oleg Yezhov was no longer under his protection. And he could uphold his agreement with Malika, who had seen Oleg driving around town and was upset enough to phone him at the mansion. The Merestkov option seemed the better choice.

'Personally, which would you prefer?' Merestkov asked.

'From my knowledge, Stolypin has played fair. But with you? Who are you? Can I trust you?'

'Agreed, we know little of each other. Maybe it would be wise for me to come down and meet with you.'

'Please do. Remember, Saturday is not business, and you are invited.'

'I will be there.' Merestkov was pleased with the phone conversation.

Grigory Stolypin was not as pleased when he became aware of Baroyev's conversation with Merestkov. He was increasingly worried that his control would be taken from him and would his life.

Dmitry was stuck for a solution. However, as he said, he wasn't sure if there was a defence. Grigory had told him there must be a solution, and he had to find it. Dmitry saw that Grigory was becoming irrational.

***

Now isolated from the polite society of Moscow, Dmitry saw that he had nothing to lose by making his intent to take a more visible role known to the senior executive of the mafia, if necessary. He realised he did not have a comprehensive understanding of how the drug smuggling operation worked and how it related to the mafia. He needed to know more if he was to make a presentation to them.

The answers were not in Moscow but in the capital of Tajikistan. He would go there for a few days at least. Grigory would object so he wouldn't tell him. He knew of only one person in Dushanbe, Yusup Baroyev. He would contact him. His phone number had been on a list that Grigory had inadvertently left at a previous meeting.

He called the number. Baroyev had answered. A brief conversation followed, with an invite to meet on Friday and attend the party the day after.

Yusup Baroyev could see that the action was coming to him. The Afghans were in the city. Ivan Merestkov was on his way, as was Dmitry Gubkin. Oleg Yezhov was already there, and Grigory Stolypin was back in Moscow.

It seemed the ideal time to sort out all the remaining issues. He could see how the plan should evolve. The only weakness in the plan was Grigory Stolypin and Oleg Yezhov. If they were out of the equation, so much the better. He would sound out Ivan Merestkov, see if he could trust him and spend time with Dmitry Gubkin – a lot of time, probably, as his reputation preceded him. He would ensure some new women for the Saturday. He could see it was going to be a boisterous day.

Yusup had phoned Malika soon after the phone call from Dmitry Gubkin and told her he had a possible solution. She was delighted and told him to make sure he came over that night, or she would come to the mansion to show her appreciation.

Oleg had made contact with her. She told Yusup that she had been polite and agreeable, but she wasn't as good at pretending as he was and was unsure how she would react the next time.

***

Ivan Merestkov had been the first to arrive in Dushanbe. Yusup had sent the Green Bentley, which Ali Mowllah had admired, to pick him up. The two Afghans drove around in a late model BMW, as the Bentley was Malika's favourite.

Merestkov was booked into a five-star hotel. Yusup offered him a woman. He declined and said he would wait for Saturday. Dmitry Gubkin arrived a little later and was offered the Bentley, a five-star hotel and a woman. He accepted all three.

Yusup wanted to meet with Dmitry Gubkin first, and after freshening up, the Bentley took him out to the mansion. To Yusup, it was the melding of two minds. There was an instant camaraderie between the two men.

'What do you reckon to either of them?' Yusup asked.

'Grigory Stolypin or Ivan Merestkov?' replied Dmitry. 'That's a difficult question to answer. Let me say that the current conflict between the two and the precarious situation of Stolypin and, by default, myself is all due to his inability to listen to me for advice.

'Killing Feliks Kalinin was a foolish move,' said Yusup. 'It was bound to raise suspicion, and then we have Merestkov killing one of Stolypin's men. I wouldn't go for either of them, but Merestkov is the smarter of the two, probably the most willing to listen to advice.'

'Can we agree on Ivan Merestkov?' Dmitry asked. It was hard to believe that two men were calmly discussing the distribution of an evil that made those involved in the trade billions of dollars a year yet subjected countless others to abject despair and misery.

'Let's meet him first,' said Yusup. 'If you are agreed, we can meet him jointly.' It was the first time in his career that Yusup had counselled advice from anyone. However, after a short meeting, he was willing to listen to Dmitry Gubkin.

***

Ivan Merestkov, duly summoned, arrived sixty minutes later. He was surprised to see Dmitry there. They had met once when Stolypin introduced him to his partners. Reticent to speak in front of Stolypin's man, he spoke carefully.

'I want to offer you the same as you have received from Grigory Stolypin.' He felt he could say that. He had wanted to say that Grigory Stolypin was a crook who should be hung out to dry, but he was reluctant to do so in front of Dmitry Gubkin, who would relay it to Stolypin.

'Please note,' Dmitry said. 'I am here in an independent capacity, not as Stolypin's stooge.'

'Why?'

'I need to decide whether to support you or him.'

'And what is your decision?'

'My decision is not made yet. You will know before we return to Moscow.'

'Why would I need you?' Merestkov asked nervously. He wanted to resolve the situation with Dmitry, but sitting in front of a third party, important as he was, discussing what to do, was not his way of doing business.

'You need a partner, and I am a precise man,' said Dmitry. 'I have detailed information that will either convict you or Grigory. The decision of who I support is dependent on you.'

Ivan Merestkov laughed out loud. He had met his match and could see that the business was too large to run alone now that Boris Sobchak was gone. A smart operator such as Gubkin would be an asset.

'You're right, of course,' he replied. 'I believe we would make a good team.'

'Gentlemen, that's settled,' said Yusup. 'Or, at least, almost settled. Ivan, tell us how you can control this.'

'It seems as if I need Dmitry,' said Merestkov. 'He obviously has the information, and if I have the support of the godfather, we will make a formidable team.'

'Agreed,' Dmitry said. He had made up his mind.

Yusup was delighted. Soon, he would have Oleg Yezhov precisely where he wanted him.

'Any plans are subject to the Bratva's godfather and our dealing with Grigory Stolypin,' Merestkov reminded them. 'Until they are resolved, no further action can be taken.'

Grigory Stolypin had attempted to contact Dmitry several times as he knew he was in the company of Yusup Baroyev and Ivan Merestkov. He saw treachery and knew that the treachery's instigator could only be Yusup Baroyev. The man had become a liability; it was time for his removal.

Stolypin realised he could not implicate Oleg in an assassination. He was now closely involved with Yusup Baroyev, and, with Denikin dead and the Afghans still in town, there was a part for him to play. Someone needed to be able to deal with the flack after the Tajik gangster had been killed, and he didn't have anyone else.

He, as Denikin had been, was still not sure of Oleg. Was he capable, or just an opportunist in the right place at the right time? Whenever he was around, there appeared to be inordinate numbers of deaths. He decided that Oleg Yezhov was his man for the time being until he could find someone else to fill the void.

What to do about Gubkin? He still wasn't sure. He would need to talk to him first; he still needed him for his defence, regardless of what deals he was cooking up with Merestkov and Baroyev. With Baroyev out of the way, it would be easier.

The upcoming presentation to the senior mafia figures was only a week away, and Stolypin knew Ivan Merestkov would be back in Moscow before then. If he had convinced Dmitry to switch sides and support him instead, then Merestkov would have been a dead man. And, if Dmitry did not support him, he would also ensure he was a dead man. Oleg could deal with that killing.

Chapter 25

Igor Rothko was a killer, one of the Russian mafia's most efficient. He was the only person that Grigory Stolypin could turn to. He would have preferred someone more familiar with Dushanbe and the intended target, but there was no one.

Rothko, a slim man with refined manners and the hands of a piano player, did not look to be an assassin. He was a fastidious man, a lover of cats and kind to children. He dressed well, took care of himself and exercised daily. In his apartment building, his neighbours believed him to be a clerk. He spoke little, never about himself, and where he went each day was unknown to them. The small case he always carried, they assumed, held his work files or maybe his sandwiches.

They would have been shocked to learn that the case carried the tools of his trade and not papers. To him, an assassination was discreet, never more than one shot. Any more than that was a waste, the mark of an amateur and one thing he prided himself on, above all else, was that he was the consummate professional.

The flight to Dushanbe concerned him little. The transportation of his small leather case did. Grigory Stolypin said he would deal with it. Rothko asked no questions other than to ask that all care be taken. His three cats were to be fed by his next-door neighbour, who gossiped and told him all the news, especially the pair who lived down the hall and their carryings-on. He had learnt to listen to her, nod in acknowledgement as she spoke, and ignore her occasional prying into his business. She looked after the cats, and that was all that concerned him.

***

When Rothko's flight landed, Dushanbe was bathed in an early morning haze. He took a taxi to the city centre and checked into his hotel. He phoned the neighbour to check on his cats. They were fine.

He had no interest in the city, only the layout and the routes that Yusup Baroyev was likely to take, the cars he travelled in and the security he carried. He had one bullet, although his weapon of choice, a VSS Vintorex, could take ten or twenty rounds, depending on the style of the clip the shooter used. It was delivered to his room at the hotel as Grigory Stolypin had said it would. It was there, placed on one side of his bed, upon his return from looking around the city checking possible assassination locations.

A small runabout from a rental company, booked by the hotel and added to his bill, suited him admirably. He had driven out to the mansion, no closer than one kilometre, so as not to raise suspicion. He had driven by the apartment where Baroyev's mistress lived and checked the frequency of the traffic lights as they changed from red to green and back to red at promising locations. Discreet inquiries at the hotel reception had informed him about the vehicles Baroyev used and the time he was likely to be seen on the street. After receiving one hundred American dollars in cash for services rendered, the receptionist was pleased to talk. The receptionist saw another one hundred if he could contact Baroyev's people to let them know an inquisitive Russian was asking inappropriate questions.

It was obvious to Rothko that Baroyev was overly confident in the city. But, as the receptionist had clearly indicated, 'Nobody messes with Yusup Baroyev, not if they want to live to old age.'

Rothko had heard such statements before, but the victim always died.

Confident as he was, he had booked a flight back to Moscow for late the following day. He had seen the best opportunity and was told that Baroyev often headed towards his lover's apartment on most evenings. The intersection, one block away, offered the best option: the road's curve caused the traffic to slow. The tree on the left-hand side of the intersection affected the visibility, which meant the driver, a chauffeur in Baroyev's case, would be forced to slowly edge out into the middle of the road to check for oncoming traffic.

To Rothko, it presented the ideal opportunity. A small, flat-roofed building on one side, isolated by overgrown vegetation, provided a platform and a clear shot. The distance was fine, no more than twenty metres, and his car could be concealed in a back street and easily accessible. If the timing were right, he could head straight out to the airport, check in, maybe wait a few hours more than usual and depart. The rifle, which had served him well over the years, would be placed in a garbage bin along the way.

***

It was a confident man who, five hours later, settled in at the small building close to the intersection - narrowly missing Baroyev's people at the hotel who had come to ask him a few questions - the case he always carried in Moscow at his side. He opened it to reveal the rifle in three sections. He assembled it quickly – daily practice had made him perfect. He fitted the night vision sight, a 1PN51, adjusted the tripod and aligned the sights. It was still early, and the weather was mild. He had a flask of tea and sandwiches he had bought in the shop next to the hotel. He did not know how long to wait, but he was sure the target was coming.

He had seen the mistress in an upstairs window, dressing in her finery, and he had assumed, correctly, that she would not be going out without his target.

Just before eight in the evening, the car carrying the target appeared. The green Bentley – Rothko had been correct in assuming it would be that one car amongst the fleet that Baroyev owned, some vintage, some incredibly expensive.

The driver, neatly dressed in a suit, steered the car to the centre of the road, a bodyguard sitting to his right. The vehicle stopped – its front bumper just over the faded centre line. Yusup Baroyev was clearly visible in the rear seat – although on the far side to where the assassin knelt, alert now, fully awake.

He lined the sights on the target. He chose the head as it was more clearly visible than the man's body, obscured in part by the imposing structure of the vehicle. He took aim.

He pulled the trigger as the vehicle slowly moved forward to cross the intersection, but he was momentarily distracted by a cat crossing the roof. A single shot, a subsonic SP-5 cartridge, its increased mass suitable for piercing the armour of the reinforced windows. He had correctly assumed, subsequently checked, on vehicles imported into Tajikistan using the Internet in the hotel, that the green Bentley was armour-plated.

The bullet broke through the window with little difficulty. It found its target, and Yusup Baroyev slumped over. The vehicle sped away.

Certain of his success, Igor Rothko made his way to the airport. The money from the one shooting would keep him comfortable for a few months.

***

The news of the shooting of Yusup Baroyev spread quickly. The chauffeur, trained for such eventualities, had taken the correct action. He had exited the immediate area and made for the nearest hospital. Once clear of the immediate vicinity, he phoned the mansion. He informed them of what had happened and what action he had taken.

Malika was notified by phone from the mansion within ten minutes. She was at the hospital within another ten minutes, almost hitting a pedestrian walking across the road as she drove recklessly to the hospital.

Yusup's men checked the area where the shot had come from. They found only a flask, a half-eaten sandwich, the imprint of the rifle's tripod and the knee marks where the assassin had knelt. With little to be achieved, they soon left the scene before the police arrived.

The scene at the hospital was chaotic; normal operations were disrupted due to the high-profile casualty. Whisked immediately into intensive care and an operating theatre, the surgeons worked to stabilise the victim. The hospital's director was soon on the scene.

The media was flocking to the hospital, and their vehicles were starting to interfere with the free movement of traffic in and out. A major figure in the country, a criminal in this case, caused a frenzy. Malika was in tears and inconsolable. Others tried to calm her, but with little effect.

'He's lost a lot of blood,' the surgeon tasked with informing Malika and Yusup's men said.

'Is he going to live?' Malika asked.

'Too early to say,' was the blunt reply. It did little to calm anyone.

The news was quickly relayed over the television and the internet. Grigory Stolypin watched the unfolding activity, relieved that at least one problem was out of the way. Rothko sat in the departure lounge at the airport, disinterested. He knew it had been a good shot. He had never failed in the past; he had not failed this time. He was supremely confident.

The surgeons focused on their patients, and the others waiting for assistance were ignored unless their ailment was serious. The assembled media throng pressed for an update.

After four hours, the surgeon, who had given the pessimistic prognosis, returned.

'He will live,' he said to Malika, who sighed with relief. Yusup's men were also relieved, as there would have been repercussions if he had died. Open warfare would have broken out amongst the other criminal gangs in the capital, each aiming to seize control of his empire for themselves. They would have been forced to take sides, maybe kill or be killed. Yusup Baroyev had given them a secure life, as much as any gangster's life could be, and they did not want it to change.

Malika was allowed to see him, heavily encumbered as he was with tubes and medical equipment. The surgeon joined her at Yusup's bedside.

'If the bullet had hit him any higher, he would have been dead instantaneously,' he said. 'Luckily, the velocity drove the bullet through the neck, the left posterior cervical, and out the other side, causing minor damage. He will fully recover, although it will be a week before we bring him out of sedation. He'll have a terrible neck ache and will not be fully cognisant for some weeks.'

'He will be okay?' Malika asked.

'He's a fit man. He should be alright.'

The surgeon omitted to say that if it had been another person, he would not have received the intensity of treatment and would not have survived.

***

Oleg Yezhov and Dmitry Gubkin, in different parts of the city, listened intently to the news on television. They had various reasons for their interest. With Baroyev dead, Oleg could see the major threat to his well-being being removed. With Dmitry Gubkin, his best hope of redemption lay with Merestkov and the man lying in a hospital bed. Unless Stolypin devised a better solution, he knew which side he would choose.

Dmitry Gubkin had seen the women that Baroyev went around with. He had decided that was the life for him. What did the society dames and their men folk in Moscow matter? He was in his sixties; he would possibly live another twenty. It was better to enjoy life at its most basic. A criminal life with a criminal's woman suited him just fine.

Ivan Merestkov was also concerned, though not as much as the others. If Baroyev died, it was an inconvenience, not a total disaster. He could always leave the drug smuggling operation the way it was as long as the Russian mafia gave him the all-clear. With Dmitry Gubkin organising and laying in the plans, he could see a successful outcome, whether Baroyev was dead or alive.

Grigory Stolypin's initial jubilation turned to despair when the updates indicated that the assassination had failed. He knew there would be reprisals, and it would not be long before he was implicated. Igor Rothko heard the news as he was boarding the delayed flight. It had been his first failure. His reputation was destroyed; he would never fire a gun again.

***

With nothing more to be achieved in Tajikistan, Dmitry Gubkin and Ivan Merestkov flew back to Moscow the next day. Grigory Stolypin was on the phone within an hour of the flight landing, anxious to discover what was happening and why Dmitry was friendly with Merestkov and Baroyev.

'Who organised the assassination attempt on Baroyev?' Dmitry went on the offensive.

'How the hell would I know?' Stolypin replied.

'You had Feliks Kalinin killed, which ultimately ended up with Gennady Denikin being assassinated. Don't you ever think these actions through?'

'I wasn't responsible for the attempt on Yusup Baroyev's life.'

'Do you imagine this is the end of it?' shouted Dmitry. 'What will happen when he's back on board, thinking clearly? He will want revenge and won't be looking for clear proof. We will all be held suspect, and from what I've heard, he is not too fussy about obtaining the truth.'

Gubkin was angry with the foolishness of Stolypin, who continued to show that he was not a man he could work with. He had to protect Merestkov, but first, he had to stay alive. If Stolypin realised the situation, he knew who would be next for the assassin's bullet.

Dmitry Gubkin weighed up the situation. If he supported Ivan Merestkov openly, Stolypin would see that as betrayal and act accordingly. If he endorsed Stolypin and then changed his support just before the meeting with the senior executive of the mafia, then he ran the risk of reprisal if Stolypin somehow survived.

He saw it clearly. Grigory Stolypin was a liability and had to be liquidated. He would speak to Merestkov and sound him out.

The conversation with Grigory had been brief and acrimonious. Dmitry was pleased when he hung up, agreeing to meet within two days to discuss the situation and his continuing support.

Dmitry phoned Merestkov shortly after. He had moved back into the house in Moscow, with the insurances of Merestkov that he would have the place watched and his contacts down at police headquarters would let him know if there was any impending move to arrest him.

'Ivan, Stolypin just phoned.'

'How is he?' Merestkov asked.

'He's not in a good mood. He sees me as disloyal. I'm sure the only reason I am still alive is that he needs my support.'

'Are you saying he should be removed?'

'If you can clear it.'

'It will only make the situation easier. Did you know about his failure to communicate with the godfather?'

'I was not aware initially that it was a requirement.'.

'Then, it is fine. If this is your advice regarding Stolypin, I will act on it.'

***

Grigory Stolypin was a man of habit. He did not exercise except to walk from the refrigerator in his house to the drink cabinet or to the restaurant every morning around midday for lunch. It was his most vulnerable time when he felt the need for some fresh air.

His security, two men, always armed, walked close by, slightly to his rear.

Ivan Merestkov had used Khasan Boqiev in Dushanbe to deal with Gennady Denikin, Stolypin's man. He had been successful, but his methods were crude, lacking the subtlety required, and an Asian-looking Tajik would have been immediately noticed amongst the staid, suited businessmen that frequented the area around the restaurant. He needed someone else.

Yegor Luzhkov was suitable, but he had just been released from prison pending an appeal for the murder of a politician. Merestkov knew that the murdered politician had failed to honour his pre-election promise to Luzhkov's boss, a particularly vicious gangster, for services rendered in disposing of the preferred candidate in a car accident.

Luzhkov was receptive to the idea when Merestkov met him at a decent middle-class restaurant.

'I owe that bastard anyway,' he said. He was a typical old-style gangster with a gangster's haircut, short and crudely cut, a two-day stubble, the smell of body odour and the look of a man who had seen it all and done it all, especially with murders, assassinations and kidnappings.

'Stolypin cheated me out of some money,' Luzhkov complained. 'I did a job for him. He complained about the payment. You get his death. I get money from you and payback.'

***

The day was overcast and threatening rain when Grigory Stolypin walked the short distance to the restaurant. He chatted to the two bodyguards as they walked down the pavement. The other people on the pavement moved to one side or stepped onto the road to let them pass.

Yegor Luzhkov stood off to the side, down a small alley. He waited for them to pass, then moved out and stood behind them. Unaware of his presence, they continued to walk. He was not a sophisticated assassin who saw the need for one shot to ensure his weapon was accurate or even to consider whether he was the best shot.

Dead was dead as far as he was concerned; for him, a machine gun was as suitable as a pistol, better if the result was ensured. A Bizon SMG, sixty-four rounds on rapid fire and Grigory Stolypin and his two bodyguards were dead, as was an elderly businessman in his sixties, returning to his office after picking up a cake for his secretary's birthday.

Luzhkov retreated down the alley, leaving the weapon and jumped into a waiting car. He felt no compunction over the deaths of the gangster or the innocent man, and he celebrated a cash payment of five thousand American dollars with a good feed at a good restaurant, liberally washed down with vodka.

Ivan Merestkov was delighted and quickly phoned Dmitry to update him.

At least, Merestkov followed my suggestion, Dmitry thought. *If he continues to, then all will be fine.*

***

Oleg did not take the news so well. Gennady Denikin was dead, and now Grigory Stolypin. There was only one more to go, and that would be three, and he was number three. Ivan Merestkov repeated several times on the phone that nothing had changed; it was business as usual as far as he was concerned.

On hearing the news, the mafia leadership decided that there was nothing to be gained by conducting an enquiry and, as long as the money was coming in, their percentage as agreed, they would let Merestkov get on with it.

Aware of the changing situation, Andre Malenkov phoned Oleg.

'What's the situation?'

'Business as usual, that's what I'm told,' Oleg replied, unsure if that was the situation. There was just too much going on to be sure.

Due to the deaths of most of the major players and the likelihood that the possible escalation in gang warfare in Russia was abating, Malenkov's superior called him back to Moscow on short notice for important meetings and an update. He left without telling Oleg whether he had done enough and was free to return to Russia.

***

Some weeks later, Merestkov was on the phone daily, and business was progressing without problems.

The Afghans, outstaying their welcome, returned to their own country. Nilufar, the lover of Ahmad Ghori, had offered to go, but he made it clear that her presence in such a conservative country would have only caused problems, and he wasn't sure if he could protect her. Besides, she wouldn't like it down there.

Oleg had kept in contact with the hospital, sometimes visiting, for the first couple of weeks to enquire about Yusup Baroyev and how he was progressing. Merestkov told him he should, but he would have preferred to keep away. He knew Malika was constantly there, and Yusup's wife had also flown back. Malika and his wife had formed a pact, and they would sit on either side of his bed while he lay sedated and barely conscious. Once he had revived enough, his wife had wished him well, spoke encouraging words to Malika and left.

At the end of the second week, the hospital brought Baroyev out of sedation. He was fine, although confused. As the days progressed, he improved immeasurably. Three weeks after the shot had been fired, he was taken by ambulance to the mansion. A fully functioning medical facility was set up at his cost, emulating what he had had in the hospital. It had cost a fortune. Malika had authorised it, as she was now in full control of his welfare.

Four weeks after returning to the mansion, he was up and walking and starting to make decisions. He called both Dmitry Gubkin and Ivan Merestkov back to Tajikistan. Malika had said it was too soon and that he was not fully recovered. Yusup stated that it was too important to be left as it was and that he would take it easy and convalesce afterwards, but she knew he would not.

***

'Dmitry, Ivan, do we have an agreement?' Yusup Baroyev asked, propped up in a comfy chair, cushions supporting him as Malika had insisted.

'You will take responsibility for the transportation and the negotiations with the Afghans,' replied Dmitry.

'Fine, then you no longer need Oleg Yezhov,' said Yusup.

'No, we will take him back to Russia.'

'Farrukh will oversee the handover. We will allow six weeks. Is that suitable?' Yusup asked.

'Six weeks appears about right,' Dmitry said.

'There is one other matter,' Yusup said.

'Yes?' Dmitry replied.

'Yezhov, he's mine at the end of the six weeks.'

'Is there any reason for this?' Ivan asked.

'It is a personal matter. You need not concern yourself.'

'Then he is yours,' Dmitry said. He was aware of some animosity and issues, but neither he nor Ivan cared greatly about what happened to Oleg Yezhov. They both knew he represented trouble.

***

Six weeks later, Malika had her revenge. A good woman in many ways, at least to the level of a gangster's mistress, she had never forgotten or forgiven what happened when Oleg caught her on her knees giving a blowjob to an Afghan. Her addiction had allowed her no other choice.

His failure to understand and his beating of her had left her virtually blind in one eye. It still gave her the occasional nightmare when she remembered that night.

Yusup kept his promise when Oleg Yezhov was picked up from outside his apartment, conveyed to a remote desert region and strung upside down over a termites nest, his head resting on the top, the termites agitated by the prodding of a stick.

Farrukh had offered to help, and he cut the genitals from Oleg and dangled them around his neck. With the blood rushing to his brain internally and the blood externally dripping into the nest, the termites, in their excitement, commenced their climb into every orifice on the helpless man's body. He would have screamed if he could have, but the gag prevented him at first and then the termites afterwards as they streamed into his mouth. His death was slow and painful.

Natasha would never know what had happened to him. Andre Malenkov would not have cared, nor would Dmitry Gubkin or Ivan Merestkov.

He had not been a good man. He had not been the worst, but fate had brought him to this place. It was fate that condemned him.

The End

ALSO BY THE AUTHOR

DI Tremayne Thriller Series

Death Unholy – A DI Tremayne Thriller – Book 1

All that remained were the man's two legs and a chair full of greasy and fetid ash. Little did DI Keith Tremayne know that it was the beginning of a journey into the murky world of paganism and its ancient rituals. And it was going to get very dangerous.

'Do you believe in spontaneous human combustion?' Detective Inspector Keith Tremayne asked.

'Not me. I've read about it. Who hasn't?' Sergeant Clare Yarwood answered.

'I haven't,' Tremayne replied, which did not surprise his young sergeant. In the months they had been working together, she had come to realise that he was a man who had little interest in the world. When he had a cigarette in his mouth, a beer in his hand, and a murder to solve he was about the happiest she ever saw him, but even then, he was not one of life's most sociable people. And as for reading? The occasional police report, an early-morning newspaper, turned first to the racing results.

Death and the Assassin's Blade – A DI Tremayne Thriller – Book 2

It was meant to be high drama, not murder, but someone's switched the daggers. The man's death took place in plain view of two serving police officers.

He was not meant to die; the daggers were only theatrical props, plastic and harmless. A summer's night, a production of Julius Caesar amongst the ruins of an Anglo-Saxon fort. Detective Inspector Tremayne is there with his sergeant, Clare Yarwood. In the assassination scene, Caesar collapses to the ground. Brutus defends his actions; Mark Antony rebukes him.

They're a disparate group, the amateur actors. One's an estate agent, another an accountant. And then there is the teenage school student, the gay man, the funeral director. And what about the women? They could be involved.

They've each got a secret, but which of those on the stage wanted Gordon Mason, the actor who had portrayed Caesar, dead?

Death and the Lucky Man – A DI Tremayne Thriller – Book 3

Sixty-eight million pounds and dead. Hardly the outcome expected for the luckiest man in England the day his lottery ticket was drawn out of the barrel. But then, Alan Winters' rags-to-riches story had never been conventional, and some had benefited, but others hadn't.

Death at Coombe Farm – A DI Tremayne Thriller – Book 4

A warring family. A disputed inheritance. A recipe for death.

If it hadn't been for the circumstances, Detective Inspector Keith Tremayne would have said the view was outstanding. Up high, overlooking the farmhouse in the valley below, the panoramic vista of Salisbury Plain stretching out beyond. The only problem was a body near where he stood with his sergeant, Clare Yarwood, and it wasn't a pleasant sight.

Death by a Dead Man's Hand – A DI Tremayne Thriller – Book 5

A flawed heist of forty gold bars from a security van late at night. One of the perpetrators is killed by his brother as they argue over what they have stolen.

Eighteen years later, the murderer, released after serving his sentence for his brother's murder, waits in a church for a man purporting to be the brother he killed. And then he is killed.

The threads stretch back a long way, and now more people are dying in the search for the missing gold bars.

Detective Inspector Tremayne, his health causing him concern, and Sergeant Clare Yarwood, still seeking romance, are pushed to the limit solving the murder, attempting to prevent more.

Death in the Village – A DI Tremayne Thriller – Book 6

Nobody liked Gloria Wiggins, a woman who regarded anyone who did not acquiesce to her jaundiced view of the world with disdain. James Baxter, the previous vicar, had been one of those, and her scurrilous outburst in the church one Sunday had hastened his death.

And now, years later, the woman was dead, hanging from a beam in her garage. Detective Inspector Tremayne and Sergeant Clare Yarwood had seen the body, interviewed the woman's acquaintances, and those who had hated her.

Burial Mound – A DI Tremayne Thriller – Book 7

A Bronze-Age burial mound close to Stonehenge. An archaeological excavation. What they were looking for was an ancient body and historical artefacts. They found the ancient body, but then they found another that's only been there for years, not centuries. And then the police became interested.

It's another case for Detective Inspector Tremayne and Sergeant Yarwood. The more recent body was the brother of the mayor of Salisbury.

Everything seems to point to the victim's brother, the mayor, the upright and serious-minded Clive Grantley. Tremayne's sure that it's him, but Clare Yarwood's not so sure.

But is her belief based on evidence or personal hope?

The Body in the Ditch – A DI Tremayne Thriller – Book 8

A group of children play. Not far away, in the ditch on the other side of the farmyard, lies the body of a troubled young woman.

The nearby village hides as many secrets as the community at the farm, a disparate group of people looking for an alternative to their previous torturous lives. Their leader, idealistic and benevolent, espouses love and kindness, and clearly, somebody's not following his dictate.

An old woman's death seems unrelated to the first, but is it? Is it part of the tangled web that connects the farm to the village?

Detective Inspector Tremayne and Sergeant Clare Yarwood soon discover that the village is anything but charming and picturesque. It's an incestuous hotbed of intrigue and wrongdoing. And what of the farm and those who live there. None of them can be ruled out, not yet.

The Horse's Mouth – A DI Tremayne Thriller – Book 9

A day at the races for Detective Inspector Tremayne, idyllic at the outset, soon changes. A horse is dead, the owner's daughter is found murdered, and Tremayne's there when the body is discovered.

The question is, was Tremayne set up, in the wrong place at the right time? He's the cast-iron alibi for one of the suspects, and he knows that one murder can lead to two, and more often than not to three.

The dead woman had a chequered history, though not as much as her father, and then a man commits suicide. Is he the murderer, or was his death the unfortunate consequence of a tragic love affair? And who was in the stable with the woman just before she died? More than one person could have killed her, and all of them have secrets they would rather not be known.

Tremayne's health is troubling him. Is what they are saying correct, that it is time for him to retire, to take it easy and put his feet up? But that's not his style, and he'll not give up on solving the murder.

DCI Isaac Cook Thriller Series

Murder is a Tricky Business – A DCI Cook Thriller – Book 1

A television actress is missing, and DCI Isaac Cook, the Senior Investigation Officer of the Murder Investigation Team at Challis Street Police Station in London, is searching for her.

Why has he been taken away from more important crimes to search for the woman? It's not the first time she's gone missing, so why does everyone assume she's been murdered?

There's a secret; that much is certain, but who knows it? The missing woman? The executive producer? His eavesdropping assistant? Or the actor who portrayed her fictional brother in the TV soap opera?

Murder House – A DCI Cook Thriller – Book 2

A corpse in the fireplace of an old house. It's been there for thirty years, but who is it?

It's murder, but who is the victim and what connection does the body have to the house's previous owners. What is the motive? And why is the body in a fireplace? It was bound to be discovered eventually but was that what the murderer wanted? The main suspects are all old and dying or already dead.

Isaac Cook and his team have their work cut out, trying to put the pieces together. Those who know are not talking because of an old-fashioned belief that a family's dirty laundry should not be aired in public and never to a policeman – even if that means the murderer is never brought to justice!

Murder is Only a Number – A DCI Cook Thriller – Book 3

Before she left, she carved a number in blood on his chest. But why the number 2 if this was her first murder?

The woman prowls the streets of London. Her targets are men who have wronged her. Or have they? And why is she keeping count?

DCI Cook and his team finally know who she is, but not before she's murdered four men. The whole team are looking for her, but the woman keeps disappearing in plain sight. The pressure's on to stop her, but she's always one step ahead.

And this time, DCS Goddard can't protect his protégé, Isaac Cook, from the wrath of the new commissioner at the Met.

Murder in Little Venice – A DCI Cook Thriller – Book 4

A dismembered corpse floats in the canal in Little Venice, an upmarket tourist haven in London. Its identity is unknown, but what is its significance?

DCI Isaac Cook is baffled about why it's there. Is it gang-related, or is it something more?

Whatever the reason, it's clearly a warning, and Isaac and his team are sure it's not the last body that they'll have to deal with.

Murder is the Only Option – A DCI Cook Thriller – Book 5

A man thought to be long dead returns to exact revenge against those who had blighted his life. His only concern is to protect his wife and daughter. He will stop at nothing to achieve his aim.

'Big Greg, I never expected to see you around here at this time of night.'

'I've told you enough times.'

'I've no idea what you're talking about,' Robertson replied. He looked up at the man, only to see a metal pole coming down at him. Robertson fell down, cracking his head against a concrete kerb.

Two vagrants, no more than twenty feet away, did not stir and did not even look in the direction of the noise. If they had, they would have seen a dead body, another man walking away.

Murder in Notting Hill – A DCI Cook Thriller – Book 6

One murderer, two bodies, two locations, and the murders have been committed within an hour of each other.

They're separated by a couple of miles, and neither woman has anything in common with the other. One is young and wealthy, the daughter of a famous man; the other is poor, hardworking and unknown.

Isaac Cook and his team at Challis Street Police Station are baffled about why they've been killed. There must be a connection, but what is it?

Murder in Room 346 – A DCI Cook Thriller – Book 7

'Coitus interruptus, that's what it is,' Detective Chief Inspector Isaac Cook said. In a downmarket hotel in Bayswater, on the bed lay the naked bodies of a man and a woman.

'Bullet in the head's not the way to go,' Larry Hill, Isaac Cook's detective inspector, said. He had not expected such a flippant comment from his senior, not when they were standing near to two people who had, apparently in the final throes of passion, succumbed to what appeared to be a professional assassination.

'You know this will be all over the media within the hour,' Isaac said.

'James Holden, moral crusader, a proponent of the sanctity of the marital bed, man and wife. It's bound to be.'

Murder of a Silent Man – A DCI Cook Thriller – Book 8

A murdered recluse. A property empire. A disinherited family. All the ingredients for murder.

No one gave much credence to the man when he was alive. In fact, most people never knew who he was, although those who had lived in the area for many years recognised the tired-looking and shabbily-dressed man as he shuffled along, regular as clockwork on a Thursday afternoon at seven in the evening to the local off-licence.

It was always the same: a bottle of whisky, premium brand, and a packet of cigarettes. He paid his money over the counter, took hold of his plastic bag containing his purchases, and then walked back down the road with the same rhythmic shuffle.

Murder has no Guilt – A DCI Cook Thriller – Book 9

No one knows who the target was or why, but there are eight dead. The men seem the most likely perpetrators, or could have it been one of the two women, the attractive Gillian Dickenson, or even the celebrity-obsessed Sal Maynard?

There's a gang war brewing, and if there are deaths, it doesn't matter to them as long as it's not their death. But to Detective Chief Inspector Isaac Cook, it's his area of London, and it does matter.

It's dirty and unpredictable. Initially, the West Indian gangs held sway, but a more vicious Romanian gangster had usurped them. And now he's being marginalised by the Russians. And the leader of the most vicious Russian mafia organisation is in London, and he's got money and influence, the ear of those in power.

Murder in Hyde Park – A DCI Cook Thriller – Book 10

An early-morning jogger is murdered in Hyde Park. It's in the centre of London, but no one saw him enter the park, no one saw him die.

He carries no identification, only a water-logged phone. As the pieces unravel, it's clear that the dead man had a history of deception.

Is the murderer one of those that loved him? Or was it someone with a vengeance?

It's proving difficult for DCI Isaac Cook and his team at Challis Street Homicide to find the guilty person – not that they'll cease to search for the truth, not even after one suspect confesses.

Six Years Too Late – A DCI Cook Thriller – Book 11

Always the same questions for Detective Chief Inspector Isaac Cook — Why was Marcus Matthews in that room? And why did he share a bottle of wine with his killer?

It wasn't as if Matthews had amounted to much, apart from the fact that he was the son-in-law of a notorious gangster, the father of the man's grandchildren.

Yet the one thing Hamish McIntyre, feared in London for his violence, rated above anything else, was his family, especially Samantha, his daughter. However, he had never cared for Marcus, her husband.

And then Marcus disappeared, only for his body to be found six years later by a couple of young boys who decide that exploring an abandoned house is preferable to school.

Grave Passion – A DCI Cook Thriller – Book 12

Two young lovers out for a night of romance. A shortcut through the cemetery. They witnessed a murder, but there was no struggle, only a knife through the heart.

It has all the hallmarks of an assassination, but who is the woman? And why was she beside a grave at night? Did she know the person who killed her?

Soon after, other deaths, seemingly unconnected, but tied to the family of one of the young lovers.

It's a case for Detective Chief Inspector Cook and his team, and they're baffled on this one.

The Slaying of Joe Foster – A DCI Cook Thriller – Book 13

No one challenged Joe Foster in life, not if they valued theirs. And then, the gangster is slain and his criminal empire up for grabs.

A power vacuum; the Foster family is fighting for control, the other gangs in the area aiming to poach the trade in illegal drugs, to carve up the empire that the father had created.

It has all the makings of a war on the streets, something nobody wants, not even the other gangs.

Terry Foster, the eldest son of Joe, the man who should take control, doesn't have his father's temperament or wisdom. His solution is slash and burn, and it's not going to work. People are going to get hurt, and some of them will die.

The Hero's Fall – A DCI Cook Thriller – Book 14

Angus Simmons had it made. A successful television program, a beautiful girlfriend, admired by many for his mountaineering exploits.

And then he fell while climbing a skyscraper in London. Initially, it was thought he had lost his grip, but that wasn't the man: a meticulous planner, his risks measured, and it wasn't a difficult climb, not for him.

It was only afterwards on examination that they found the mark of a bullet on his body. It then became a murder, and that was when Detective Chief Inspector Isaac Cook and his Homicide team at Challis Street Police Station became interested.

The Vicar's Confession – A DCI Cook Thriller – Book 15

The Reverend Charles Hepworth, good Samaritan, a friend of the downtrodden, almost a saint to those who know him, up until the day he walks into the police station, straight up to Detective Chief Inspector Isaac Cook's desk in Homicide. 'I killed the man,' he says as he places a blood-soaked knife on the desk.

The dead man, Andreas Maybury, was not a man to mourn, but why would a self-professed pacifist commit such a heinous crime. The reasons aren't clear, and then Hepworth's killed in a prison cell, and everyone's ducking for cover.

Murder Without Reason – A DCI Cook Thriller – Book 16

DCI Cook faces his greatest challenge. The Islamic State is waging war in England, and they are winning.

Not only does Isaac Cook have to contend with finding the perpetrators, but he is also being forced to commit actions contrary to his mandate as a police officer.

And then there is Anne Argento, the prime minister's deputy. The prime minister has shown himself to be a pacifist and is not up to the task. She needs to take his job if the country is to fight back against the Islamists.

Vane and Martin have provided the solution. Will DCI Cook and Anne Argento be willing to follow it through? Are they able to act for the good of England, knowing that a criminal and murderous action is about to take place? Do they have an option?

Steve Case Thriller Series

The Haberman Virus – Book 1

A remote and isolated village in the Hindu Kush Mountain range in North Eastern Afghanistan is wiped out by a virus unlike any seen before.

A mysterious visitor clad in a spacesuit checks his handiwork, a female American doctor succumbs to the disease, and the woman sent to trap the person responsible falls in love with him – the man who would cause the deaths of millions.

Hostage of Islam – Book 2

Three are to die at the Mission in Nigeria: the pastor and his wife in a blazing chapel; another gunned down while trying to defend them from the Islamist fighters.

Kate McDonald, an American, grieving over her boyfriend's death and Helen Campbell, whose life had been troubled by drugs and prostitution, are taken by the attackers.

Kate is sold to a slave trader who intends to sell her virginity to an Arab Prince. Helen, to ensure their survival, gives herself to the murderer of her friends.

Prelude to War – Book 3

Russia and America face each other across the northern border of Afghanistan. World War 3 is about to break out and no one is backing off.

And all because a team of academics in New York postulated how to extract the vast untapped mineral wealth of Afghanistan.

Steve Case is in the middle of it, and his position is looking very precarious. Will the Taliban find him before the Americans get him out? Or is he doomed, as is the rest of the world?

Standalone Novels

Malika's Revenge

Malika, a drug-addicted prostitute, waits in a smugglers' village for the next Afghan tribesman or Tajik gangster to pay her price, a few scraps of heroin.

Yusup Baroyev, a drug lord, enjoys a lifestyle many would envy. An Afghan warlord sees the resurgence of the Taliban. A Russian white-collar criminal portrays himself as a good and honest citizen in Moscow.

All of them are linked to an audacious plan to increase the quantity of heroin shipped out of Afghanistan and into Russia and ultimately the West.

Some will succeed, some will die, some will be rescued from their plight and others will rue the day they became involved.

Verrall's Nightmare

Jacob Montfield, regarded as a homeless eccentric by the majority, a nuisance by a few, had pushed a supermarket trolley around the city for years.

However, one person regards him as a liability.

Eccentric was correct, a nuisance, for sure, mad, plenty thought that, but few knew the truth, that Montfield is a brilliant man, once a research scientist. And even less knew that detailed within a notebook hidden deep in the trolley, there is a new approach to the guidance of weapons and satellites—a radical improvement on the previous and it's worth a lot to some, power to others, accolades to another.

And for that, one cold night, he died at the hand of another.

Inspector Tremayne and Sergeant Clare Yarwood are on the case, but so are others, and soon they're warned off. Only Tremayne doesn't listen, not when he's got his teeth into the investigation, and his sergeant, equally resolute, won't either. It's not only their careers on the line, but their lives.

ABOUT THE AUTHOR

Phillip Strang was born in the late forties, the post-war baby boom in England; his childhood years, a comfortable middle-class upbringing in a small town, a two hours' drive to the west of London.

His childhood and the formative years were a time of innocence. Relatively few rules, and as a teenager, complete mobility due to a bicycle – a three-speed Raleigh – and a more trusting community. It was the days before mobile phones, the internet, terrorism and wanton violence. An avid reader of Science Fiction in his teenage years: Isaac Asimov, and Frank Herbert, the masters of the genre. Still an avid reader, the author now mainly reads thrillers.

In his early twenties, the author, with a degree in electronics engineering and an unabated wanderlust to see the world left England's cold and damp climes for Sydney, Australia – the first semi-circulation of the globe, complete. Now, forty years later, he still resides in Australia, although many intervening years spent in a myriad of countries, some calm and safe – others, no more than war zones.